Praise for *From These Dark Depths*

"Rasanen delivers epically in this sequel…"
—Rachel L. Schade, author of the *Cursed Empire* series

"Phenomenal sequel! It's literally everything you could want out of a pirate book with fae!"
—Emily Schneider, author of the *Ash and Smoke* series

"I was swept away by the longing and romance in this tale like a ship drawn to the distant horizon line."
—Natalia M. Lucia, author of *Girls of Salt and Sea*

"If you thought the first story made you feel all the feelings then gather all of your comfort items before diving into this one."
—Vicki Gannon, beta reader

from these dark depths

Aisling Sea Book 2

VANESSA RASANEN

CRAB APPLE BOOKS

Crab Apple Books
P.O. Box 4220
Cheyenne, WY 82003
www.crabapplebooks.com

Visit the author's website at www.vanessarasanen.com

Dust jacket and case laminate design by Maria Spada
Map and chapter illustrations by Dimension Door
Character artwork by Ana Damar and Elina Iatsenko

ISBN 978-1732765252
Also available in paperback, ebook, and audiobook

For Joel, who loves me unconditionally,
and for all who have felt the sting of betrayal.

BLACK SOUND

TYSHALY

CAPROTHE

CREGAH

TO LARCSPOROUGH

TURVALA

DAORNA

THE AISLING SEA

HAVIERN

...LES ISLAND

BINBRACKEN MOUNTAINS

PORT MORSHAN

THE COUNCIL

FOXHAVEN

Pronunciation Guide

CHARACTERS

Declan: DEK-len
McCallagh: muh-KAH-luh
Mikkel: mih-KELL
Aoife: EE-fuh
Lani: LA-nee
Melina: muh-LEE-nuh
Cait: KATE
Maura: MOR-a
Bron: BRAHN
Naeve: nave
Callum: CA-luhm
Halloran: HA-lor-en
Csintala: sin-TAH-luh
Carthach: KAR-hekh
Ada: AY-duh

PLACES

Cregah: CRAY-guh
Morshan: MOR-shahn
Larcsporough: LARK-spur-uh
Turvala: tur-VAH-luh
Daorna: day-OR-nuh
Haviern: hav-ee-AIRN
Caprothe: cuh-PROHTH
Tyshaly: tih-SHAH-lee
Aisling: ASH-ling
Helles: HELL-es

OTHER

Muirnaughton: MEER-not-en
daemari: day-MAH-ree

1

DECLAN

It never got easier. Even after seven years of avoiding this, Declan McCallagh's stomach still clenched in protest, his feet shifting on the pine needles that covered the dirt path. They hadn't told him who. They never did, only providing a time he needed to be here, ready.

Here wasn't marked by anything more than a large boulder off to the side of the road, whose black soil was divided into two wheel ruts with a strip of grass between them trying desperately to survive. To the infrequent traveler it was an inconsequential rock, not unlike the ones that could be found along the coasts of Cregah. But to Declan it meant doom.

Not for him, thankfully, but for the poor soul who had crossed the Council.

Whether he was the only pirate who struggled with this arrangement between the Council and the lesser pirates, he didn't know. He'd never asked anyone and never would, not when his reputation hung by a quickly fraying thread, all his hard-won prestige at risk of being dissolved by the Pirate Lords targeting him one after the other.

Declan forced himself to remain still, steeling his expression as the rumble of carriage wheels hit his ears, still faint but growing louder. They were coming fast. Faster than usual.

Urgency wasn't typically part of this gig as most of those found guilty and sentenced to *exile* came along willingly, either unaware of their true fate or accepting their martyrdom for their rebel cause.

But this. This one was different.

The pounding of hooves against the hard packed soil reverberated in his head even before he could see them.

Drawing in a deep breath, his fingers itched to hold the familiar steel of his dagger that remained concealed at his waist. Silly how they expected him to dispatch of their *exiles* while still holding to the forbidding of weapons.

He ignored the urge to reach for his blade, putting on a bored expression as he crossed his arms over his chest and continued leaning against the rock. The door flew open as the carriage skidded to a stop directly in front of him. Standing, he prepared to grab the exile so he could escort them to their fate, but he stopped and waited, watching as a mess of red hair filled the doorway to the carriage. The woman's back was to him, her hands gripping the edges of the opening, screaming with desperation as her captors tried to push her out.

Declan might have found the display humorous if he didn't know what the woman faced, what she fought and screamed to avoid. Pity and remorse brewed within him, tightening their grip on his throat.

You're a damned pirate! Get it together!

With a clearing of his throat, as if he were about to speak, he dislodged the invading emotions and stepped forward, wrapping his arm around her waist as the women inside the carriage worked to get her fingers loose from the carriage.

She continued fighting, kicking and flailing, screaming and writhing, as Declan carried her away toward the boulder. He'd need to hold onto this one. More than the others he'd dealt with.

"Good luck with this one!" One of the women called. The door hadn't even latched shut before the driver sent the horse off with a flick of the reins.

Declan pulled her close against him, ignoring how her hair crowded his face. He needed to get her to calm down or he'd have to find some way to knock her unconscious. He probably should have, especially with this feisty one, but something within him pushed him to avoid that move.

Still, time was against him here. Even under the cover of these tall trees, he could see the sun already nearing its highest point. Gavin and Tommy would be arriving at the pub in a matter of hours. He needed to get this over with.

Holding her tight he tried to coax her to quiet down, whispering against her hair to relax. A laugh echoed in his head at the absurdity of his request. Would he have relaxed in her position? Would he have gone without this same fight?

He waited for her body to tire itself out, for her growls to quiet. When he felt she had finally given up, he loosened his hold on her. But before he could move her to face him, her foot came down hard on his, her elbow landing in his gut at the same time.

That was unexpected.

But he was no amateur, and he regained his hold of her waist, growling as he did.

"Hey!" he barked at her. "Stop it. Now. Fighting will do you no good here."

But she continued to buck against his hold, her feet scrambling for purchase against the black soil. This was not going at all as planned. Perhaps another tactic would work.

"Let's stop. Talk. Relax a bit. This doesn't have to go badly."

His words must have surprised her—as intended—because she froze and turned her head to look at him over her shoulder. Her glare pierced him, searching to see if there was any deception in his words.

"Of course it has to go badly," she spat at him. "I know what you do for them."

"Aye," he replied, allowing the remorse he'd shoved aside earlier to return and soften his expression. "Doesn't mean I like it. Doesn't mean it has to hurt."

"So you want to talk?" she asked and started to pull away from him.

Though he eased his hold, he kept his guard up, ready to grab her again if she tried anything again.

He dipped his chin. "Aye. Let's talk."

When he was sure she wasn't going to dart off—not that he wouldn't be able to catch her if she did—he lowered his arms and took a step back. She turned fully to him now, her arms crossing defiantly across her chest. Despite her curves having filled out, this girl was no woman. She couldn't have been more than twenty years old, if that. The smooth alabaster planes of her face—framed by deep red waves of hair—showed little weathering. She didn't get outside much.

She scowled at him, but didn't make to move away. Standing there, her arms still crossed, she eyed him. Seconds went by and then minutes, with them facing off in silence.

Declan searched the blues of her eyes, wondering what this girl—a girl so young—could have possibly done to be marked for *exile* by the Council.

What do you care?

Giving his head a shake, as if it could whisk away the scolding words, he started to say something. But she spoke first.

"Well? You wanted to talk? What about?"

He had originally planned to ask her who she was and what she had done. But something churned in his gut, warned him about getting too—not attached, but—involved. His mind whirred with an ominous feeling that this job, this *fee* he had to pay to the Council, was one he should complete and forget as quickly as possible.

But could he do that? Eight names repeated in his head, and with each one, a face appeared, some scared and begging for mercy, others at peace with their fate.

Taking a life wasn't against his moral code. He did so when he needed to, but he preferred it to be his own rival or in defense of his crew. Being hired to dispatch those who posed no threat to him and had done him no wrong gnawed at him.

No, he didn't care. He couldn't. Wouldn't. But then he couldn't quiet that part of him that insisted everyone had a right to be remembered. Even if only by their executioner.

Shifting his feet, he forced himself to relax a bit, hoping it might put her more at ease with him. The thought caused him to laugh internally, though he was careful to keep it from escaping. As if she could or should be at ease with the man tasked with...

He cut off the thought with a question. "What's your name?"

The girl's brow shot up in surprise, but she blinked it away quickly before answering. "Lani. You?"

"Declan."

"And you're a pirate."

He answered with a mere nod.

"Hired to take *care* of me."

"That's one way to put it," he said. "And you? What landed you in such a... predicament?"

She didn't respond immediately, but instead swallowed hard. Her eyes glazed over as if lost in a daydream. Tears began to form, but she blinked them away before they could spill over. Taking a deep breath, her whole torso shifting as she filled her lungs, she lifted her face to the tree tops. When she looked back at him, there was no longer any trace of the emotion that had been there a moment ago, her blue eyes now frozen over.

"I fell in love." Her jaw tightened before she added, "And I trusted the wrong person."

"Classic blunder, that," Declan said. "The trusting part, that is. Though I don't know why love would warrant such a sentence from the Council. Did you fall for one of the Lords? Or perhaps had an affair—"

Lani lifted an arm, keeping the other tucked tight across her ribs, and examined her nails, as one might do when bored. And then ever so slowly, she turned her palm toward him, exposing the delicate white of her forearm where the unmistakable design lay in stark contrast, its twists of smoky shadows seeming to creep from beneath her sleeve down to her wrist.

Declan's gut tightened, but he somehow maintained his bored expression as he spoke. "Ah, I see. And I take it you didn't fall for one of the Lords you were to be matched with?"

Once more crossing her arms in front of her, she gave him a small shake of her head.

"Well, this is certainly a first for me."

Her chin snapped up, her eyes burning with surprise.

"Not my first... well, you know," Declan said, as his mind chided him for being such a bumbling idiot. "But it is my first time with an heir to the Council."

Lani pursed her lips. "And what did you do to deserve such an *honor*?"

"Wrong time, wrong place," he said, and lifted his hands to the side in a shrug. "And no money."

Her eyes went wide for a moment before she uttered a quiet *interesting*.

"So the heirs don't know then," he said, not quite sure why he bothered going down this path in the conversation, but then again, any information was worth having. One never knew when one might need leverage of some kind.

"No." The word was barely over a whisper.

"But you knew."

Dipping her chin she said, "I had my suspicions. And I guess I was right, as we are nowhere near the docks and a ship to take me away."

"Aye." Declan gestured with a nod to the nearly invisible path that twisted through the trees beyond the boulder, noticeable only by those who knew it existed. "That trail doesn't lead to any ship, but it is a different sort of freedom perhaps."

Lani looked over her shoulder briefly, and when she turned back to him tears lined her bottom lashes. He waited for her to break down, but then this girl didn't seem the type to shy away from, well, anything. She lifted her chin, squared her shoulders, and lowered her arms until her hands were clasped together before her waist. "Well, let's get it over with then. You probably have other things you need to be doing."

Declan led the way through the trees, walking the entire twenty minutes in somber silence, with only the sound of their footsteps on the bed of pine needles that covered the ground. Until the sound of the Aisling Sea—usually a comfort to him—joined in, faint at first and growing louder as they neared their destination.

Her sharp inhale broke the silence—and echoed in Declan's chest—as they stepped into a clearing in the trees.

The sight never got easier to behold.

Not ten feet ahead of them, the ground simply disappeared. Stretching fifty feet to their left and right, it was no more than twenty-five feet across at its widest point—which lay directly in front of them. The trees didn't venture near the edge, as if the drop made them as uncomfortable as it did Declan. Lush grass filled the space between the pit and the forest, and the clearing might have been pleasant if it had existed anywhere else.

Lani approached the cave on careful toes, testing each footing to see if the ground gave way before putting her full weight into her step. Declan could have told her there was no point in doing that. The ground here might as well have been stone. When he'd come here all those years ago for that first exile, he'd wondered how such unforgiving soil could support this forest, but every visit since then simply left his stomach dropping into a pit of its own.

"How deep is it?" Lani asked, the words coming out barely audible over the sea's waves below and the breeze that had begun to pass through the trees above, as if the trees themselves were bidding her a farewell.

"I don't know, myself, but—" He stopped short.

"What? What were you going to say?" Lani had turned to look over her shoulder at him, her blue eyes boring into his, forcing him to look away.

What harm was there in telling her the truth?

It would terrify her unnecessarily, he thought.

But there was nothing about this situation that would warrant anything less.

"I, well." He paused to rub the back of his hand across his brow before finally meeting her gaze once again. "I imagine it's rather deep. Over a thousand feet at least."

She turned back to the black void that lay inches from her toes. "And how could you guess that?"

"Based on the length of their screams." He winced as he watched her arms begin to tremble. So many times he had imagined what the fall would feel like, to feel the air rushing past you, to not be able to see what awaited you until you...

When she spoke again, there was no hint of the fear that still coursed visibly through her body, and in any other moment he might have marveled at the control and poise she exhibited. "You said it didn't have to hurt. How? I can't imagine being thrown onto solid rock—or whatever awaits down there—from this height would be painless. So, how?"

"There are ways to kill..." He nearly added *you,* but stopped himself again. "...that are quick and relatively painless, as far as I am aware. I have, after all, never experienced them myself."

She gave another glance over her shoulder. "But you've done it often enough to assume."

"Aye. After the first exile I was tasked with, after hearing those first initial screams as they fell, it affected me more than I had expected. Haunted me. More than I care to admit. A pirate shouldn't have a problem with it, but there I was, facing nightmares after throwing them over that edge. So after that, I offered each a choice."

"Who would choose to be alive for that fall?" she asked as she turned fully away from the drop off to look at him.

"You'd be surprised. Some welcome the chance to feel the wind upon their faces one last time. Perhaps they want to be reminded that they once lived, that there are things of beauty in this world—even if just in the feel of air on their skin."

"You're rather poetic for a pirate. You don't meet too many of those."

And you won't get the chance to meet another.

He kept that thought to himself, at least, but he let the silence stretch out between them. He could have offered a witty remark, a word to tear down the Lords and their fleets. But the darkness behind her seemed to widen, gaping like a yawning mouth, reminding him time was quickly fading.

Taking a cautious step toward her, Declan opened his mouth to speak, but Lani cut him off.

"Is it time for me to make my choice?" While her expression held its steeled composure, her words quivered, betraying the fear she was trying so hard to contain.

"Aye. Only delaying the inevitable, and I do have other things I need to do today."

That's an understatement. Why are you being nice to her? Just push her in and get it over with.

It's what any other pirate would have done.

"Why are you being so nice to me?" Her question echoed his own thoughts.

"Would you rather I be mean? In addition to the whole killing you thing." He narrowed his eyes at her, taking another step toward her until there was no more than a foot between them. Close enough he could reach out and shove and be done with it.

But he didn't.

"Still. Why? You're a pirate."

He couldn't stop from pulling his mouth into a smirk. "As if I could forget."

"I suppose it makes sense, though," she said, her lifting a

shoulder before relaxing more than she ought to given the situation. When he didn't respond, she continued. "No need to worry about your reputation with me. Not like I'm going to have the chance to ruin your *good* name. Still, I'd think it'd be easier to do this, be less traumatizing for you, if you gave yourself over to the pirate within. I mean at this point I'm starting to wonder if you're a real pirate at all."

He gritted his teeth as her words struck a nerve. She was right. He wasn't acting much like a pirate here.

She inched toward him, her expression calmer than it had any right to be. "I wouldn't be surprised if you simply stepped aside and let me go."

Declan grabbed her then, the force causing her to stumble back, though he kept her from going over the edge. "Don't let my politeness fool you, Lani." He hardened his gaze at her, searching her eyes for any of the fear that should be swimming there. "I might have more manners than the other pirates, but I am still a pirate. Now, make your choice. And quickly. Because if you don't, I will make it for you."

Lani stared back at him, confident at first, as if she were still testing him, searching for the cracks in his hard exterior. But she would find none. He'd wasted enough time here already. His plan had been to get her to calm down, and he'd done that.

When she still hadn't moved or spoken, he tightened his fingers around her arms, and stepped forward again, edging her heels past the edge of the drop until she stood on only her toes with her body leaning slightly over the darkness. She grabbed his jacket, that desperation for survival kicking in, fear rushing into her eyes, her head gave tiny shakes, begging him to be different from the rest, to not do what was required of him.

He could say he was sorry, but it would do him no good to

let that piece of him out. He'd already allowed it to breathe for too long outside the wall he'd built around it. He shoved it back, securing it once again.

"Choose."

"Don't," she whispered, her terror increasing as he let her body angle away from him more.

"Now. Or I will."

He counted five seconds before he tensed his muscles, preparing to push her and be done with it, readying himself for the inevitable screams, knowing he wouldn't forget them soon enough.

"NO! I'll choose." Her words stopped him in mid-motion, and he raised his brows at her, a silent request for her answer. "Not like this. I don't want to know I'm falling. I don't want the air or whatever it is the others seek. Just end it. Quickly. Please."

Declan pulled her a few inches away from the edge, and without another word, he released one hand, keeping her firmly held with the other as he reached for his blade. She closed her eyes and breathed deeply, one last breath before the end came.

He didn't look away as he lifted his dagger. He looked her over one last time, this girl who had done nothing more than fall in love with the wrong person and dare to dream of a life she could never have, and pulling the air, ripe with the scent of the sea and the pine trees, he drove his blade in just behind her collar bone and pulled it out in one clean motion.

She gave a gasp, her eyes flashing open so he could watch the light in them dim quickly. With the dagger still in hand, her blood smearing across its smooth surface, he closed her eyes with the edge of his hand before letting her lifeless body fall away into the darkness.

He backed away from the edge, forcing coldness into his features, as if there was anyone here to witness his reaction. Wiping her blood from his dagger with the sash around his waist, he turned, not to go back to the road, but to pass around the massive hole. Eventually he would go back—back to Morshan, back to the pub, back to his men and his ship—but if he was going to focus on the next task, he needed to clear his head.

And he knew just how to do that on this island.

2

AOIFE

All of Aoife's dreams started the same. Every time she closed
her eyes, her mind whisked her away to the forest path leading to Morshan from the council hall. The scene mirrored that day
down to the most minute detail. The whisper of the wind through
the trees overhead. The puddles of dappled sunlight she disrupted
as she walked.

And Lani.

*"I don't know how you didn't know, Aoife," Lani said, her tone void of
any derision or disdain. Rather, she spoke the words with gentleness. "With
how curious you always were, why did you question everything but this?"*

*Aoife swallowed hard. There was so much she wanted to tell her sister,
strings of apologies and remorseful pleas for forgiveness, though she knew forgiveness was impossible now. At least from Lani. But the air thickened around
her, slowing her legs and constricting her lungs so that no sound could be made.*

Squeezing her eyes shut, she shook her head back and forth slowly, telling herself it wasn't real. She wasn't suffocating. She wasn't back on Cregah.

And Lani wasn't alive.

That thought forced her eyes open to verify it was a dream and that Lani and the forest had disappeared. But as she looked around, her heart quaked at the sight of Lani standing before her in a grassy meadow. The Aisling Sea was close enough that Aoife could hear its waters crash against the cliffs of her home.

The darkened sky scared her, but not nearly as much as the figure beside her sister. A man.

Aoife wanted to close her eyes, to save herself from having to witness this scene and accept it as truth, but her body refused to obey. When she was finally able to take a breath, she nearly recoiled at the familiar scent of sea mist and rum. Even if she had been able to shut out the image before her, she wouldn't have been able to ignore that smell, as it called up images of wet footsteps in black sand, the sharpness of a stone wall at her back, the tickle of his breath in her ear, the touch of his fingers along her neck, and the sound of her name on his lips.

As much as she wanted to ignore it all, she also yearned to hold on to each sensation like a treasured gift that needed protecting from a world that would rip it from her and destroy it.

But he has already done that, *her mind reminded her, and as if on cue, the man beside Lani turned.*

It was ridiculous to hope for the man to be someone else. It was always him. Always Declan.

But not as she had last seen him.

This was the Declan who had mocked her in the cove and accosted her in the alley. This was the Declan whose gray eyes gleamed not with hopeful love but callous apathy. A smirk turned up one side of his lips, and he winked at Aoife before turning to Lani, who waited calmly beside him.

The blade appeared in his hand, from where Aoife didn't know, but when he raised it toward her sister, she didn't run to stop him. She didn't call out to warn Lani. She didn't do anything but stand there, frozen.

Declan turned his head back to her, his blade still pointed at its target. "It might as well be you standing here." He flipped the dagger and caught the blade carefully in his hand before offering it to her, his eyes alight with excitement. "Would you like to do the honors?"

Aoife frantically looked between Declan and Lani as her chest tightened with the understanding that he was right. Her carelessness with her sister's secret had been as effective a weapon as the knife he now held out to her.

She whispered her answer to him, declining his grotesque offer. In an instant he righted the blade in his opposite hand and swept it across Lani's neck.

Blood sprayed across Aoife's face in the same alarming way it had on that beach in Foxhaven. Still, she couldn't move, other than to look down where Lani now lay, not in the clearing but in the council library. Blood pooled around her, as it had the servant who had helped them.

Aoife remained silent, unable to utter even one sound of surprise or grief, as she stared down at her sister. If anyone else was with her in this vision of the library, she didn't know. It was just her and Lani sharing a moment as the guilt suffocated her. That was what she deserved, to be killed by her guilt. Everyone else suffered for her mistakes. Why shouldn't she?

Declan had killed Lani. In every dream, over and over, he did it again and again. It was like her mind needed her to understand the truth and not foolishly give in to the hope that it hadn't been real and he had found a way to keep Lani alive while tricking the council.

But he was a pirate. And this was what pirates did.

From the shadows, Declan reappeared, whispering her name.

Blood soaked his clothes, covered his face and his hands. His eyes brimmed with tears of remorse that threatened to spill over at any moment. He held his hands out to her, not reaching but begging with palms up, as if her forgiveness was something tangible she could place in them.

"I love you," he whispered with blood-smeared lips.

Aoife woke with a start. A million tiny legs crawled over her chest with the weight of a person, crushing her and making it impossible for her lungs to take in the air she desperately needed. Placing a hand on her chest, she pressed her fist against her sternum, wishing it would be enough to quell the attack.

But it refused.

Her fingers pulled the chain at her collar, and she lifted the glass vial of black sand from underneath her shirt, squeezing as hard as she could. But the panic only pressed harder, slithering over her skin faster.

Breathe, she commanded herself. She longed for Declan to comfort her—like he did before—and then cringed from shame. She shouldn't want him or his help. Not after he had lied to her and betrayed her.

I love you.

The words from the memory and the dream collided within her chest, and she gasped just as she had in the cove.

If he truly loved her, he would have been honest. But he'd kept it from her.

Every time the wave of ire began to ebb, that fact would barrel its way through her thoughts, pushing her back into the depths of her bitterness.

Aoife was sure she was going crazy.

Her mind constantly shifted from wanting to forgive Declan to wanting to make him feel as betrayed as she did. She wanted to hurt him in return, but then her guilt surged once more, reminding her she was not the only person to ever have been hurt, nor would she be the last. Even knowing he was likely on his way to his death in the Black Sound, her heart held its iron grip on her misery. All while some small part of her wanted to forgive him, yearned to throw all of the anger into the depths, to grab hold of him and never let go.

Around and around her emotions twirled her, her broken heart like a life raft caught in a tempest.

She didn't know which way was up. Which choice led to happiness. If any of them would.

Tommy had insisted she try to get some rest. It would take several days to get to the Black Sound, and Gavin was pushing the crew to sail as quickly as possible even though the winds weren't cooperating.

All her attempts to rest had failed. She couldn't shut her eyes, so she simply stared at the wooden ceiling above her bed—their bed—as she had done so many times during her short stay on the ship. But she couldn't avoid the emptiness of the cabin any more than she could avoid the chaos in her mind.

She didn't dare look at his side of the bed. That wouldn't help her panic attacks.

Breathe, she reminded herself, clenching her teeth when she heard it not in her own voice but in his.

Tightness clutched at her chest, taking hold until she felt she might collapse into herself. Maybe that was what was best for everyone.

She'd helped no one.

Not Lani.

Not Tommy.

Not the poor servant.

Not Declan.

She'd begged him to let her help. What had she been thinking? That a week on a pirate ship could suddenly undo a life's worth of awkwardness and stumbling? Had she thought she could simply wish herself to change? To be different? Better?

Tears should have welled at all these thoughts, but they seemed trapped inside a vault within her, incapable of being conjured up.

Numbed by the overwhelming emptiness.

A throat cleared from across the room. How had she not heard the door open and shut?

"Not able to sleep?" Tommy asked, his voice stronger and less weary than she'd expected. Here his best friend was heading toward certain death, and he was speaking as if it was any old day.

Perhaps this was any old day for him though. What did Aoife know about pirate life after only one week?

Pushing herself up into a seated position, she kept one fist clenched to her chest as she worked to stretch out the discomfort between her shoulder blades before meeting his eyes. She didn't say anything but offered a quick shake of her head in answer.

"You should try."

Irritation bubbled up from its coffin within her, and she glared at him, jaw clenching as tight as her fists.

"It's not like I haven't tried, Tommy."

She shouldn't be so short with him, but she couldn't help it. Feeling frustration—even if unwarranted—was oddly comforting.

Though it did nothing to quell the anxiety that made this exchange even more cumbersome.

Breathe, Aoife. Just breathe.

But Tommy—the ever-patient saint that he was—didn't appear bothered by her biting tone.

"I know." He remained in the doorway, not leaning against the frame as Declan had done so many times during their talks, but standing awkwardly like he was itching to get away from this room. "You should still try. Maybe the sisters could do something to help you rest."

"Damn fae." The words fell from her lips in a sharp whisper.

"What?"

With a shake of her head, she dismissed his question. Her

issue with the trio of fae had little to do with their actions or their personalities. It had nothing to do with anything they could control. It was simply them being what they were created to be.

Graceful. Beautiful. Helpful.

Perfect.

Tommy wouldn't understand, nor could Aoife ever admit to anyone how she felt wholly insignificant beside them. It was her problem. Not theirs. Not his. She was the problem. Like always.

The phantom attack at her chest intensified, but she managed to draw in a deep breath, close her eyes, and focus on breathing. Surviving.

"Maybe rum then?"

She flashed her eyes open and turned her chin in question.

"That always has me sleeping like a baby." Though he offered a lopsided shrug, his words lacked their typical relaxed quality, and his eyes seemed dimmer than usual. He apparently wasn't as unfazed by the situation as Aoife had assumed.

"And it leaves me with a nasty headache." Her words dripped with bitterness. A bitterness that coated her tongue and singed her heart.

You're being unfair.

She was. And she knew it. But she couldn't control it. The irritability had taken on a life of its own, and it seemed to feed off the wounded parts of her heart, growing bigger and stronger and more formidable with each negative thought.

Maybe I am going crazy.

It seemed the only explanation for the complete lack of control she had over her emotions and thoughts. How could it be possible to *know* your thoughts were extreme and damaging and unproductive yet have no ability to stop them from attacking you? Even her mind had betrayed her.

"You okay?" Tommy's quiet question eased its way around the sea of grief that was drowning her. Such a simple question. Two words. But they were like a lifeline tossed toward her, and all she had to do was grasp it, let it pull her back in.

Tommy must have taken her silence as more irritation, because he rushed to explain. "It's a dumb question, I know. None of us are okay."

Aoife drew in a steadying breath. The tightness at her chest increased, but she fought it back with the words Declan had offered.

It's not you.

You aren't broken.

It doesn't control you.

While the feeling remained, she finally managed to wriggle herself free—as free as she could be from such internal torment. She stared down at her hands. "Do you think we'll reach him in time?"

Tommy's silence drew Aoife's attention to him. He roughed a hand over his mouth and along his stubbled chin before he lifted a shoulder. "I don't know. But I hope so. Even if we don't, we won't be too far behind them. And we have the fae. They can help us save him."

"And help us get the dagger."

"Aye. That too."

Aoife shifted in her seat, failing to ignore the way the anxiety had settled within her. "Maybe the dagger could help me overcome...this." She pressed a hand to her chest once again.

"The panic?" He offered a comforting smile. "Don't look at me all surprised. You're not the first person I've seen plagued with it."

"If it's enchanted to bring victory—"

"Victory over adversaries. I don't think it helps much against the enemies we carry inside ourselves."

Aoife breathed deep, but the rush of air did nothing to quell her unease. "If it did, even more people would be seeking it."

"Aye. Not everyone desires success in battle campaigns or political contests. But none of us are free from the demons within."

Desperate to change the subject, Aoife asked the first question she could think of. "How is the rest of the crew doing? Are they going mad having the fae aboard? Are they pushing you to throw us all overboard?"

Tommy gave one of his signature laughs, though it lacked its usual heartiness. "They are managing well enough, if only because they have no other choice. Even the new crewmen were so impressed by Declan's welcoming them the other night that they're as determined as the rest of us to get him back, even if it means having the fae around. And having to bunk with me and Gavin."

"You poor guys, giving up your quarters to wallow with the common crew." Aoife had meant for the comment to be funny, but it fell short. Still, Tommy laughed again, most likely from pity rather than actual humor.

"Aye. I don't know if we'll get much rest either with how loud they all are. Half of them snore like an anchor being raised from the depths. Others mumble and talk in their slumber. I've had to stick bits of cloth in my ears to get any sort of rest, regardless of the time of day."

"Well, if you're desperate for rest, you can always sleep in here if you want." She cleared her throat and felt her cheeks warm. "When I'm not in here, that is. We can take shifts sleeping."

"I might have to take you up on that offer." The mention of sleep must have reminded him of his own need for it, because his jaw dropped open into a yawn he failed to hide behind his hand.

"Seriously, Tommy," she said and stood up from the bed. She

motioned to the feather mattress with her arm. "I'm not getting any rest at the moment anyway. Lie down. Close your eyes. I'll head out and see what I can do out on the deck. Maybe I'll find someone to teach me to sail."

Tommy drew in a deep breath, and Aoife waited for him to refuse her offer, but he didn't. Instead, he walked past her and seated himself on the edge of the bed, his gaze settling on the floor beyond his boots.

"Thanks, Aoife. I appreciate it. But do me a favor?"

She hummed in response.

"Don't fall overboard. Declan would have my head if I let anything happen to you."

Aoife tried to swallow the ball of emotion that rose to her throat at the mention of Declan's name. But it wouldn't budge, preventing her from voicing any kind of response.

Tommy didn't seem to mind though. He pushed himself back onto the bed, crossed his arms behind his head, and closed his eyes.

She listened to his breathing lengthen into soft whispers before she turned to leave as quietly as she could.

At least one of them could sleep.

I'll sleep when I'm dead. Or after we get Declan. Whichever comes first.

3

TOMMY

The sound of Aoife's footsteps had long since faded away. Still, Tommy couldn't sleep. He'd closed his eyes and tried to concentrate on his breathing, but when the door had clicked shut, he'd allowed his eyes to flash open and study the wooden beams above Declan's bed.

His whole body felt heavy, slow, and his eyelids wanted to slide closed, but he forced them to remain open. He couldn't face what awaited him. Not yet.

He hadn't explained his fatigue to Aoife, and thankfully she hadn't asked. No doubt she assumed it was merely due to the stress of Declan heading toward ravenous sirens and the challenge of having to step into a leadership role he'd never wanted. And while he could have claimed his sleep was plagued by bad dreams— which was true—he didn't trust his tongue to not divulge everything. Especially with this exhaustion clouding his senses.

If only nightmares were the only thing he avoided. That would have been far less embarrassing.

Whenever he dared close his eyes, it wasn't the pirate slashing him across the chest he saw. It was her face. Maura. Youngest sister. Tormentor of his heart. Fae.

After he'd been wounded by Captain Madigen's man, the sisters had taken turns overseeing his healing, resting to replenish their powers before taking up where the other had left off. He had been unconscious at first, but when he came to, it was Maura's face he saw first, her golden eyes shining down at him as if she were studying him rather than mending his injuries. She'd said nothing as his eyes opened but smiled in an almost shy way. It had seemed contrary to his understanding of fae—which was admittedly quite limited.

They'd remained there in silence, her hands lightly pressed against his bare chest, as he took stock of his physical state. Nothing hurt anymore. No trace of the burning sharpness that had settled into him once shock had released its grip on his mind. No aching in his muscles. No throbbing of his head. Surely, he'd thought, his healing was complete, and her touch was unnecessary. But when he'd opened his mouth to tell her as much, he hadn't been able to push the words out. He'd swallowed them back down, where they sank beneath the waves of indecipherable emotions crashing against the edges of his heart.

Certainly it couldn't have been more than an involuntary reaction to a pretty face. He knew nothing about her. Yet, Tommy had seen many a pretty face—and plenty of other pretty feminine features—during his travels on the sea without the conjuring up of such a strange tension. Tension in certain parts of him, sure. He was only a man, after all. But never in his chest, his throat, his head.

Tommy had heard stories of the wounded or ill developing a

connection with their healers, and he was certain that was all it was.

A passing feeling.

A common, albeit strange, phenomenon.

Nothing more.

Yet the feeling hadn't passed, and it showed no signs of waning. If anything, it seemed to be strengthening even as he avoided her at all costs. But try as he might, he couldn't avoid her in his sleep, and part of him wondered if her powers included intruding into one's dreams. Or perhaps bewitching men into falling for her. He couldn't deny something had happened to him, though he didn't know exactly what to call it.

Love was impossible. The thought of it happening so fast was absurd. Everyone knew that wasn't how it worked. Love didn't happen instantaneously. It developed with time, conversation, touch, and—at least in Aoife and Declan's case—a bit of arguing and frustration.

While his mind urged him to avoid Maura, something within him seemed to seek her out, as if a void had been created in his chest and only she could fill it. He wanted to know everything about her. What life had been like before her imprisonment. What she had missed most while locked away. What haunted her dreams and what moved her to rise in the morning. Her favorite smell, color, memory. Everything.

There was far more to her than eyes of melted gold and a sweet yet devilish smile. Her beauty was merely the ornate entryway into a world he knew nothing about, a world he'd only caught glimpses of while he'd been healing. A world he wanted to step into, to explore, and to call home.

He shook his head desperately, his eyes closed tight. None of this would help them save Declan. But neither would being sleep-deprived.

One way or another, you'll have to face her eventually.

The thought echoed in his mind as he succumbed to the lure of sleep, letting the weariness take over. He was too tired to keep fighting the dreams.

When he opened his eyes once more, he found Maura standing before him. Even in his sleep, he knew it wasn't real. They were in an empty room. Whether it was on a ship or on land, he couldn't tell, couldn't see much past her. It was as though she was giving off her own light. She smiled—a coy yet somehow innocent curve of her mouth—as she raised her hand and beckoned him forward with a graceful wave of her fingers.

His feet moved against his will, taking him forward until he was close enough to feel the warmth emanating from her. Searching her eyes, he silently asked her the question he couldn't utter aloud.

What is happening to me?

As if this were an ailment or an infection that only needed the right poultice to be cured.

He shouldn't be dreaming of Maura. Not when Declan was missing. Not when they had so little hope of reaching him in time.

He tried to back away from her, but he hadn't made it a half step when her arms lifted, her hands cupping his neck. Despite her intensity and swiftness, it wasn't an aggressive gesture but a caring one. Loving.

Tommy swallowed hard. Maura's thumbs brushed against his ears as she ran her fingers through his hair.

It's not real. It's not real. It's only a dream.

But even as he repeated these words, he knew he was lying to himself.

When he woke up, she would disappear, but the feelings wouldn't. He'd be left with this yearning to be near her and to know her, to care for her and to live life beside her. A yearning for something that could never be, could never work.

He was human.

She was fae.

And she was heading to Larcsporough after all of this. If they survived.

He couldn't follow her. He couldn't abandon Declan and Gavin and the *Siren's Song* to follow Maura south. His place was here, on the ship, on the Aisling. And Maura belonged with her kin. While he didn't know why she was needed, he couldn't shake the sense that it was rather important.

No matter how much he hated it, they were from two separate worlds. Worlds that could never truly mix.

There was no point in torturing himself by allowing this to go anywhere. Even in his dreams. So when she leaned into him, he steeled himself, using all his strength to not glance at her mouth, where her tongue moistened her lower lip in anticipation. He didn't want to hurt her, couldn't dream of hurting her, but if he pursued this, if he let himself take another step into her life, that was what would surely happen.

Lifting his hands, he grabbed her arms below her shoulders and pushed her away as gently as he could. She didn't fight him, didn't argue, but allowed her fingers to slide away from his neck and drift back down to her sides, where they clenched the fabric of her dress. Her gaze burned into his, and the passion he'd seen in her eyes moments before had been replaced with a deep mourning that pressed into his chest so powerfully he expected his heart to be crushed against his spine.

"I'm sorry," he whispered. Again and again, he offered up his apologies as he backed away from her. And with a jolt, she disappeared, along with the room they'd been in, leaving him surrounded by nothingness.

His eyes flew open.

The ship had stopped.

And there were only a few possible reasons why. None of them good.

Forcing the intense longing and bitterness to retreat to some far corner of his consciousness, he rose from the bed and made his way across the cabin. He was acting captain. Whether he knew how to fulfill the role or not, he needed to focus, and he couldn't do that with her haunting him in both reality and his dreams.

He needed to end it—whatever it was—and soon.

4

DECLAN

The tang of iron coated Declan's tongue, as sharp as the metal that dug into his wrists behind his back. How long he'd been here, in the dark and rank innards of the *Curse Bringer*, he wasn't sure. When he'd come to, he'd been confused and half-thinking he was back on his own ship. The only clue to the contrary had been that he was cold, uncomfortable, and alone instead of in his bed relaxing with Aoife beside him.

Aoife.

Her name instantly conjured up images against his will. The look in her eyes when she'd denied him the forgiveness he'd needed. The way her expression had twisted in confusion and disbelief when those damned words had spilled from his mouth.

I love you.

He hadn't meant to say it. He hadn't even known he could say it until that moment.

She probably thought it was a disingenuous attempt at getting back into her good graces after what he'd done to her. Another lie to get what he wanted.

His head ached, the pain throbbing behind his eyes and radiating down from his ears before settling into the base of his skull.

The knot on the back of his head where they'd struck him begged for attention, but with his arms shackled behind his back, there was no hope of checking to see how bad it was. They must have hit him rather hard though, because he could sense a sticky mess of blood in his hair; it pulled whenever he moved his head.

Where they were taking him he wasn't sure, but given how angry Callum had been about his deception, it was no doubt somewhere undesirable.

Like everything in my life.

He chided himself for the thought. Now was not the time to get depressed. If he had any hope of getting off this blasted ship and back to his own, back to his crew, back to Aoife...

He shoved the image of her away as best he could. Replaying her disapproval over and over wouldn't help him. Not now. He could deal with that later. But now he had to devise an escape.

Heavy boots sounded on the ladder at the far side of the room, and Declan lay his aching head against the side of the hull, closing his eyes.

The footsteps were slow but determined. Whether it was Callum, his quartermaster, or another member of the crew, he couldn't tell, but he was certain they weren't coming to see him for anything good.

Declan slowed his breathing as he counted the steps. When they stopped, he focused on the breathing of his visitor—low, raspy, labored. Whoever Callum had sent, it wasn't someone in peak physical shape. But he was likely one of the larger men, especially if he'd come down here alone. Callum either underestimated Declan, or this crewman was tough enough he knew he could handle Declan on his own.

Unless he's just bringing you food.

His stomach grumbled at the thought.

A loud clang rang through the room, reverberating through the floor and up Declan's spine, and he squeezed his eyes tighter before lazily opening them. He'd been right. Standing before him was a rather large individual, half as wide as he was tall. He was, in fact, quite huge, having to duck his head to fit into this small section of the ship.

Although he certainly had the advantage of size, being in such a confined space might even the odds in Declan's favor.

Declan mulled over his different options for attack even as he asked, "Can't a man get some sleep here?" He kept his words slow and coated with grogginess.

The man huffed out a gruff laugh—or what Declan assumed to be a laugh, despite no mirth showing on the man's face. It was either a laugh or the man had a sudden tickle in the back of his throat that needed clearing.

"Cap'n wants to see you."

Declan looked around the brig before meeting the crewman's gaze again. "He knows where I am. He could have come down himself."

This time there was no doubt the man laughed. "You think he would come down to the dregs of the ship for you?"

"Perhaps he should take better care of his ship then?"

"The brig isn't meant for comfort."

"Aye, I've had better," Declan said, once again looking around, but this time with a twist of disgust playing on his lips. "So I am to come to him then? I'll need help standing."

The keys to his iron cage rattled in the man's large paw of a hand. The sound of the lock snapping open and iron scraping against the wooden floor sent a spark of hope through Declan's bones. Not that he'd let it show. He didn't need to force the wince onto his face as the man grabbed him by the elbows and hoisted him up to his feet, which were surprisingly steady given how long he must have been sitting here.

The scent of sweat and grime from his escort mingled with the musty odor of his surroundings, twisting the wince on his face into a grimace. He might have spent over a decade on pirate ships, but each had its own distinct scent, and the *Curse Bringer* was proving fouler than any he'd boarded before.

The man clamped his hand around Declan's elbow and shoved him beyond the iron bars toward the ladder. The tightness of his grip at least distracted Declan from the pain in his head, but only slightly.

Stop being a baby. You've had worse.

He turned his chin over his shoulder. "It's a tad difficult to climb a ladder with my hands bound."

In response, the man put his bulky hand between Declan's shoulder blades and pushed him once again. "Climb."

"First time for everything, I suppose," he said under his breath as he stepped up onto the first rung.

Each step was painfully slow. As he moved his feet carefully from rung to rung, he was forced to trust that the big oaf behind him would keep him upright.

"This would go faster if you unchained me, you know. I'd hate to keep Captain Grayson waiting."

"He can tolerate your slow-ass ascent more than he could tolerate you trying to escape. So, no."

"Escape?" The word came out strained as he moved another

foot, his head now popping up into the next area of the ship—the munitions hold most likely, though in the darkness he couldn't make out much more than a few stacks of crates. "How could I possibly escape? Your crew would cut me down before I even made it on deck."

"Aye, that's true. But still. We won't risk it."

When Declan stepped onto a solid floor again, he waited for his escort to meet him.

"You know," he said as he took a step toward the stairs, "it makes little sense that the brig is only accessible by a ladder. How do you get your prisoners down there? Seems like it could have been better designed."

"Not my concern. I don't question Cap'n's choices for ship setup. Or anything for that matter. I simply drop sorry lots like you into the brig and drag your sorry asses into that cage where you belong."

Declan trudged up the stairs slowly, though not so much on purpose as from necessity, his legs still burning from having to climb that damn ladder without use of his hands.

"I suppose that explains all this pain then. Hit over the head and then dropped down a ladder. Some way to treat a friend."

A scoff sounded from behind him. "Friend. Ha."

Declan waited for the man to say more, but they continued their walk up a few more flights of stairs before arriving on deck. He blinked as they emerged into the pale light of dawn. It wasn't midday as he'd expected, and the mellow pinks and purples on the horizon were easier on his eyes than the bright sunlight would have been.

They were moving at a fast clip. North. His stomach clenched at the realization. Callum couldn't be this stupid.

Or he could be. Likely is.

The crew only afforded Declan passing glances as they continued their work to keep the ship sailing on their current heading despite the wind wanting to push them in the opposite direction, as if it knew where they were headed and was using all its effort to prevent them from doing so. Declan made his way across the deck, marveling at the efficiency with which Callum's crew worked. Had he not been shackled as a damned prisoner of the bastard, he might have complimented Callum for how the ship was run. But as it was, he had no desire to extend such pleasantries.

Callum's quarters were tucked away under the quarterdeck as Declan's were, except instead of being accessible from the center of the deck, the entrance was off to the starboard side. Anyone not familiar with a ship might have thought it was a door to a storage closet, as it was rather nondescript, shabby, and worn from the years at sea.

Declan stopped before it, not bothering to step aside. He glanced over his shoulder at his escort, who stood uncomfortably close.

"Shall I knock then? Or did you want the honor?"

The man rolled his eyes, but before either of them could lift a hand to the door, a voice bellowed from behind it, "Get in here!"

The beefy hand of the crewman pushed past Declan and shoved the door open before forcing Declan inside.

"Leave us!" the voice boomed again, and Declan found himself thrust further into the cabin. The door closed behind him.

Keeping his eyes forward, locked on the man seated before him, Declan took in what he could of his surroundings, taking stock of what this captain valued, how he lived. Anything that might prove advantageous. But there seemed to be little help here. Little of anything really. He'd expected Captain Grayson to be the type to hoard riches in his cabin, to take the best of the plunder for himself and display it around his quarters to bolster his pride.

But the quarters were sparse. Simple and understated. The room held only a simple desk—worn and tired. No rug on the wooden floor. No shelves. In one corner of the room lay a small mattress. No separate sleeping quarters. No separate dining area.

"Your hospitality is sorely lacking, Captain," Declan said.

Callum leaned back in his chair, his head tilting to the side as he examined Declan, his fingers ripping into the rough skin of a round fruit Declan had never seen before. He dropped the pieces of the rind onto his desk before tearing off a segment and sending its juice spraying into the air in front him—its sharp scent filling the room—then popped it into his mouth.

"It seems you've forgotten what we are, McCallagh, if you think *hospitality*"—he spat the word, spittle and juice and bits of fruit flying from his mouth—"is something to be concerned with."

"Regardless, I would have thought our years of—"

"Of what?" Callum said sharply. "Camaraderie? Partnership? Perhaps you haven't forgotten what we are, after all, since you saw fit to treat me so."

Declan chewed on the inside of his lip, contemplating how to respond, but he came up empty.

Callum snickered. "What? No smart-ass quip this time? My man must have hit you harder than I thought."

Declan huffed a short laugh. "Well, such treatment sure-ly doesn't help one's ability to perform. My head still hurts, you know."

"I'm not concerned with your comfort."

"And what is it you're concerned with then?"

"I'm sure you've guessed by now."

"Aye, I have my suspicions."

"I know it's in the Black Sound, McCallagh. I also know you

had this information before sending us on that useless hunt."

"What can I say—"

"Nothing. Keep your damned mouth shut." Callum's eyes narrowed on him, sheer rage washing over his face for a moment before he pulled it back, took a deep breath, and settled back into his usual quiet but menacing state.

Declan merely stared back. Waiting.

"Past actions aside, you can make it up to me now."

Declan flashed him a questioning look, though he already knew what Callum wanted.

"You will help us retrieve the dagger from the sound."

"If you know it's in the sound, then you also know—"

"Aye. The sirens."

Declan's eyes went wide with a silent question.

"You were heading there yourself, McCallagh, so don't play me here. I know you know how to get past them. So you'll do so. But for me."

"Aye, I do know how to get past them. But that knowledge alone won't be any good when you've stolen me away from those who would make it possible."

"And who is that?"

Declan shifted his weight, refusing to break away from the stare Callum had him trapped in. How much could he tell this captain? How much could he reveal? Could he afford to divulge his secret? And did it even matter? If they continued on this course, he'd be dead within minutes of their arrival anyway. They both would be.

"The fae."

Callum burst into laughter as his head fell back. When he snapped forward again, the amusement remained, dancing in his eyes and across the devilish smile that made the ghastly scar that ran across his face more prominent.

"You expect me to believe that, Declan? Seriously? The fae are gone. Resting at the bottom of the Aisling or hiding in Larcsporough like the cowards they are."

"Not all fled or died. Three remained. Sisters. Imprisoned by the council."

Callum sobered up quickly as he leaned forward. Tossing the orange fruit aside, he propped his elbows on the desk and steepled his fingers under his chin.

"And that's why you were in Morshan. Why you failed to meet me."

Declan gave a nod. The men studied each other for a silent minute, maybe two, before Callum barked out another laugh. "No."

"No, what?" Declan asked, honestly unsure what the man meant.

"I don't believe you. You're simply trying to delay the inevitable, convince me to turn around, where I'm sure your crew is waiting to ambush us to get their dear captain back. It won't work, Declan. You know a way past them, and you will help me get that dagger, or you die."

"If you don't listen to me now, I'll be dead anyway. We all will."

"It's a risk I'm willing to take."

"Then you're stupider than I thought."

Silence fell between them again. Callum rose from his seat and walked around the desk until he stood inches away from Declan, who did his best not to flinch away from the forced proximity and the stench of perspiration and filth that stung his eyes.

Callum lowered his voice to a whisper as coarse and rough as his weathered face. "You will do this, and you will get me past those ravenous bitches. Try to escape before we arrive? Try to jump overboard? Try to harm yourself to avoid this? And I'll pay that sweet sister of yours a visit. She looks like she could offer up a bit of sport before I spill her guts all over that pub floor."

Declan looked Callum in the eye, searching for any hint that the man was bluffing, though he knew the effort was pointless. Of course the man was telling the truth. He'd heard of him doing much worse for far milder infractions.

Images rushed into his mind of Cait struggling in Callum's grasp, fighting and punching to get free, falling to the ground. His chest caved in, crushed in a vice he hadn't experienced in years. Before his mind could conjure up the images of her blood spilling out, he shook everything away and broke Callum's stare, glancing lazily around the captain's quarters.

Raising his shoulders into a shrug, he asked, "And how would that be possible? You run a tight operation here. No doubt I wouldn't get far if I attempted an escape."

Callum wagged a finger in his face, narrowing his eyes before pulling one side of his mouth into what might have been intended as a smirk. "I know you, McCallagh. You'd find some way."

"Ah, I'm flattered. But alas…" Declan rubbed his chin against his collarbone to quell an itch that sprang up, hoping he wasn't being infested with parasites on this disgusting ship. He locked eyes with Callum, once again forcing himself to stand as tall and proud as possible and not shrink away from the ripeness of his host. "Despite any familial drama, my sister doesn't deserve to pay for my own stupidity in getting caught. So, I suppose I have no other option than to help."

His muscles tensed in response, protesting the concession, fighting against the inevitable demise awaiting them in the Black Sound.

How are you going to get yourself out of this one, Declan?

5

CAIT

The morning light filtered through the wavy panes of the old window, bright enough that Cait McCallagh couldn't justify sleeping any longer. Not that she'd slept much as it was. Her eyes slid open a fraction before scanning the small apartment she'd grown up in with her parents and Declan. While she had gotten used to spending most nights at her office underground, she had decided Declan's operation at the council warranted due diligence in keeping up the ruse that she was merely a pub owner managing the family business.

Kira had rushed into the pub in the early morning hours, her frantic state nearly giving her away as a Rogue as she approached Cait with the news that she'd seen Declan taken by Callum and his men. Cait had attempted to keep her face impassive as she'd dispatched Lucan to get word to Declan's men as quickly as possible.

She hadn't been able to relax after that but had filled drinks and made small talk, her carefully constructed mask firmly in place despite the panic tightening her chest. It had only loosened its grip a fraction when Lucan returned and gave her an almost imperceptible nod to let her know he'd delivered the message.

The night had been long, and it had taken every ounce of her willpower to not kick every patron to the curb and lock up early so she could collect her thoughts.

It wasn't like this was the first time Declan had been in trouble, but it had been nearly twelve years—when she'd learned he'd run off to be a cabin boy—since the last time she'd worried about his well-being to this extent.

He's a pirate. And a good one.

She tried to remind herself of these two facts, but the unease wouldn't leave her alone. Not completely.

When the last of the customers had finally ambled out the door mere hours before dawn, Lucan had helped her up the stairs to her apartment. She'd seen the offer in his eyes, the offer to stay, but she'd given a shake of her head, insisting she'd be fine and would see him later for lunch.

Not that she could even think about food.

But she couldn't bear to have him doting on her. Not now. She just needed quiet. Peace. Time to think.

To plan.

What had happened at the council hall last night? Lucan had confirmed they'd gotten the fae sisters out. So at least something had gone according to plan. But why had Declan been separated from his crew? Why had he been alone in those dark streets? Such an idiot.

What have you gotten yourself into, Declan? Why did you bring Callum, of all people, into this job?

She threw her questions at the dust motes floating through

the dim rays of light.

The sound of a door opening pulled her away from her questions.

She sat up, her hand reaching for the dagger she kept in her right boot that she hadn't bothered to kick off before lying down. The back door to the alley clicked shut, and two voices whispered at the bottom of the stairs.

Idiots. Why were they here? And together? She'd need to get firm instructions to her team if they were going to manage to avoid being detected by the council and its hired goons.

They knew better than to come up the stairs at least.

With a steadying breath, she rolled the tension from her shoulders before making her way down to meet them. Cait let her irritation be known with each stomp of her feet on the stairs. Lucan stood at the bottom like a tightly wound coil of nerves ready to explode at any moment.

He hadn't been in such a state a few hours ago.

"What happened, Lucan?" Cait said by way of greeting.

He didn't answer but motioned to the alley door, where a young girl stood, worrying her fingers in the hem of her shirt.

"Eva, what is it?" Cait took a step forward but didn't get too close, as it looked like she might run off if spooked.

"Maggie." The girl's eyes dropped to the floor just as Cait's insides did the same, crashing down into her feet. She'd known this was possible when she'd assigned Maggie to that station. And Maggie had gone willingly, eagerly even, knowing the high stakes and the importance of the information it would give the Rogues.

"She's—" Cait couldn't seem to utter the word. All air was sucked from the room until she didn't know how she even managed to remain upright and conscious.

But it was Lucan who answered, his tone low and cautious,

ever aware of the possibility of spies everywhere. "Aron saw her this morning, just before dawn. You know we're always watching the paths from the council hall. He saw them taking her body, or *a* body, but they screwed up, and the cloth they had wrapped her in blew off in the morning breeze, and he saw her red hair. It was her, Cait."

The room spun against her will. What kind of leader couldn't keep it together when the inevitable happened?

No. She would lead. She wouldn't break.

"I need a drink," she said and plodded over to the bar, not bothering to motion for them to follow her, but she knew they'd be cautious and likely wouldn't.

She grabbed a glass and a bottle of rum from beneath the bar and poured a dram, downing it quickly before pouring another. The alcohol didn't burn away the bitterness as she'd foolishly hoped, but it snapped her out of the stupor that had taken hold.

Straightening her shoulders, she turned to find, as expected, Lucan and Eva standing cautiously in the doorway of the back storeroom. Given the strict regulations regarding business hours, being seen with patrons at the bar could bring unwanted attention.

She took a few steps toward them and shooed them back. "Upstairs. Now." She gave one last glance over her shoulder to ensure no one was looking through the front windows.

Once upstairs, with the door to the apartment shut, she motioned for them to sit at the old dining table that sat in one corner of the main space.

"Do we have any information on what happened?" Cait asked, willing her nerves to remain calm.

"How could we?" Lucan answered, his tone carrying more desperation than irritation. "She was our one set of eyes in there."

"Fair enough." Cait's mind rushed through all the facts of the situation, and she considered how this incident would affect the next step of their operation.

Eva cleared her throat, and Cait nodded for her to speak up.

"Well, this is the first time we've ever seen actual physical evidence of their work, right? At least evidence tying it directly to the council. Until now, we've only known it's the pirates doing the killing. Now we have a clear sign that killing is happening with the council's own knowledge."

Lucan added, "They've gotten sloppy."

"I can't figure out how that helps us though. Unless we push them out into the open," Cait said, shifting forward to rest her elbows on her knees, her fingers an anxious mess of movement and her eyes seeing nothing but the apartment floor.

"They had to have figured out who she was working for," Lucan said. "Declan wouldn't have risked killing someone unless he absolutely had to."

Cait snapped her face up to look at him. "Declan didn't kill her."

The sharpness of her words had Lucan recoil as he stumbled to explain. "I didn't say he did. Merely that he wouldn't have allowed them to get into a situation that would have gotten her killed…"

Rolling her eyes, Cait waved away his lengthy explanation with a hand.

"What are we going to do?" Eva's voice was timid.

"Stay the course. It's what Maggie would have wanted. We'll be flying relatively blind now that she's gone, and I doubt the council will be too keen on hiring anyone new. Assuming they know who she was working for."

"Is it possible they don't know?" Lucan asked. "That she was just an unfortunate bystander? Wrong place, wrong time?"

"Possible, perhaps," Cait said. "But it's best for us to assume the worst. No way to confirm either way, so we move forward under the assumption that the council knows the Rogues got a spy in their walls and that they likely know what we're after."

They sat in silence for what felt like an eternity. And yet, it wasn't nearly enough time for her to sort out all the thoughts rustling around in her mind. Lucan's toe tapped against the wooden floor—a nervous habit of his when he was lost in thought. Normally it was endearing. Today it was a thorn in her side.

Cait punched to her feet and began pacing the room, shaking her head from side to side as she analyzed the situation from every angle.

Worst case, they'd been caught by the council. The council had killed Maggie. But then they'd let Declan go.

Why? Why not kill him for infiltrating and kidnapping the fae?

The fae. She'd forgotten about them. She stopped her pacing and spun on her toe to face Lucan again.

"The fae. They got out?"

Lucan gave a quick set of nods. "Aye. I saw them aboard Declan's ship."

Cait rubbed her hand across the back of her neck. "Well, at least that's to our advantage."

"But your brother. Why would they let him go?" Eva echoed Cait's unspoken question.

"If I had to guess, they want him to get the dagger for them. It's the only thing that makes sense. Get to it before we can. Whether they know he's working for us or not? Doesn't matter. But likely they sent him to go get it."

"But Callum..." Lucan said, his toe no longer tapping.

"Aye. Let's hope Declan's crew can intercept them before they arrive at the sound."

"Do we think the council knows who you are?" Lucan asked. "Who any of us are?"

"If they did, I'd likely not be breathing right now. They'd have some pirate knocking down my door already—"

As if on cue, a loud bang sounded from downstairs as someone entered the pub and slammed the door behind them.

Cait lifted her finger to her lips, instructing them to keep quiet before she whispered, "Stay here. Don't move. I'll be right back."

6

AOIFE

Aoife shut the door to Declan's quarters behind her, careful to keep it quiet so as not to disturb Tommy, though it was likely unnecessary, as the sound of the crew bustling around on deck had been impossible to ignore from within. Still, she refused to add to the noise.

"She lives!" Gavin's voice bellowed from where he stood at the helm on the quarterdeck, and he flashed her his bearded grin, his eyes twinkling as if they weren't on a race against time to rescue their captain from certain death at the jaws of evil sirens.

Aoife smiled in return, though it was contrived. Gavin didn't seem to notice though, and he motioned for her to join him.

She'd never been allowed on the quarterdeck and hadn't dared request permission after Tommy had yelled at her for nearly stepping foot on it before.

The view of the sea—even from this vantage point, a mere

seven feet above the rest of the ship—sucked the breath from her. Teal water spread out before them, still vibrant despite the billowing clouds in the skies casting shadows across its surface. The vast emptiness was both freeing and suffocating, beckoning her with promises of adventure even as it warned of the dangers that lay ahead. Aoife saw no hint of land, no hint of any other ships. She'd always imagined the Aisling teeming with ships. So many crews and ships to keep straight in her mind, and that was only the lords and their fleets. Perhaps she'd failed to grasp how large the Aisling really was.

"You seem to have found your sea legs, Miss," Gavin said, giving her a nudge with his elbow.

"Please, Gavin. It's Aoife. And yes. Thankfully."

"It'll be Miss for now. I mean, you're practically the quartermaster."

"But you never called Tommy by any such formality." Aoife pulled her brows together.

"That's what you focused on? Not that I just gave you a title?"

Aoife shook her head and laughed. "Well, that too. I mean, both are absurd. One, for me to be a quartermaster, I'd have to be a pirate—"

Gavin made a point of looking her over from head to toe before flashing her a questioning glance.

Aoife ignored him and continued. "And if I were the quartermaster—which I am not, because, come on, Gavin—I'd expect similar treatment as Tommy. So you'll call me Aoife. Okay?"

"No offense, *Miss* Aoife, but you're not as scary as Tommy, who gave a rather convincing threat to anyone who dared call him anything but his first name."

Aoife couldn't even imagine Tommy offering any sort of threat or looking menacing in any way. And this was after witnessing him take down a handful of Lord Madigen's men in the library.

She settled her forearms against the railing and breathed in the sea air, pulling it into every inch of her body, wishing it could clear her thoughts and wash away everything she now faced.

After a few minutes of watching the horizon in silence, she asked, not bothering to look at him as she did, "Why would you call me the quartermaster?"

"Well, Miss Aoife, if you recall, I said *practically*. And am I wrong? You're sleeping in the captain's quarters—not that that's typical of quartermasters, mind you—but you are also a pivotal part of the decision-making."

"Am I? I don't feel like I am. I feel like I'm still just an annoying stowaway."

"An annoying stowaway who plundered our captain's heart though. And you claim you're not a pirate."

Aoife's chest tightened involuntarily as Declan's *I love you* echoed once again in her mind. "Still, that shouldn't grant me any special rank. Don't you have to work your way up to such titles?"

Gavin shrugged through a laugh. "Eh, yes and no. Every ship is different. But it's not unheard of, although 'tis rare for a captain to lead his crew with his love by his side, not necessarily as equals. But close."

"But I thought women aboard were seen as a curse."

"You'd be surprised how quickly that becomes a non-issue when it's the captain's lover."

Aoife cringed as her face grew warmer. Did everyone on this ship consider her that? Had Declan told them all? "I don't know that I'm..." She abandoned that, deciding it didn't matter one way or the other. "Even so, I doubt the crew likes the idea. I don't even know how to sail. Or fight."

"Aye, you are a rather unconventional choice. But to be honest, we're all happy to see the captain happy. Or we were. Until whatever happened last night."

A familiar rush of numbness froze her veins, spreading from her chest out to all her limbs. Guilt. Her old friend, who tensed her insides and pulled her into a void where nothing existed except her and her mistakes. So many mistakes.

Gavin's elbow nudged her again. "Apologies. I didn't mean to throw it in your face."

"It's not your fault. It's mine."

Gavin let out a short whistle, and Aoife turned to see a crewman walk over from where he'd been standing at the other end of the quarterdeck. Gavin entrusted the helm to him and then gestured for Aoife to join him on the opposite side of the stairs. He rested one elbow on the railing as he looked at her, and she realized she had underestimated him, writing him off as an inconsequential member of the crew.

His encouraging smile had his blue-gray eyes twinkling with kindness. "If I may... It's not too late. There's time to make amends. To make things right."

"How can you be sure?" Aoife asked, pushing herself away from the railing. The quiet numbness was giving way to prickling panic. She flung an arm out, gesturing to the sea before them. "He's nowhere in sight, and he's headed to certain death. How can it not be too late?"

Gavin pulled in a deep breath that sent his shoulders slumping.

"Aye. I admit it doesn't look promising. But if we don't have hope, what do we have?"

Aoife looked back to the horizon as she pondered his words and focused on the clouds that were swirling in a slow but powerful dance. She'd never seen such beauty from the black sands of Cregah. The council hall was too guarded by trees to allow for a good view of the skies, and the cove gave a far more limited view of the sea than she had here.

She didn't know how long they remained there not speaking, but she found herself thankful for Gavin's intuition, his knowing when not to push further.

Hope.

She had to cling to that, to the hope that she'd get her chance—when she was ready—to offer Declan the forgiveness she could never receive from Lani. Yes, there was time. There had to be.

Beside her, Gavin muttered a curse, sharp but quiet, before rushing away. He bellowed down to the crew, "Heave to!"

Aoife glanced at him and then at the crew, who didn't question the order or hesitate as they worked the sails and prepared to carry out whatever Gavin's command had meant.

"Ready to heave to!" Gavin called.

The crew answered with a "Ready!"

Aoife watched as Gavin spoke with the man at the helm. He guided him through a maneuver while shouting commands to the crew. She stared in awe as the men worked the ropes and sails with a grace as beautiful as any dance she'd seen by the troupes the council invited for festivals and holidays. Gripping the railing as the ship turned past windward, she worried she might lose her balance with the movement.

But then everything stopped. The ship seemed to come to a standstill, bobbing along the waves, nearly as steady as when in port.

Gavin rushed for the stairs, motioning for her to follow.

"What is it?" she asked, nearly tripping down the steps in an effort to keep up. Something troubled him; of that she was certain. But Gavin didn't answer. He strode around the staircase and made for the crew's barracks.

Aoife called after him again. "Tommy's not down there."

Gavin whirled around.

"He's in Declan's cabin." Gavin's brows twitched, his head tilting slightly with that familiar look of curiosity she often received from people when she misspoke. Her hands fidgeted, as did her feet, and she moved quickly to explain. "He was exhausted. I told him to take the bed for a few hours to rest."

Gavin breathed an "ah" before starting off again, careful to avoid colliding with her. She turned and followed, her heart thumping against her sternum and her mind whirring with what might have Gavin so worked up.

Before they made it to the door, the fae sisters met up with them on silent feet.

"Why have we stopped?" Renna asked.

Gavin, normally a perfect gentleman—or as perfect a gentleman as a pirate could be—with the sisters, gave them little more than a sideways glance and no verbal response. But he didn't stop them from following him into the cabin as he pushed open the door, not bothering to knock.

Aoife followed the sisters inside, shutting the door behind them.

"Tommy!" Gavin shouted on his way into the sleeping quarters. He stopped short when Tommy appeared in the doorway, his eyes blinking against the sleep that had been interrupted.

"I'm up. Felt us stop."

"Aye. Storm brewing ahead. And quickly."

A curse fell from Tommy's mouth. "I was afraid of that. Hoped our luck hadn't completely abandoned us."

He walked around Gavin toward the map still laid out on Declan's desk and cleared away the books and other odds and ends Declan had left there.

Leaning over, bracing himself with his arms, he studied the seas. He didn't look up as the others joined him around the desk. Aoife wondered if this was a typical situation and whether Tommy and Gavin were unnerved being here with her and the fae instead of Declan.

But if it bothered them, they didn't show it at all.

Tommy pointed at a spot north of Cregah. "We're here, aye?"

Gavin mumbled a confirmation. Tommy lifted his hand to his chin and spoke through his fingers. "We can assume they're on the other side of this storm, that it didn't come up until after they'd passed through—"

"How can you assume that?" Aoife interrupted.

Tommy met her gaze from under his brow, not bothering to lift his chin. "The Aisling is known for creating these storms quickly and powerfully. Sailors and crews become quite accustomed to finding themselves in the middle of a squall with little warning, if any. That is, if they survive at all. With this one just starting and with the lead they had on us…"

Gavin traced his finger along a path off to the west. "We could go around it, pulling in closer to Haviern, where the seas are normally calm this time of year."

Tommy shook his head. "It takes us too far off course. We'd lose any chance of reaching him in time."

Aoife's gut clenched at the words, and she swallowed the protest that nearly escaped her lips.

"Well, that leaves us with only two options: brave the storm or risk the waters near Tyshaly," Gavin said, and Aoife could have sworn she saw him blanch slightly at his own words.

The fae sisters still hadn't said anything but were standing around the desk like statues, though they studied the map along with the others.

"What's the risk there?" Aoife asked.

Gavin and Tommy both drew in a breath, but it was Maura who answered for them, her light voice taking on a dark tone. "The beasts that live beneath the surface."

Aoife felt pinpricks dance along her arms and creep up her neck.

"Aye. It's why Tyshaly's main port was built so far south," Tommy answered. "Closer to their enemy to the south, but it kept the merchant vessels safer from the dangers lurking below."

Aoife didn't know if she wanted the answer, but she asked anyway. "What manner of beasts?" She knew of the sharks that lived off the coast of Cregah and had heard the pirate lords' stories of the black whales they'd seen attack smaller fishing boats off the Turvala coast. But this wasn't a fishing boat, and neither of those beasts seemed likely to cause the fear she now saw on her friends' faces.

Again it was one of the sisters who answered. Bria this time. "A creature of great size and strength, with many arms that can grip a ship and pull it to the depths before the crew even knows what is happening."

Aoife shuddered. "The kraken is real?" Her eyes widened as she glanced at each face around the table.

Tommy dipped his chin slightly.

"I thought it was only a tale, a myth!"

Tommy said, "All myths are based on a bit of truth. This one turns out to be no myth at all."

"Well, we can't go that way!" Aoife looked at each of them once more, but everyone's focus had returned to the map.

Tommy didn't bother to lift his face as he answered. "We don't have much of a choice though, unfortunately. There are no good options here. We either risk the storm's wrath, the delay to the east, or the—"

"The *kraken* to the west," Aoife said, finishing his sentence for him.

"If I may?" Maura said. "We could help."

Tommy shook his head, looking from sister to sister until settling on Maura. Aoife could have sworn she saw something shift in his eyes as he looked at the youngest sister, but she must have imagined it.

"We can't risk you using your powers up before we arrive at the sound. We'll need to go in, and you'll have to promise not to use them. At all."

Gavin straightened as he asked, "What's the likelihood we can get past without coming across the creature? That we can get through undetected?"

"I don't know, but we have to try."

Dread pooled in the pit of Aoife's stomach. Nothing about this felt okay. No good options.

"How long will the storm last? Can't we wait it out?" she asked.

It was Gavin's turn to shake his head. "They come on quick, but they don't dissipate as fast. It's why it's so dangerous to have one hit on top of you."

"So we have to go west? And risk the…" Aoife couldn't say the word again, the mere thought of the creature sending another shiver through her shoulders.

"Unfortunately," Tommy said, "it's the best option we have."

He turned to Gavin. "Have Mikkel get the crew ready."

"Won't they panic?" Aoife asked, even as Gavin walked past her and out of the cabin. "I mean, they're a superstitious bunch already. Won't this shake them?"

Tommy chuckled, which seemed oddly out of place for the situation, but Aoife noted how his eyes didn't dance with amusement as they usually did when he laughed. "They may be superstitious, but this is the type of danger they expect in this line of work. We need them ready."

Aoife wondered how anyone could prepare for a giant, multi-armed creature that ate ships for fun, but she had to trust Tommy.

Looking to the fae sisters, she searched for a sign they shared her trepidation, but they were the epitome of calm. Even facing such danger, they looked the opposite of how she felt, and her bitterness echoed in her mind.

Damn fae.

7

TOMMY

Tommy leaned against the desk, his arms spread wide as he stared down at the map with unfocused eyes, trying to ignore the four women who remained in this cabin with him. How did Declan do this? Slowing his breathing, he tried to calm his thoughts, even as they hammered against the edges of his mind.

Kraken. Storm. Time.

No good options.

There never were, were there? But normally it wasn't him having to make the call, and he hated that he had to now.

Advisor. Confidante. Friend. That was what he preferred to be. Not responsible for all the lives aboard the ship.

Where are you, Declan? How the hell did you do this?

Some things could be decided by vote, but other decisions, like this, had to be made solely by the captain. And this was precisely why he'd pushed for Declan to be voted captain all those years ago on that distant shore. Declan had the head for this, the guts, while Tommy...

A growl of frustration rumbled within him, and it took a second for him to realize it hadn't been internal but had escaped into the room and brought all eyes to him.

He looked up, his gaze shifting nervously from face to face.

Renna spoke first. "Are you sure we——"

"No." Tommy stopped her short, lifting a hand to emphasize his refusal to let them use their magic.

"Tommy," Aoife started, and he snapped his attention to her. "Can we at least consider it?"

His jaw clenched, his chest tightening. Why didn't they listen to him? Why were they pushing for this? Was he that awful at filling in as captain that they didn't respect his word?

No. How many times had he challenged Declan? This wasn't a rebuke of him. It was desperation and fear of the monster they'd soon face.

Taking a deep breath, he turned back to Renna, hoping no one noticed how he avoided Maura's eyes.

"Renna," he said as he roughed his hand along the back of his neck, "is it possible for you and your sisters to use magic through these waters and still have time to replenish it before we arrive at the sound?"

Before the fae could answer, Aoife added her own question. "What are your powers, anyway? Are they all the same?"

"Some powers we share, like the ability to heal. Ourselves and others, as we did with Tommy," Renna explained.

Bria chimed in, her voice noticeably harsher than Renna's, though it was still softer and more refined than that of any human. "Our magic—as you humans tend to call it—courses through our veins; it's part of our blood."

"Can you feel it?" Aoife asked, that familiar curious look Tommy always found amusing passing over her features, tightening her brow over eyes alight with curiosity.

"Yes. In a way," Maura said, but Tommy could sense her eyes were locked on him rather than Aoife. "It's hard to explain, not that I've ever tried. But it's like a tingling, a pulsing, a burning?" She turned to her sisters. "I'm not describing this right."

"It's as if it's alive," Renna said.

"Within us," Bria added.

"But we each have our own unique powers, just as we are our own unique selves," Renna said.

Bria cut in. "For example, I have power over the elements. Fire. Earth. Water. Air. I can manipulate them. Control them. Move them to my will."

Tommy nearly laughed at the way Aoife's jaw nearly dropped open, but he managed to contain his amusement. "And you, Renna?"

"The mind."

She must have seen his shock—or was it fear?—because she added quickly, "Not compulsion. At least not as you likely envision. I can see your thoughts, fears, dreams. And at my strongest, I can shape them a bit. The more I attempt to control though, the less powerful the result is."

Her explanation brought little comfort, and he hoped she didn't notice how a shiver crawled up his spine. Could she see the discomfort in his mind?

He began to vocalize this question, but Renna spoke first.

"I can't hear or see you unless I focus on you, and I have to be relatively close. I've had many centuries to practice tuning out the minds of those around me. Otherwise I'd have gone mad long ago."

Still, knowing his thoughts were subject to her intrusion made him feel exposed, naked before her. Another shiver shook his shoulders slightly.

"And you? Maura?" Aoife asked.

Tommy let himself look at the youngest fae as she answered, "Glamour."

Maura had turned to look at Aoife, her rich brown hair falling over her shoulder, hiding the delicate features of her face from him. The three sisters were all beautiful. There was no doubt about that. Any man on this ship—or anywhere, for that matter—would be daft not to notice their otherworldly beauty. But this one, the youngest, she had a quiet beauty about her. She was not as terrifying and harsh as her sisters.

He was still uncomfortable being in the same room as her, acutely aware of her presence and her gaze whenever it fell on him.

Did Renna sense it?

He shook that thought aside as he heard Aoife say his name.

"Tommy? You with us?"

He glanced down at the desk, trying to avoid Renna's stare, hoping she hadn't seen where his mind had drifted. He looked back to Aoife. "What? Sorry. My mind was elsewhere."

"I thought that only happened to me," Aoife said with a quiet laugh. "Maura was explaining how she can manipulate what others see, change the appearance of people or locations or even ships."

"Well..." He blinked at Maura. "That would come in handy—"

Maura finished his sentence for him. "If one needed to get past, say, a monstrous creature lurking below? Aye."

Indeed. This must be why the Rogues had determined these sisters to be the best way past the sirens to the dagger.

Running a hand through his hair, he asked the obvious. "What state are your powers in now? I mean, how strong are they? You spent the past however many hours healing me, so I'm assuming they aren't back to full capacity?"

"In ideal circumstances," Renna said, "as in, had we not been imprisoned and subjected to centuries of only using our powers once every generation, we can replenish them within twenty-four hours."

"But we are still regaining our strength, waking up the magic, as it were," Bria added.

Maura concluded their explanation, saying, "It can take up to thirty-six hours if we've depleted them completely."

"And what happens if you do that?" Aoife asked.

Maura answered, "We collapse, losing consciousness, waking only when our powers are back to half strength. It is rather painful for it to build back up from that level, so we don't like to use our powers to that point if we can help it."

"Which," Tommy said, "is precisely the reason we need to find another plan of attack here."

Roughing a hand over his stubbled chin, he directed his attention back to the map—not that it held any answers for him, but it was a good distraction from everyone's stares. If only they had some kind of explosive, the type used for opening up the earth for the excavation of minerals and metals. But those weren't easily acquired, and they hadn't come upon a ship carrying such cargo in years.

"Can we use the cannons?" Aoife asked.

He looked at her from beneath his brows and gave a quick shake of his head. "With this type of creature, it's unlikely it would present us an ample target above the surface. We can try, but we shouldn't expect that to be our best option here."

"So what is then?" Aoife asked, her voice shaking. "Our best option, I mean."

Leaning forward, he braced himself against the desk with both hands. "We attempt to get through undetected. Keeping quiet. No movement on the deck. Pray we don't alert it to our presence."

"And if we do?"

"We'll rely primarily on our blades, I'm afraid. And our wits," he said.

Seeing her "we're doomed" look, he quickly added, "Don't worry, Aoife. We're not as dumb-witted as some might think."

Aoife fumbled with her response. "I didn't... I trust you... I mean. I just don't see how blades can be an adequate defense against this monster."

Tommy offered a shrug, ignoring how the eyes of the fae sisters bored into him and wondering if Renna was fighting the urge to use her powers to nudge him toward allowing their use of magic. "They might not be. But it's all we have."

"Can we at least maybe agree to let the fae use their magic as a last resort?"

"And who would decide when that moment—"

"Trust us to know when that moment is," Maura said, remaining as still as a statue.

A gorgeous statue.

No. That kind of thinking would get them nowhere.

"If I did that, you'd be using them right now. You'd have Bria calling upon the wind to fill our sails and get us through faster. You'd be conjuring up a glamour along the surface to hide our hull from the beast. You'd even have Renna giving my brain a shove toward agreeing to this."

"And how do you know I'm not already?" Renna said, though her tone showed none of the jest her words might have suggested.

Dropping his chin to his chest, Tommy squeezed his eyes shut, as if doing so might help him feel her powers poking and prodding at the edges of his mind. Would it be so bad to let them help? It would be the best way to get past the beast unseen, but then, it would put them at risk of arriving at the sound unprepared and unarmed against the sirens. Put them at risk of not being able to save Declan, of not being able to survive.

"Well, I certainly can't stop you, Renna." He paused to run a hand over his face once again, but it couldn't clear the weariness and concern he knew showed plainly in his features. "And if you're using them on me now, which I hope you aren't, then I suppose there's nothing I can do against you." Even as he spoke, his mind growled at him for being too soft and not taking charge of this situation as a captain ought to.

But I'm not a captain! he shouted back. And yet, he was—at least temporarily.

He clenched his jaw and drew in a deep breath. With his eyes firmly fixed on Renna's, he said, "I may not know why you and your sisters agreed to leave with Declan, but it must have been rather important if it convinced you to ignore a centuries-old promise to the council. And as long as you are on this ship, you will obey its captain. And until we get Declan back, that is me. You *will* obey me. Is that clear?"

"Yes, Captain," Renna agreed with a smile, albeit a patronizing one.

"Good." Tommy straightened. "Now, if you'll excuse me, I need some fresh air." He moved around the desk, giving the sisters as wide a berth as he could. As he passed by though, Maura's hand reached out, her fingers brushing his bare forearm lightly. A shiver ran through him even as she pulled away. Without pausing—without so much as a glance at her—he continued walking.

"Fresh air sounds like a good idea," Aoife said behind him, and her footsteps rushed toward him as if she were as eager to be away from the fae as he was. But even as he opened the door and stepped out onto the deck, Aoife shifted and called behind them, "Sisters, it would be inappropriate for you to remain in these quarters without the captain present."

It was perhaps the first time Tommy had heard her take on the air of a councilwoman.

A quiet "Of course" followed him out the door, and he didn't need to look over his shoulder as he strode away to know the fae had obeyed and exited. He could only hope they followed orders when it truly mattered.

8

MAURA

The sea mist hit Maura's face as she stood at the starboard rail. After centuries locked in the council hall, fresh air—its feel and its scent—mesmerized her. She had forgotten how freedom tasted. And she hadn't realized how much she'd missed it.

Running her fingers along the wooden rail that was smoothed by the years of sailing, she marveled at how warm it felt compared to the cold stone—and iron—of the walls she'd lived within for so long. She closed her eyes as she raised her chin toward the sky, soaking in the warmth of the sun as it shone down on her, enveloping her in a hug as warm and sweet as a loved one welcoming her home.

She'd given up any hope of enjoying the fresh air and the sun's rays many years ago, accepting that she and her sisters were the last remaining fae with no purpose beyond serving the council. Why had she accepted that as her fate? A life spent locked away, used by those who had saved them from the war. How much living had she missed out on over a lie?

Now's your chance to make up for lost time! You're free!

Despite the symphony of noise created by the water slapping against the hull and the sails adjusting with the wind carrying them forward, the unmistakable sound of her sisters' footsteps cut through her thoughts. Half a millennium locked up together brought familiarity beyond anyone's comprehension.

It also brought an excess of frustration. The near-silent footfalls of Renna and Bria against the ship's deck felt like a light hammer pinging within her head.

"Don't say it, Renna," Maura said, not bothering to turn and look at her older sister as she stepped up beside her. In her periphery she saw Renna's jaw lower to release a response, but Maura cut her off. "And don't try to claim ignorance. It's not a good look on you."

But it was Bria who responded, coming to stand on her other side. "We are worried about you. That's all."

Maura gritted her teeth. Her jaw throbbed as she clamped it tighter and tighter, trying to keep her words—the nasty, spiteful, bitter, angry words—from escaping. The last thing they needed was a sibling squabble interfering with their efforts to rescue Captain McCallagh. Taking a deep breath, she kept her focus on the horizon, as though studying that distant line where two worlds met but never crossed would calm her down. It didn't work.

"There's no reason to worry," she offered finally, but her voice was choked off by the damned ache that had started in those dark, frantic hours of healing Tommy.

"That almost sounded convincing," Renna said, sliding her hand along the rail to rest it atop Maura's. The touch, though tender and meant to be reassuring, did nothing but inflame her inner torment like a breath upon a dying fire.

"You know as well as I do, Renna," she said, squeezing her sister's name out through clenched teeth, "I have little control over this." She couldn't keep the agony and despair from tainting each word, but she refused to let these blasted emotions show. She would not cry. She would not fall apart. She was a fae. Centuries old. Powerful.

And broken.

"You're not broken," Renna reassured her.

Maura spun on her sister and ripped her hand away. "Stay out of my damn head, Renna!" Her tone, although harsh and angry, remained quiet enough so as not to alert any of the crew of the drama brewing between them.

"She only means to help," Bria said from behind her, but she at least knew not to lay a hand on Maura. Not now.

"I don't need her help. Or yours," Maura said with a sharp glance over her shoulder.

But before she could turn her attention back to the horizon, she spotted Tommy standing on the quarterdeck and looking out over the rest of the ship. What he was watching, she didn't know. Only that it wasn't her. And she shouldn't want it to be.

He was a pirate. Thrust into the role of captain—a role he had obviously never wanted—beaten down by worry for his best friend's safety and that of their crew.

"I think you do though," Renna said, and Maura turned back to her sister, willing herself to not give in to the intense bitterness, to remain calm. It was only barely working.

Her blood thrummed as it traveled through her veins, an exhilarating and nearly forgotten sensation after all the years spent in the iron-infused walls of the council hall that had kept this magic, this power, subdued. It had been freed as sure as her body had, and even with the bit she'd expended while healing Tommy, her magic seemed almost giddy as it was replenished and strengthened.

"Of course you think that, Renna," Maura said. "You know best, right?"

"Well, not best, but I'm not the one whose judgment is clouded by emotion at the moment."

Such an understatement.

"Don't pretend at all to know what this feels like."

Renna stared her down. "And don't you pretend to know anything about this man."

"I may not know everything, but I—"

"You what? You cannot fall for the first handsome face you see."

Maura straightened. "Technically I saw Captain McCallagh's face first, so…"

"You know what I mean, Maura. Stop being so difficult."

"Stop treating me like a child."

"Then stop acting like one."

Maura's teeth gripped each other hard enough to spark pain at her temples. Somehow she resisted the temptation to let her eyes roam over to Tommy once more, instead turning them to the sky.

"Why should I expect you to understand?" she whispered to the wisps of clouds before dropping her chin back down. "You have no idea what this feels like!"

Renna moved toward her—so fast it would have been imperceptible to any of the humans observing them—until she and Maura stood almost nose to nose. Her blue eyes blazed with an anger that mirrored Maura's.

Through gritted teeth, Renna growled in a vicious whisper, "Don't you dare pretend to know all aspects of our lives, sister."

They hadn't been together for their whole lives. Even though they had spent the last five hundred years together, they had not always been so close, only having reunited on Cregah a few decades before the end of the war. The memories of that time forced a shudder up her spine.

"Care to enlighten me then, *sister*?" Maura infused the last word with the spite that coursed through her along with her magic.

"You are not the only one to ever fall. But I did. He didn't. Such is the risk of it."

"Who was it?" Maura couldn't contain her curiosity at this confession.

Renna gave a lazy shrug. "It doesn't matter. It never had a chance. Unrequited love may be painful, but it has its advantages. The hope it creates is like an early morning mist, a soft whisper easily dispersed when the light of the sun reveals the truth. But your—"

Renna's lips clamped shut, and regret flashed briefly across her face.

"My what?"

"It's one thing to love someone, accepting they will never love you, Maura. But to love someone, to have them love you, knowing you can never be together? That? That is the pain that only comes from shattered hopes and destroyed dreams. If I could spare you that pain, I would, but I may have to settle for lessening it. Walk away while you can, Maura." The final words came out more as a desperate plea than the command Maura might have expected. She rested her hands on Maura's arms with uncharacteristic tenderness.

But Maura only tensed.

"How can you possibly know he—" Maura clamped her mouth shut. "You didn't."

"I did, and I'm not sorry for it either. Despite what you might think, it wasn't for your benefit. I merely wanted to be confident he could be trusted to lead, to see if he might need to be helped a little."

"Don't you dare." Once again Maura's rage sparked. "You leave him alone, or—"

"Or what? You can't stop me from doing what needs to be done. But all of that is beside the point. He's falling for you too. Not as intensely as you—obviously, since he's only human—but he is struggling against it. It's there, and you cannot pursue it. It is doomed from the onset. You know what is expected of us in the south. You know how much our kin need our help. You cannot turn your back on your kin."

Maura couldn't suppress the groan that rumbled in her chest. "I know. And I'm not. I'm not against helping them! But this is about more than him."

"Is it?" Renna asked, unconvinced.

"I want to *live*, Renna. Don't you? Don't you want more than just to be at the beck and call of others? Don't you want a life that you get to choose?"

But her sister was already shaking her head.

Bria chimed in. "We have our roles, Maura. If we don't help, who else would? Or could?"

Within Maura's chest, the fibers of her heart began to fray, torn in different directions, toward different paths and dreams. Her gaze drifted to the western horizon, then behind them to the south, before swinging back up to where Tommy still stood. There was a life beyond the walls of the council hall, beyond the shores of Cregah, beyond the Aisling, and beyond even Larcsporough. She'd spent most of her life confined, and now that she was free, her bones ached to take advantage of it.

She wanted to live. And to love.

"I know you want to spread your wings, Maura," Renna said

gently. "But we still have weeks aboard this ship before we can travel south. If you pursue this with him"—she waved a finger discreetly between Maura and Tommy—"things will only get more complicated and difficult as you feed that hope that has kindled within you."

Even as Maura moved to deny it, that tiny but strong flame flickered within her heart. Renna warned of the risk of being burned by it, but Maura was more fearful of the emptiness that would result if she snuffed it out.

Her sister meant well. Logically, Maura knew that, but emotionally, she only saw her older sister trying to control her as she always did. She might be free of her ties to the council, but escaping her sister's authority wouldn't be so easy.

Still, she had to try. "While I appreciate your concern, it is my life—"

"No, Maura! It's the life of every fae!" Renna yelled, all gentleness gone. She barely kept her words from being heard by all on deck. "Their lives depend on us. That includes you!"

Stepping around Maura, Bria tried to appease both her sisters, placing her hands on their shoulders. But Maura ignored her.

"Don't be so dramatic!" she spat.

"Don't be so selfish!" Renna's blue eyes burned into Maura's.

Neither sister backed down, but even as they stared at each other, Maura sensed the attention of the crew on them.

"Sisters," Bria said, allowing only a brief pause to see if they would turn to her. They didn't. "This isn't exactly the most becoming of displays. Especially for who we are. This is not going to be resolved here and now. That much is obvious. Emotions are high. Let's not make any decisions rashly."

Bria. Always the voice of reason and calm, she provided a nice balance to Renna's authoritative nature and Maura's passionate personality.

"Fine," Maura whispered with a bit of a growl.

Renna merely nodded before turning to leave.

As Renna and Bria walked away, leaving Maura alone once again at the rail, Maura risked a glance up at Tommy, who was now in conversation with Aoife. Their voices were too low for Maura to make out from this distance.

It had already been complicated, trying to balance her duty in Larcsporough with her urge to head off on her own. And then Tommy had been thrown into the mess that was her heart. She had not planned for any of this when she'd sat down to help heal him. Just as she'd given up all hope of freedom while living at the council hall, she'd abandoned all thought of love or companionship beyond her sisters.

But something had happened between them in that small cabin.

Like her heart had been given new life as she had saved his. Like it had been precisely tuned to his somehow, leaving it feeling empty when he wasn't nearby. Renna was right. Maura didn't know much about him beyond what she had observed over the past few days. Where had he grown up? Where was his family? Why didn't he want to lead? What drove him to be so different from most pirates?

She wanted to know all these answers and then some, and the thought of denying herself the chance to understand him as well as she knew herself only twisted that pang deep in her chest.

You had to fall for a human, didn't you? her mind teased her.

She could have picked a far worse human to fall for than Tommy. Even with all the stress he was under, there was something about him, something she couldn't quite pinpoint, that put his sense of loyalty and devotion on clear display. He was like no one she'd ever met, in all her six hundred years. A man who would always do what he needed to for a friend.

For a loved one.

But would he go with her to Larcsporough and beyond? Could he?

If Renna was telling the truth, Tommy was falling for her too. If Maura was responsible, she'd leave him be, let him have a life on the sea he loved with friends who needed him, not ask him to give all of that up for her.

But that flicker of hope within her heart—that spark she'd thought her years of captivity had surely killed—would not be ignored. As she watched Tommy, the flutter in her chest quickened, and she knew she couldn't heed her sister's warnings. She would risk a lifetime of pain and heartache for a single chance—not to simply know this man but to love him and be loved by him. No matter how short a time she was granted.

You also risk inflicting pain on him. Whether he follows you or not, you will part ways. One way or another.

9
DECLAN

Callum backed away from Declan, his face relaxing into an easy smile that Declan found more disconcerting than anything else. While he didn't know how long he'd been unconscious in that damn brig, they couldn't have been sailing for more than one or two days, which left only a few more before they reached the sound. And their inevitable demise. With Callum refusing to listen to the truth, he'd need to come up with some semblance of a plan.

"Sit, McCallagh," Callum commanded. With a jerk of his head, he pointed out the chair a few steps to Declan's right.

Declan angled his hands away from his back while turning slightly. "A bit hard to do that when I'm—"

"I'm sure you can manage. Sit." The captain's eyes narrowed.

"What is your worry exactly, Captain?" Declan asked, easing himself into the chair, his bound hands forcing him to sit straight up as if he were enjoying tea at a palace instead of being held captive aboard this pirate's ship. "Surely you don't think I could best you. Especially since you've taken my blade."

Callum leaned back against the edge of his desk, his legs relaxing in front of him, ankles crossed. He reached behind him. "Ah, yes. This blade," he said, lifting the dagger in front of him as he turned back to Declan. "You never did tell me how you acquired it. That's got to be quite the story."

Declan smacked his lips lazily. If he looked away, Callum would see his lies, so he kept his eyes forward, allowing only a brief glance down to his weapon, which was now being turned round and round in his captor's hands. "Same ol' story, I suppose. Pulled it off a merchant ship's captain who didn't know how to listen."

A laugh rumbled from Callum's chest, though it didn't show in his eyes. "That doesn't match the stories others tell."

"You, of all people, should know not to trust gossip."

"Perhaps," Callum said as he used the dagger's point to clean out the grime from under his fingernails. After several seconds of brutal silence, he spoke again, his eyes locked on the blade in his hands. "How did it feel, Declan, to watch both of your parents be dragged away within days of each other?"

Declan's gut twisted at the words, but he shoved the memories back, refusing to let them take hold of him. He wouldn't fall for Callum's play here, and regardless of what changes Aoife had stirred in him, his years of perfecting this mask wouldn't go to waste. He offered a lazy shrug, though Callum couldn't see it with his face still lowered. "Was a long time ago. I don't readily recall."

"Ah, but I think you do. And I think it still hurts." Callum lifted his chin, his dark eyes burning into Declan's. "Hurts knowing you couldn't do anything, doesn't it? To feel helpless? Useless? Insignificant."

Declan swallowed hard and channeled all his tension into his hands, clasping them tightly until his knuckles ached. He couldn't let anything show on his face, couldn't give Callum further ammunition. He released a sigh, his body relaxing with the breath, and said, "I was only a kid. Not much I could do."

Pulling his mouth into a half-smile again, Callum said, "Is that what you tell yourself to curb the guilt? How's that working for you?"

A familiar tightness gripped his chest, as if Callum had summoned the years-old guilt from where Declan had tried to force it to rest. He mentally stamped it down before answering, though he wasn't sure how long he could keep it at bay. "Well, I was doing just fine until you knocked me upside the head and dragged me aboard your ship."

"Oh, yes, it certainly seemed that way." Callum let out a loud guffaw as he looked toward the ceiling. "Is that why that little bitch of an heir was stomping her way back to your ship—to your cabin perhaps?—crying and red-faced? What did you do? Nothing good, I imagine."

Declan ignored the goading, hardened his features, and refused to turn away from Callum's stare. Even if he had the words to respond, he couldn't trust his voice not to betray the emotions Callum conjured up inside him.

"Did she finally see you for what you are?" Callum continued. "A pirate? A killer? A liar? A brigand? That's it, isn't it? She saw the real you under whatever mask you were using on her."

The grip he had on his features was slipping; the strength he needed to continue appearing emotionless and bored was slowly waning with each verbal jab from this captain. Declan's hands itched to be free from their bonds, free to strike the bastard before him. But that's what Callum wanted. Leverage. Any emotional reaction Declan offered would be used against him. It was what

Declan would have done if the situation were reversed.

Clearing his throat, Declan lifted his chin and responded, "Such is our lot, isn't it, Callum?"

"And what lot is that exactly?"

"Loneliness. Lovelessness." Declan hoped his words were coming out as steady as he needed them to.

"There are places"—Callum gave his hand a whirl in the air before him—"to satisfy such longings. Or are you too good for such establishments, McCallagh?"

"Ah, but do they satisfy? Truly?"

A sadness clouded Callum's expression, but only briefly, like a wisp of cloud passing in front of the sun on a summer breeze, gone as quickly as it had appeared. But it had been there nonetheless. "They satisfy well enough."

Declan cleared his throat and shifted his weight in the chair, silently cursing the manacles at his wrists that made it impossible to get comfortable. "I'm not sure I believe you. Especially after the stories I've heard about your own past."

"What was that you were saying about not trusting gossip?" Callum's tone tightened around his words, but it was forced, strained.

"I never said not to trust it. Sometimes the gossip turns out to be true. So, is it?"

Callum's stare bored into Declan, as if he could, with just a look, strip away every layer of his being until only his true self remained.

Thankfully, that's not possible.

After too long a silence, Callum whispered, his voice rough with anger, "Is what true?"

"That your cold heart is capable of love. Or it was. Once." If he could unnerve the captain, get him on edge, force his past to overwhelm him, perhaps Declan could play to his sympathies to give them some chance of surviving. And if not that—as this was a long shot, indeed—he could at least buy himself some time to devise a plan. Any plan would be better than none.

Callum turned to drop the blade onto his desk before moving toward Declan. He stopped close enough that Declan could kick him if he wanted to. Not that he would. Callum would expect such a move. When Callum remained silent, Declan relaxed his head to the side and raised a brow. "What was her name?"

Without warning, Callum's fist slammed into the side of Declan's face, sending his jaw swinging to the right. His vision darkened, and silver stars appeared before his blinking eyes as the pain registered. Nose. Cheek. Jaw. Declan shook his head as he turned forward. He could already feel the corner of his eye beginning to swell, but he couldn't stifle the laugh that bubbled up. Ignoring the sting of the air against a fresh cut, he licked blood away from the corner of his mouth. Callum slowly came into focus before him. He didn't seem at all amused.

"My apologies. I shouldn't assume," Declan said before spitting blood and saliva onto the floor at his feet. "What was *his* name?" This time he saw the blow before it came and managed to shift away, though his ear took some of the impact, and he winced at the pain that sprang up. "Don't tell me it was an animal. I mean, to each his own."

Before he could continue, Callum leaned toward him, stomping on Declan's foot. With his hands gripping the chair's arms, he forced Declan backwards.

"My past is mine, McCallagh," he said in a low and menacing tone. "And mine alone. Rumors exist, but I don't owe you or anyone else my story. Push the matter again, and I won't stop with your sister. I'll track down that heir of yours. Give her a test of a real pirate, and I'll make it hurt. Understand?"

The threat struck Declan as intended. His gut tightened at the possibility of Aoife being the object of this captain's wrath, but he slipped the mask over his features even as he swallowed back the fear of anything happening to her.

"Understood," he offered. "Now, if there's nothing else you need, I'd appreciate being allowed to retire back to my accommodations. My head could use the rest."

Callum retreated to the desk and—with his back still turned to Declan—lifted the dagger, turning it lazily upon its tip. Declan slowly drew in a breath, thankful to be free from the physical intrusion.

"Of course," Callum said, still turning the blade, refusing to look at Declan. Was the man ashamed of something? Ashamed of having real emotions? Or simply ashamed of reacting to Declan's provocation?

The door to the cabin opened, and the big brute from earlier stepped inside and hoisted Declan out of the chair by his arm.

"Easy there," Declan complained, turning his chin up toward the massive man. "Not all of us like it rough."

The man only harrumphed before dragging him toward the door. Before they stepped outside, Callum called after them. "McCallagh, be ready tomorrow to discuss your plans for the sirens. I don't want to be caught unawares, so you will be honest next time. Aye?"

Declan couldn't even sigh in response before he was shoved over the threshold and back into the sunshine, the freshness of the sea air a welcome change from the stuffy cabin. He hadn't taken more than one breath, though, before the big oaf's hands had him moving along the deck toward the ladder. He dug his feet into the wooden floor to stop their progress.

"Mind if I catch a bit of a breather here before I'm forced back into that hole?"

The man turned to him, studying him, searching for any sign of mischief.

"I don't know if you've noticed, but my head has seen better days, and—as ashamed as I am to admit it—I'm not adjusting to the sea quite as I normally do. Now, I suppose if you want to risk me hurling what little is in my stomach all over you or this meticulously kept deck, that's your choice. Though I would rather do so over the railing." Declan pretended to stifle a retch, swallowing down the phantom bile he hoped the man would believe to be real.

The big hand tightened on Declan's arm before dragging him not toward the ladder below but to the starboard side. With a shove, the pirate sent Declan stumbling into the railing while still keeping his grip on him.

"Thank you," Declan offered, once again forcing himself to fake another wave of nausea. The key to a ruse was to play it right up to the point of excessiveness, to sell it without overdoing it. He looked out at the horizon, swallowing, hoping the oaf was buying his act of needing to quell an uneasy stomach. While the cabin and the brig had indeed been ghastly and offensive to his senses, his stomach had long ago become so accustomed to such that he had begun to believe the years at sea had turned it to steel.

You thought the same about your heart.

Declan didn't have to fake the cringe that thought invoked. Thinking about Aoife excessively would not help him. She was his reason to survive this suicide mission, however he could manage that, but if he let himself focus too much on her and on their last moments together, their last words shared…

Involuntarily he turned his attention to the right, risking a glance behind him, allowing a bit of hope to spring up that his ship would appear on the horizon. But there were no sails to be seen. Only darkness brewing with a ferocity he had only seen in a handful of storms here on the Aisling. So that was the rumbling he'd heard in the distance. He should have known this wouldn't be easy. Nothing about this endeavor was proving easy.

"Hope your crew isn't risking their necks in there for you," the man beside him said, and Declan didn't need to look at him to know he was referring to the storm behind them. "You're not worth it."

The man was right. Declan wasn't worth heading into that storm, and he could only hope Tommy—and Aoife—had not been in the middle of it when it had come on. But that left them with only two other options: the longer way, near Haviern, or the decidedly more deadly one close to Tyshaly. He hoped Tommy had chosen their course wisely, but knowing his friend—knowing what he himself would have done in his place—he could be certain they weren't taking the safer route.

Damn pirates.

10
CAIT

Cait forced herself into a slow, steady gait, shuffling her feet in uneven steps so this unexpected guest would believe she'd been upstairs asleep. Her mind rushed through all the people she might find in her pub, devising a response for each possibility. No matter who it was, her greeting would be the same, at least, so she started speaking even before she turned the corner at the bottom of the stairs.

"Can I help you?"

She nearly stopped short at the sight of the young woman standing just inside the door, but she recovered quickly, striding behind the bar and grabbing for a towel. As silly as it was, it helped to have something with which to occupy her hands whenever she found herself in uncomfortable situations. Not stopping to wait for a response from the newcomer, she proceeded to wipe down the bar, though it had been thoroughly cleaned earlier that morning when the last patron had left.

"Are you Ms. McCallagh?" The girl sounded as youthful as she appeared. She couldn't have been more than fifteen years old. Cait quickly recognized her as one of the girls employed by the council; her cloak was doing very little to hide the council garb she wore. And even if it had succeeded in concealing her clothing, the presence of the cloak at all in the middle of summer would have been enough for anyone to realize something was amiss.

"I am. And I apologize, Miss, but we don't open for another few hours. Council rules."

The girl shifted her weight as she looked around the empty pub, her hands clenched tightly before her. "Then why is the door unlocked?"

"I would have thought you'd know, given..." Cait waved a hand in the girl's direction before changing the course of her words. "Another council rule. With violence being forbidden, all business-es in Morshan and on all of Cregah—as far as I'm aware—are forbidden from having locks in use. To do so would be to display a distrust in our dear councilwomen and the peace they provide for us."

The words ran bitter over her tongue—so rehearsed, so coat-ed in faked reverence for the sham the council peddled. The girl didn't seem to catch the lie, though, merely mouthing a silent *oh* and allowing herself to look around the pub.

Cait stood up, leaning a hip against the bar, the towel keep-ing both her hands busy as she continued. "Per council rules, of course, I'm not allowed to have patrons here prior to allotted busi-ness hours. So if there's something I can do for you, I'll need to know straightaway."

"I wondered... Well, you see, I'm looking to buy something for a friend." The girl paused, her chin dipping down to her chest as she fidgeted with the edges of her cloak at her waist. "Do you possibly know where I can buy a cookie for my friend?"

The air stuck in Cait's throat at the seemingly random question, and she had to remind herself to continue breathing, though she didn't allow herself to relax. As she found her mental bearings, she fought the urge to roll her eyes at the ridiculous words Lucan had insisted upon all those years ago. *"What? It's perfect. It's unusual enough that few people will ask it but not so odd that it would seem out of place."* Cait had conceded, but even so, this was the first time someone had ever uttered the passphrase, the first time someone had sought her out.

Cait drew in another breath to calm her nerves. She wracked her brain for the asinine response Lucan had devised, but it had been years ago. *Really? Years? That long?*

Before she could utter one word, though, a man's voice filled the room. "And who is this friend you're gifting this to?" Lucan stepped around the wall and settled into one of the stools at the bar, refusing to make eye contact with Cait as he angled himself toward their guest.

Cait was going to kill him. He was supposed to stay hidden. She had it handled. But did she really? Why was she so averse to accepting his aid? It was true she had forgotten her line, and if she were being honest, she was less angry with him than she was with herself for failing to even notice that he had come down the stairs at all.

With nothing to add to the conversation, Cait looked toward the girl, who was once again fidgeting with her cloak. Her eyes darted from the floor to the walls, to Lucan and Cait, and then back to the floor before she finally—with a breath so deep Cait could hear the air rushing into her lungs from across the room—answered him. "For a friend who works with me. She's a bit...

under the weather."

Lucan turned to Cait with the same smug attitude he always got when he was proven right, then returned his attention to the young girl.

"I see. And what kind do you think might help her?"

Cait gnashed her teeth together until her jaws hurt. Sands, no one would ever buy this ridiculous exchange. She would need to have a talk with Lucan later to change these blasted code phrases to something more refined and less foolish.

For a brief moment, Cait wondered if the girl had actually been sincerely asking for cookies, though, and not using this secret—and absurd—method of making contact with the Rogues. Once again her breath caught, her body unwilling to let any air pass her lips until the girl answered.

"Chocolate, I believe," she said, trying to control her trembling hands. "With mint chips."

That was it. That was all Cait needed to hear. The girl had been sent here. That much she knew from the whole cookie nonsense, but chocolate meant the one who had sent her was in danger. Mint meant death. As ludicrous as this whole cookie business was, she had to admit that it had worked——though she wasn't sure she'd give Lucan the opportunity to gloat over it.

"I see," Cait said. "Come 'ere." She waved the girl over and motioned for Lucan to offer the stool beside him. The girl sat on the edge of the seat so her feet still touched the floor, as if this were a trap she needed to be prepared to escape from.

Lucan lifted his chin at her. "We will get you directions to the best bakery in Morshan."

The girl's expression seemed to hold a mix of confusion and gratitude, as though she wasn't quite sure if Lucan and Cait had gotten her message or if they really were going to point her toward a pastry shop. She mumbled a "Thank you" nonetheless, and Cait cleared her throat to get her attention.

Cait spoke slowly. "Should be easy enough. We don't need to write it down. The best cookies come from a woman who lives outside Morshan, actually. Take the path northwest, not more than a half-mile. You'll know it when you see it. But"—she looked at the clock behind her above the bar—"she won't have the cookies ready this early. I recommend heading that way in, what"—she turned to Lucan—"an hour or two?"

"Aye," he said with a string of easy nods. "Closer to two, I'd think."

The girl was looking back and forth between them uneasily.

Cait raised her chin and looked toward the door of the pub as she spoke again. "I wish we could chat more, but alas, the council really does not like it if we entertain patrons outside hours."

"Of course," the girl said, standing and rolling her shoulders as she straightened, and for a hair of a second, Cait had a nagging suspicion that this girl had played them for fools; her confidence had appeared only after they'd basically given her the key to discovering the Rogues' identities. Had they played right into a trap set by the council? Had Maggie divulged their secret before they'd killed her?

But no sooner had Cait asked herself these questions than the tension returned to her guest's face, her next words coming out shaky and unsure. "Thank you, Ms. McCallagh." She turned to Lucan. "And Ms. McCallagh's friend. I will look into your recommendation in a couple of hours after I finish the rest of my errands."

She pivoted on one of her feet and walked briskly toward the door. Without a word, she was gone.

Lucan burst into laughter. His loud guffaws filled the room

until Eva came rushing from the stairway where she'd been hiding, her brow wrinkled with worry, her lips tight with concern.

Cait threw her towel at Lucan's face. "Stop that laughter, you buffoon! Someone will hear you!" She ignored how much she sounded like her mother. How could she move on from her grief when every day she exhibited some mannerism that mirrored her mother so perfectly?

Lucan snapped his mouth shut before mouthing a silent apology.

"Do you think it was a trap?" Eva asked. At least she was smart enough to keep her words barely audible.

"I don't know. I hope not, but it is possible. I hope the baker outside of town can help her out."

Lucan sobered quickly at those words, straightening in his seat, his eyes once again clear and determined. As hilarious as he'd found his whole cookie idea—and she would no doubt get an earful about his enjoyment later—at least he'd been working with her long enough to know when it was time to get to work.

"I'll be back later. Maybe I'll bring a cookie or two back for you," he said, flashing Cait a wink before turning toward the door, waving at Eva to join him. "You coming?"

A silent nod was the only reply he received.

Cait watched her two closest friends head out the door and into Morshan, away from the relatively safe walls of her pub. As if anywhere was truly safe on this island.

Whether the girl was a spy or not, only time would tell, and she had to trust Lucan and Eva to handle the situation while she played up the ruse of being the devoted pub owner and model Cregahn businesswoman.

This seemed to be her lot in life. In charge, running the show, running the pub, sending others out to have all the fun, to face all the danger. Maybe once the council was gone, she could leave this all behind, get a ship of her own, and set out for other seas, for an adventure all her own.

But not yet.

11
AOIFE

Thunder rumbled in the distance as Aoife pushed her short legs after Tommy, who was taking the steps up to the quarterdeck two at a time. She didn't hear the fae following them—not that she would have, with their obnoxious way of walking silently—and she hoped their hundreds of years of existence had given them the ability to sense when they were no longer welcome.

As she turned toward the spot at the railing where she had last stood with Gavin, her breath escaped her in a sigh. The sisters were huddled together on the deck. Tommy stood at the rail, his forearms digging into the edge of the wood, his eyes staring blankly at Mikkel, who was preparing the crew for what lay ahead.

Bumping Tommy's hip with her own, she took up the spot next to him and flashed him as genuine a smile as she could muster, though it melted away when he didn't so much as glance her way. He flexed his jaw.

"So," she started, not sure what to expect from him now that he was the acting captain. Would he snap at her with some rude comment as Declan had so many times? Would he ignore her as he had just done? Or would he be the kind friend she'd come to see him as? "The crew seems to be okay with me now."

Silence.

Well, his response could have been worse.

She continued, "Gavin says I'm practically the quartermaster now, but I told him that was nonsense, as I'm not even a pirate. But still, it's nice to not have so many eyes staring at me all the time. Collins even waved to me earlier. That was nice. You know, even though I don't want to be stared at, you could still look at me? Maybe?"

She'd been rambling far longer than she'd intended, but he hadn't reacted at all. No laugh. No roll of the eyes. Not even an exasperated sigh.

They remained there for a few more minutes in silence as Gavin relieved the man at the helm and shouted out the commands that would get them underway.

Toward death. A multi-armed death.

Aoife risked another look at Tommy from the corner of her eye and then whispered, "I'm sorry, Tommy."

She was almost sure he hadn't heard her, not over the flap of sails in the breeze or the shouts of men as they maneuvered the ship. But he turned to her then. Not fully, but a pivot of the head was far better than being ignored.

"For what?" The words came out strained, as if the stress of the predicament had sapped the life from his voice.

"For leaving Declan at the cove. If I had just forgiven him when he requested, he would be here now, and you wouldn't be under so much stress."

At this, Tommy stood fully and turned toward her, and though his stance was relaxed, his hip resting against the rail, arms crossed loosely in front of him, tension rolled off of him.

"Should you have forgiven him?" He answered his own question with a shrug. "I don't know. Only you can decide whether that was even possible at the time. But you aren't to blame for this. This was Callum's doing, not yours. Even had you left the cove together, Callum would not have let Declan get off Cregah any other way but in his brig. Of that, I'm certain. No doubt Declan would have been just as distracted with you by his side as I'm sure he was when Callum came upon him. And had you been with him? I would still be stressed. Perhaps more so. Because I'd be worried about you both. Chasing after you both."

Aoife took in a deep breath, filling her lungs with the refreshing sea air. It didn't help her digest what Tommy had said though.

After a moment, he turned back to his original position, like a gargoyle who had come to life during the night returning to its stony resting place with the daylight. Aoife followed suit.

She opened her mouth to speak, but her words were cut short when Tommy nudged her with his elbow and said, "But you don't get to be quartermaster though."

At first, his face remained so stern, she wasn't sure if he was teasing or if he was serious, but then that sweet smile she'd grown so fond of spread across his face.

"Well, you'd better inform Gavin of that before he tells the entire crew."

The thunder in the distance continued its throaty growl as lightning spread across the wide swath of clouds, like wispy fingers reaching out to find something to destroy. If it wasn't forcing them to take the dangerous route to the west, Aoife might have thought it beautifully mesmerizing. She could imagine sitting on the shores of some distant land, safe and warm, watching the lights, imagining they were created just for her. And Declan. It wouldn't be—it currently wasn't—as nice without him.

"How long until we... " She couldn't bring herself to finish the question.

"Meet the kraken?" Tommy asked, and she merely gave a small nod in reply. "A couple days. Maybe more. But that's just until we arrive in its territory. We'll take it as slow as we can without forfeiting Declan to his demise, and hopefully it will be slow enough to not alert the beast to our presence."

Aoife wasn't sure how that logic would pan out. It seemed to her the monster would be able to see the hull of a boat at the surface no matter what speed it was moving. But she trusted Tommy to know what he was doing. He had been doing this job far longer than she had, after all. That thought caused a breath of a laugh to escape her lips, prompting him to flash her a questioning look, but she merely shook her head.

She needed to change the subject. Anything to move his attention off her. "So, Tommy, what was that between you and Maura, huh?"

That's what you're going to bring up? Have you learned nothing from your past mistakes?

Her thoughts screamed at her, and she froze with the realization that she had probably asked the worst question possible of her friend. She didn't dare breathe as she waited for him to react, but the lack of oxygen in her lungs quickly foiled that plan, forcing her to greedily suck in more air.

Fainting would be embarrassing.

She expected him to brush it off as nothing, deny what she had most definitely witnessed between them in Declan's quarters.

Instead, after running his fingers across his brow and then

through his hair, he simply asked, "You noticed that, did you?"

Aoife looked around, as if there might be someone else he could be asking, before stammering out, "Um, were you both trying to hide it? Because you did a piss-poor job of it if you were."

"To be honest, I don't know that she's as intent on hiding it as I am. If she is at all."

"You can't tell me there are no feelings there though. I mean, the sparks were nearly visible."

"It's impossible to have such strong feelings so quickly though. Right?"

Aoife lifted a shoulder. "Only seems impossible because it happens so rarely. And even then, I don't think it's as rare as people make it out to be. It happened for my sister, after all." Her throat tightened at the mention of Lani, and she raised a hand to where the necklace still hung beneath her shirt.

"I suppose. But, possible or not, I won't encourage some dream of love and companionship that I can't have." She moved to interject, but he held up his hand. "I know. You and Declan. Yes, that can work, and has for a handful of partnerships. But she's fae. I'm not. She has her kind to get back to, to be reunited with in the south. It can't—"

"Well, not with that attitude, it can't," Aoife said, hoping her words conveyed the lightheartedness she intended.

"It would never work, Aoife. I belong here. On this ship. With this crew. And she's needed elsewhere. I won't get my hopes up for something that is impossible."

"You know, Tommy, a smart pirate named Gavin once told me, 'If we don't have hope, what do we have?'"

Another deep breath, and Tommy huffed out a sighing laugh. "Gavin. I swear. Going to him for wisdom now, are we?"

"What? Even a blind seagull finds a fish now and then, right?

Why can't our silly Gavin have some wisdomous moments?"

"Wisdomous?" He raised a brow at her, his lips fighting back the smile she missed seeing.

"Hey, I'm practically quartermaster. I get to make up words if I want to."

He wagged a finger in the air at her. "Nope. I denied that title, remember?"

Aoife feigned surprise and pushed herself back from the railing, nearly falling over as the wind caught the sails, rocking the boat at just the right moment. "Then, I'd best get off the quarterdeck. I don't believe we mere deckhands and stowaways are allowed up here."

"Nah, you can stay. You have this interim captain's permission to go anywhere on the ship you please. You may not be the quartermaster, but you are our esteemed guest. You are still sleeping in the captain's quarters, after all."

"Well," she said, bowing her head, "this lowly stowaway turned esteemed guest thanks you for your kindness."

He nodded in reply before turning back toward the railing once more, but she couldn't let him sink back into his brooding just yet.

"Tommy?" she asked, and he hummed in response. "What shall I be doing when—I mean, if—the kraken spots us? Am I to hide in the cabin and hope to the ends of the Aisling that we survive? Is there no way for me to be of help? And if not with the kraken, then in the sound? I'm going to need some preparation. I can't always be the prim and proper council heir sitting on the sidelines, especially not in this attire."

"I don't think even Declan would have you hiding anywhere, not after we witnessed your courage back at the council hall. We don't have much time to make you great with a blade, but we can at least make you better than you are."

"That shouldn't be hard. I know nothing at the moment."

"That's not true," he assured her with a shake of his head. "You do know what end goes in your hand."

"Even children learn that quickly."

"True, true. But still. We can get you introduced to some basic handling skills. It's better than nothing."

"So when do we start?" Aoife asked, standing taller, though it didn't improve her confidence at all.

"Not *we*, you..." Putting two fingers to his lips, he whistled down to the main deck, pointed at a man, and waved for him to come join them. "...and Collins. I believe you've met before?" he asked just as the tall pirate came up beside Aoife with an eager look on his face that had her wondering what duty he expected Tommy had summoned him for.

"Yes," Aoife said, addressing Collins now. "I never did thank you for not throwing me off the ship when you first caught me."

A silent nod was his only reply.

Turning back to Tommy, she asked, "So Collins will train me with a blade?" Collins's expression lit up a bit more at this news.

"Aye, he trains all of our younger, newer recruits who get hired fresh out of the ports with little-to-no experience. He has quite the knack for teaching novices quickly and efficiently."

"Good," she said with a sigh, and before Tommy had completely turned away from them, Collins was already motioning for her to follow him down to the deck.

She knew she needed at least somewhat of a fighting chance against the kraken and the sirens, but looking at Collins's towering frame, the hard lines of lean muscle trailing down his arms and across his shoulders, she wasn't so sure she'd survive the training itself. But she had to try.

12

DECLAN

The large crewman-turned-jailer proved no gentler as he returned Declan to the brig. The grumbling scoff he unleashed at Declan's request for a bit of food was as rough as the scruffy beard along his jaw.

"I'll win you over yet!" Declan called after him, and although the man didn't bother with any verbal response, Declan was satisfied enough with the slight shake of the head the man gave him before disappearing back up the ladder.

Within minutes, the silence of the brig became too much, and even with the constant sound of the sea against the hull, the absence of all other noise threatened to suffocate him.

As if silence could actually do that. You're such an idiot.

He answered his own thoughts aloud, "Indeed I am. I've certainly gotten myself into a shitty mess now, haven't I?" He swept his eyes around the small cell. The wooden floor was entirely bare save the faint signs of where he'd been forced to relieve himself.

He had little desire to sit on the filthy floor again, but he also couldn't stand still. The silence seemed to have taken on a life of its own. So he began to pace, counting out the sound of his footsteps as he walked, forward and back, and then around and around. Counting gave him some idea of how long it had been since the man had left, but more importantly it kept his mind from wandering back to that cove.

At least for a moment.

Every few paces, the image of black sand in the moonlight flashed in his mind, and he counted louder in his head, as if he could wash away the visions like a tide washing away a message in the sand.

But they never stayed gone for long, with Aoife shoving her way to the forefront over and over again.

Well, if she wasn't going to leave him alone to think, there seemed little point in expending what precious energy he had trying to fight her. In his mind, he pulled out a chair, proffering it to the imagined version of her.

You really have lost it, haven't you?

Still, inviting Aoife to stay on the edge of his mind rather than trying to shove her away and lock the memories up tight helped him focus on the matter at hand. Maybe having her there, keeping him company—even if only in his imagination—would remind him of all he had to fight for.

So, with Aoife watching, he set to examining the predicament he'd gotten himself into.

He needed a plan. Of that he was sure, but no matter what angle he viewed the situation from, he could see no way past the sirens without using the powers of the fae. Perhaps he could convince Callum of that truth, but even as he thought it, he knew that would be a fruitless effort. The pirate was as stubborn as he was stupid.

But what kept Callum from listening? It wasn't merely his stubbornness, though that was formidable, to be sure.

You conned him. He won't trust you.

"But he trusts you enough to escort him into the damn sound?" he asked himself aloud, no longer caring how crazy it was to be talking to himself. At least half the conversation remained in his head, and that felt slightly less awkward. But only slightly.

Still, he couldn't deny that Callum obviously harbored some bitterness over Declan's last play. It had been a risk, of course, but that was what this job entailed. Time and time again, risk at every turn. And at the time, it had seemed better to risk angering an old friend than to see Aoife taken as a prisoner and hauled back to the council hall.

It would do no good to focus on what might have happened had he chosen differently. What was done was done, and the plain fact remained that he was stuck in this damn cell, hands bound behind his back, with no blasted clue how he was going to survive the next chapter of his cursed life.

Trying to mentally sort through all the scenarios that could play out once they arrived in the sound didn't prove to be of any comfort either. Every possibility was just as bad as the last, each of them ending in a bloody death. No chance of being reunited with his crew, his ship, and Aoife.

Aoife.

If she arrived in the sound, if they didn't catch up to the *Curse Bringer* before they entered those waters, what would happen to her? Declan told himself to trust Tommy and the fae to handle the situation, but the thought of her being devoured by the monsters waiting for them...

Too much.

But those images only dissolved into similarly devastating ones of her drowning as the many arms of the kraken tore through his ship. She didn't deserve any of this. The lies, the deceit, the danger, the risk, the heartbreak. She should be living a life of ease, free from worry and death and pain.

Not that that type of life exists anywhere, here in the Aisling or beyond.

He nodded to himself, his lips tightening into a line. Life wasn't easy, no matter the circumstances. Life was instead a grotesquely beautiful combination of pain and love, tragedy and triumph. Though, at the moment, he and everyone associated with him seemed to be enduring more of the former.

No, he had made a promise to himself, and he would have voiced it to Aoife too, if she had given him the chance. He would make things right. He would make it all up to her. He would make amends for lying to her.

But you won't be able to do that if you don't bloody survive.

With a huff, he kicked the iron bars of his cell, regretting it at once when his toes took the brunt of the impact. A grimace spread across his face, and a string of curses fell from his mouth as he hopped away, nursing his aching foot. But his bound hands threw his balance completely off. His leap away from the offending bars sent him falling backwards, and his fingers were crushed between his backside and the floor.

"Well," a voice said around a scratchy laugh, "you aren't at your most graceful, are yeh?"

Declan raised his chin so he could see his guest, hiding his wince so the man wouldn't see his embarrassment and pain. No wonder he hadn't heard him approaching; he was nearly the exact opposite of the previous crewman who had come for him. This one was slight, and though he looked to be close to Declan in age, his eyes carried more wisdom—and kindness—than Declan would have expected from anyone aboard this ship.

"Sadly, no. You are not catching me at my best," Declan said as he tried to maneuver himself into a more comfortable position.

"No kidding. You're proving all the stories we've heard of the great young Captain McCallagh to be naught but folly. How did you manage to make such a name for yourself if you also got caught and thrown in our brig?"

"Just bad luck, I suppose," Declan answered with an exaggerated sigh. "So, to what do I owe the pleasure of your visit? Callum not trust me in this cell? Not like I can do much here, like this." He tried to lift his shackled hands as far around to the side as he could.

"Well, trusting you doesn't seem to be high on his list, but he did instruct me to bring you your rations. Can't be encountering the sirens with you all weak and feeble." The man stepped forward, and for the first time, Declan noted the bundle the man held at his waist. He might have kicked himself for being so inattentive, but the dim light plus the blow to his head were viable reasons for his failure.

"Thank you. I wondered if Big Boris had heard me when I requested food," Declan said with a nod of his chin toward the ladder.

"Big Boris?" Even in the darkness, Declan could see the man's dark brows pull together over his light blue eyes. "Oh, you mean Reggie. You're not likely to get much out of that one. He's more the quiet type. And I don't mean vocally," he added, tapping a finger at his temple a couple of times.

Declan let out a light laugh as he caught the man's meaning. "And you are?"

"Oh, I'm all well and good in that department."

"Good to know, though I was actually asking your name."

The man took another step forward until he was mere inches from the bars and shook his head, dark strands of hair falling over his face. "Well, you should be clearer. People can't read your mind, you know."

"Sands, I'm glad for that." Declan attempted to stand, but the man waved for him to stop.

"No need to get up," he said, instead lowering himself down to sit on the floor, pushing the hair back behind his ears. "I'm not permitted to free your hands, so unless you want to eat it off your lap or"—he gestured to the floor—"off whatever the hell is coating this disgustingness, I figured I could help."

Clearing his throat, Declan eyed the man, trying to figure him out. "Well, I've never been fed by another man."

"First time for everything."

"I've heard that before. Aboard this ship, actually. But okay. I'll accept your help, but only after you give me your name. Feels weird to have a stranger do such a thing."

The man gave another throaty chuckle. "I would think it would feel weird, friend or otherwise, eh? But the name's Boris."

Declan gave him a once-over and tried to ignore the itch that developed along his jaw again. "No, it's not."

With a roll of his eyes, the man let out a breath. "Fine, it's not. I should have known I couldn't pull one over on you. It's actually Killian."

Declan clicked his tongue as he looked to the ceiling, his mind searching for dim memories and coming up empty. "I swear I knew a Killian once."

"Oh? Fellow pirate, was he?"

"I don't think so, though my memory isn't what it used to be. Used to frequent the pub and entertain folks with stories from his home beyond the Aisling. Tales of magic and death, great battles and…a horse. That I remember. He always talked about his black horse."

He blinked and looked back at Killian to find a quizzical expression on the man's face. Declan cleared his throat before saying, "Not that any of that has to do with you. But you're not from the Aisling, are you?"

Killian unwrapped the bundle in his lap as he responded. "The accent give me away?" He didn't wait for an answer. "South of here. Came north when I was a young man to get away from the conflict that was brewing."

"South, as in Larcsporough?" he asked before opening his mouth awkwardly to accept a piece of the same fruit he'd seen Callum eating earlier. The burst of juice when he bit into it surprised him as much as its sweet, tart flavor, and Killian laughed lightly, shaking his head.

"It's called an orange. Never seen one? They come from the south actually. And yes, Larcsporough. But it's been nearly twenty years since I've set foot on that land."

Declan shifted closer to the bars. While he doubted anyone was listening in, it was better to take care, so he said in a low voice, "So you know of the fae?"

The man lifted a hand to his head, rubbing away whatever tension had built up at his temple. "Aye, I know 'em."

"I sense some not-too-fond feelings toward them," Declan said. The information Killian could provide might not aid him in his current situation, but if he'd learned anything from his years at sea, it was that all information was valuable. Eventually.

Killian dropped his gaze to the floor and drew in a breath. "You could say that."

Declan waited, and somewhere deep inside him a slight laugh echoed at how different his situation had become. He'd been so stressed by the deadline Cait had given him, and now it no longer seemed to matter. Not that he'd had any control over circumstances before, but here he had none. It did him no good to fret over it, and so he could wait for Killian to provide the story.

Offering him the last segment of the fruit, Killian said softly, "For centuries my people lived in Larcsporough, ruled peacefully by our royal family. But when the war up here ended and the fae moved in, it all changed. At first we lived in harmony, equally sharing the lands. We integrated well, perhaps too well, because we let our guard down."

"What do you mean, too well?"

"How much do you know about fae history?"

"Only the basics. Much was lost and forgotten with the belief they had all perished in the war."

Killian sighed, nodding. "Well, then you don't know that only fae of the royal bloodline have magic, or what they call *daemari*. The fae who survived the war sought a way to avoid the destruction in the future. So they instituted new laws. They broke apart the royal families. Decided the best path forward was to lessen the *daemari* as much as possible."

"So they forbid royal fae from bonding," Declan said.

"Aye. And it worked. While the original royals survived the war and their powers remained strong, they paired with lesser fae, so their children's *daemari* was less potent, if they received any at all. And after spending a century or two living with us humans, those children—the lesser fae—began to bond with mortals."

"Bond. Like something they can't resist?"

Killian straightened up, his face contorting as if he had tasted something bitter. "What? No. Has that become part of the lore?"

Declan gave a nod. "One book I read talked of how they can't control who they pair with, and there is no breaking it once the bond has formed."

The man shook his head with a breathy laugh. "Not surprising how the truth gets twisted over time. No, what we might see as being a firm bond is merely how intensely the fae feel. Humans fall in love—if they're lucky—but fae? There is no word for what they experience. Can they deny it? Walk away from it? Aye. But it rarely happens."

"And they were allowed to take humans as—"

"Encouraged to, in some cases," Killian said. "Some fae lines resorted to forcing their offspring into marriages with mortals."

"To ensure their powers—the *daemari*—would die out?"

"Aye."

Declan's mind worked to piece all of this together, but something was missing. "But how did this lead to you fleeing? What was the danger?"

Killian was silent for a moment, and the tears forming in his eyes shined. But with a blink, he managed to keep them at bay. "The lesser fae didn't know the history. And some felt their elders had exaggerated the stories to keep them from having more power, more wealth, more of what they felt they deserved. After centuries of being denied what they saw as their right—land and riches and control—they started to rebel. The fae are nothing if not patient, and their bitterness and resentment festered for another century and a half, with small steps being taken little by little to create division throughout their kind. I was only a babe when the first camps were built."

Declan froze. He'd never heard of such a thing, but Killian's forlorn tone and solemn demeanor indicated it was far from good. "Camps?"

A dip of the chin was all Killian offered, silence settling between them. Declan wracked his brain as he tried to digest this revelation. What had the fae done to Killian's people? What had happened to Killian's family? Before he could decide how to ask any of his questions, the man was talking again.

"All humans were taken from their homes. First in the east. We heard about it up north where I lived, but news came too late. We had only heard whisperings of families being dragged out in the middle of the night, forced to give their homes and belongings over to the fae."

"Was it all fae? Some of them were wed to humans, though, right? Did they participate? Or…" Declan thought he knew the answer, but he hoped he was wrong.

"Forced to choose between their fae heritage and their human partners and their demi-fae children. If they chose their families over their brethren…" His eyes glazed over as if he was reliving some memory, seeing a vision of some past event replaying in his mind. "It was not pretty. Those who chose to join their fae kin were forced to prove their loyalty by slaughtering their spouses and children. If they refused, they were punished, made to watch as their loved ones were tortured and killed."

Declan's stomach turned. He'd seen his share of violence, had inflicted pain upon others himself, had done so without regret or remorse, but he did not do it for sport—not like some of the more ruthless in his profession. Rather, it was simply a necessary part of achieving some goals.

"And you? Where does your story fit into all of this?" Declan asked, trying his best to keep his tone neutral and not let any of his shock show.

"We were one of those families. The fae had reached a nearby town, and one of my father's close friends—a human—had managed to get his family out in time. He came to warn us. They decided we needed to leave Larcsporough, make a new life in the north, in one of the lands of the Aisling. But the nearest port was a day's walk away. My father urged us to leave, vowing we would have a better chance of reaching a ship and sailing to safety if he stayed behind and stalled the approaching fae. My mother refused to leave his side, and he finally agreed to join us. But it was a lie. He never intended to come, I don't think. We made it to the port. He secured us passage on a merchant ship, but just as we had stepped foot aboard, he stopped and rushed back to the dock. I watched him disappear as my mother wailed, nearly falling over the edge. The crew had to restrain her and give her a tonic to help her calm down and sleep. I don't know what happened to him. I never heard. I was only sixteen at the time, but even then I had no idea how to help my mother. By the time we reached Ludlam, she had fallen into such a grave depression over my father's absence, we could barely tell if she was still present in her mind. My younger sister insisted on staying there with her, to take care of her and to hopefully build a simpler life away from the hatred and persecution. But she was only eleven, with no skills, and I refused to let her do the work many young girls end up in. I got hired onto the first crew that would take me."

Declan blinked, his eyes opening wide as he tried to find the proper words. He had so many questions, each of which itched to be voiced first. He snatched at the first one he could mentally grasp onto and blurted out, "Callum's crew?"

A nod. "Though it wasn't always Callum's. He was younger than me when I first signed on. I've known him a long time."

"And you said your family was one of those being—" Killian nodded sharply, as if the man couldn't bear to have it said aloud again. "That would mean one of your parents was a—"

"A fae. Yes. My father."

"So you're a... What are you exactly?" He cringed at the ridiculous way he had worded the question, but thankfully Killian didn't seem to notice or care.

"Demi-fae, technically, but most of my father's fae qualities went to my sister, so for all intents and purposes I consider myself human."

Propping himself up against his bound hands, Declan leaned back. "And what of the humans who had no ties to the fae? Do I even want to know?"

"The camps. They were strictly for the humans. What they did with them there, I never heard, but I doubt it was anything good."

"No doubt. No wonder you have such animosity for them." Declan wondered how Killian would react to the knowledge that he had planned to work with the fae to achieve this goal.

He worked his way through all he'd just learned, debating how any of this might help him in his current situation, but nothing presented itself.

Except for one thing... Not that it helped him in this festering brig. How it would help in the future, he didn't know either, but he tucked the information away into the corner of his mind for safekeeping.

Only the royal fae had powers.

So the Bron sisters were royals.

13
AOIFE

Aoife tried to ignore the blatant stares she received from the crew as she strode out onto the deck, but it was difficult not to notice how they cleared the area and took up spots around the railing as if they didn't have anything better to do. Like prepare to meet the kraken.

Collins stepped forward calmly, his shoulders back, his dark eyes gleaming with confidence. Aoife could fake that, surely. Rolling her shoulders, she forced herself to grow a couple of inches with better posture, and then she drew her dagger from where she kept it at her waist.

"No," Collins said. But not rudely. More like he was declining a cup of tea instead of giving his new pupil a command.

"What do you mean, no?"

"We don't use real blades." Before she could protest or ask for clarification, he added, "Not when first learning. Last thing we need is for you to be not only untrained but also injured."

He motioned to a man Aoife didn't recognize, who tossed him what looked to be a few sticks. Holding them before him, Collins flashed her a wink. A week ago, that gesture would have been unexpected. Two weeks ago, it would have made her bristle. But now it felt as natural as an eyeroll from Lani.

Slipping her dagger back into its spot at her side, she motioned for Collins to toss her one of the wooden practice blades. When he did, she reached out with both hands, hoping at least one of them would be able to catch it. Snickers erupted around the deck when it clattered at her feet, but they stopped with such an abruptness that she knew without looking up that Collins had warned them to knock it off. She grasped for the dagger, curling her fingers around what she hoped was meant to be the handle. To pick it up by the wrong end would no doubt earn her more ridicule.

"First off, you need to loosen up a bit. You're standing too stiff," Collins instructed.

Aoife forced her joints to release some of their tension, but she didn't understand how she was to do any sort of fighting with her body as limp as a drunkard after a long celebration.

"Closer," Collins said, walking over to help her out. He slipped his own practice blade into his waistband and reached for her arms. Giving them a small shake, he said, "This is good, but this?" He grabbed her wrists and shook them around, and her hands flopped like fish in a net until her stick fell to the deck. "Causes that. You need to keep yourself loose so you can move quickly—especially with the beast we're going to encounter—but not so loose that you can't hold on to your weapon."

Aoife retrieved her bit of wood and tried again. "Like this?" But when she tightened her grip, it stiffened her whole arm. She corrected herself before he could speak. "Wait, no." Another roll of her shoulders, and she focused on relaxing her shoulder, her elbow, and her wrist while still keeping her hand in control of the sparring weapon.

"Yes, Aoife. Like that, except you'll need to practice that so it doesn't require so much concentration to achieve." He backed away a few feet, and Aoife could have sworn she saw him trying to suppress a laugh or a smile, but she refused to let it bother her. This was what she wanted. To learn. To be useful. And if achieving that meant dealing with a bit of embarrassment, then so be it.

"Okay. I'm loose, but not too loose. Now what?"

Pulling his practice weapon out once more, he waved her forward. "Attack me."

Aoife hesitated. Surely he should tell her how to do that before forcing her to, but he was the trainer. He must know how to teach, so she would listen. Thrusting her weapon in front of her, she lunged forward, covering the distance between them in a handful of steps. She hadn't even seen his tall form move when she felt the strike against her arm and heard her weapon fall onto the deck again.

"Good," Collins said.

"But I failed. How was that good?" she asked as she bent down once more to retrieve the wooden blade, forcing herself to ignore how her forearm hurt where he had struck her.

"Aye. But you tried. That's the first step. Failure in training isn't a bad thing. The faster you fail, the faster you'll learn how the correct movements feel, and the faster you'll learn overall. It would have been worse if you'd hesitated or refused."

"Okay," she said, not sure she quite understood his logic. "So what did I do wrong?"

"A few things." He must have seen how his words deflated her, because he flashed her a smile that melted away some of her apprehension. "Don't take it personally, Aoife. These are common errors. Nothing I haven't seen before. First, you were focused only on striking and didn't anticipate needing to guard yourself. You came at me squarely, but you'll want to shift your body like this." He moved one leg back until his body was at an angle to her.

"But doesn't that make you more exposed?"

"Only if I were facing multiple attackers, but right now we're focused on one. This allows me to prevent you from striking in my more sensitive areas."

Her face warmed at his words, and she cringed more at her own reaction than at what he'd said.

"Remember, you are both on the offense and the defense. You can't succeed in attacking if you aren't ready to guard yourself from their response. You won't be striking an unconscious person—or a sleeping beast, in this case—so you have to be prepared for them to defend themselves."

Aoife gave a nod. "What else? Did I approach wrong?"

"It was predictable. Not that this will be as big a deal against sea monsters and all. So instead, I want to focus on energy conservation. If you use too much force too early, you'll tire too quickly. Adrenaline can only help you so much."

"So how do I conserve that? If I don't put enough force behind my strike, it won't do any good, right?"

"Part of it is practice. As your body gets used to the movements—gets used to moving at all, really—it'll be easier to only use what you need."

"But we don't have—"

Collins held up a hand, and Aoife snapped her mouth shut.

"No, we don't have much time. So I'm not going to focus on the hand-to-hand fighting I normally would. Instead, I need you to be able to move quickly, react instantly, and not drop your weapon so easily when struck."

Aoife mimicked his angled position as Collins moved forward to show her how to keep her guard up. For hours they worked through the basics, striking and blocking so many times that the clacking of their wooden blades became as familiar a sound to her as the rush of the air past her ears. The feinting and quick movements proved more challenging than she'd expected. How did these pirates make it look so easy?

She was so focused on his instructions—and her own frustrations over how difficult it all was—that when they finally stopped, she was surprised to find the crew had all gone back to their regular tasks. When she moved to offer the wooden sparring blade to Collins, he once again held up a hand to stop her.

"Hold onto it. You'll want to be practicing what we worked on as often as you can. Even if only by yourself."

With a nod, she made to walk off toward the captain's quarters but turned and asked, "Will we practice again today?" While her mind insisted this would be best so she could improve as quickly as possible, her muscles screamed in protest, her legs and arms aching from the fatigue of being used in such an unfamiliar way.

"Nope. I don't want to break you too badly this first day. We'll train again tomorrow. I'll have someone bring some food in for you." He jutted his chin toward the cabin, encouraging her to retreat and rest.

After being out on the deck with the whistling of the sea breeze in her ears, the clattering of wood on wood, and the thudding of her body hitting the floor, the quiet in the quarters seemed to press in on her from all sides. While it wasn't her first time alone in this room since they'd left Cregah, the discomfort hadn't lessened any. Any forgiveness she had begun to feel for herself had been replaced with fresh guilt over abandoning Declan on that beach. No matter what Tommy insisted, she should have been there with him.

Running is what you do best though.

Tears sprang up, and she closed her eyes to keep them at bay. Crying wouldn't help anyone. She hadn't even been strong enough to face her pain as Declan pleaded with her in the cove. But she could be strong now.

She nearly laughed at that thought. Her whole body felt like a washcloth being wrung out for the hundredth time, squeezed and pushed until there was nothing but emptiness.

As soon as she sat on the edge of the bed to kick off her boots, she heard someone enter the cabin. She tried to identify the visitor—who hadn't even bothered to knock—by their gait alone, but her mind was as tired as the rest of her, unwilling to put forth much effort. She could call out, but there seemed little point, given that no one on this ship would do her harm, and they'd make themselves known soon enough.

All she wanted to do was to lie back and take a long nap, and she might have, had her stomach not grumbled in reaction to the smells of salted meat, cheese, and bread that now filled the room. Before she could move to rise, Tommy appeared in the doorway, a single plate of the food in his hand.

"No doubt you're hungry. I could hear your stomach from the other room," he said, offering her food to her.

Noticing his empty hands, she asked, "You not eating?"

"Not here. I'll take mine with Gavin and Mikkel over our strategy session in a bit."

"Shall I join you?" Even as she asked the question, she hoped he'd decline, not wanting to move any more than she had to. She wasn't even sure she could move if he requested her presence.

"No. I think you need to rest a bit—and stretch out those

muscles—or you'll feel even worse in the morning."

"Worse? I don't know how that's possible." The tears returned, and she felt all the more ridiculous for reacting in such a way. How could she possibly expect to engage the kraken, let alone the sirens, if she couldn't even handle one day—not even a whole day—of training?

"Oh, it is. But it will get easier. And who knows. If we're lucky, you won't have to use any of those moves on the monster."

"I don't think luck has proven to be on our side thus far."

"Aye, but the past can't completely predict the future. All it can do is teach us so we make better decisions next time around."

Tommy's expression darkened a bit, his jaw tightening and his gaze softening as if he was standing somewhere else instead of in his best friend's quarters. Nibbling on a bit of the meat, Aoife watched him. The carefree charm she had come to associate with him had been absent since Declan's capture.

"What's eating at you, Tommy? Other than the obvious."

"Nothing," he said with a wave of his hand, shooing away her concern as he would a sand fly. "Just the obvious."

Aoife eyed him, but something about his tired appearance kept her from pressing for the truth.

Before she could think of anything more to say, he was backing away from the sleeping quarters and muttering something about needing to meet up with the men. With the door closed and the cabin once again empty and quiet, Aoife could have spent time pondering what could be bothering Tommy. But her mind and body both begged for rest, and without finishing the last of her food, she lay back onto the feather mattress and fell into a dreamless sleep.

The forests northwest of Morshan might have been peaceful if not for how eerie the silence was. The trees in this area lay thicker than to the south, as if they had crowded around to hide what happened beneath their branches. As silly as that notion might have been, it held some truth to Cait, as it was here she had found these ruins all those years ago on one of her explorations. Stone walls—or what was left of them—marked the entrance to a small clearing barely larger than the pub's main room. The clearing was otherwise empty, with the wall separating it from the rest of the forest all the way around. Some sections were nearly up to Cait's shoulders, while others were barely above her ankles. What the area had been used for, she had no idea. Some holy spot for a long-dead religion perhaps, or merely the remnants of an old home. Whatever it had been in the past, now it provided Cait and the Rogues the perfect hideout.

While Cait had initially balked at Lucan's half-brained cookie exchange idea, she had to admit it did work rather well. A small, abandoned house on the outskirts of the port town provided the perfect location to send those who made contact. Its original owners had left the area when Cait was too young to explore on her own, and no one had since moved in or claimed it for their own. Whether people thought it an ill omen to take up residence in an abandoned home, she wasn't sure, but even passing it on her way here had sent a shudder up her spine. Had the residents been exiled? Possibly. Or had they simply moved on to another land?

It was in that building that Lucan and Eva had met the girl from the pub to hear the rest of her story. A story so similar to others on the island. Family disappearing. Wealth being stripped. Hunger. Pain. Sickness. Until the only option she'd had was to look for work. She'd originally intended to use a position on the council staff to get close enough to gain an audience with them. She'd hoped they would be willing to hear her family's case and maybe have an investigation opened to discover what had become of them and who was responsible.

But before she'd had a chance to request such a meeting, she had witnessed the exile of the middle heir. Most of the newer and younger staff had remained in the staff quarters as instructed, but curiosity had pushed her toward a window that overlooked the main drive to the council entrance. The terror in the girl's eyes and the force they'd used against her had raised the girl's suspicions, eventually bringing her to the pub.

When Lucan had returned after lunch with the girl's story, he had suggested they call a meeting. Cait hadn't been keen on the idea, as it was too risky to have all of the Rogues in one place. They hadn't gathered in nearly two years, when they had planned Maggie's infiltration of the council's staff. Since then, all communication had been done via couriers. They were neither official members of the Rogues nor privy to the secrets within the messages they delivered, but they were satisfied with the extra ration cards or copper coins they received for their assistance. The steady stream of jobs Cait and her crew provided kept the men they employed from wagging their tongues to the council.

Still, with Maggie dead, Cait hadn't been able to deny the benefit of having a new set of eyes within the council hall, and she had quickly granted Lucan's request.

Although Lucan had left before her, Cait was the first to arrive at the ruins. Leaning against a corner of the wall where two tall sections met, she tried to exude the calm confidence her role demanded despite the quick, heavy beating of her heart against her sternum. It was so loud it echoed in her ears.

Her mind began to wander as she waited. How was Declan faring? Had his crew intercepted Callum yet? Was he safe, or was he already dead? Her throat constricted at that thought, and she forced her mind to move past it.

What of the dagger? If Declan didn't... Would his crew pick up where he'd left off? Or would her mission—the one thing that could help take down the council for good—fail before she could even really put it into action?

A throat cleared behind her, and she glanced over her shoulder to see Lucan and Eva approaching through the trees, stepping around the bushes and undergrowth. Between them, the girl, with a burlap sack over her head, trembled in their grasp. Lucan's grip was notably looser than Eva's, who, by the scowl on her face, did not agree with the decision to bring the girl into their confidence.

With a nod, Cait gestured for them to bring the girl into the enclosed area before pointing to a low section of wall where she should sit.

"Can you take this off yet?" the girl asked, her voice muffled by the bag.

It was Eva who answered, gruffness etched into the single syllable. "No."

Lucan added, "It won't be long. Hang in there."

Over the next half hour, the other Rogues arrived, most alone, but some in pairs. Wives with their husbands. Sisters with their brothers. Or simply best friends who had—Cait hoped—not met up until they were well hidden in the trees. All arrived just as Lucan had—silently, moving like phantoms who haunted the forest. Their greetings remained equally quiet. Most simply nodded to one another. Others whispered into ears while offering quick embraces.

Cait watched the arrivals, not moving from her spot in the corner but merely offering silent nods of acknowledgement to the newcomers. While she saw many of them in her day-to-day life, there were a handful she hadn't seen in a while, and she made a mental note of who looked too thin or too sickly, promising herself she would get them the extra food and medical care they needed. But none of the Rogues had aged well since their last meeting. Most looked as haggard as Cait felt, and yet none had surpassed middle age.

When all eighteen members were accounted for, she stepped forward into the quiet circle of her brethren. She would need to address them, but the words were trapped behind the emotions wedged in her throat. Though most of those gathered hadn't known Maggie as well as Cait had, their sense of loss was written plainly on their faces.

Waving to Lucan, she motioned for him to bring the girl over to where she stood.

"What's your name?" Cait's question came out rougher than

she would have liked.

The girl seemed to flinch before finally answering in a voice barely louder than a whisper, "Naeve."

"And how did you know how to find us?"

There was no hesitation this time. "Maggie."

Murmurs rose around the circle of rebels, and Cait didn't have to guess what they were all pondering, for it was the same suspicion she had been chewing on since this morning. Had Maggie double-crossed them? Had the council learned who she was and used her against them?

Naeve addressed those questions as if Cait had voiced them aloud. "You needn't worry. Maggie was loyal to you up until the end."

"How do we know that for sure?" a young man named Jameson asked, his deep brown eyes narrowing.

More whispers rippled through the assembly, and then multiple people began asking questions at once, the discussion reaching a concerningly high volume as they talked over each other. Lucan stepped into the center and raised his hands up at his sides, like the leader of one of the musical groups that sometimes visited to entertain travelers.

Everyone quieted at once.

"Because of this," Lucan said, his voice sounding soft after the ruckus they had made with their questions. He held up a piece of paper that was folded and smudged with dirt and what looked an awful lot like blood.

Naeve stiffened beside him. Although the girl didn't exactly exude confidence, her stance demonstrated how hard she attempted to portray it anyway. If Lucan was pausing for some dramatic effect, it only worked to make Cait and the others more frustrated.

"And?" Cait asked, not bothering to hide her annoyance.

With a glance over his shoulder, he said, "It's from our Maggie."

Cait reached for it, and thankfully Lucan didn't try to stall in that moment or she might have dropped him on his backside for being a pain in hers. The circle of Rogues tightened an inch as if they could get a glimpse of the message—not that Cait would afford such an intrusion. And it was good they couldn't see it. Had they discovered then and there that the message was, in fact, blank, it would not have ended well.

For either Lucan or Naeve.

"I see," she said, folding the note and slipping it into her shirt between her undergarment and her breast, not willing to risk putting it in a pocket. "Before we discuss further, I need to have a chat with Lucan. Eva, hold onto her."

She gestured for Lucan to follow her around the walls and away from the ruins, ignoring the hushed grumbles of protest chasing them into the trees. Every member had agreed, upon joining this crew of rebels, to the hierarchy, understanding that Cait and Lucan worked closely together to decide strategy and determine the group's course of action. But she couldn't blame them for their frustration with the current situation. She would have felt the same in their position.

When she was sure they were out of earshot, she rounded a large tree and pushed Lucan against the rough bark. After looking around the trunk to ensure no one had followed them, she turned her attention back to her second, only to find him smiling that wicked grin he donned when he was about to make some smart-ass remark.

"About time you pushed me up against a tree, Cait," he whispered.

She didn't have the energy to roll her eyes at him, not with a potential spy in their midst. How could he have been such an idiot? How could she have been stupid enough to trust him?

You made him your second for a reason. You trust him for a reason.

Drawing in a breath, Cait focused on the scent of pine and dirt that washed over her. She settled her nerves enough to speak without hissing at him. "Why the blank paper?"

"I trust her, Cait." His expression sobered as all humor fled from his eyes, replaced with a seriousness she'd seen only a handful of times.

"Your gut." It wasn't a question. This was why she'd chosen him. Not simply because he was the first one she'd met when forming this band—or reviving it, as it were. But he had proven himself—and his instincts—time and time again. He had such an uncanny way of feeling out a situation, preemptively identifying danger, keeping the Rogues from being discovered.

He offered a single nod but didn't say anything more.

"And you knew they wouldn't trust your instincts as I do."

"You are a rare breed in that regard. If they weren't all on edge with Maggie's death, if things weren't so unsettling, they might have taken my word alone. But as it is, they needed *evidence.*"

"And what if they ask what Maggie wrote to us? What if they demand to see her words?" Although Cait had already begun formulating a lie to tell her people, she preferred having someone to help shoulder the responsibility. As independent as she'd had to become, she found comfort in having a friend beside her to keep her in check and support her decisions.

"First off," he said, relaxing against the tree as Cait backed off a step to allow him some space, "you're the leader of the Rogues. You don't have to show them anything. Just tell them the less they know the less chance the council might have evidence against them."

Running her hand across her brow, she tried to chase her thoughts from option to option, to nail down the right decision. "That could work. So how do we use her? In what capacity do we have her help?"

The laughter returned to the chocolate browns of his eyes. "Really? I'm pretty sure you know."

"Well, yes, of course she'd be our eyes and ears within the council. But we can't have her meet the same fate as our Maggie. We need to be smart about this."

"I suggest we ask her then. And it would behoove us to let the others offer up their ideas as well. Even if they're all awful and worthless, it will help them trust us, and her."

With a nod, Cait shifted to start the short jaunt back to the ruins, but a flash of movement from her right made her go still. Lucan eyed her as he stood equally frozen in place, not even daring to look in the same direction. It might have made Cait laugh, that he could possibly think anyone wouldn't notice them simply because they had stopped moving, yet she was doing the same thing.

Narrowing her eyes at him, she willed herself to speak louder, loud enough for whoever was watching to hear. "Go on and start getting their ideas out in the open. And let her meet the team officially. I need to use the *facilities*. Too much coffee this morning."

As he moved around the tree and headed toward their crew, she pivoted and strode off in the opposite direction, thankful for how thick the woods were on this part of the island. Moving behind a bush and out of sight of whoever had followed them, she lowered herself down and crept on silent feet, circling their position. She still hadn't gotten a glimpse of who it was, but given the scarcity of animals here and the absence of any breeze, it had to be a person, and that person couldn't be allowed to discover the

Rogues.

When she was sure she had gone far enough around to flank the intruder, she risked looking around a tree. Her eyes scanned the forest, looking for any movement, but everything had stilled, as if the trees held a collective breath, waiting to see what she would do.

She had nearly convinced herself it had been nothing, a figment of her imagination or her eyes playing tricks on her, when the sharp tip of a dagger pressed into her back in the perfect spot for a quick kill. She stilled, her mind whirring as she cursed the council's ridiculous rules against weapons and her stupidity in adhering to them. She turned her chin to look over her shoulder at her attacker, but she froze before she could catch a glimpse. Warmth spread across her entire back as the person stepped closer, invading her personal space. Hot breath crept across the back of her neck, and the scent of sweat and leather and seawater surrounded her.

A familiar scent after growing up in a pub filled with traveling sailors and weary pirates.

Cait let her body shudder with a shaky breath and whispered a plea for mercy. She didn't need to be armed to take care of herself, especially if the man fell for her act. But he didn't budge. Instead, his blade dug deeper into her flesh, and his other arm moved around her to rest on the tree, blocking her exit.

"Begging for mercy from a pirate, love?" His taunting words came out in a rough breath with more humor than anger. His *tsk-tsk* filled her ear.

Damn pirates.

With that thought, she sent her elbow into his arm, pushing the blade away from her back just enough that she could whirl around to her right. But before she could get away, he grabbed her hair, yanking her head back with a quiet growl.

Cait gritted her teeth to suppress a cry of pain. While making noise might prompt Lucan and the others to come to her aid, she didn't need them. Not yet.

Her attacker used her hair to pull her against the tree until the rough bark dug into her spine. He moved his hand to her shoulder so quickly she wondered how anyone could move like that. She tried to raise her other arm to strike him, but as it was her non-dominant side, her blow was ineffective and clumsy, easily blocked, and his blade now pressed below her ribs.

She could try again, but she had to admit—albeit reluctant-ly—that her body was out of shape, incapable of fending off a pirate who spent his time honing his fighting skills while all she had done recently was wipe down tables and pour drinks. Making a mental note to start training with Lucan—*If you get out of this, you mean*—she breathed a sigh and let her shoulders relax.

"I give up. You win."

He didn't loosen his grip, didn't move at all except to raise his brow at her.

He wasn't much taller than her, and his piercing blue eyes trapped her for a split second. How many lasses had fallen under their spell? She wouldn't be one of them though. His face was not altogether unpleasant, his strong jaw covered by a beard he kept cut close to his face, unlike most of the sailors she'd seen, who grew theirs into long, unattractive scraggles of hair they would braid or leave completely unkempt.

No, this man had a different air about him than the men she knew. Her eyes trailed the lines of his face, taking in the waves of blonde hair, the sides shorn short above his ears in a style the younger pirates preferred. She'd thought she knew most of the pirates who graced the Cregahn shores, but his face was foreign to her, which meant he was either new or he wasn't one to visit the pubs and eateries in port.

He wore no colors around his neck like many of the men did, but when she glanced down at his waist to check his sash, he released another breath, once again sending heat over her ear and neck. "This isn't my best angle, love."

She ignored the way his rough voice sent her core fluttering, clenching her jaw in an effort to push the sensation away. At his waist she found nothing but a worn leather belt.

"Aw," he said. "Trying to see which crew I'm with, are ya?"

She didn't respond except to meet his gaze, forcing her annoyance at being trapped against this tree to edge out the other feelings that had built within against her will. The silence between them filled with tension as they remained locked in the stare.

Cait didn't have time for this nonsense though, and she needed to end whatever game he was playing with her so she could get back to planning. "No colors means either you're a liar, a loser, or a spy. Or all three."

A gruff laugh escaped him, once again sending that irritating warmth creeping through her body. "Aye. All decent assumptions, I suppose."

"So which is it?"

Giving his head a slow shake, he said, "You'll just have to find out."

"And why would I care to, exactly?"

"Oh, because you, Ms. McCallagh, can't risk your merry band of criminals being caught by the council or having your plans foiled by a handsome pirate."

"Well, if I see a handsome pirate anywhere, I'll be sure to tell him to go away and leave us alone."

"I'm waiting."

"For what?"

"For you to tell me to go away and leave you alone." How the light danced in his eyes when there was so little of it here under the trees, she wasn't sure, and it took all her will to pull her attention away from them. All these years she'd ignored the devilishly attractive men who had graced her pub. She could do so now.

She glared up at him. "You think quite highly of yourself, don't you?"

"It beats the alternative. I've never been one for self-loathing."

"Ah, yes, at least one person in the Aisling should like you. Might as well be yourself."

Shadows crept through the blues of his eyes, like clouds passing over the sea, and if she hadn't known better, she would have thought his mind had wandered away to some other place. Had she been prepared for such a reaction, she could have used the moment to break out of his hold, but it quickly passed, his expression returning to the annoyingly flirtatious one he'd had for the past several minutes. But he didn't say anything.

Cait dropped an ear to her shoulder. "So, to what do I owe this visit then? You see, I'm rather busy."

"I want to help you," he said matter-of-factly, like he was ordering a rum in the pub instead of offering to help overthrow the council. Though perhaps he meant to assist in a different capacity.

"With what exactly?"

"The council," he said and then lowered his voice into a gruff whisper again. "I want them gone."

"And who says that's my goal?"

"You think the council doesn't know about you and your rebels? Doesn't know what you're planning?"

How did *he* know about the Rogues and about her position within them? How could he know what the council had discovered? How could...

"You've been with the council? You're on a lord's crew."

"Was."

"Did they kick you out for being an ass?"

"I guess you could say we wanted different things."

"And why should I trust you? I don't even know your name," she said, not fully expecting him to actually provide it.

"You'll just have to follow your gut, I guess." One corner of his mouth lifted into an easy smile that brought out a dimple in his bearded cheek. "And the name's Adler."

The sky had darkened considerably by the time Tommy had finished his discussion with Mikkel and Gavin on the quarterdeck. The location of their meeting was far from ideal, but with Aoife nursing her pains from training and the sisters doing who knew what in the officers' quarters, they had few options that would allow for any privacy. The quarterdeck was as good a place as any.

Even after several hours of planning, they had little to show for it. He'd had to shut down Mikkel several times for continuously mentioning the powers of the fae. They could definitely help—that Tommy couldn't deny—but he couldn't stomach the thought of allowing it and having them not recover enough before they reached the sound. If he did everything to save the crew only to fail at the very end, he'd never forgive himself.

But if you lose the crew to the kraken, you'll be fine?

His thoughts warred within him as he strode toward the stairs, leaving Mikkel and Gavin to continue their chatter. No doubt they were cursing him for refusing to budge on the matter. He took the steps more quickly than usual, and with his mind preoccupied, he didn't notice the person walking into his path until it was too late.

"Watch where you're—" he said, starting to reprimand the clumsy crew member who had dared get in his way, but his words were cut short at the sight of Maura.

"Apologies, Tommy," she offered, not showing any sign of embarrassment. In fact, had he not known better, he might have thought she'd planned this as an ambush.

Way to let your guard down.

"I should be the one to apologize, miss. I—"

"Please, Tommy. It's Maura. I can't have you calling me miss in the middle of a skirmish with the kraken or the sirens. How would we know which of us you were speaking to?"

As much as it irked him to admit it, she had a point. He gave a curt nod and whispered "fair" before moving to get around her. But with unnatural speed, she stepped in his way, her slender body uncomfortably close to his. It sent a warmth from his core to his head, and he hoped her fae sight didn't allow her to see how his complexion reddened in her presence.

"Excuse me," he muttered. "Maura, I really need to check on Aoife and perhaps get some rest of my own."

"Of course," she said, though she made no move to let him pass. Something in her eyes sparkled, catching the last rays of sun as it dipped below the horizon. While Maura had always seemed the more innocent of the three sisters, Tommy was starting to wonder if he had underestimated her. She still had a demure air about her, yet something about her was far from sweet and modest.

He didn't have time for whatever game this was, but some

part of him urged him to play along. The door to Declan's cabin opened then, pulling both his and Maura's attention in that direction. Aoife stopped short at the sight of them.

"Oh, am I interrupting something?"

"No," Tommy said. He gritted his teeth, pursing his lips, hoping Aoife would see how perturbed he was in this moment and give him an out. He silently pleaded with her to rescue him.

But Aoife's lips curled into an easy smile as she stepped aside, reaching her arm out in an invitation to the cabin she'd exited. "I needed some fresh air for a bit, so you're welcome to take your conversation to a more private location."

He might have hit her had she not been, well, Aoife. His friend. Though he was strongly reconsidering that title for her.

Just as he opened his mouth to decline the offer, he was cut short by Maura answering for them. "Thank you, Aoife. That's greatly appreciated." She turned to Tommy, her golden eyes inviting him in, not just into the cabin but...

No! You don't have time for this.

"I really don't have time—" he said, pushing his thoughts out into the open, but it was Aoife who interrupted him now.

"Nonsense, Tommy. We have another day before we get to, well, you know. And avoiding Maura here won't get us there—or to Declan—any faster." Walking past him, she mouthed a "You're welcome" as she took her leave.

Maura was already entering the captain's cabin before he could protest further, and with a not-so-cleansing breath and a painful attempt to swallow his discomfort, he followed her, trying to force himself to be confident, commanding, assertive. Like Declan.

What would Declan have done in this instance? No doubt make some sarcastic remark to put this fae in her place. But Tommy wasn't Declan, and did he really want to be? While his captain was his best friend, one he would follow to the ends of the Aisling, Tommy knew he'd never be like him. Not that it was a bad thing. There was only room for one brooding man on this ship.

But he's not on this ship.

Tommy grimaced at the thought.

"Are you going to come in?" Maura's words snapped him back to the situation. She was standing in the dim room, a single lantern on the desk behind her casting her in shadow. "Aoife insisted it was inappropriate for my sisters and me to remain in the captain's quarters alone, and I'd hate to go against her on that."

"Yes," he said, though the word held none of the assertiveness he'd intended. Stepping inside, he shut the door behind him but didn't move closer to Maura, instead leaning his back against the wall in an awkward stance.

Maura's laugh danced through the still air. "You look so uncomfortable, Tommy."

"Indeed. I am." There seemed little point in lying to her. The fae's perceptiveness wasn't worth fighting. He wouldn't be surprised if she could see his thoughts even without the power to read them directly. "What did you want to speak to me about?"

"Who said I had speaking in mind?"

While he couldn't see her clearly, he had no trouble picturing the coy smile she flashed him.

Running a hand through his hair, Tommy scratched the back of his head to buy time to think. Normally he would have had an easy quip to brush aside the discomfort, but that night at the council hall had thrown everything askew.

Injury. Recovery. Kidnapping. Storms. Kraken. Sirens.

It all weighed heavily on his shoulders. This entire crew—including his captain—was relying on him to lead them to success and to ensure they survived. He missed his easygoing attitude, which was being sufficiently subdued by the gravity of the situation.

Explains why Declan is so moody, huh?

Maura cleared her throat.

Him. Maura. Alone in the dark in Declan's cabin.

"Well," he said, swallowing, "speaking of propriety. I don't believe using my captain's quarters for non-speaking would be altogether proper either."

Once again, her laugh—light, airy, like a feather floating on a breeze—greeted him. He was glad he couldn't see her clearly. Sands knew how his body might react against his will if he could see her face, angelic with that hint of mischief. She pushed away from the desk and walked toward him, mesmerizing him with her graceful movements.

Holding his breath, he waited, unsure of what she planned to do. He had an idea, of course, but the notion of it seemed so far-fetched.

And yet it didn't.

"Can't you feel it, Tommy?" Her words came out barely above a whisper. She closed the distance between them until mere inches separated them.

"My personal space being invaded? Aye. I feel that."

She laughed. And that laugh might very well be his undoing. But she ignored his flippant comment and moved closer still.

"Can't you feel the emptiness that creeps in when we're apart?" she asked, and Tommy struggled to ignore the sweet scent that clung to her. "Can't you feel the warmth when we're close?"

"Well, that warmth is pretty standard whenever I'm with a woman." He tried to sound nonchalant. He needed to stop her pursuit. It wouldn't do anyone any good for his attention to be divided in such a way, especially for something that had no possibility of a future. None of this would end well.

Maura stood so close now that he could see her delicate features despite the darkness. Keeping her chin down, she peered up at him from beneath her lashes. "Ah, but I'm no mere woman, Tommy."

He risked touching her, putting his hands on her elbows and moving her away from him as gently as he could.

"I can't deny something is happening. Whatever it is, it doesn't matter. We cannot act on anything. Not with Declan missing and the dagger needing to be retrieved and the kraken... I have to put the needs of my crew and my captain and my home above my own desires." His voice lost all power on that final word, which seemed bizarrely insufficient to describe the feelings building within him. Something had ignited, though he had no name for it, and now he'd admitted as much to her, all with some ill-found hope she reciprocated.

Not that it mattered if she did or not. It couldn't happen.

Stepping back, she lifted her chin as she challenged him. "Then let me help. Let me cloak the ship, create a glamour to keep us hidden from the monster below."

"Just because I can't be with you doesn't mean I don't care about you, Maura." He tried to rush past the admission of his feelings, but the words hung in the air between them, electrifying it. He swallowed again. "If you do this to get us through these waters, you won't have time for your magic to replenish before we reach the sound."

"I think you underestimate our magic. You underestimate me." Her tone came out flat and empty.

"What do you mean?"

"The longer we are away from the iron they had in those walls, the stronger our magic becomes and the quicker we are able to recover after using it. It will still drain, of course, and we will certainly need to rest afterward. Every moment we don't use it, it grows and strengthens."

"But you've only had a couple days to rest after healing me. If I'm to believe what your sister said—that you needed days, not hours—then you may not even be at your strongest by the time we enter its territory. And what happens if you push yourself too far, if you use too much too fast?"

"I've never experienced it myself, but I've witnessed it. Once."

"And?"

Maura hesitated, though she didn't look away. "Burnout. And not the type you humans experience when you've overexerted yourself for too long. Burnout for a fae is an extinguishing of their magic. We have to monitor it, because if it goes out completely, it's like an ember that's died. It can't be rekindled. There's no recovering it if we get to that level. And once our magic is gone? Our long life is shortened, our days numbered."

"Then there's no reason to even discuss this." He pushed away from the wall, taking the risk of getting too close to her. It didn't matter, if this was what he needed to do to convince her not to insist on using her magic.

"With all respect, Tommy, I don't answer to you."

Balling his hands into fists, he narrowed his eyes at her. "You do as long as you're on this ship and as long as I'm the acting captain."

"And how will you stop me, Tommy? Keep me prisoner? Lock me in the iron cage of the brig below decks? Or maybe tie me down?" He could have sworn he saw her wink at him, and he forced himself to ignore the imagery her words conjured.

"If it comes to that, perhaps. But I'd rather not be forced to repeat the council's tactics here."

She breathed deep, exhaling her sugary scent into the space

between them, a breath of a sigh that sent tingles up his spine. And then she whispered, all hint of mischief gone, "I will do anything, Tommy, to protect you. Whether it's against the kraken or the sirens or whatever unforeseen danger awaits you. You may not want to pursue what we have, but you don't control my feelings any more than you can control my actions. If your life demands me extinguishing all my magic? It's a price I'm more than willing to pay."

Before he could protest further, to tell her how ridiculous she was being, how his life wasn't worth her risking her own, she was lifting herself onto her toes and leaning forward. His breath caught as he waited to see what she intended, ready to stop her once again if necessary. But her lips simply brushed his cheek, and she whispered, "Before this is all over, you'll understand your own worth, Tommy."

If she meant the words to be a comfort, they provided none, instead sending a wave of panic through him. His mind brought forth images of her and her sisters collapsed on the deck, unconscious, unmoving—images that threatened to cut off all air to his lungs. If she cared for him as she claimed, wouldn't she respect him enough to listen? Or was he the one letting fear blind him?

The cabin walls pressed in on him. Maura's golden eyes pierced him with a look that threatened to gut him, not because they held any malice or ill intent but because they were hers, and she could never be his, no matter how strong their feelings were for one another.

He tried to swallow, to push the stress and panic and despair and confusion down, but when he opened his mouth to speak, his words came out strained. "I need some time alone."

He stepped to the side and opened the door for her, beckoning her to exit as his attention fell to the floor, all ability to face her gone.

16

DECLAN

Once Killian had left, taking the scraps of the bizarre fruit with him, Declan couldn't do much more than listen to his own thoughts. He pondered all that the southern pirate had told him. How had none of this information traveled up to the Aisling before? Surely, with merchants traveling between the two regions regularly, some news would have been transported with the goods.

That mystery bothered him more than it probably should have, as it was too far removed from his current predicament. Or was it? That letter he'd given the fae, had it carried information about the conflict brewing? Had it requested their help? And if so, who had the request been from? Their fellow royals? The lesser fae?

The questions swarmed him, swirling around in his mind, churning like the sea during a storm.

He paced as he dissected each one. No way would he resign

himself to lounging in the filth of the brig. But the more he paced and the more he pulled apart the history of the fae and considered the role the sisters might play, the less confident he was about understanding any of it.

Too many variables. Too many possibilities. Too many distractions.

His shoulders throbbed from being held back awkwardly by the bonds at his wrists, and no matter how many times he tried to roll them and stretch them out, the ache wouldn't let up.

Is anything going to ease up for you? Doubtful.

For some reason, the thought conjured up his last view of Aoife. Her walking away from him, leaving him there with those blasted words hanging on the salty air. Had Callum's actions done anything to shift her heart toward him, gain him any sympathy, or move her to forgive him?

Declan wasn't afraid to die, whether by a cutlass or a siren or the sea itself. It was part of life for him. His father had often said, "To live fully is to be ready to die at any time." Declan hadn't understood that until many years later. It was a bizarre lesson to teach a young child, and it had done nothing but confuse him at the time. But after that misty night and the bloody dagger and his parents' deaths, he found those words running on repeat through his mind. And when he had ended up on that shore with Tommy, watching their captain walk away and abandon their crew, he had come to understand it better. Fear of death came to those who were afraid to live, afraid to take chances—qualities not conducive to a life of piracy.

And so here in the brig of Callum's ship, pacing the small cell, it wasn't the fear of death that brewed within him. It was the fear of dying without her forgiveness, of being left with a remorse that would surely haunt him for eternity.

He should have listened to Tommy's incessant nagging to tell Aoife the truth. How many times had he told himself the same thing? Yet he'd never followed through. He should have told her. Should have known it would be brought to light. Should have planned for that possibility.

Perhaps this was why marriages in the pirate world happened so rarely. Because love made you blind. It made you reckless. It made you stupid.

Live fully.

His father's words continued to echo within, successfully pushing out the myriad of others that had been in the forefront. His parents hadn't survived the council's wrath. But he could. Tommy had almost fallen to it. But he wouldn't. They had very nearly failed entirely. He wouldn't let them.

There was only one option, one way to survive this fool of a mission. He needed to stall. Give Tommy and Aoife enough time to catch up to them, to bring the fae so they could use their powers as planned. Maybe then he'd have an opportunity to spend the rest of his life earning back her trust.

But first he needed a way to buy time.

His head hurt, and only partly from the knock on the head they'd given him, which had been hard enough that it still ached days later. The pungent smell of the ship's belly didn't help matters, consistently distracting his thoughts as he paced. He couldn't think in here. He needed to get out, to breathe fresh air.

You have gone soft, haven't you?

These conditions wouldn't have bothered him before. Yes, they would have been annoying, but he had always had a knack for tuning out all the distractions and discomforts to focus on what needed to be done or decided. But now, it took every last bit of his energy to try to ignore it so he could think clearly. Maybe they had hit him harder than he'd thought.

Or maybe you're losing your edge.

A muffled commotion far above his head sifted down through the wooden floors—shouts sounding like the distant caws of a dozen seagulls. The sudden shift in the noise had Declan frozen in place, straining to listen, though it was unlikely he would be able to hear anything from down here.

His stomach twisted into a knot. Had they arrived at the sound already?

A thump behind him made him spin toward the ladder. Killian, having just jumped to the floor, rushed over, keys in hand, his face flushed and shining with sweat, his eyes wild with that familiar mix of excitement and nerves that all pirates got before some action.

"Guessing you didn't come down to bring me more fruit," Declan said.

"No," Killian said, his clipped answer followed only by the sound of the lock clicking open and the door creaking on its rusted hinges.

"And it'd be presumptuous of me to think Callum has come to his senses."

"Aye, presumptuous indeed," Killian said. "Turn around, unless you want to be fighting with your arms bound."

Declan obeyed, even as he asked, "Fight whom exactly? We haven't arrived—"

"No," Killian said quickly. "Not there yet. But we've got company, and it's doubtful it will end in a handshake and a laugh over a shared bottle of rum."

"So, Callum wants my help early then?" He laced his words with skepticism. It certainly didn't sound like something Callum would do. He was far more likely to leave Declan in the brig to drown if they lost, simply to keep him or anyone else from gaining the spoils he sought.

"Of course not," he said. "He'd leave you here."

Declan rubbed and rolled his wrists as he turned back around. "You take a lot of risk here then. More than necessary."

Killian scoffed, shoving a cutlass into one of Declan's hands. "No man should die in such a way. And I'll face whatever consequences knowing I did the right thing." He reached into his boot and withdrew a blade Declan recognized at once.

But Declan hesitated when the man offered it to him. "How is helping me the right thing?"

Killian forced the dagger into Declan's other hand as he answered, "Because I'd like to see you succeed here to get the Bron sisters back to Larcsporough after all this dagger business is over and done with."

"What? I never—"

"You didn't need to tell me. It wasn't hard to figure out your plans, especially with all your curiosity about the fae history. Everyone in the south knows of the three sisters trapped in the north, held prisoner on Cregah."

More questions flooded Declan's mind, but Killian dashed them away with a wave of his hand, signaling Declan to follow him to the ladder. Hopefully he would be willing to answer all of his questions when and if they made it out of whatever awaited them atop.

Declan's heart sped up with the excitement that always hit when a fight was imminent, and with each ladder they claimed and each set of stairs they ascended, the sounds of orders being yelled by the bo'sun and quartermaster got louder.

Blinking against the afternoon sun as he emerged onto the deck, Declan noticed two things: they had stopped, and no cannon fire had started. Was this a friendly stop?

As friendly as when you stopped for Callum, most likely.

Killian led him to the quarterdeck, where Callum stood with his quartermaster, his face as calm as though he were basking on a beach rather than waiting for his ship to be boarded. Calm until he saw them. His eyes narrowed as he stomped into Killian's path, barreling his chest into him. But he kept his voice low and menacing, more like a rumble of a growl than the speech of a man.

"What in the sands are you doing?"

To his credit, Killian didn't flinch or cower beneath the glare of his captain but offered up his answer in an almost bored tone. "We need every blade we have aboard if we're going to take on Roberts's crew."

Declan stepped forward, his eyes wide. "Roberts? As in Pirate Lord Roberts?"

"Aye," Callum said, the word clipped as if he hadn't the time for even the single syllable.

Killian looked over his shoulder to provide more of an explanation to Declan. "Roberts has an uncanny way of knowing where we're sailing, interrupting our course every week or two."

"And I dread every encounter," Callum muttered to himself.

It seemed an odd thing for this menacing pirate to admit, but perhaps he hadn't realized he'd said it aloud. Off the starboard side, a ship of moderate size approached.

"So why stop?" Declan realized a second too late that he'd voiced the question aloud, and Callum let out a throaty laugh devoid of any humor.

"Same reason you stopped for me, I gather." The captain didn't turn to Declan as he spoke but kept his attention on the other ship. Declan worked out his own strategy in his mind. It was a gamble, but Callum was right. It was the same one he'd taken. It did them no good to risk Roberts firing his cannons at them, especially when he hadn't proven to be an adversary. Yet. That could cripple them, leave them stranded at sea, or send shrapnel ripping into Callum's crew. The only option was to wait for the approaching pirate to show his hand.

Surveying the crew around him, Declan noted that Callum's strategy differed from his slightly. The men of the *Curse Bringer* didn't hide their blades, instead choosing to make a display of how well-armed they were. The deck was so full of armed men, he nearly wondered if the entire crew had been called above for this show of force, but no doubt a fair number of men waited below with the cannons ready to use at their captain's call.

Roberts's ship, the *Revenge*, had come close enough now that Declan could make out the pirate lord himself, who was not standing on the quarterdeck as expected but at the port-side rail, his men ready to extend a plank between the ships.

Tension roiled through Callum's crew, like a pulsing thrum of energy covering the entire deck. Declan's palms grew sweaty around his own weapons, and he scolded his body for acting so when this was far from his first altercation. But it had been years, many years, since he had not been the one in command. His mind whirred with the possibilities and the different outcomes that could arise here.

The *Revenge* swung around so their port side met with the *Curse Bringer*'s starboard side, and the ships scraped together, the impact forcing Declan—and everyone else on board—to brace themselves. Stumbling around certainly wouldn't display the confidence they needed to exhibit in front of this lord's crew. As Roberts's men dropped the plank to make a bridge between the two vessels, Callum headed down the stairs to greet them, his cutlass still in its sheath and his hand at the ready to draw it quickly if needed. Though he hadn't motioned for them to follow, Killian and Declan

trailed after him almost on instinct, meeting up with Callum's quartermaster, Dominic, at the bottom, whose mouth was twisted into
a sneer that Declan thought could be as much for him as it was for
the lord who now boarded the *Curse Bringer*.

Two things seemed odd to Declan as Callum stepped forward.
Roberts's crew was not behaving as Callum's men were. Their deck
was not crowded with men; it was far emptier than Declan would
have expected. On one hand, it made sense. There was no need
for Roberts to make a spectacle of his strength. His reputation as
a lord preceded him. It was well known the lords didn't partake
as often in their own battles and skirmishes anymore, leaving that
messy business to the ships within their fleets.

Perhaps that has made them soft.

Declan chewed on the thought, but again his skin prickled
with unease, his mind searching for a thread of a clue that could
explain what Roberts's play was here. Putting himself in the lord's
place, he worked quickly through strategy after strategy, searching
for one that might fit.

Declan backed away slowly through the crew, inching away
from Killian, who didn't seem to notice his departure. The *Curse
Bringer*'s deck was packed with men, all of them quiet and tense,
as if their very limbs itched to draw blood and cut men down. He
couldn't keep moving backward without stepping on someone's
toes, which might lose him an appendage or two. Some glanced at
him out of the corners of their eyes as he turned, but most kept
their attention ahead on the pirate lord stepping onto the deck.

At the sight of the lord, Declan stopped.

He'd never met Captain Roberts, and though he often joked
about the lords' lackluster personalities, he didn't have any firsthand knowledge of what they were like. It was merely an assumption born from contempt and frustration. And perhaps some bit-

terness. The lords might not be as free as they could be—tied to the council per the treaty—but their lot was notably better than the other pirates sailing these waters. They enjoyed the prestige that came with the title, had the pleasure of the councilwomen's company, and had free rein, at least in the Aisling.

How the lords had managed to receive such a position, Declan couldn't say. Possibly a mix of pedigree and luck. Everything he knew about the lords he'd gleaned from rum-soaked rumors. Supposedly some passed the title to a son, on the off-chance a lord's union with a councilwoman produced one. But that happened so rarely that most lords selected from among their crew who then had to be approved by the ruling council.

Declan hadn't heard how Lord Roberts had gotten his title, but it certainly wasn't for his looks. The man's nose had been broken far more times than one would expect for a lord, leaving the bridge of it crooked in two places. His mess of long blonde hair was tied back and hidden under a tricornered hat that lacked the wear and tear most often seen in pirate attire. His less than intimidating height was countered by his muscular build, again contrary to what Declan would have expected for a pirate in his position. Needless to say, whether Roberts was a bore or not, he did not appear to be an easy adversary, not one you took on without a plan or skill.

All of this Declan assessed in the time it took the lord to stride over to Callum and extend his hand in greeting. Declan waited to see how Callum reacted, and when the captain took the lord's hand, albeit with some reluctance, Declan continued making his way to the other side of the ship. His stomach churned. He hoped no one would think he was using this as a chance to escape and try to stop him, but thankfully everyone was glued to the quiet exchange taking place between the two captains. Without another glance back, Declan maneuvered his way through the stinking bodies of the crew until he saw the railing. It was a long shot, of course, but every instinct told him he needed to be sure.

He had just broken free of the mass of crewmen when the first hands appeared on the port-side railing. Before he could open his mouth to alert anyone, men were hauling themselves over, landing on the deck with quiet skill. Declan pulled his dagger out and threw it at the pirate directly in front of him as he shouted the word, "Behind!"

Callum's crew turned just in time for their blades to meet those of the invaders. Retrieving his own from the fallen pirate, Declan slit the man's throat before turning toward the next closest, who was busy fighting one of Callum's men. He swiftly thrust his dagger into the man's side, up and under his ribs, making him a far easier opponent for the crewman who worked to finish him off.

Declan didn't check to see who fell and who succeeded. He tried to see over the swarm of men as they bustled around him, rushing past him to meet the oncoming threat, but he couldn't see what had become of Callum and Roberts.

Someone lunged for him, and he had his dagger lodged in the man's gut before he realized it was one of Callum's crew. He didn't have time to fight the man, and despite his being held hostage on this ship, he also didn't want the man to suffer, so he pulled the blade out and, with one smooth motion, severed a large artery, causing the man to fall to his knees. His blood gushed out around the fingers he pressed against the wound in a feeble attempt to stanch the bleeding.

Declan didn't wait to see what became of him but instead pushed his way through the crew, blocking strikes as he needed, wincing as blades nicked his forearms. Where the hell was Callum? Had Roberts bettered him? Had Callum heard his warning and taken out the lord in time?

The scene was utter chaos as more of Roberts's men swarmed the deck, seeming to come from all angles, climbing over the railing, rushing across the plank that still bridged the ships.

There. Declan spotted him.

Callum's face was splattered with blood that seemed to accentuate his scar. He was facing off against Roberts. Callum had lost his blade somewhere and was doing his best to block Roberts's strikes with his arms, now streaming with blood from the numerous cuts his opponent's dagger had inflicted, but he was still managing to get his fist in contact with the lord's face now and then.

Declan could let them be, take his chances with whoever survived, but the thought of helping a lord, the same pirates who aided and abetted the council, the same lords who were responsible—even if not directly—for the deaths of so many innocents, including his parents… No, he couldn't have that. Even if Callum wanted to risk Declan's life to get the dagger, Declan would rather die helping this independent pirate than serving the lords in any way.

"Roberts!" Declan shouted, pulling the lord's attention away and distracting him long enough for Callum to snatch the dagger from his hand and land another blow across the lord's face. Roberts stumbled back but righted himself quickly, his mouth pulling his face into a grotesque scowl. With a growl, he lunged for Callum, pouncing more like a wild animal than a refined pirate lord.

Declan rushed forward, tripping as a body fell into him but still managing to leap onto the lord's back. He weaved his arm under Roberts's chin, gripping his body with his legs and hoping they didn't tumble over the railing into the water below but not particularly caring if they did.

The lord stumbled about, trying to free himself, but Declan

only tightened his hold on the man's neck. With his legs wrapped around the lord's waist, Declan used his last bit of energy to thrust himself backward, pulling the lord off-balance until they fell backwards. Declan refused to let go even as they hit the deck.

Declan's back rammed into the ground with the full weight of the pirate on top of him, and he lay there hoping Callum would return the favor and lend him a hand. But just as Callum came into view, two men appeared behind him, ready to attack.

"Watch out!" Declan yelled, still working to hold the lord.

Callum turned in time, howling as his attackers' blades cut into his already torn-up arms. Despite his injuries, he was able to subdue the men. He sliced one across the belly, and the man's knees fell into his own innards that spilled onto the deck. Callum brought his weapon around. In one smooth motion he slashed the other man across the chest and pushed him into the sea.

Lord Roberts still flailed atop Declan, who was growing tired from trying to wrangle him. He wondered how the man could still have so much strength left in him. The lord was so preoccupied with trying to pry Declan's arm from his throat that he didn't see Callum coming toward him or the flash of the sun reflecting on the blade as it came down to cut him across the upper leg, a strategic blow to sever a major artery.

The lord's scream tore across the deck, and to Declan's surprise, Robert's crew stopped and turned toward their captain, who now moved his arms to reach for his wounded leg, though it would be of no use. The wound was severe enough he'd be dead within minutes.

The fighting around them ceased as the lord went still, and the air rushed from Declan as the lord's dead weight pressed down on him. With great effort, his muscles burning, he began to shove the man off. A hand was extended toward him. He was surprised to find Callum offering to help him stand, but he was more surprised by how the crews had responded to the lord's death.

This was not typical. Declan had never seen this in all his years on the sea. No matter how much a crew admired their captain, they did not simply stop fighting if he fell. But just as surprising was how Callum's men, too, stood still and waited, seeking their captain's command. Even his own crew didn't show this level of restraint or respect. Was Callum a better captain than him? Had Declan misjudged him?

Rising, he stood beside Callum as he faced the men, many bloodied and clutching their wounds while trying not to step on the fallen at their feet. They waited. What would happen now? Lord Roberts was dead, and the *Revenge* was in need of a new captain, up for grabs. Declan's mind whirred, the plank connecting the ships beckoning him, urging him to take this moment to flee and get back to his own ship. But he couldn't sail without a crew, and it seemed unlikely that any of Roberts's men would agree to sail under him after he'd played such a role in the lord's demise.

No doubt Callum would catch him before he could even move the ship away, and there was also no way he could make his way over to the ship without one of the crewmen calling him out. He might have been released from his cell and chains, but he remained a prisoner nonetheless.

Still, Declan couldn't stop the smile from tugging ever so slightly at one corner of his mouth. They were stopped, not likely to be underway any time in the near future. Whatever Callum had in store for him, Declan could face that later. For now he was simply thankful for the delay he'd needed.

17
AOIFE

High above Aoife's head, wisps of clouds drifted across the full moon, throwing the deck of the ship into shadow for a moment before moving on and allowing the light to return.

Reclining on this wooden step, it was impossible not to remember the last time she'd been sitting here. But instead of jovial singing, an eerie silence greeted her, even though the deck was far from empty. Some of the crew worked to keep the ship on course while others stared out across the water or conversed in hushed tones, not loud enough to be heard over the ship's hull cutting through the waters, the only indication of their conversation being the movement of their lips.

Tommy was going to be angry with her for what she'd done, forcing him to be alone with Maura, but she could handle him and whatever attitude he might show her.

Why had she done it? Certainly for the hope of securing a

happy future for her friend, but also because she hoped Maura might be able to persuade him to allow the use of fae magic once they entered the kraken's territory. It seemed their only chance for survival, and Tommy was stubbornly refusing. For good reason, she had to admit, but he needed to at least be open to the option if worse came to worst. If nothing worked, would Tommy choose to lose the crew rather than rely on the possibility of draining the fae's magic too much before reaching the sound?

And would that be a disaster? Would that secure their defeat? What was at stake? They either fell to the kraken and failed to reach Declan in time, or they got there and had to get past the sirens with fewer weapons in their arsenal. It seemed an easy decision to Aoife, but then again, she was no strategist. And no pirate. But could Tommy's judgment truly be trusted here? His priorities seemed askew. What was driving his utter refusal? With the possible scenarios laid out in her mind, she could not fathom that he was solely driven by his desire to save his captain.

Declan.

His name tumbled around in her mind, and she turned to the space beside her where he had sat that night, too far away for her liking but still closer than he possibly should have been. He had seemed so different then. Less moody. More carefree. More himself, she assumed. She reached her fingers up to her cheek, hoping she'd never forget the moment when he'd brushed her tear away. But it had only been a few days ago, and already the memories were fraying. That hadn't been the first—or last—time he'd touched her, but she cherished it all the same. In her mind she saw that gentle smile he only seemed to offer her, heard his soothing voice as he talked her through her panic attacks.

But then the memories shifted. To sand and blood and his strained and weary plea for her forgiveness. His declaration of his feelings for her. Her chest tightened, and she shut her eyes against the images, though she knew it was impossible to force them away by simply doing so. The voice within her whined, *You should have forgiven him.* This was followed by the equally insistent part of her that silently growled, *He lied to you. Like everyone else.*

She'd hoped Tommy could help guide her, tell her which part of herself to heed, because even with Declan in danger, she wasn't sure which was correct. She loved him—that much she was sure of—but was it enough? Was this something she could move past? Or would it taint whatever future they might pursue, like mold permeating a loaf of bread?

It could never work.

But even as she settled onto those words, she remembered how Tommy had insisted the same regarding him and Maura. She had pointed him to the importance of hope. Could Aoife take her own advice? Again, the two sides of her warred internally, one side begging her to give him a chance, the other trying to wrap a protective barrier around her heart.

To her right, the door to Declan's cabin opened, creaking on its rusting hinges.

The door thudded against its frame, and Aoife peered around the railing to see Maura standing there, her elegance a stark contrast to the way her shoulders slumped with a sigh.

Tommy hadn't exited with her, and although Aoife was sheltered and naive, she could still recognize the disappointment written on the fae's face. As Aoife wrestled over whether to speak up or not, Maura's chin lifted, her golden eyes finding Aoife's easily.

"Aoife," she said, the word coming out with a tinge of surprise. "Have you been sitting out here this whole time?"

Pulling her mouth into her best version of Declan's smirk, she lifted her shoulder as she said, "Aye. But don't worry, I couldn't hear any of what was said behind those doors. Even in this deathly silence. Not that I was hoping to listen in. Simply trying to put—"

Maura's light laugh floated on the sea breeze between them, and she soundlessly moved closer. "No need to explain, Aoife. I trust you. May I sit?"

Scooting over a few inches, Aoife proffered the seat. "Of course."

For a few moments the silence enveloped them while Aoife pondered what to say or whether to say anything at all. Her muscles itched to move, and she shifted her feet against the wooden deck several times, clasping and unclasping her hands in her lap, all while Maura sat as still as the figurehead on the front of the ship. But before the fae could tease her for fidgeting, she cleared her throat and asked, "So the chat with Tommy went well then?"

Maura's head fell back, and she let out an exasperated groan, her whole body relaxing as if released from some spell that had kept her frozen in place. She rolled her head to one side and back, taking a moment before responding.

"I'll win him over yet."

Aoife caught her eye. A spark of mischief gleamed in those otherworldly eyes, which was entirely at odds with the defeated posture she now exhibited. She raised her brow. "Romantically or..."

Another laugh bubbled up from Maura's lips as they curled into a coy grin. "Any way that I can."

"Well, as much as I'd love to see Tommy think about his own happiness and all, we should probably focus on getting him on board with the whole magic plan. Right?"

Maura pursed her lips, frowning. Turning her chin, she looked out across the deck, watching the crew. She took a deep breath but didn't answer right away.

"I'm not sure which I desire most though."

Aoife scoffed. Rolling her eyes, she shook her head a couple times. "Seriously?"

Maura turned back to her. "What?"

"So much for fae perception, eh?" Maura didn't say anything but simply waited, staring. "There's little point in winning his heart if we all fall prey to the kraken."

Her voice had risen enough that several of the crew stopped what they were doing to glance over at her, sending another wave of color to her face as she cringed.

"Fair point, Aoife. Fair point. And not one I hadn't thought of. But the heart wants what the heart wants, and mine is set on that sweet roll of a pirate."

"Sweet roll?" Perhaps the centuries spent within the iron walls of the council hall had done damage to more than just this fae's magic, because Aoife could not, for the life of her, figure out what she meant.

"Oh, you know," Maura said, smacking Aoife's arm with the back of her hand, "he's the sweet one. He might have a few browned, crispier edges, but most of him is kind, gentle—"

"And delicious?" Aoife hadn't intended to say the word aloud, but before she could apologize for saying something so inappropriate, Maura was laughing again.

"Why, yes, actually. I mean, I can only imagine he is. I haven't had the pleasure. Yet."

They'd gotten off topic, and Aoife needed to steer them back. "Well, as I said, no point if we don't survive the next few days."

Maura hummed a response. Lowering her head, she moved closer to Aoife and whispered, "Can you keep a secret?"

Aoife stiffened as a pang of guilt tightened around her insides. "I wouldn't trust me to."

It was Maura's turn to roll her eyes, and she opened her mouth to speak. Aoife rushed to cover her ears, nearly smacking Maura in the face, and began humming to herself to keep from hearing whatever the fae wanted to divulge. She wasn't about to take on another secret that would very likely require she lie to a friend. She could not be responsible for the death of someone—anyone— else if her tongue betrayed her again.

When she dared to steal a glance at Maura, she discovered the fae wasn't speaking to her. No, she was laughing. Of course she was laughing. Aoife stopped humming, testing to see if it was safe to remove her hands. With caution she uncovered her ears, ready to replace her hands if this damn fae showed any sign of spitting out the secret. But Maura simply sat there. Her laughter eventually eased, her lips settling into a friendly smile.

"Don't," Aoife said and pointed a finger toward her companion. "Don't you dare."

"Dare what?"

"Don't tell me any secrets. And don't mock me for protecting you and everyone else."

Maura cocked her head to the side, her forehead crinkling with a question.

Aoife released a breath before adding, "I get people killed."

"Well, that's a tad dramatic."

"Perhaps, but true all the same. If I hadn't, my sister—"

"Would have been caught and killed anyway," Maura said, finishing her sentence with words that caused Aoife to freeze in place.

"How did you know about—?"

"Lani?" Aoife nodded. "Same way we knew Declan's name before you stumbled into our room at the council hall."

Aoife mulled over the explanation for half a moment before shaking her head. "But Lani had a plan. She was smarter than me.

She would have made it."

Shifting, Maura leaned back until her elbows rested on the step above her before stretching her slender legs out. She crossed her ankles one way and then the other, finally relaxing again.

"You underestimate your mother, Aoife."

"You mean the council."

A graceful shrug and then, "I said what I said."

Aoife's gaze fell to her lap as she tried to process this. What did Maura mean? She'd always seen her mother as taking the lead on the council, but everything she'd been taught indicated the councilwomen ruled as equals.

Because everything you were taught was true? What's one more lie?

Looking back at Maura, she asked, "What do you mean though?" She certainly didn't want to jump to any conclusions.

"Your mother isn't—" Maura's words were cut short by the sound of boots approaching. Tommy was coming toward them. Aoife all but forgot that Maura had been about to tell her something important.

"Aoife," Tommy said, pinning her with a glare. His face was stern, despite the friendliness still present in his eyes. "You should get some rest." With his head he motioned toward the captain's quarters. Aoife glanced from him to Maura and then back. Before she could respond, he was speaking again. "You'll need it for your training time with Collins tomorrow."

The words pulled a groan from Aoife's gut, and her joints and muscles began aching again. She'd forgotten the torment they'd gone through earlier until he'd brought it up. Rising, she tried to keep from bumping into him, and thankfully he stepped back to give her room. She turned to Maura and bid her goodnight before looking up at Tommy.

"I'll see you in the morning?" She didn't know why she'd

worded it as a question, and relief hit when he dipped his chin in a single nod, looking everywhere but at Maura.

Aoife stepped slowly, pretending to be sleepy. She glanced over her shoulder, hoping to see Tommy and Maura in discussion again, but Tommy had started up the stairs, bypassing Maura and leaving her behind on the lowest step. Aoife slowed her pace while continuing to watch them, curious how the two would continue this awkward dance they'd found themselves in.

Maura rose and turned in her graceful manner to follow Tommy up to the quarterdeck. Aoife held her breath, waiting to see how he'd react. Did he even hear the fae's near-silent steps behind him? Would he allow her up there? She didn't have to wait long for her answer. Within seconds Tommy spun around to face his pursuer.

"You're not allowed up here." His voice was firm but calm, quiet enough it hadn't attracted the attention of anyone else on deck.

Maura didn't stop, though, and continued up the stairs until she stood on the same step as him. "Can't we talk some more?"

"If you had more to say, you shouldn't have left the privacy of the cabin. I have nothing more to discuss with you."

"But I—" she started.

Tommy cut her off with a glare and a sharp "No" that had Maura flinching as though he'd slapped her. "Not tonight, Maura. I'm done."

He left the fae standing in the middle of the stairs as he continued up to the quarterdeck, not once turning back to look at her. Maura took longer to retreat. As Aoife watched them part ways, she hoped the tension—which was as thick as the black sands of Cregah—wouldn't cause them more problems than they already had.

18

CAIT

Cait kept her stride short with slow steps. While this pirate, Adler, might think she did so out of caution, it was more that she needed to buy time to figure out how she would explain this—explain him—to her people. But she remained at a loss. She could ask Lucan to trust her and her gut, but the others would not understand.

She didn't even understand it. But that was how intuition worked. It often went against reason and sense. Despite all logic, something often pulled her toward one path or one decision. She had long ago stopped doubting it.

But that didn't make it any easier to ask others to trust it. From the corner of her eye, she watched Adler's long legs match her pace.

"So what are you going to tell them?" Adler asked, and although he kept the words hushed, they were still too loud in the looming silence of the forest.

"I'll figure something out."

He jutted his chin out. "And hopefully soon. Sounds like we're getting close."

Indeed, the voices of the Rogues drifted toward them, though still too quiet for her to make out what they were saying. She had already asked so much of them regarding Naeve's inclusion, and now she had the audacity to ask even more of them. All while they still mourned the loss of one of their own.

Cait came to an abrupt stop and turned to Adler. He showed no sign of surprise, but those blue eyes of his seemed to sparkle with excitement once again.

"How did you find me?" she asked.

A smirk pulled at his lips—an expression that was quickly beginning to irk her. "A question you probably should have asked before leading me to your secret meeting spot, love."

Cait glowered at him in a silent prompt for him to answer the damn question.

"It wasn't that hard, to be honest—once I knew who to follow, that is. There are plenty of rumors about who leads the Rogues. You've done quite the job keeping suspicion off yourself, but I have a unique skill set, you could say."

"So you followed me."

A mischievous nod. "Though I didn't know you were the mastermind. Got lucky with that one. Shouldn't have been surprised, though, given your family name and all."

"And you want the council gone," she said, struggling to keep up with her mind as it processed all the information. He remained quiet and waited for her to continue the thought. "But as a pirate, the council works in your favor."

He offered a lazy shrug but didn't bother to correct her.

"Who was it?" Cait's eyes snapped up to his. Her brow contracted. She'd expected some reaction from him, some clue that she was on the right track, but he remained annoyingly hard to read. "Brother? Sister? Parents?" She ignored the way her heart flinched and hurried on to add, "Or a lover?"

There. The slightest flash of his jaw tensing. Though his face didn't betray his feelings, she'd been working in the pub long enough to tell when a man was on the verge of revealing his secrets.

"Who was she? Or he?"

Adler's jaw tensed again, longer this time, but his blue eyes dulled. He still didn't say anything.

"Look, Adler, it's none of my business, and as much as I would love to have some juicy bit of information to use against you when needed, I have enough drama of my own. No reason I need to take on yours as well." Cait moved to take a step forward again but stopped. Nodding ahead toward the Rogues who awaited them, she added, "But they will want to hear your reasons. They'll need to know if you—and whatever pain you carry—is worth the risk of trusting you."

Dropping his eyes, Adler stepped closer to her. Uncomfortably close. Close enough she could feel the warmth emanating from him. Close enough it caused every muscle in her body to tense in anticipation. Of what, she couldn't pinpoint.

With how close he stood, she would have had to angle her chin up to look into his eyes. But she couldn't. Somehow he had entrapped her without even a touch. Focusing on her breaths, she drew them in slowly to keep herself grounded.

He cleared his throat, and she looked up at him through her lashes. "Yet you trust me without hearing."

"Who said I trust you?" Cait challenged.

"Either you trust me enough to bring me into your circle of

friends or you're an idiot. And you don't seem like a dumb lass to me, love."

She should step back, should put some space between them, but he would expect that. And she hated taking the predictable path, so she closed the last inches between them until her breasts pressed against his broad chest. Lifting her face to his, she leaned closer until she could almost feel the hair of his beard brush against her cheek. And then she whispered in his ear, "Trust is earned, but I'll use you if I can."

Before he could say anything in response, she moved away and resumed walking toward the others. The Rogues' eyes widened as she passed through the entryway with Adler on her heels. Lucan stepped into her path. But he wasn't looking at her. His stern gaze was firmly fixed on the man behind her, and while it was an expected reaction, she couldn't help but roll her eyes at him.

Waving her hand over her shoulder, she introduced them. "Lucan, this is Adler. Adler, Lucan. My second."

Adler stepped forward, his hand extended before him in greeting, but Lucan didn't move or relax. Adler gave a shrug and lowered his hand as he said with a laugh, "Nice to meet you too, Lucan."

Lucan's eyes snapped to Cait's, wide and silently demanding an explanation, but she didn't answer him, instead addressing the entire assembled group.

"Adler has asked to join us." She paused, allowing the protests to rumble for a minute before cutting them off with a raised hand. "And I have agreed to allow him."

More complaints filled the small area, but it was Lucan who now hushed them. His stare bored into Cait as if he was searching for some hidden message. Or maybe he was waiting for some intuition of his own to guide him.

He didn't look away even as he spoke to everyone. "If Cait trusts him, then I do too. Because I trust her." He paused, his jaw tensing as he pinned Adler with a hard look and then returned his attention to Cait. "But as we've asked a lot of you all today, with Naeve and now…" He stopped again and leaned forward toward Adler so he could ask, not bothering to lower his voice into a whisper, "What was your name again?"

The pirate laughed at Lucan's ridiculous behavior but played along by offering his name once again.

Lucan nodded before resuming. "Yes, Adler. As we've asked a lot of you all today, I think it only fair that he tell us his reasons for wanting to join our efforts."

Cait stepped forward now, squaring her shoulders as she confronted her second. "We did not require this of Naeve, Lucan."

"We could, of course. I'm sure she has no problem recounting her story again as she did for me and Eva."

As the Rogues murmured their agreement, impatience shot through Cait, and her limbs became antsy. She was eager to get past all this drama and start doing something productive.

"We don't—" she started, but halted mid-sentence when Adler placed a hand on her shoulder. She peered back at him.

"It's okay, love. I don't mind."

Cait didn't try to stop him as he stepped into the center of the group. Looking from face to face, she observed how they reacted to him. Some showed nothing but suspicion. Others seemed at least partially curious. And Kira looked at him as if he were as tasty as the rum she poured for patrons when working in the pub.

"As Cait correctly guessed," he said, his eyes pausing on Cait for a second before continuing on around the circle, "the council took a loved one from me, as I know they have done to many, if not all, of you. I was a member of Captain Tiernan's crew."

A few muffled gasps interrupted his words, but he paid them no attention as he continued.

"Months ago, while visiting the council hall, I met someone. One of the heirs. She was…" He paused—whether for effect or from genuine emotion, Cait couldn't tell. "Well, it doesn't matter now. They discovered our plan to run away together, and they punished her for it."

"And why didn't they punish you?" a woman asked from the far corner, suspicion coating every syllable. Others echoed her question, pushing him to answer.

Adler lifted a shoulder as a hollow laugh spilled from him. "We were in Foxhaven, not due to be back on these shores for another month, when we heard of an heir running off. You can imagine who I thought that was, even if the timing was off, but alas, it wasn't her but her sister. Lani had already been discovered. The council had found out—somehow—and they had her killed."

At this, a young man to their left countered, "But the council would never let that information out. We only knew because—"

Another voice interrupted. "Yeah! How would you have heard of it in Foxhaven?"

Cait answered for him. "Oh, come on. You all know how pirates are with gossip. No one can keep a bloody secret to save their lives."

Another halfhearted laugh rumbled within Adler's chest. "Indeed. It's true. Once I heard of my Lani's fate, I left. Took all the money I had saved up to start our life together and bought my way out of Tiernen's crew. Ditched my colors and caught the first vessel I could get passage on to these damned shores."

Lucan spoke now, distrust dripping from his words. "And we're just to believe you want to take down the council. The council that kept you well fed and your pockets filled."

"Aye. Not all pirates choose the profession out of greed. Some of us do it out of necessity."

That brought an image of Declan to Cait's mind, but she pushed it aside as quickly as it had appeared. No time to worry about him at the moment. Nothing she could do for him here and now, especially not when she had Lucan acting like a jealous lover.

That's a bit unfair. He's just looking out for you. All of you.

As Cait swept away her thoughts, Lucan inched forward. "You seem rather at ease for someone who claims to have lost their one true love." The last word came out clipped with disdain. Like a challenge.

Adler turned lazily to face his accuser, and the corner of his mouth lifted into a smirk. "I never said she was my one true love, friend." Lucan opened his mouth to speak, but Adler continued. "Do I love her? Yes. Always will. And do I want to make those haughty bitches pay for what they did to her? Absolutely. But is Lani my only and my last? Sands, I hope not. I'm much too young to live the rest of my days alone and in mourning."

Lucan pressed closer still, pulling his shoulders back and jutting his chin forward, and glared at the pirate. "But you had only just met her. Seems highly suspicious that you'd form such a bond with one glance or one conversation." Cait had raised her foot to step in and intervene, but at Lucan's last statement, she hesitated, dropping it back to the ground. Why hadn't she caught onto that?

The murmuring questions ceased, and the group grew quiet, watching Adler with collective skepticism. Cait could have kicked herself for believing him, but even still, something told her to trust him. She searched his expression for any hint he was pulling one over on them, duping her to lead them into a trap. What such a sign would be, she wasn't sure. Surely her gut would point it out as it had so many times before.

Adler didn't answer right away. His face remained neutral, with not even a flicker of tension as he decided on his next words. The silence stretched on into an uncomfortable void. Cait had just decided she couldn't handle it one more second when Adler cleared his throat with a gravelly sound.

"I didn't think it was possible either," he said, his strong, confident voice filling the space. "And yet, it happened."

Cait narrowed her eyes at him, but still she found no indication he was covering up some ulterior motive. His deep blue eyes mesmerized her. Had she been a few years younger perhaps, she might have found herself wavering in their intensity, the world around her falling away until only the two of them remained... But that was before her whole world had crumbled.

A lost family. A lost future.

She blinked slowly to regain focus.

"You can't possibly believe him, Cait. It's absurd," Lucan said in a deep whisper.

The air was thick with tension. Something pushed her toward Adler at the same time it pulled her away from him. Another slow blink helped to distract her from the strangeness of the invisible opposing tugs on her body, and she gave a nod without turning away from the newcomer. "I might, though I can't explain why."

Lucan's exasperated sigh called her attention back to him. A mix of confusion and defiance played across his features.

Lowering her voice, she said, "We don't know him, no, but you know me, Lucan. Trust me."

"I do. But..." Lucan flung his hand in Adler's direction. His shoulders rose as he sucked a breath deep into his lungs before slumping in defeat. "But never mind. My trust in you is stronger. So that's what I'll hold onto."

Eva raised a hand, like she was a kid in a schoolroom instead of a rebel plotting a coup. "So what's the plan exactly? We now have two new resources at our disposal in Naeve and Adler. How do we put them to use?"

Cait hesitated a moment, not sure how the Rogues would respond to her plans. "We have been taking a very careful approach the past few years. Biding our time. Strengthening our numbers. We have never taken the fight to the council, and it's time to do just that."

"What does that mean, *take the fight to them*?" a girl to Cait's left asked.

Adler stepped forward. "If I may?" he asked and waited for Cait to give the nod to continue. "How did the pirate lords come into power? Why do some become lords and others become fish food?"

"I'm not sure how a pirate history lesson is supposed to help," Lucan said, his annoyance made clear in every syllable.

But Adler ignored the interjection. "They are smart. They use strategy. They understand their adversaries, and they know how to use their weaknesses against them. And, when needed, they are ruthless."

His words mirrored what Cait had been feeling since she'd gotten the word about Maggie. They needed a plan, and they needed to be willing to do anything to pull the council from power and free the people. And they needed to be prepared to do all of that without the magic of the dagger to ensure victory. As much as she wanted to embrace the hope flickering in her belly, she had to be realistic. The mission she'd sent her brother on had always been an unlikely gamble. Not because Declan couldn't handle it, but because of the odds were stacked against them.

Hushed whispers and mutters rippled through the Rogues as they contemplated what this might mean, what they might have to do, and what they were even willing to do.

"Let's start with what we know," Cait prompted, thankful when her words managed to bring their murmurings to a halt.

Adler offered, "The council knows you're seeking the dagger."

Naeve, speaking for the first time since Adler's arrival, added, "And they have asked Captain McCallagh to bring it back to them."

"But he was intercepted by Callum," Lucan said, "who we assume is heading after the dagger under the assumption that Declan is the key to retrieving it."

"Wait." Adler's chin rose. "Where is the dagger?"

Lucan gave a breathy laugh. "Well, at least that bit of gossip hasn't managed to make it to the far ends of the Aisling."

Cait dove into the abridged version of the dagger's location and her brother's need of the fae to retrieve it. When she finished, Adler said, "I see." It certainly wasn't the reaction she'd expected, but little about this pirate seemed to match her assumptions.

"At least the fae are aboard the *Siren's Song*," Lucan said. "So if Declan's crew can get there, we still have a chance of getting the dagger."

Once again, Naeve's timid voice chimed in. "But why does everyone want this blade? I've heard the legends, of course, but we won't be fighting the council in battle." Her eyes went wide. "Will we?"

Cait shifted her weight. "Not in the sense you may be thinking. Unless we have to. But if the legends are true, then the dagger's power isn't limited to combat but brings victory in any conflict. If possible, we will avoid unnecessary bloodshed." She paused and looked around at her people. "I think it best if we plan on not having it. Adler's right; we'll need a strategy, and we'll need to know what each of us is willing to do to see this through to the end. The council wants nothing more than to keep our people under their heel, under their promises of peace, but we know the truth, the truth they don't want to be made public. We know they have spies among the populace, and we know those spies hide well. But they aren't all spies, and not everyone is complicit in the council's ways—if they know of their true nature at all."

Adler's eyes shone with humor and anticipation. "You'll need to figure out a way to get the silent to speak and the blind to see, all while avoiding the council loyal."

Cait motioned for everyone to gather closer, and she began to lay the plan out for them, accepting worthy suggestions from anyone who expressed them.

After a few hours, her back aching from the hunched position she'd assumed for the planning session, Cait bid each of the Rogues farewell as they headed off to their agreed-upon assignments. Naeve headed back toward the council hall, where she would resume Maggie's intelligence gathering from within. Although the girl's quiet air had made Cait suspicious at first, the sorrow in her face when they spoke of Maggie's death seemed genuine. Genuine enough to earn Cait's trust.

They all would need to keep pretenses up, going about their daily lives as normal. Any major change could mean disaster if the council got wind of it.

"And what about me?" Adler asked as he joined Cait by the entrance to the ruins. Most had left already, staggering their departures so as not to bring any suspicion upon themselves when they returned to town. Only she, Adler, and Lucan remained.

Lucan, her ever-present bodyguard and shadow.

He hovered a respectful five feet away, but Cait could feel the tension rippling off him even at this distance. Her second had agreed to trust Adler for her sake, but it wouldn't be easy. She couldn't blame him either. Not with what they now faced—a stranger with a dubious story, a questionable past, and a suspiciously convenient arrival. Even as she'd acknowledged the inner voice that urged her to trust this stranger, she'd promised the other side of herself—the guarded and jaded side—she would be vigilant in case her instinct proved false.

"The council knows who he is," Lucan said. "It's not as if he could just get a job somewhere in town and start his new life here. Too many questions. Too much suspicion. Too much risk of having someone from his old crew discovering him."

Cait contemplated the point and debated the options silently in her head while the men looked on and waited, more patiently than she had expected.

"Aye," she finally said and turned to Adler. "The council knows you?"

He dipped his chin slightly, but that smirk returned to his lips. "They know my name. They know I was a member of Tiernen's crew. But as far as I've gathered from the whisperings going around, they don't know my connection to Lani."

Lucan was shaking his head, eyes closed. "Still, someone could have easily seen you with her. Or she might have confided in someone. I wouldn't put it past the council to keep the knowledge of your name under wraps until they can use it to their greatest advantage. We can't chance someone recognizing you."

Cait heaved a sigh. "I assume there's no convincing you to hide in the attic or the basement for the next month?"

Adler only shook his head, his mouth quirking up into another smirk instead of a frown.

"And disguises are out," Cait said.

"There's no hiding these good looks anyway, love," Adler said.

Cait shook her head. "Well, at least you're humble. That will help."

"Don't lie."

Lucan took a step closer to them. "Are you two done flirting, or can we hurry this up? The pub needs to open soon."

Cait was about to protest the insinuation when Adler said, "I'm done if she is."

She suppressed a swear and instead veered the conversation back to the matter at hand. "How were you hoping to help us? You must have had a plan."

"And my plans always go so well," Adler said. "Truth is, I hadn't expected you to allow me to stay. Or to even hear me out."

At this, she raised a brow. "And why is that?"

"You're a McCallagh," he said. As if that was sufficient explanation.

Despite the urgency of their situation, her curiosity got the best of her, and she wondered what he—and the lords—had heard of her family. "What do you mean?"

With a shrug, he said, "I refuse to believe you don't know your brother's reputation."

"Afraid I don't, actually."

"So you haven't heard of the brutality his crew inflicts upon merchants he comes across? Burning them alive once the ships have been stripped clean of any valuables? Or his treatment of Captain Susset who sailed as part of Tiernen's fleet?"

Cait feigned confusion with a purse of her lips, an act she'd perfected over the years from having to play dumb when pirates came into the pub with too many questions. "That can't be Declan."

"So you haven't heard how he tied Susset to the mainmast before breaking each of his fingers? Story says your dear brother removed the man's tongue and ears before leaving him to sink with the ship. It was our crew that came upon the survivors he'd allowed to row away and pass along the tale."

Those were indeed just a handful of the stories she'd heard about her brother, but she had never completely believed them to be true. Even now, hearing them from Adler, she trusted her instincts that insisted Declan had conjured the rumors to build his reputation.

"Why else did you think the lords were targeting him if it wasn't in retaliation of his attack on Susset and others within their fleets?" Adler asked.

"Boredom? Jealousy?"

Adler laughed, a big booming laugh that bounced off the canopy above them instead of being absorbed by the leaves. "I suppose those are both good reasons. Regardless, I digress. Point is, I hadn't gotten that far in my own planning."

"How convenient," Lucan muttered.

"I don't have to be locked in a basement to remain hidden, you know."

Cait couldn't keep her eyes from dropping to his feet and trailing back up his entire six-foot frame.

"Subtle ogling there, love," Adler said with a flirtatious smile. "Aye, I'm no small prawn of a man, but you don't have to be of slight stature to be stealthy. You'll find we pirates are quite adept at it. Some of us, anyway."

"So what do you recommend?"

"Hire me in the pub."

Lucan choked on nothing, but Cait shared the underlying sentiment that the suggestion was absurd. She nearly laughed but managed to hold it back. "You. In the pub. The pub where pirates gather. Yes, of course. No one could possibly recognize you there."

"Aye, you're right. Pirates drunk on your spirits have impeccable memories. I had heard the rum on Cregah actually heightened one's senses rather than dulling them. I simply didn't believe it to be true."

Cait clenched her jaw. If only she had a blade on her, she could teach him a lesson for being so annoying.

Yes, because that's not an overreaction at all.

"Fine," she said as she forced her jaw to relax.

"What?" Lucan looked to the sky, exasperated. "This is the dumbest idea ever!"

But Cait ignored him and said to Adler, "You start tonight. Let's go." She turned to leave and got about ten paces before calling over her shoulder, "Also, you're staying with Lucan."

She could have sworn she heard one of them mutter, "Now that's the dumbest idea ever," but she wasn't sure which, and she didn't particularly care. She had a pub to run and a council to take down.

19

DECLAN

D eclan's body jerked involuntarily, waking him. Based on the smell alone, he knew he was back in the brig, but here in the bowels of the ship, he couldn't discern how long he'd been unconscious this time.

Everything ached. The bruises on his face from his first day on this ship had begun throbbing again, courtesy of the blows he'd taken during the ambush. He winced at the pounding within his head only to groan when the movement pulled his wounds taut, aggravating them as well.

Opening his eyes, he tried to assess the rest of his body, but the only light, weak and minimal, came from the opening above the ladder, making it nearly impossible to see what state he was in. He scooted himself closer to one set of bars and—lightly but firmly enough for him to register any discomfort from bruises or cuts—he began to press one arm against the metal. Starting with the wrist, he moved gradually up his arm, finding only one spot on his bicep that screamed in pain when it came in contact with the iron. There was no telling how deep the cut was, and there wasn't much he could do about it anyway with his hands bound. Scooting around, he continued on the other side. When he didn't find anything of concern beyond a bit of soreness, he began to examine both legs, his neck, and his torso with his hands and forearms. The exercise was pointless of course, but he completed it all the same if for no other reason than to keep himself busy.

And to keep his mind from wandering off to other places, other moments, other people.

The more Declan tried to distract himself, though, the more insistent the images became in his mind. He focused on the creaking of the wooden hull, which groaned with each swell of the sea beneath him, and counted his breaths in time with its rhythm.

In...one. Out...one. In...two. Out...two. In...

I can't.

Aoife's voice interrupted, and his breath hitched. His chest tightened around his sternum, and it began to ache so much that he wondered if the moaning of the ship wasn't actually coming from his body being ripped apart by the memory.

A curse. A growl. A bang of his head against the iron bars.

He started again.

In...one. Out...one. In...

How could you?

This time he had been prepared for the words to barge in and push him around.

"I'm a pirate," he said aloud, as if the sound of them might be enough to ward off her voice.

I know you're a pirate, but you are different, Declan.

She was right, in some ways. He wasn't like most of the other pirates, his upbringing having given him a much different start than the others, but he wasn't different in the way she thought. The way she hoped.

And he didn't know if he regretted that or not.

He'd vowed to ensure she was safe—from the council, from the pirates, from whatever—whether that came with her forgiveness or not. He hoped it would, but then, he didn't want to disappoint her. Again. He couldn't be the man she thought she saw. The man she wanted him to be would have found a way around killing for the council. That man would have helped the exiles escape, faked the deaths, and worked closely with the Rogues to undermine the rulers.

But he hadn't.

He'd killed them.

Perhaps more civilly than other pirates did, but he'd killed them all the same. And their names—etched into his mind—acted as a constant reminder of how he'd become a tool for the council. The council who had killed his parents and ended his childhood. The victims' names haunted him, reminding him of his failure to save his parents, to stop the council, to become the man his parents always hoped he'd be.

No, the council had killed that good man on that foggy night, and he wouldn't be resurrected. No matter what walls Aoife managed to conquer within his heart.

I love you.

It was no longer her voice but his own, and he replied to it with a groan through gritted teeth. He was about to resume counting his breaths, this time aloud, when footsteps thundered down the ladder.

"Hey, you. Time to go." It was the oaf of a man who had come for him the first day.

Declan stood. "Where's Killian?"

The man only grumbled as he lumbered across the space.

"I see," Declan said and tapped his toe impatiently. "Not talkative at the moment?"

A laugh rumbled, short and coarse, before the man said, "You won't be so yappy either in a moment."

Declan's mind whirred through the possibilities of what awaited him above deck. Another beating? He could handle it, though he didn't look forward to it. Torture? He winced. That was far less appealing, but his thoughts took a jab at him.

It's what you deserve, isn't it?

Once again, he was forced to climb the ladder awkwardly, but he kept quiet this time, his throbbing head making any quip or retort elusive.

They were met by a wall of pirates whose backs were turned toward them. His escort bellowed for the men to move, and the group parted to let them pass, revealing Callum standing by the mainmast with Dominic beside him. Killian was restrained nearby. Declan worked to keep his expression blank as he took in the scene before him.

This was not good.

"Ah," Callum said, "you've arrived at last."

"I would have been here sooner had you not thrown me back in the brig."

Callum's nostrils flared as he spat out, "Which you should never have been removed from to begin with." Dominic punched Killian in the gut, forcing the man to double over, a strangled groan escaping his lips.

Declan shrugged as best he could with the shackles still in place. "Aye, but then who would have saved your life?"

"I would have managed."

"Of course you would have. How silly of me to think you'd be grateful for my help." The crew snickered but quieted quickly.

Ambling toward Declan, Callum rested his hand on the hilt of his cutlass, which had been returned to the scabbard at his side. His wounded arms had been treated, but aside from the slight tinge of blood peeking out from the bottom layers of his bandages, Callum's body showed no indication he'd just been ambushed and killed Lord Roberts and much of his crew.

"You think so highly of yourself, don't you, McCallagh?" Callum asked menacingly as he approached.

The corners of Declan's mouth fell, and he gave another shrug.

"What? No quip? No boastful words from the young captain?"

Callum now stood inches from Declan's face, and the offensive reek of sweat, blood, and salt rushed into Declan's nose.

But Declan didn't answer the goading questions. Instead he peered over Callum's shoulder and gave a quick nod. "What is happening here exactly? Am I to get a cellmate?"

Whatever Declan had been expecting from Callum, it was not the outburst of laughter that now exploded from him, which went on for a solid minute. Declan bit back his growing impatience and frustration, pushing all the tension into his shoulders. This display was meant to unnerve him, to make him squirm. He wouldn't give Callum the satisfaction. Even if internally the tactic was working to pull his gut into small knots.

"You wish that were the case. Unfortunately for your friend here, his fate is far worse than having to spend the remainder of this voyage in such close proximity to you."

They were still two days—or more—away from the Black Sound, so Callum could not have been planning to sacrifice poor Killian to the sirens. Only one thing Declan could think of would cause Killian to stand here as white as the caps on the Aisling's waves. Declan struggled to prevent his eyes from going wide, to stop his jaw from dropping open. He hoped his own face hadn't lost all color.

Not good, not good, not good.

That's an understatement.

Declan must have failed in his attempts to mask his reaction, because Callum gave another laugh—albeit less dynamic than the last—and said, "I see you've guessed then." Keeping his eyes locked on Declan, Callum raised his hand and circled a finger in the air, shouting, "String him up, boys!"

Four of the crewmen rushed forward, ropes in hand, while the rest of the men straightened, as if they were all eager to witness the spectacle about to take place. Declan wanted to look away, to avoid capturing another memory that would surely haunt him, but he steeled himself. He met Killian's terrified stare for mere seconds before the men threw him down on the deck and tied thick ropes to his already bound arms and legs. Together, they lifted him and hauled him to the starboard side.

Declan tried not to turn as Killian passed him, but Callum grabbed his arm and swung him around, dragging him forward. "You deserve the seat of honor, McCallagh," he hissed in his ear.

At the rail, they stopped, turning Killian to face the crew. The four men stood to Killian's right, Callum and Dominic on his left. Some of Killian's usual color had returned, and all his previous fear had somehow washed away as his features turned to stone—cold, accepting his fate.

Callum clasped his hands before him and rocked on his feet before finally speaking to his men. "This man, right here, took it upon himself to defy my command, to go behind my back, and to betray me and this entire crew by releasing our prisoner from the brig. This kind of behavior will not—cannot—be tolerated on this ship."

He drew his cutlass now and swung it up until the blade stopped just short of Killian's neck, and Declan flinched internally with the movement despite knowing it was merely for dramatic effect.

"I could slit his throat and be done with it," he said. "And perhaps I should. After all, he is an old friend and has served under me for many years. But that is exactly why this betrayal cuts as deep as the Aisling, and why my response must be as equally painful."

Dropping his blade but not returning it to the scabbard, Callum gave the signal for his men to proceed. Declan closed his eyes so he wouldn't have to watch the one kind person on this ship be subjected to such treatment. But Callum refused to let him avoid this. His rough hand gripped Declan's chin, hissing at him to open his damn eyes and witness the consequences that came from double-crossing him.

Declan's eyes slid open just in time to see Killian kicked over the edge of the ship, the rope tied to his arms rushing after him.

"Heave!" Callum bellowed. Declan looked around to find, as expected, a line of crewmen pulling a sopping wet rope from over the port rail. The entire crew remained wordless, the silence filled only by grunts of exertion as the men worked to drag the rope onboard. Their struggle intensified as a waterlogged Killian broke the surface and scraped along the side of the ship. Other crewmen dragged him onto the deck, dropping him in a wet and bloody heap.

Killian's body lay there, a mangled mess of torn rags, darkened by the seawater and his own blood. Flesh, blood, and bone peeked through the gashes in his clothes where barnacles had ripped him apart as he'd been dragged across the hull. His face was in an even worse condition, shredded down to the bone. One corner of his mouth had been torn away to reveal his jaw and a couple of missing teeth. The flesh along his cheek and nose were simply gone. Only a few bloody scraps of muscle hung onto his skull.

Declan nearly sighed with relief that Killian had perished with one pass under the keel and wouldn't suffer any further. But then the man blinked his one working eye, and his chest lifted with a sudden gasp for air before continuing to rise and fall rapidly as he panted. Bile lurched up Declan's throat, but he forced it back down. It would do him no good to lose it here with Callum and his crew watching, and it was not like this was the first keelhauling he had witnessed in his twelve years at sea. But the practice was—as far as Declan knew—rare, reserved only for the most heinous of crimes and performed only by the most vicious of captains. Declan himself had never called for it, but then, he'd never felt the need.

Even early on in his role as captain, when he'd let all his anger and pain come out against the unlucky crews and captains of the ships he overtook, he had never subjected anyone to this brutality.

"Again!" Callum's voice broke through the silence. Not one of the crew seemed surprised by this command, and they moved to obey without delay, ignoring how the flayed man groaned in pain when they hoisted him into their arms and carried him back to the starboard rail, where they flung him over the side once more.

Declan braced himself for another painfully silent and eerie passage of time while the men pulled their disgraced crewmate under the ship. It should have been Declan under the water being ripped open by the sharp barnacles covering the keel. He had been the one to initially betray Callum.

You also betrayed Aoife.

Squeezing his eyes closed, he swallowed hard against that truth. Yes, if anyone deserved such treatment, it was Declan, not

179

Killian. But Callum would never have offered it to him, because as barbaric as this torture was, there were easier ways to inflict pain upon Declan.

An elbow knocked into Declan's ribs, and he lifted his chin to the side to see Callum grinning at him like a madman. "This your first hauling, McCallagh?"

Declan's throat remained too tight to allow any words to pass, so he offered a shake of his head.

"Oh, that's too bad. I had hoped to be your first."

Killian was once again hauled aboard and dumped onto the deck, his torso little more than crude strips of flesh somehow still clinging to his bones. Declan forced himself to look the man over, to verify he had died on this second pass. His eyes glanced quickly over Killian's midsection, where his innards were now visible through his tattered clothes, and settled on the gruesome sight that was his chest. Still. Unmoving. One eye had been ripped away from his skull. The other lay open, unblinking.

"Again!" Callum commanded, and Declan glanced sharply at him.

He waited to see if any of the crew would protest, direct their captain to the fatal state of their crewmate and insist his body not be desecrated further.

But no one spoke. No one even flinched at the order. They simply repeated the movements they had performed twice before, and Declan wondered—if only briefly—if it was worse to die by Callum's hand or by that of the sirens.

It was near morning when Tommy finally ambled back down from the quarterdeck. After flatly refusing to sleep, despite his bo'sun's insistence he do so, he'd finally been forced by Gavin to retire below when he could no longer deny the heaviness in his eyelids. For the last several hours, he had wallowed in his thoughts, fighting himself over all the decisions he had made and had yet to make. He had gnawed on every word Maura had said to him, memorized every emotion he had seen in her eyes.

Such bravery. Such stupidity. Such stubbornness. Such confidence.

Confidence. That was what he needed. To make a decision and believe in it. Even if it turned out badly, the crew and Declan and everyone needed him to step up and take command.

At Declan's cabin door, Tommy knocked, more out of habit than as a courtesy to Aoife. He leaned against the doorframe, trying desperately to keep his eyes open long enough for her to answer. When nothing happened for several minutes, he knocked once more, louder this time. On his last stroke, the door swung away from his hand, and he nearly stumbled in as a result.

"Tommy," Aoife's sleep-logged voice croaked. She looked as tired as he felt. "What is it?"

"Gavin says I need to sleep. But he's crazy," Tommy said.

She looked him over. "Not crazy. He's absolutely right. You're barely still conscious as it is."

Something grabbed his arm. The world moved beneath his feet and went dark around him. "I don't know what you mean. I'm wide awake."

"Then why are your eyes closed?" she asked. "Have you been drinking?"

"What? They're not closed." He could quite clearly see Aoife's face before him. But then her freckles faded away, her eyes lightened to a golden yellow, and her ears became pointed at the tips. Realizing she spoke the truth—because last he knew, Aoife was not a shape-shifting fae—he forced his eyelids to part. Aoife had led him into the cabin and was about to help him settle onto the bed when he remembered her second question. "And no, unfortunately, no drink. Not until we get Declan back."

Aoife nudged his shoulder down with a soft word of instruction to sit and rest. Looking up at his friend, Tommy searched for something to say, some words of encouragement, but he came up empty.

"Why are you such an idiot?"

Her sharp tone snapped him to attention and caused his eyes to grow wider.

"Excuse me?"

"Look, Tommy, I'm an expert at screwing up. I make mistakes

more than anyone should ever be able to in one lifetime. Perhaps that makes me more than qualified to note when someone else is in danger of doing something beyond stupid."

Tommy tried to parse through her words, but his exhausted brain was too slow to keep up. "What?"

"Maura. That's what."

His body tensed at the mention of her name. Aoife had taken note of whatever connection had grown between them, but as he'd told her before, there was nothing to be done about it. It was a doomed future.

"Why won't you let her help?" Aoife asked.

"Wait. Huh?" So this wasn't about their mutual affection but about Maura's powers and the kraken they were fast approaching.

"You didn't ask for my advice, I know, but you're being an imbecile. She—and Bria—are our best chances of getting past the creature alive. And you know it." Aoife displayed none of the sweetness he had become accustomed to, and though he was proud of her for finding her inner toughness, he wasn't sure he liked having it directed at him.

"We can't risk it," he said, more softly and less convincingly than intended.

"We can, and we should. It's the only—"

"No." Tommy straightened. Aoife stepped away from him, shock and confusion and anger swirling in her eyes. If he was going to be taken seriously as captain—even if only temporarily—he needed to find confidence.

"No? And why not exactly?" Bitterness swam in her green eyes, visible even in the dim lantern light.

Because I said so! His thoughts screamed inside his head. He wanted to simply demand that Aoife respect him and stop pressuring him to do something he knew to be too dangerous and risky.

Instead, he calmed himself with a quick breath so he could explain.

"Because"—he cleared his throat—"if they use up their magic in the kraken's territory, they may not have time to restore it by the time we arrive at the Black Sound. And if they push their magic to its limit—use too much too fast—they lose it completely."

Aoife was quiet for a minute, searching his eyes. Finally she shook her head and huffed out a breath. "I don't like it, Tommy. It seems like not using their magic puts us at a greater risk of becoming kraken food and never making it to the sound at all. You must see that. I'm sure they can learn to manage without their powers."

"It's not just their special abilities they lose if they burn out. Their ability to heal is lessened. Their long life is shortened. I won't risk her—them."

"But it's a risk she's willing to take, isn't it? Why can't you respect her wishes? Why can't you trust her to know her limits and to help?"

"I just can't, Aoife," Tommy said before hiding a yawn he couldn't fight. "Now, if you really want to help, you'll let me sleep. I believe Collins should be ready for you soon too."

"Fine," she said and crossed her arms in front of her. "Get your sleep, Tommy. Hopefully you'll be thinking more clearly when you've had some rest."

She hadn't even made it out of the bedroom before his eyes were closed and he was falling onto the bed. He was asleep before he could hear the cabin door click shut.

Sitting on the quarterdeck stairs as she had last night, Maura forced her attention to remain on Aoife, who was in the center of the deck running through drills with Collins, a tall and lanky pirate who seemed to be one of the few who wasn't completely put off by the presence of three fae on board. Though she appeared to be watching the lesson intently, Maura's vision had long since blurred as she stared, her mind wandering to the cabin behind her and the man who slept within.

She understood Tommy's hesitance to allow her to use her powers, and unlike Aoife, she didn't take it as any personal affront. But Aoife couldn't feel the fear emanating from him like Maura could. Whether it was because of her sharp fae senses or her connection to him, she wasn't entirely sure. It didn't matter why or how, but she could tell there was far more bothering him than he'd ever let on.

While Aoife trained to help her fight the monsters waiting for them, Maura spent the morning wondering how to convince Tommy that things—especially things between them—weren't so dire, complicated, or doomed. But he'd been quite clear in his cabin. And again on these stairs.

He had no intention of being with her. Or even listening to her, apparently.

And though he admitted to caring for her, he wouldn't act on it.

How he could ignore it, she couldn't understand, even knowing her emotions exceeded anything he would ever experience. His rejection had stung far more than she'd expected it to, and though she'd been able to keep her words calm and her attitude nonchalant back in the cabin, she hadn't had the strength to refrain from trying to speak to him again when he'd eventually exited.

If his dismissal in the privacy of Declan's cabin had hurt, it paled in comparison to the gut-squeezing pain of him publicly pushing her away.

Renna was right.

At least about the pain this *predicament* destined her for.

But Maura refused to believe in the impossibility of it. Of them.

Except there is no chance for you two in Larcsporough. You're fae. He's human.

That inconvenient truth remained, twisting the fibers in her chest so tightly she had to press a hand to her sternum to calm it. When she and her sisters eventually traveled south to their kin, they would be expected to sacrifice their own dreams and plans to help stop another war. And that sacrifice didn't allow for Tommy's inclusion.

But where had her kin been while they were locked away in

that room by the council? What did she—or any of them—owe the other fae when they had forfeited them to a life in prison?

They likely thought you were dead, just as you believed them to be.

She frowned. How dare her thoughts be so logical when all she wanted to do was sulk?

A weight crushed her chest, forcing her shoulders to round as she folded in on herself. Her face fell into her hands, and she propped her elbows on her knees. There were no good options. Either she betrayed her entire race or she betrayed her heart. No middle ground. No possibility of pursuing both. Even if Tommy would leave this ship and this sea, what waited for her in the south...

No, she couldn't ask him to go with her.

And she was beyond selfish to keep pursuing such a ridiculous hope that could only end in heartache.

It's not like you're soul mates. It's not like you don't have a choice here.

While her thoughts again rang true, it didn't make her choice any easier. She'd seen friends—who had been forced to sever ties and abandon the ones they loved during the war—struggle with that loss. Even though it was their choice to make, they were never the same afterward. Like a piece of themselves had been cut out, discarded, destroyed.

Was she strong enough to do the same?

Maura wasn't so sure, not when the only thing she'd ever dreamed of, in all her centuries of life, was finding someone to share life with. Bria, sweet as she was, had teased her for being such a romantic. Hopeless in her idealism of love and partnership. Perhaps there had been a chance for such a future before the Aisling War had broken out. But war changed things.

During those five centuries of imprisonment, Maura's dream had faded, as if the iron infused into the stone walls had snuffed out more than just her powers. But like her magic, the dream had not been completely extinguished. Her magic had roared back to life as they'd fled the council hall, stronger and more vibrant than it had ever been before. Even as her magic waned with her work to heal Tommy, warmth filled every part of her, pulling the sun from the sky and placing it within her chest, where it continued to shine.

It had shone until Renna brought in the clouds with her warnings, until Tommy had pushed her away and ignored his mutual feelings.

"You okay?"

Maura looked up to find Aoife—her face red and covered in sweat—standing before her.

A smile couldn't be helped as Maura answered. "Perhaps I should be asking you that."

Aoife took a few more ragged breaths. "I'm not sure how I would answer that, honestly. Not sure if it's helping me in the slightest."

"Better to know a few things than nothing at all, no?" Maura asked with a raised brow and a half-smile, hoping they effectively hid her inner turmoil. "Do you want to sit?"

Aoife gave a shake of her head. "I think I just want to lie down, actually. After I have some food." She shifted to her left, starting for Declan's cabin.

All of Maura's muscles urged her to stand, but she managed to quell it in time, forcing herself to remain seated even as she raised a hand to grab Aoife's arm, stopping her before she could walk off. Aoife tilted her head in confusion.

"Sorry. I think Tommy's still sleeping in there."

Yes, better to pretend she didn't know exactly where he was. That would appear less creepy.

"Ah," Aoife said, her shoulders slumping in disappointment.

She looked around the ship, chewing on her bottom lip as she did. "He did look rather beat. Do you think he's doing okay?"

Maura's breath hitched at the unexpected question. Weaving her fingers, she stared at her hands. "I don't know."

"Then I guess I'll sit after all," Aoife said, already moving to sit beside her. The familiarity sent a disconcerting shiver up Maura's spine so strong she was sure Aoife had noticed. But if she had, she gave no indication, allowing their shoulders to touch with the closeness of good friends instead of new acquaintances. Maura hadn't had a friend in ages. Sisters, yes. They were a type of friend in themselves, she supposed, but sisterhood—even on good terms and in good spirits—had always felt too intrusive for Maura's liking.

It would be nice to have a friend.

"I'm worried about him," Aoife said.

I'm sure he's fine.

That's what Maura should have said, but instead her tongue betrayed her before she could stop it. "I am too."

Silence fell, and neither of them moved, both staring straight ahead. Maura should have sensed how Aoife was doing, emotionally speaking, but it seemed her preoccupation with Tommy had hindered her perception. She didn't know what to say or if she should even say anything at all. So she simply sat and counted breaths as they baked under the midday sun.

When Aoife spoke again, it came out as a whisper. "Can you tell a lie?"

Maura fought a laugh and smiled, but her amusement faded as soon as she saw Aoife was serious. "No. I mean, yes, we can. No, that rumor is not true. It's a myth."

Aoife's shoulders lifting with her breath before dropping, and she turned forward again. "I suppose that's a good thing."

"Why do you say that? Seems like that particular bit of lore came about to provide some comfort to men who feared fae over-powering them." A bunch of nonsense, if anyone asked Maura. Fae had no desire to rule over men. At least no fae she'd ever met.

Aoife fidgeted. "Sometimes the truth isn't always what we need."

Maura pondered the words for a moment, but Aoife continued before she could devise a response.

"I know it sounds silly, especially after Declan didn't tell me about..." She shook her head in a futile attempt to erase the end of the sentence from existence. "I would rather someone choose to tell the truth rather than be compelled to. Perhaps I'm naive, and it would be better to always know the truth in all instances. But I want to know I've earned someone's trust. Not have them confide in me simply because they couldn't avoid doing so."

"That doesn't sound silly at all, honestly." While Maura had never given this concept much thought, she had to admit Aoife had a valid point. How nice it would be to have control over what she shared with her sisters rather than having their keen perception and sisterly intuition give them such access into her life and her emotions.

"I've wondered," Aoife said, "will I be able to forgive Declan if—when—we rescue him?"

The question cut into Maura's heart and had her wondering how she would handle it if she and Tommy were in that position.

But Aoife wasn't Maura.

And Declan wasn't Tommy.

So while Maura—with this intense and sudden devotion—could not imagine withholding forgiveness from Tommy, for any infraction, she knew Aoife would struggle with this. Given her up-bringing and the level of betrayal she'd experienced from her own family, Aoife understandably struggled with forgiving Declan, no matter how much she loved him.

"I think," Maura started, waiting to ensure Aoife was listening, "you'll have to ask yourself if you can accept the risk of being hurt again." Aoife's breath hitched, and Maura moved to continue before the girl got the wrong idea. "Thing is, though, life is inherently risky. Pain exists, and there is no way to avoid it entirely. The question becomes: is your love for him stronger than your fear that he'll betray you again? And I'm not saying you need to know the answer now. But it's something to think about as we travel. He gave you time, yes?" Aoife's chin dropped slightly. "He didn't chase after you. He didn't force you to give him an answer then and there. He honored you. And yes, I know he made a mistake in keeping the truth from you. More importantly, he knows it was a mistake."

Maura had no idea if she was helping or if her words were making any sense at all. And Aoife offered no sign either way. After another breath of silence, Maura moved to speak again.

"Remember, Aoife, forgiving him is not condoning his actions. It's not admitting what he did wasn't wrong or hurtful. It's choosing not to let those actions rule over your heart any longer. Sands, you don't even need to commit to a future with him in order to forgive him. And from the few moments I spent with him—watching him with you at the council hall, seeing his desperation when he brought Tommy back to the ship, witnessing him wrestle with whether to stay with his wounded friend or go after you—I can say with utmost sincerity, I believe he will accept your forgiveness with no strings attached. He will respect whatever boundaries you need. He may be a pirate, but he's a rare sort."

"Like Tommy," Aoife muttered, and for a moment Maura wondered if the girl hadn't heard anything else she'd said, only picking up on the last line. "You're right though. He's not like the others. He's done despicable things—and will likely do so again before his end—I can't imagine my life without him."

"But?" Maura could sense Aoife was holding something back, though she vowed to herself she wouldn't pry if she chose not to share.

"I just don't know when—how soon—how much time I might need before I can—"

"And you don't need to know that yet. He will understand."

Aoife donned a half-hearted smile.

Maura shook her head and said, "I'm no seer, and I can't read minds like my sister, but he will wait for your forgiveness. I would bet my last breath on that."

◦◦◦

Hours passed, and the sun, flirting with the horizon, washed the sky in streaks of bright orange and vibrant pink. Aoife had accepted Gavin's offer to take her meals on deck with the sisters rather than in the captain's quarters, and now her barely stifled yawns betrayed her exhaustion. The girl would need a bed soon, and Tommy still hadn't left Declan's cabin.

"You should probably get some rest," Renna said to Aoife. "We all should, actually."

Aoife glanced around at the fae. "You mean fae sleep?"

"What kind of—" Maura started to ask, but she stopped when Aoife's face lit up with a smug grin. Maura rolled her eyes at herself for being so gullible.

"I'm really not that tired," Aoife said to Renna before promptly covering up another deep yawn.

"Clearly," Bria muttered with the hint of laughter in her eyes.

Aoife glanced toward the door of the captain's quarters.

Although Maura knew their agreement to alternate sleeping shifts between them, she hoped Aoife wouldn't push to have him give the space up for her. Tommy would never knowingly let himself take the rest he needed, and he would likely decline further hours of sleep if he were to be wakened.

"I can't ask Tommy to move," Aoife said, almost to herself, though the three fae could hear her regardless.

Trying not to sound too happy, Maura counted to five before adding her agreement. "The continued sleep would do him good." She ignored the heat from her sisters' glares and their silent accusations. It wasn't as though being concerned for someone's health was crossing any line, was it?

"She could share our cabin, couldn't she?" Bria offered, her eyes alight as though she were planning a social gathering rather than simply figuring out sleeping arrangements on a cramped ship.

Aoife protested with a shake of her head. "You only have the two bunks though. I couldn't put you out any more than you already are."

"Nonsense," Renna said. "It was Maura's turn to have the floor space anyway, and I'm happy to relinquish my cot to you."

"You'd do that for me?" Aoife's mouth fell open, though it could have been from the subsequent yawn and not surprise.

Renna gave a short laugh. "Just for one night. Let's not get crazy. My ancient bones can only take so much discomfort curled up on the floor."

"I couldn't accept," Aoife started, but Renna raised her hand, and her expression hardened.

"You can, and you will. End of story."

Tension coursed through the small group. No one spoke for quite some time with Aoife looking to Maura and Bria in turn.

Maura forced her own laugh out. "So serious, sister. She won't want to take up our offer if you scare her away like that."

"Like what?" Renna demanded, her back straightening.

Her reaction seemed so perfectly comical that Maura couldn't prevent a smile from spreading across her face.

"Exactly," Bria said and turned to Aoife. "Really though, Aoife. You are more than welcome. One night sharing a bed on the floor will be cake for these two."

"Says the one who gets the bunk," Maura said, though she actually had no preference.

"Well, if that's settled," Renna said as she stood, "we really should retire for the night. If Gavin's estimates are correct, we will have a busy and stressful day tomorrow. Starting early."

In silence the three pushed to stand and follow Renna to the officers' cabin. When Renna opened the door and walked in, followed by Bria and Aoife, Maura remained in the doorway. She'd forgotten just how tiny this space was. Barely large enough for two men. Tight for three. Absurd for four. Even with Aoife being on the smaller side.

"We will make do, Maura," Renna said in her commanding tone. "Now come in here and shut the door."

"I think I'm going to spend a bit more time out here while you three get settled," Maura offered, ignoring how Bria and Aoife both cocked their heads in response.

"Very well then." Renna turned and met Maura at the door, standing as close to her as she had at the railing the other morning. "But remember what I told you. Don't be tempted. Don't—"

A growl rumbled in the back of Maura's throat, and she backed out, shutting the door with a heavy slam. She hoped it hit her sister in the face but immediately regretted that thought. Renna was only trying to help. But while some small part of Maura understood that, more of her had already succumbed to the overwhelming emotions that threatened to consume her.

Stalking to the center of the deck, she lowered herself onto the deck and leaned back against the mainmast. Minimal crew remained on deck to maintain their heading. A pirate Maura didn't know manned the helm while Gavin took his leave to sleep a few hours in the barracks below.

Tommy's fine. He just needs the extra sleep. You needn't worry about him.

Maura repeated the thoughts to herself, but failed to convince herself that Tommy was okay. Her earlier conversation with Aoife replayed in her mind, and she began to ponder what she would do if it Tommy had killed on of her sisters. And lied about it.

Would it be any more difficult than your current reality?

Perhaps not more difficult. Just different.

And would it even matter if Tommy lied to her, if they could never be together anyway? Perhaps that simple fact—that she and Tommy could never be—prevented them from being hurt by possible betrayal.

Maura shook her head at herself.

No. Even if they had to ignore their feelings, those feelings would remain, and betrayal could still damage them.

Throwing her head back against the sturdy wood of the mast, she examined the sky, a deep blue velvet, speckled with what appeared to be a random spattering of stars. But she knew they were anything but random, placed there at the creation of their world. Before her time. Before war. Before enchantments. Before corruption. Before heartache.

When she was younger, Maura had found the view of the stars to be a freeing and exhilarating indication that anything was possible. But now, looking at the expanse spread above her, feeling the weight of a million could-have-beens and what-ifs crushing her chest, she saw no magic of possibility. Only the reminder that all she wanted, although visible, was out of reach. An impossibility.

With each passing moment, the sky deepened until it had lost all color and settled into a rich black. She must have been sitting at the mast for hours, and her backside ached from the uncomfortable wood beneath her.

Not that sleeping on the floor of the officers' quarters would have felt any better.

With a glance around, she stood and stretched out the stiffness from her joints. None of the crew on duty seemed to notice her as she began to pace the deck on weary feet. From one side of the ship to the other, she walked, counting her breaths, listening to the slapping of the water against the hull, contemplating the unfamiliar tune one of the crewmen whistled quietly. By the third passing, though, she could barely keep her eyelids open any longer and knew she needed to concede and join her sister on the floor in the small cabin.

Pulling the door open, she peered into the darkness. Renna had left some space on the floor for her, and from the sounds of their steady, slow breathing, her sisters and Aoife had been asleep a while. She should go in, shut the door, lie down, and sleep as best she could.

But she couldn't move from the doorway, like some force was pulling her away from these quarters, beckoning her elsewhere. She listened a few moments more, and then, convinced they were indeed sleeping soundly, she backed away on her toes and closed the door softly once more.

This was dumb. She was stupid. This was exactly the opposite of what she knew she should do. And yet, her reason stood little chance of winning an argument with the force now driving her back across the ship, around the quarterdeck stairs, and toward the captain's cabin.

Her fingers landed on the handle, and it took every ounce of self-control she could muster to stop herself from barging in. No, she needed to think this over. She wasn't going to do anything. She merely wanted a more comfortable space in which to rest. That didn't mean she was going to curl up in the same bed as Tommy.

The mere idea of doing so had her shoulders tingling.

Just go in. Grab a blanket. Lie down on the floor.

She walked herself through the plan, but her traitorous mind wouldn't cease its dreaming.

Go in. Crawl onto the bed. Lie down beside him.

"Balls!" The word fell out of her mouth with a frustrated thud, and she pulled her hand away from the door. Pivoting on her feet, she gasped at the sight of Aoife standing a few feet away, her brow creased with concern but her eyes sparkling with curiosity.

"Aoife! You scared me," Maura said, trying to keep her voice low as she risked a glance over Aoife's shoulder. If Aoife had woken up, it was quite likely her sisters had too.

"I could say the same about you." Aoife stepped closer. "Thought you'd be sleeping by now."

"And why aren't you sleeping?" Maura hoped her question didn't sound accusatory, though with her nerves wound so tight, it likely did.

Aoife shrugged and dropped her gaze to the floor where her toe shuffled against the deck. "I was. But I don't sleep well these days." When she lifted her face, the hint of curiosity had been replaced with what Maura could only interpret as worry, regret, and weariness.

Reaching a hand toward Aoife, Maura offered a tight smile before saying, "We'll catch up to Declan. We'll get him back." But when Aoife didn't respond or react, she wondered if perhaps she'd misinterpreted. Maybe Aoife was worried about something else? Her mother? Tommy? The sisters? Herself?

With a sheepish look, Aoife said, "Not if Tommy remains so stubborn."

She wasn't wrong.

"Maybe he'll feel better after he's rested," Maura said with a half-hearted shrug.

"I hope so. Speaking of. I'm heading back. You coming?"

Maura hesitated, her words stuck in her chest, her breath trapped in her throat. Pulling in a deep breath, she searched for the best answer, except she hadn't quite decided for herself. When Aoife's brows rose, she scrambled one last time and said the last thing she'd planned to say. "I think I'm going to keep an eye on Tommy."

Aoife's expression shifted as her curiosity returned, pulling the corners of her mouth down. At least she didn't look angry, as Renna undoubtedly would have. Maura's heart pounded, and she waited for her friend to say something. Anything.

"Okay then," Aoife finally said with a smile Maura hoped was genuine. As silly as it was to be preoccupied with remaining on a mere human's good side, Maura couldn't deny she hoped she and Aoife would become close friends.

"Thanks, Aoife."

"Of course. But"—she quirked up a brow—"I'm not saving you from your sister's wrath in the morning."

Maura released a breathy laugh. "Nor would I ask you to."

Aoife turned to leave but stopped once to look over her shoulder. "Oh, and take care of him."

Before Maura could respond—or even react—Aoife was walking away, back toward the borrowed bunk in the cramped room. What she'd meant by that, Maura wasn't sure. With how much the girl carried on her heart already, it amazed Maura that she would have any energy to be concerned for Tommy's well-being. But then again, humans never ceased to amaze her. Their lives might be short, but the amount of cares and worries they could carry within them seemed as innumerable as the stars still glittering above her head. Maura had often wondered how they managed to survive as long as they did with the amount of baggage the hauled upon themselves.

But if Maura could help ease Tommy's burdens, she would. Whether he ever opened his heart completely to her or not, she would do everything in her power to see him not only survive but thrive.

22
TOMMY

Tommy opened his eyes to find the sky still dark, with dawn not yet lightening the eastern horizon. Groaning and rubbing his knuckles over his eyes, he sat up, cursing internally over the minimal sleep he had gotten.

"It's about time you woke up."

The words, despite having been said by the sweetest voice he'd ever heard, had Tommy's eyes flashing open and his hands hovering in the air before him. Maura sat on the end of the bed with her legs crossed under her in the same way he used to sit as a child.

"What are you doing here? And what do you mean, it's about time? It's still the middle of the night." He flung a hand out toward the window and turned to ensure the world outside was indeed still dark and he hadn't imagined that a moment ago.

"You've been asleep for nearly a full day."

His eyes went wide, and his jaw felt heavy, like it would flop open at any moment if he didn't keep control over it. He looked around the room—from the window to Maura, then to the desk out in the main area and back to the window.

"What did you do to me?"

Pain flashed across her delicate features, tugging at the corners of her eyes, but she recovered quickly. Straightening, she raised her chin and pinned him with a glare.

"I don't know what you believe I'm capable of, Tommy, but it's certainly not putting men into comatose states. So don't you dare accuse me of *doing* something to you."

Her words were as sharp and clipped as the icy daggers she shot at him with her eyes, and he flinched as if they had actually pierced him. He slumped his shoulders and dropped his chin to his chest before pushing a hand through his hair.

"I'm sorry, Maura. I'm just—"

"Stressed."

He offered a nod but didn't look at her, instead keeping his eyes cast down onto the blanket in front of him.

"Maybe I can help," she said.

His exasperation escaped him in a groan before he could hold it back. "We've already been over this."

She shifted closer to him, uncrossing her legs and kneeling beside him. She still wore the simple dress from her time at the council hall, a purple so deep it looked almost black until a beam of light hit it just right. Her eyes contrasted with it so dramatically that the gold in them seemed to move, simmering away like honey melting into a cup of hot tea.

Tommy lost all knowledge of how to breathe as she inched closer. He sat, waiting, unsure what her intent here was exactly. But given her forward nature earlier that night—or, rather, last night—

he could only assume she was looking for something he could not give her, no matter how much a part of him wanted to.

She placed a hand on his knee and moved it cautiously up to his thigh. He closed his eyes, not sure where this was going, not sure what she was planning, and not sure he could stop it if it continued like this.

The bed shifted as she moved, but still he kept his eyes closed.

Why are you such a nervous wreck? Seriously. Declan would mock you endlessly if he saw you!

He shook his head at himself—a small, almost imperceptible movement to quiet his thoughts.

"I wasn't talking about my magic, you know." Maura's voice floated toward him from much further away than he'd expected, and he risked a peek at her, trying not to think about the way her hand still rested on his leg.

In one quick, graceful motion, Maura turned around until she was seated beside him, her left leg pressed against his right, her shoulder resting against his own. And though her hand now lay in her own lap, the way her body was nestled alongside his was almost more intimate.

Too intimate.

He should get up. He should figure out what had happened while he was sleeping. He should look for Aoife and see if she needed a chance to sleep or seek out Gavin and find out how close they were to those dreaded waters.

But he couldn't.

Her warmth. Her scent. The gentle rise and fall of her chest as she breathed. He was trapped, transfixed, mesmerized, frozen.

"Do you want to talk about it?" Maura asked, turning her chin slightly so she was looking at him from the side.

"About what exactly?" His mind skipped and hopped among

all the various problems that lay before him, until it all fell away, leaving him with a blank nothing that must have shown plainly on his face, because she laughed. Short. Sweet.

"Take your pick, I suppose. It's no wonder you slept for so long with the number of things you're juggling and the new role you're filling and the new...feelings you're fighting."

He ignored that last thing and once again ran a hand through his hair. It seemed cliche to sigh, and yet his body seemed to do it on its own, like the release of air could somehow soothe all the tension pulling at his nerves.

"I mean," she continued when he didn't respond, "I'm content in silence as well, but I doubt that would ease your stress much."

After a full day of sleeping, Tommy had woken up more re- laxed. The edge of the cliff he'd been lingering on for the past several days had seemed a bit further away. Until she'd spoken. Then it was as if a force had pushed him forward, his toes once again hovering over that emotional edge.

His chest tightened.

The air was slowly leaking out of this cabin.

He couldn't breathe.

Maura wanted too much from him. The crew needed too much from him. It was all too much. A crushing weight even a restful sleep couldn't lessen.

He had been quiet for so long, he didn't know how to break the silence. In fact, he usually didn't know how to talk to her at all. Others, yes. But Maura? She fascinated him and—not that he'd ever admit it, not even to Declan—she intimidated him. Why she wanted him was beyond comprehension.

But then she had told him he'd see his own worth one day.

Was that really what his problem was? Was that why he al- ways sought to be second and not in charge? To be the follower rather than the leader? Was it simply a lack of self-confidence and self-worth?

He cringed at the slew of questions pinging around his brain. It was too early to tackle any of that. If he ever could.

"This is nice," Maura whispered and lowered her head onto his shoulder, her soft hair tickling his cheek.

A "Hmmm" was all Tommy could manage, not trusting his voice not to crack.

"It could be nicer," she said with a hint of mischief. Her hand returned to his thigh, higher this time. Tommy went still, even as every nerve in his body seemed to move, causing a not unpleasant tingling down to his toes, along his shoulders, and elsewhere.

He wanted her to back away. To give him space. But also to never stop touching him.

He wanted her to be just another barmaid in a distant port that he could bed once and move on from. But also to be the only one he took to bed ever again.

He wanted to ignore the warmth that gathered within him, to remind her—and himself—it wasn't an option. But also to give in to it all.

Before he could think better of it, he had her in his arms and was lifting her up and over until she was seated on his lap, her dress pooling at her thighs as her legs straddled him. He lost himself in the welcoming light of her eyes, which shone with the same hunger that simmered within him and held none of the surprise he had expected.

Her hand traveled up his torso, setting more of him on fire. He couldn't stop his arm from winding around her back, pulling her closer, and moving her forward so the warmth of her body enveloped him.

Tommy was swimming in honey—the golden, luscious, sweet

honey of her eyes. She sat so close to him now, there was no hiding the effect she was having on him. Yet he didn't care.

Her hair spilled around her face as she leaned toward him. His eyes dropped to her lips. What would it feel like to kiss her? To take her here and now? To give in to everything he knew was wrong?

Even if he could untangle his thoughts enough to form coherent sentences, he didn't think his tongue could manage to utter them.

What are you doing?!

He shouldn't do this. Couldn't.

I don't fucking care.

With everything else in his life turned upside down, why couldn't he claim something good? Something just for him.

Ignoring all the silent warnings, his eyes traveled back to hers, memorizing every perfect detail of her face. He ran his hands down her back to her waist, his thumbs grazing her curves beneath the fabric of her dress. He couldn't pull his gaze away from hers, even when he ran a hand over her shoulder and let his fingers trace the length of her neck and down her jaw toward her inviting lips.

Everything about her enticed him. He lost all concept of anything outside of this room, this bed, this small space they shared.

All he saw was her beauty, strength, and feisty spirit. All of it caused a thrill within his heart. She'd been right about them. Whatever had happened during his healing, whatever spark had been ignited would not be ignored.

And he didn't want to ignore it.

He only wanted her lips on his.

To taste her.

To feel her.

To do anything she asked and then some.

Maura hovered close enough now that her breath warmed the

sides of his nose and the top of his lips. Sliding his eyes shut, he closed the distance between them.

Her lips brushed against his, a touch so light yet so amazing it sent another shiver through him. It should have excited him. In any other situation, it probably would have. But now it seemed to wake up that responsible part of himself he'd shoved aside earlier.

Tension shot through his limbs, stopping him before his lips could devour hers.

Gently he moved her back—the motion uncomfortably reminiscent of his dreams. The distance between them now brought him a refreshing chill, like stepping out of a crowded, stifling pub.

Still, he kept his eyes clamped shut, afraid of how she might react.

He was a coward. Too scared to see how his sudden rejection might hurt her. He braced himself for the slap of her hand or the cut of her sharp tongue—two rather unpleasant but familiar responses he'd been the recipient of in the past—but they didn't come.

Instead, her sweet laugh—a laugh he hoped to always remember—embraced him, carrying none of the pain or resentment he'd anticipated. When he opened his eyes, she was looking at him as though he hadn't just refused to kiss her. Love and endearment and care shone at him, more than he'd ever deserved, so intense it scared him.

Except it wasn't her feelings he feared but the fact that he sensed the same emotions crying out from the dark corners of his soul where he'd discarded them.

Gone were the questions of what was happening to him. It was painfully—so painfully—obvious. This was no simple attraction, no basic human desire. It was more, much more, and the only question now was *how*. How could he be falling in love with someone he didn't know? A war raged inside him, until he thought his heart might crack in two. One part of him wanted to give everything and more to this amazing woman—this *fae*—but the other frantically worked to protect him from the pain they'd both suffer when things inevitably ended.

"Tommy, love," Maura said as she swept a stray hair from his forehead.

Could she see the fear in his eyes? He wasn't even trying to hide it at this point.

Some captain you've turned out to be.

Reaching both hands out to touch his face, she cupped his jaw and slid her fingers behind his head. "I have waited for you a long time. I will wait as long as I have to. Even if I have to wait forever."

Forever.

He swallowed the word down, accepting it like the medicine his mother used to force on him whenever he got ill. Just like that medicine, the word coated his insides in the same disgusting taste, but he knew—no matter how much he hated it, how much it hurt, how bitter it left him—it was what was best for him.

Tommy could never allow himself to build an impossible future with her, and he moved to tell her as much. But he didn't get a chance. She leaned forward, and her hair once again draped around his face. He snapped his mouth closed, ready to ward off her advances.

You're making the right decision.

As much as he wanted to trust his own thoughts, when she pressed her lips to his in a kiss so light and sweet and soft and full of love and patience, he wondered if he'd made a mistake. Before he could change his mind, she was gone, all her warmth taken away as she slipped off the bed and out of the room.

A oife found herself surprisingly less sore than she'd expected, especially considering the cramped quarters. Sleep had
remained elusive though, if only because of the intimidating
company.

You didn't have to take them up on their offer.

She grumbled as she rolled over on the small mattress and sat
up, forgetting about the bunk sitting low above her borrowed bed
until her head hit the wooden edge hard. Wincing, she bit back a
cry of pain. She'd shown enough of her less-than-graceful side
already, and there was no way she could bear to lose any more of
her pride.

Especially among the fae.

As she rubbed the tender part of her scalp, she listened. No
movement. The blankets Renna had used to set up her bed on the
floor had already been neatly folded and placed under the small

table that sat in the corner opposite the bunks. Aoife stood and risked a timid glance toward the upper bunk. Bria was nowhere to be seen, having already tidied up her bed as well, likely in the most orderly fashion these accommodations had ever seen.

Aoife rushed to the small porthole. Its single pane was too grimy to allow her to see much detail outside, but she was at least able to determine that the sun was up. And she had overslept. Gavin had expected to enter the kraken's territory shortly after sunup, and from what Aoife could tell, it was well past that now. Without another thought, she made her way across the room and out the door, stopping short once she had stepped onto the deck.

She noticed two things immediately: it was silent, and the entire crew seemed to be above deck. Unmoving. Not talking. Simply waiting. Watching. Some turned to glance at her, fear worn plainly on their faces. Others seemed ready, eager even, to take on the giant below.

No one said anything to her though, and she scanned the crowd of tired, sweaty, grungy, nervous men for one of her friends. As silently as she could manage, she tiptoed forward.

With a glance up to the quarterdeck, she confirmed Tommy and the others weren't there. Something tapped her shoulder, and she nearly yelped from surprise but quickly clamped a hand over her mouth to keep any rogue sounds from escaping. A large burly pirate, whose name she didn't know—though she recognized him as being one of the new Foxhaven recruits—lifted a finger to his lips before pointing the same hand toward the captain's quarters.

If the officers and fae were in there, perhaps things weren't quite as dire as they seemed.

At least not yet.

Aoife opened the door without knocking and found them standing around Declan's desk much in the same manner as the day they'd gathered and chosen this course. Except now Maura wasn't bothering to keep her distance from Tommy, standing close enough to him that their shoulders nearly touched. Not that he seemed to be bothered by it. Or to even be aware of it.

Six faces looked up to greet her as she joined them. Tight smiles came from the men. Nothing but blank stares from the fae.

Although she had started to warm to Maura, especially since their talk on the stairs the other night, she couldn't quell the jealousy she harbored toward her and the other fae for their elegant grace and calm demeanor in the midst of strife. They wore their serene masks expertly, and Aoife wondered if they thought doing so put people at ease, because the empty expressions plastered onto their perfect faces was anything but relaxing.

Tommy dipped his chin to her with a whispered "Good morning." The man didn't look like the extra sleep he'd enjoyed had helped him. In fact, he almost looked worse off.

You could have slept in your own bed last night, and it would have been just as well.

Biting back the thought, she focused on Tommy's eyes, hoping he would understand her question without her having to voice it. While she trusted herself to be able to whisper, it seemed better if she didn't have to take any unnecessary risks.

"Obviously," Tommy said, continuing in a whisper, "you can tell we are keeping ourselves as quiet as possible. This makes sailing a bit more difficult—"

"A lot more difficult," Gavin interjected, also in a whisper.

But Tommy ignored him. "So far we've had no signs of the creature, and we are moving on as quickly as we can, as silently as we can."

Aoife stepped closer until her hips rested against the edge of the desk. She leaned forward. "How are we sailing at all when the deck is packed full of men? Men who are more for decoration than anything else."

Tommy released a slow sigh. Running a hand through his hair, he gestured to Mikkel with the other. The man turned without question and slipped out the door, likely to give whispered commands to the crew to disperse and get back to work as best they could.

"Thank you, Aoife," Tommy said, "for allowing me the extra rest. I know it wasn't what we had agreed to, and it was far from ideal to squeeze four of you into the small officers' quarters, but I appreciate the consideration all the same."

Aoife snapped her attention to Renna, the eldest, but she and Bria both stared straight ahead, as if they were off in some dreamland instead of present in this meeting. Maura, though, looked at her and offered a small shrug as the corner of her lips pulled back in a sheepish grin. Maura's brows rose, and her golden eyes pleaded with Aoife to not mention how she had slept in here near Tommy all night.

He thought the four of them had slept in the officers' quarters. Maura hadn't told him otherwise.

And now Maura was asking her to keep it a secret from him, one of her only friends in the world.

Another damn secret.

But Maura was her friend, too, and she could talk with her later about the importance of honesty. Sands, life had become complicated now that she wasn't isolated and basically alone.

She turned back to Tommy, and her whispered "You're welcome" was as much for Maura as it was for him. Whatever was now happening—or not happening—between those two could wait until tomorrow. If they lived that long.

"Gavin," Aoife said, turning to the helmsman, "at the rate we are sailing at the moment, will we—"

A shake of the man's head cut her words off as sharp as a cutlass would have. "No, unfortunately. Wind is not cooperating with us. There's still some, but not enough to give us the speed we need. It's like the wind avoids these waters as much as sailors do."

Glancing around the small group, Aoife asked, "So this is our plan then? Glide slowly across the waters as quietly as possible in hopes the shadow of our ship doesn't catch the attention of a gigantic beast who swallows vessels whole?"

"Basically, yes," Tommy answered.

"Well, that's stupid."

"Look, it's the best—"

"No, it's not, Tommy, and you damn well know it." Aoife struggled to keep her anger from pushing her volume up above a whisper. With all her recent mistakes, she didn't want to add *alerted the kraken* to that list.

Tommy didn't move, didn't say anything as his lips formed a tense line.

"And you're okay with this, Gavin?" The sharpness in Aoife's tone lingered.

Gavin kept his eyes lowered to the desk as he answered, "Captain's orders, Aoife."

Aoife bit back her frustration. "There has to be a way for Maura and Bria to help without burning out their magic. You have to consider it, because at this rate, at this pace...Declan will be dead before we even make it out of the kraken's cursed waters!"

She had at least stopped herself before pinning Declan's impending demise on her friend, but Tommy still looked as if he wanted to toss her to the monster himself. His amber eyes, full of anger and hurt, bored into hers, but she refused to back down.

"And what do you care, huh?"

"That is unfair, Tommy. Just because I was hurt doesn't mean I want him dead. Just because I didn't forgive him immediately doesn't mean I never will. You're being ridiculous."

Tommy's chest rose with a deep inhale before he spoke, his words barely more than a hiss. "Regardless, you haven't exactly shown the best judgment, Aoife."

Aoife flinched but stepped once more toward the desk and pressed her fisted knuckles onto its worn surface. "That may be, but you're the one whose judgment is being clouded by—"

"That's enough." It was Maura who interjected, looking from one to the other. "Both of you need to cool down before you throw away your friendship out of spite and bitterness."

She was right of course, though neither Aoife nor Tommy eased up, continuing to glower at each other. Aoife's heart raced, the blood rushing to her face. The sound of ragged, sharp breathing filled the cabin.

Aoife's mind bounced between thoughts and questions, tactics and possibilities. She was no strategist, and although she might have been naive, she was not stupid. Neither was Tommy, which made it all the more frustrating that he wouldn't listen, couldn't see it wasn't as black and white as he believed.

In her periphery, Aoife noticed Renna's head turn toward her. "That's not a bad idea, Aoife."

All attention shifted to the eldest fae.

Renna clarified for them all. "Aoife was just pondering why my sisters couldn't use their talents sparingly, not to their full power but just enough to give us an edge. It could be the best solution we have, allows us to benefit from their magic with less risk of pushing themselves too far."

"But there is still some risk," Tommy said.

Renna nodded. "Everything carries some risk. It's not perfect, but it's better than anything else anyone has offered."

Bria and Maura exchanged a glance before they both nodded and spoke in unison. "It could work."

Tommy's shoulders slumped, and his head fell forward as he leaned over the desk, defeated. Aoife nearly felt bad that she had pushed her friend so far on this, but Declan's face flashed in her mind. Yes, it was all her fault. All of it. But that was why she needed Tommy to make this decision, so she could have the chance to make everything right.

"Fine," Tommy said finally, the word barely audible to Aoife. He lifted his gaze to Maura, and even from the side, Aoife could see the intensity with which he looked at her. "We try it. But, Maura, if—" He stopped speaking as she touched his forearm lightly. A silent conversation seemed to happen between them then, and Tommy said nothing more.

Aoife let relief spread through her as she breathed deep. They would have a chance. Declan would have a chance. They weren't doomed. Everything would be okay.

Cait's feet ached more than they had in ages. She had been going nonstop all day even with the extra help from Adler at the
pub. Last call had been announced an hour earlier, and despite the
few men still nursing their drinks by the window, she slumped into
a chair at one of the tables and thudded her boots onto the one
opposite her as she closed her eyes and laid her head back.

It had been one of the busiest nights they'd had recently.
They'd served a somewhat even mix of pirates and locals, which
might have been interesting to Cait if she hadn't been so exhausted
from all the orders and the noise and the running around. Having
locals wasn't unusual in itself, but they typically visited in the early
hours after opening, leaving before most of the surlier patrons
began trickling in after dusk. But last night, the locals had not been
deterred. And many of the parties had stayed well into the night,
with more women coming in after supper, their husbands or other

male companions in tow.

"So, when do you normally kick out the stragglers?" a hot breath muttered in her ear, and Cait snapped her eyes open to find Adler standing much closer than was proper in public.

Sitting up straight, she placed her feet back on the floor, ignoring how they protested, and turned her chin toward the window and the pirates quietly chattering away between sips of rum.

"Hey!" she called over to them. "Manny! Will! Gus! Five minutes before I take back whatever you haven't downed and kick you out on your asses!"

The three men lifted their faces and glanced around the now empty pub before finding Cait. Two of them threw back the last dregs of their glasses, while the third, Will, gave her a nod and muttered an apology, his gaze flitting between Cait and Adler before he too finished off his drink.

Cait couldn't help but laugh. "I said five minutes, not seconds. You had some time left."

They all stood, and it was Manny who provided an explanation. "Aye, Cait, but we know as well as you do how we lose track of time, and we prefer to walk out the door of our own volition rather than being tossed."

"You mean kicked," Adler said, correcting him. Cait turned to glare at him for the ridiculousness of his statement, but Manny only laughed.

"Right, right. Kicked. That's far worse for our reputations," he said as he shoved his companions toward the door, each of them offering their goodbyes and thanks as they stumbled over the threshold.

When Cait settled herself back into a relaxed posture, Adler walked around toward the door but stopped before reaching it. "Do you not need to lock it?"

A breath, tired and slow, seeped from her lungs, and she answered with her eyes once again closed. "With what? There are no locks in Morshan. Or anywhere on Cregah, except perhaps in the council hall." She opened one eye and peeked at him. "I'm surprised an astute pirate such as yourself wouldn't know that already."

She watched him scratch his bearded jaw a few times as he pondered the information before going back to resting her eyes. She could have sighed with contentment at the sheer luxury of being able to put her feet up, but when her new employee still hadn't spoken, she said, "Sit, Adler, and stop thinking so hard. Let's relish this first successful night of your anonymous employment here."

Heavy, tired footsteps moved closer, and a chair scooted across the wooden floor. A deep exhale filled the air as the chair creaked under the weight of the massive man dropping into it. Still, he didn't speak.

Cait soaked up the silence, but after several minutes had passed and she remembered she was not sitting here alone as she normally did, she turned her attention to him once more. He was staring blankly at the table before him, hands in his lap. Not tired. Not worried. Not happy. Just empty, cold, dead. She regretted the question even before it left her mouth, but the silence that had been comfortable seconds before was becoming prickly and tense.

"What are you thinking?" she asked.

He didn't look up from the table but only shook his head a couple of times. "Nothing."

"Doesn't look like nothing," she countered, even as her mind told her that was exactly what his features showed. Nothing.

"Well, nothing that can be remedied anyway." After a few more minutes, his blue eyes lifted, but he remained stoic and unreadable.

Come on, Cait, it's not that hard to figure this out. He just lost his love, the one he was going to run away with to start a new life.

"Well, you did a good job tonight."

A slight sparkle shone in his eyes at her words, and one corner of his mouth quirked up. "Was that a compliment, love?"

She rolled her eyes. "Don't let it go to your head."

His smirk shifted into a true smile, and Cait wondered how she hadn't noticed before how his dimples peeked through his beard when he did so. Something sparked inside her against her will, like a flash of a faded dream or a hope long since tossed aside and ignored but not forgotten.

"And what are you thinking?" He hiked a brow as he turned the question back on her.

"Oh," Cait started as she glanced toward the bar. She could almost catch a glimpse of her mother and father there cleaning up after a long night, laughing and teasing and tickling one another. With a blink, the memory was gone, replaced by the sight of glasses needing to be cleaned and spills needing to be wiped up. "I don't know. Missed chances, I guess. Paths blocked. Futures upended. Dreams scattered."

"So, happy things then."

Cait's chest tightened, and silence filled the space between them. It had been so long since she'd let those thoughts out of their cage, and the shock of their sneaking up on her here, now, and in front of him, had caused her to be more honest with her answer than she'd intended. Such deep sentimentality felt out of place for the leader of a rebellion.

Some rebellion.

Nothing was going as planned, and Cait ground her teeth to keep that truth from rising to the surface in the form of tears and a trembling chin. She'd already humiliated herself when he'd surprised her in the woods. She didn't need to give him any additional fodder.

But perhaps the tide was turning with his arrival and Maggie's death. The fire had been stoked and now burned even brighter than it had when she'd revived her parents' rebellion.

A rumble broke the silence as Adler cleared his throat. "So, am I to find Lucan's on my own? Or will—"

"He'll be by shortly to show you the way," she said, letting her head loll to the side so she could look at him. "And I expect you to not kill each other."

"What about a bit of maiming?" That smirk returned, and she reminded herself he wasn't that attractive when he did that.

"Just keep it minimal. I'd prefer limbs be intact if we're going to succeed with our plans."

Adler nodded, and the corners of his mouth turned down.

"But seriously," she said, "be nice."

"I'm always nice. It's him—"

The door opened, and a pair of boots thudded into the pub, accompanied by a bellowing voice. "Where's my new tenant? Is he ready to go at least?" Lucan seemed as annoyed as Adler was amused. With that obnoxious grin once again on his face, Adler flashed Cait a wink.

"Right here," Adler said. "And I'm ready as long as the boss doesn't need me to help with the cleanup." He rose to his feet, pushing his chair back under the table as he did so.

Lucan looked past Adler to Cait and, with a raised brow, asked, "Can he leave? I'd rather get this over with, but if you need—"

"No, go. It's surprisingly clean. Won't take me long to straighten up before I head to bed."

"Well, be sure to get some rest. You look like crap lately," Lucan said. His smile dimmed when Adler laughed at his poor attempt at humor. Waving a hand toward the door, Lucan indicated to Adler it was time to leave.

With three long strides, Adler was at the door, where he turned to flash another smile at Cait, this one smaller but more genuine, it seemed. "Good night, Cait."

Before she could respond, Lucan had shoved the larger pirate out the door and was offering her a lazy wave as he headed out into the street.

Silence once again enveloped Cait, and she allowed herself one more cleansing breath before she pushed to her feet—which screamed at her as she did. The pub wasn't going to clean itself.

She had barely made it behind the bar when a noise—subtle but noticeable—came from outside. Following the sound to the back door, she glided as quietly as she could past the stairs and beyond the storeroom. Her gut tightened at the memory of the last time she'd answered this door.

She inched the door open and peered out to see what was happening in the alley behind her pub.

A woman she'd never seen before, dressed in bright clothing that stood out conspicuously even in the dimly lit alley, was being pressed up against the pub's wall by two large hands Cait recognized.

"Adler. What are you doing?" Cait hissed as she rushed out to meet him. "Where's Lucan?"

"I'm here." Lucan's voice came from the other side of Adler at the same time his head became visible.

The woman made no sound. She didn't even struggle against Adler's grip. Both seemed odd, considering the situation.

"We found her slinking around. Followed her back here. Caught her trying to break into the pub," Adler explained.

"Is that true, Lucan?" Cait asked, cringing internally at her openly questioning Adler's story when she had claimed to trust him. Thankfully, Adler didn't seem bothered by it.

Lucan nodded. "Aye, that's what happened."

"Do you know her?" Adler asked, his eyes now shifting to meet Cait's.

Cait shook her head and addressed the woman. "Care to introduce yourself?"

"I'm looking for Captain McCallagh," she said, her thick accent a mix of several nations—Haviernese, Turvalan, a bit of a Foxhaven lilt. Possibly others Cait couldn't quite place.

Cait stepped closer as she asked, "What makes you think he'd be here?"

"Name on the sign. Lucky guess."

"We have a front door. Why try to enter through the back? And without invitation?" Nothing about this woman set Cait at ease. Her gut churned in warning.

"You were closed. Didn't want to get you in trouble with the council. And I wasn't trying to break in. I was going to knock." The woman's brown eyes wandered to the two men who had stopped her.

"Last I checked," Adler said, "knocking on a door didn't involve picking the lock with your hairpins."

Cait huffed a laugh, despite not finding any of this funny. "Perhaps they have a different method of knocking where she's from." She glanced at the woman again, brows raised in question.

"Foxhaven. And fine, I lied. You must be used to that with all your dealings with pirates."

Turning on her heel, Cait said, "Bring her inside. The alley is no place to talk."

Once inside, Lucan dragged a chair from the main room into the storeroom, and Adler promptly and firmly dropped the woman into it before securing her with a rope Cait handed him.

Lucan stifled a yawn, and Adler mirrored the move.

"You're both tired," Cait said. "Why don't you head on out and get some sleep. I can handle her."

Both men shook their head in unison, mouths tight, and Cait muttered a "fine" before turning back to their unexpected guest.

"Let's start easy. What's your name?"

"Could I get some water?" the woman asked.

"No. Answer the question."

"I'm parched."

This was going to be a long night.

"Not too parched apparently," Lucan muttered under his breath.

Cait repeated the command. "Name. Now."

With a roll of her eyes and an exaggerated breath, she answered, "Lucy."

"And you're a friend of Captain McCallagh's?" Cait was too tired to hide her skepticism. Declan had few friends, and they were all part of his crew.

A nod was all Lucy offered, causing one of her curls to fall loose from where she'd had them pinned atop her head.

"Why are you looking for him?"

"To apologize."

"That's a long way to travel for an apology. What did you do to him?"

"That's between me and Declan."

Cait's hand itched to slap the smugness out of this woman, but she managed to refrain. She was already taking a risk tying her to a damn chair in her storeroom.

"I believe it stopped being between the two of you when you attempted to break into my pub." Cait couldn't determine this woman's game, but every one of her internal alarms was sounding.

Lucy offered a lazy shrug. "Still, I prefer not to break a friend's confidence. I've already done too much."

They were getting nowhere, and it was clear Lucy had no intention of providing any information. While Cait had heard of pirates using extreme measures to force a captive to talk, she had no desire to do that here and now.

She stepped back. "Let her go."

"What?" Lucan asked, his eyes wide.

"You heard me."

Still, Lucan didn't budge, so Adler moved around him to loosen the bonds.

When Lucy was free, she stood and rubbed her wrists. "I'm assuming he's not here."

Cait shook her head. No benefit in lying about that. The woman could get that information easily enough.

"Very well then."

"You could leave him a note, if you wish," Cait offered.

Lucy breathed a laugh. "And have you read it? I think not. Better for me to wait around and stay."

"Well you can't stay here," Lucan said.

Cait placed a hand on her friend's arm, hoping to ease his frustration. "We can direct you to a boarding house, and once Captain McCallagh returns, we can send a message to you."

Lucy's lips pursed. She appeared to be mulling over the offer. Like she had any better options. Finally she clasped her hands together in front of her hips. "I appreciate that. Thank you."

"Lucan here will show you the way. It's not far."

If Lucan had an issue with this, he hid it well, thankfully. "This way," he said, offering Cait a tight-lipped smile as he passed, Lucy close behind. Once they were out, Adler moved to leave, but Cait grabbed his arm. He paused, looking down at where her hand tightly clasped his muscles, and smiled. Before he could make any remark about the close contact, she flashed him a stern look.

"Get word to Aron and Eva. We need to watch this Lucy woman. Find out what she's up to."

"Will do, love."

And he slipped out into the early morning darkness, leaving Cait to wonder what dealings Declan could possibly have had with that woman, and what infraction would drive her to take a three-day journey to make amends.

Assuming she's telling the truth.

No part of Cait thought she was.

25
DECLAN

Four times Killian's body was dragged under the *Curse Bringer*, and each time, the razor-like creatures clinging to it cut him apart a little more. No doubt Callum would have called for another pass, but finally his men hauled up remains that were totally un-recognizable as human.

"Let him loose!" Callum said, and his men quickly cut the lines from what was left of Killian's limbs before discarding his remains over the port rail as if they were leftovers from a meal going into the garbage. Turning to Dominic, Callum said in a low his voice, "Have the deck cleaned, and tell Pepperwood to get us underway. Then I might need your help with this one."

With that, Callum snatched up Declan's arm and pulled him past the crew, which had begun to disperse and head back to the barracks or to the jobs Dominic and the bo'sun doled out. Declan assumed he'd be led back to the brig but then remembered what the crewman had said about Callum never stooping so low as to go there himself.

"Get in there," Callum growled as he shoved Declan through the open door and into his cabin. While the air was a tad stuffier in here, Declan appreciated the break from the noise and the closely packed bodies he'd endured out on the deck.

"You know," Declan said, trying to scratch behind his ear with his shoulder, "I didn't ask to be let out of the brig."

Callum pulled a bottle of rum from behind his desk and poured a hearty serving into a tin cup that was probably as clean as the man who used it. He took a long sip as he relaxed back against the edge of his desk.

"I do know." Callum stared into his cup as he swirled its contents. "You didn't have to follow him though."

"You and I both know that's not true." Declan shifted his weight, though it was impossible to find any comfortable position in these circumstances. "Hard for a pirate to turn down an invitation to a good fight."

Callum choked out a laugh into his mug. "You're such a poor excuse for a pirate, McCallagh. It's a wonder you managed to fool everyone on the Aisling into thinking you were someone to fear."

"All it takes is a few well-crafted stories—"

"Stories!" Callum laughed again, though it didn't reach his dark eyes. "You could have been great, Declan. You had such potential. When you got that first crew, you were… Let's just say, I was impressed. What you did to Susset and his crew? I didn't even know you, and I was proud. Such a young captain, already so dastardly. And those merchant vessels—"

"I was there, Callum. I remember." Declan might not be the good man Aoife thought he was—the good man she deserved—but that didn't mean he wanted to be some cruel villain either. A mere six months of heinous acts had been enough for him. It was Tommy who had suggested he could build the reputation without the deeds, and from then on, they'd relied on his past record and carefully and methodically relayed stories in pubs at different ports.

Callum clucked his tongue. "Do you though? Seems you've been out of this brutal game a bit too long."

"What do you mean?"

"I saw you when Killian first went over that rail." Callum's low laughter grated on Declan. "You looked like a youngster on his first sailing through a squall. Thankfully we hadn't fed you enough to allow for you to make too much of a mess had you not been able to control it."

The door behind him opened and closed, but Declan didn't bother to turn.

"So, keelhauling. Your crew seems right familiar with it. Is that what passes for entertainment on your ship?" Declan asked.

His question was answered with an elbow to the center of his back. Declan fell forward but remained standing. A couple of well-placed kicks to the backs of his legs caused his knees to buckle before slamming onto the wooden floor.

You're losing your touch, McCallagh.

He looked up to see Callum sneering down at him. The man's eyes raged, but Declan refused to look away.

"That's a no then?" Declan asked. "Or a yes? I'm sorry, I didn't quite catch the answer."

The other man moved to hit him, but Callum's voice stopped his arm in midair. "Dom, that's enough." It wasn't barked or bellowed as his commands had been on the deck. This calm, casual tone was more intimidating, like the hiss of a snake before it struck.

Stepping away from the desk, Callum lowered himself until he was kneeling, bringing that burning stare closer. "We will reach the sound by tomorrow night," he said, pausing to scratch his bearded jaw.

Had Declan miscalculated? Had he lost a whole day while he was unconscious below decks? While part of him insisted it didn't matter, another part knew if Callum had found some way to travel faster, it was unlikely Tommy would catch up to him in time. Even with Lord Roberts's interruption, they were still too far ahead.

"I need you to tell me how you intend to get past the sirens, McCallagh. No tricks. No surprises. I won't be going into that sound unawares."

Declan let out a small groan before responding. "I've already told you."

"Yes, I know. The fae. Magic. A bunch of hocus-pocus nonsense."

"Refusing to believe it doesn't make it any less true," Declan said, and for a moment he let himself ponder the truth of those words, how relevant they were to his life—a life he'd never get back now.

The back of a hand slammed into the side of his face, causing him to spit blood.

"You will tell me," Callum growled again as he punched the wooden floor.

Declan worked the ache out of his jaw—to no avail—and peered at Callum from the corner of his eye. "Contrary to what you might think, hitting inanimate objects—or even hitting me— won't get me to divulge information *I don't have*." He stretched out the last three words for emphasis, but he could see, even from this angle, that it had little effect.

"You think I'm going to trust you after what you did?"

Declan turned fully to Callum now with eyes wide. "So we're going to play this little game again? You hit me. I tell you the same thing. And round and round we go. You know, it's really a shame you don't listen. Or is it that you simply can't comprehend the words that are coming out of my mouth?"

Callum let him prattle on for far longer than expected, and it wasn't a punch or a kick that got Declan to stop talking. Instead, Callum stood and walked away. Declan risked a look up to see the pirate settling into his chair. He gave a nod, and Dominic had Declan standing in an instant, his hands gripping his arms like a vice.

"What do you know of the sirens, Declan?"

The cordiality of Callum's question caught Declan off guard as much as the question itself did.

"If this is going to be a long conversation, might I request a chair? I'm rather fatigued after saving your life and all."

To Declan's surprise, the quartermaster didn't pummel him for his disrespect, instead placing a simple wooden chair behind him. The man's hands yanked him down into it with more force than necessary.

"Thank you," Declan said, smiling over his shoulder. "You are most hospitable, Dominic."

Dominic snickered.

"I see your tongue isn't fatigued," Callum said.

"It's been a long while since I've found someone who could meet that challenge."

Callum huffed out a breath but otherwise ignored the comment. "The sirens. You obviously know about them, or you wouldn't be so scared."

"You obviously don't, or you would be."

"Fear is a pirate's downfall."

"I find blades to be more so, but we can agree to disagree."

Pressing his elbows against the top of the desk, Callum leaned forward and spoke around his fisted hands. "What do you know?"

Declan leaned back and drew in a deep breath. He wasn't sure where this would lead or how his knowledge of the sirens could help them survive, but what other choice did he have?

"Same as everyone else, I suppose. Sirens are bad. They live in the sound. Don't go there."

Callum didn't react to his ridiculous answer other than to drop his head to the side and continue to stare at him. For a moment Declan wondered who could maintain the silence the longest, but he gathered that any attempt on his part to do so would result in another visit from Dominic's fist.

"The sirens are ancient creatures. Some say they predate the fae in this region, though who can really know for sure. They're confined to one area of the sea—the Black Sound—thanks to some curse placed on them that prevents their leaving."

"And you know what they do, I take it? Since you are so afraid."

"They kill," Declan said.

"How?"

He took another long breath. Not because this topic was at all difficult to discuss—though he wasn't particularly looking forward to meeting those creatures—but because the longer he remained here chatting, the less time he had to spend in that dank hole below decks.

"In short? They eat people. And from what the legend says, it's not all that fun. For the people. I wouldn't know how it is for the sirens themselves. Now, I don't know if this part is true or if it is some wild fable someone concocted to keep people loyal, but supposedly the sirens have quite the taste for the despicable souls. And not just any type of despicable, but the betrayers. Those who made promises only to break them. Whether it's true or not has no bearing on us though, as they'll kill us regardless. But a betrayer?

They are the delicacy the sirens crave."

Callum was slowly nodding. He seemed to be contemplating all that had been relayed, though Declan had no doubt it was nothing the captain wasn't privy to already.

"You know your legends. At least that wasn't a ruse. But I do believe you're missing a piece of the story."

"They are immortal, ancient, and bloodthirsty, with a magic of their own. And they have the Csintala dagger. What more is there to know?" Declan asked, hoping his acting skills hadn't been hurt by his poor treatment aboard this ship and that Callum would buy that he knew nothing more. He might have been stupid enough to get captured, but he wasn't about to divulge information needlessly. Even if it might earn him the same treatment as Killian.

"Much more, in fact," Callum said. "And while it may not be pertinent to our plans of retrieving the dagger, one would be a fool to not understand the enemy as well as he could. You're right about their taste for betrayers, to a point. It goes beyond that. They feast on pain. Not just any pain, but the type that scars your heart and burns your soul. The type that can't be remedied with trite words."

"I didn't know you had such a way with words," Declan said, if for no other reason than to lighten the mood and perhaps distract himself from the rather personal way Callum's words bothered him. But Callum continued as if he hadn't said anything.

"Some betrayals are nearly impossible to forgive, and the pain from having forgiveness withheld? Well, I don't need to explain that to you, do I?"

Declan froze, unable to swallow and struggling to breathe. His brow wrinkled against his will, and Callum took advantage of the tell.

"Hard to hide. Even from me. Will be impossible to hide it from the sirens."

Steadying himself with a long, slow breath, Declan refocused on his host. "What you're saying, then, is what I've been saying all along. We're doomed."

Callum angled his head, clicking his tongue before his lips turned up into a cunning grin. "You mean *you're* doomed. Your brooding soul provides quite the distraction."

"Why did you—"

"You really must have a low opinion of me, McCallagh, if you haven't pieced this together by now."

Callum was right, of course, but it didn't make Declan's head hurt any less or his thoughts become any less jumbled. He winced as the throbbing returned at his temples.

"As much as I enjoy watching you struggle," Callum said, "this conversation has dragged on far longer than intended." With a quick word, he sent Dominic away to get a status update from the helmsman and the bo'sun. Something about this move piqued Declan's interest. This gruff captain could have had Declan thrown back below, could have had his quartermaster do that on his way to carry out the other orders, but he'd allowed Declan to remain here.

He debated whether to play the sincerity card, set the conversation up so Callum would divulge whatever was on his mind without reservation, or go with his usual tactic of poking him until he was so agitated he let information slip by accident. The latter would have won out had Callum not broken the silence first.

"You are actually quite good at hiding your baggage, Declan, behind the irritating words and the forced cynicism."

"I wouldn't say it's forced."

"Most wouldn't recognize this pain you bear, but..." Callum's attention fell to where his hands were folded atop his desk, his thumbs moving around and around each other in lazy circles. A wave of grief flashed across his features, darkening them before his face hardened once more into its usual indifferent mask.

"You've experienced this." Declan didn't bother making it a question. The change in Callum might have been brief, there and gone in the matter of a breath, but Declan had no doubt what it indicated, because it was the same grief he had experienced after Aoife left him in the sand.

Callum gave a nod, his dark eyes hardening into stone. "But I wasn't as stupid as you."

"That's not very nice of you to say."

"I told you as much last week on your ship. I can't be faulted for your refusal to heed my advice, for you falling for the girl."

Declan started to protest, but Callum raised a hand to stop him before he could even utter a sound.

"And that falling is going to get you killed."

"You mean eaten." He tried to find the humor in those words, at the absurdity of such a fate, but the sense of dread pressing down on him remained. "Seems to your advantage though."

"Oh, indeed. I'm not complaining about my good fortune. I simply thought you should know, as you face your own demise, that you could have avoided this. It was all within your power. Betrayal paired with love? It'll get you killed one way or another."

But Declan hadn't wanted this, had actively tried to avoid it. He hadn't wanted to grow close to her. He hadn't wanted to need her help. Perhaps Callum was right though. He could have denied her passage. He could have tossed her into the sea. He could have found another way to retrieve the fae.

"Unfortunately," Callum said, "it is much too late to undo it now. Love has that way about it, much like a siren in that sense. Preying on the weak, the desperate, the hurting. It offers you warmth. It promises all that you seek, but it lies to you with visions of a future that cannot exist."

"It can exist." Declan hadn't meant to say the words aloud, and he mentally kicked himself for slipping up. This conversation was getting to him, as Callum likely intended.

Callum narrowed his eyes. "When did you become such an optimist? I would have thought you'd know better by now that all good things rot in this world. Either by an external force taking a life—or two lives as happened with your parents—or by our inner demons hurting those we believe we love. It all falls apart. It all decays. It all festers and fails."

Images flashed in Declan's mind. His mother being dragged away into the fog. His father's body lying motionless and cold on the cobblestones. Aoife backing away from him in the cove.

Declan cleared his throat and straightened his back against the chair in a poor attempt to ease away a knot that had formed below his ribs. "You certainly know how to give a motivational speech. I'll give you that. No wonder your crew is so disciplined and successful."

Callum leaned forward. "Joke all you want. Hope won't save you in the end, not when you look into the eyes of the siren queen and she drags all mistakes from these dark depths." He tapped a finger to his own chest. "Your hope will die in that sound right along with your body."

"And hopefully it takes long enough for you to snag the dagger away from them."

With a nod, Callum stood and walked around his desk. Lifting Declan out of the chair, he pushed him back through the door and called for the oaf, Reggie. As Declan stumbled back down through the bowels of the ship to his accommodations, he couldn't set aside Callum's words.

Was hope truly a fool's mistress?

There are worse mistresses to entertain.

26

TOMMY

Tommy hated this plan, hated the risk it posed, hated the position he was in and the decisions he had to make. But fretting over it did them no good either. So desperate to find an alternative, he had almost gone along with Gavin's joke about inviting the kraken for a drink and getting it so intoxicated on rum it would retreat to sleep it off.

Unfortunately, getting a kraken drunk was as unlikely to work as getting through the waters unseen on their own. Yet, he had still not been able to stomach allowing Maura to be put in such danger. While he'd turned down her advances, he'd never denied his feelings for her, and if he couldn't devote himself to her in the way she desired and deserved, he wanted to at least ensure her safety.

But Aoife was right.

If they continued on at this slow pace, they'd never reach Declan in time. And if they risked going much faster without any precautionary measures from Maura and her sister, they would most certainly alert the monster to their presence and find themselves worse off.

This will work. This has to work.

The breeze picked up, filling the sails so they billowed smoothly, soundlessly. To Bria's credit, the ship didn't jerk forward but glided along with ease, as if it were being moved along by the water itself rather than the wind.

Gavin let out a sigh and seemed to relax his grip on the helm, his knuckles returning to their normal coloring. Smiling tentatively, Gavin gave Tommy a nod to let him know they were good.

So far.

Around the deck the crew stood still, more silent than they were even when asleep. Some moved to tend to the lines as they sailed, careful to keep their steps as light as possible. Others maintained a watchful eye on the teal waters, which lay eerily still, showing no indication that a monster of nightmares and legends lurked below.

No sign of it.

No sign of anything, actually.

The water stretched out to the horizon, smooth as glass, unsettlingly still this far from land.

Tommy turned slowly to study the water all around. When he turned to the aft side, though, he stopped short at the sight of Bria and Maura standing together, eyes closed, leaning against the rail more casually than he had expected.

They looked as though they were relaxing on holiday and soaking up the afternoon sunlight, not tapping into invisible powers to thwart a beast. On closer inspection, though, he noticed their faces were far from relaxed. Their jaws were tense, their temples pulsing. While their elbows hung loose by their ribs, their hands gripped the railing as if that was the conduit their magic used.

From this vantage point, Tommy couldn't tell if Maura's glamour was in place, and for a moment he worried she'd already used too much of her power while healing him and didn't have enough to carry out this plan. The wind was eerily quiet even as it moved them through the water at an unimaginable speed, and in that near silence Tommy heard a gasp as Aoife leaned over the railing beside Maura.

He rushed over as fast as he could, his hand ready to draw his cutlass quickly if needed. But when he joined her in looking over, he nearly gasped as well.

It was one thing to know what a glamour was in theory, but seeing it in practice was extraordinary. He blinked once to ensure he wasn't imagining what he saw below them, but the illusion remained. Below the row of windows, the ship simply disappeared, and only teal water, smooth and unmoving, lay below them. There were no ripples in the sea betraying their movement, and the *Siren's Song* made no shadow on the water.

Tommy might have laughed at the sight had the situation not been so dire. Aoife's elbow knocked into his, and he turned to see his friend's tentative smile. It conveyed both triumph and worry. Tommy could understand the dichotomy, as it warred within him as well. Though he wanted to return her positivity, something kept him from giving himself fully over to the hope that had sparked with this first victory.

"It's a good start," he whispered to her, risking a glance at Maura before walking away.

For the next two hours he crisscrossed the quarterdeck, monitoring the sisters as they worked and checking in with Gavin to see how the *Siren's Song* was progressing. Aoife remained beside Maura, her hand never leaving the dagger at her belt. A hint of hope remained in her eyes long after her lips had grown tired of holding her smile. As Tommy settled himself once again beside Gavin, this time facing away from their heading, his attention fell firmly on Maura, who had not shown any sign of fatigue since they'd started.

"You're wrong," Renna whispered as she stepped up beside him.

"About what?" He hoped Renna hadn't tapped into her magic to pry into his thoughts. There were a number of things she could be speaking to.

"You and her." She turned her chin toward him, her vibrant blue eyes as warm and friendly as his mother's had been. Or his sister's. "You can never be."

All the warmth drained from Tommy's face, and bitter hopelessness returned. He tried to ignore it, blink it away.

"That's what I've told her," he said.

"But your mind is shifting now." A statement, matter-of-fact. There was no hint of doubt in the fae's tone, and the certainty she displayed sent a shiver through him.

He didn't bother to ask her how she knew—by reading it on his face or pulling it from his thoughts. Either way, there was no point in denying it.

Renna spoke once more. "What changed? Why now?"

"Don't you already know?"

"I try not to listen in for longer than needed. I much prefer to gather information from willing parties."

"Didn't seem to stop you from invading my thoughts earlier." He hadn't intended for it to sound like such a challenge, but stress had taken its toll on his self-control.

A soundless laugh escaped her before she smiled at him. "Fair. Though, it doesn't take magic to see how you look at my sister." If she held any disapproval, it didn't show. She almost appeared sympathetic to his plight.

"You don't seem surprised."

"Oh, I knew well before you did. You were unconscious a good while as we worked to heal you. It was not difficult to sense that emotional bond weaving its way between you."

"But if we have some irresistible bond—"

"I never said it was irresistible."

"That's not true—fae bonds and soul mates?"

Another hushed laugh escaped her lips. "I suppose I can understand how that falsehood came to be. Fae pairings must appear as such from those looking in. But no, it is not true. There is no otherworldly power at play here, not beyond the very normal, common yet mysterious phenomenon we call love. But for fae, all our senses are heightened. Our emotions—just like our strength, grace, beauty—are magnified." She turned back to look at Maura, who was still focused on maintaining the protective glamour. "So yes, she's intense and persistent, because for her this tie between you runs deeper than the Aisling."

He looked back at Maura, the brown waves of her hair blowing in the breeze behind her. He didn't take his eyes from her as he repeated Renna's earlier words. "But we can never be."

"Unfortunately, no. She is needed in Larcsporough, as is Bria. As am I." Before Tommy could interject, she added, "And what is expected of her—of the three of us—leaves no place for you in her life. You must understand. Our kin need us. A war has been brewing while we rotted away in those quarters, and they need us to help stop it."

"She knows this?"

A nod preceded her next words. "And she was ready and willing to step into her role. Until you."

Tommy's gut twisted around those last words. *Until you.* He had known any future together was unlikely, and he had known about the fae's plans to travel south after the dagger business was completed. But Maura had never told him her presence was required.

"What is her role in Larcsporough exactly?" He asked the question not quite knowing if he wanted the answer.

"Same as mine. Same as—"

Before Renna could finish, the sound Tommy had feared cut her short. His feet had him at Maura's side in a few paces, his knees hitting the wood hard, though no pain registered.

"Maura!"

Tommy should have kept his voice low, but the sight of her body crumpled on the ground drew her name from his lungs with such force there was no controlling it. Lifting her body gently, he pulled her to him, brushing long strands of hair back from her face.

In his periphery he could see Bria still standing.

Why had Maura collapsed?

The question swirled around his mind as he searched her face. Her eyes remained closed. Her breath came in short, shallow gasps.

"Maura, can you hear me?" His voice sounded odd to his ears, like someone else was calling her name. Like someone else's hand was cupping her face and stroking her cheek. This wasn't supposed to happen. She shouldn't have even been close to her limit. Had she broken her promise and pushed herself too far?

Glancing up quickly, he found Aoife watching them in icy silence, her mouth gaping behind shaking fingers.

"Aoife, water. Now," Tommy said. Aoife blinked away whatever shock had held her in place and, with a string of nods, stormed down the stairs.

Renna knelt beside him and, wrapping a hand around Maura's wrist, let out a breath that sounded almost relieved.

"She is okay."

"How can you say that?" Tommy asked, unable to control his nerves.

"Because she is."

"But—"

Renna gently pried Maura away from him, and though she offered a small smile, Tommy was far from reassured. "She just needs rest."

"Did she—will she—"

Renna's face hardened, but a moment later warmth shone in her eyes once again. "Not burned out. She collapsed because she gave in to the fatigue rather than pushing past it. Had she forced her magic to continue beyond that, then..."

"We need to get her to the captain's cabin," he said as they stood, but when he moved to help carry her, Renna stopped him.

"I will get her there. I'm more than capable. But right now, you need to stay here. You need to be ready."

She was right, of course, but it didn't make it any easier for Tommy to watch Maura, unconscious and limp as a ragdoll, be dragged away.

She'll be okay. She is okay.

Though he repeated the words to himself, it did nothing to quell the sense of doom that grew within him. He looked to Bria, half-expecting to see her ready to collapse onto the deck as well. But she stood as strong as she had for the last couple of hours, as if summoning wind and pushing them through the water was no feat at all.

He had only made it a half-turn toward Gavin when he noticed a handful of the men leaning over the port-side rail. He assumed they were merely observing the lack of glamour hiding the hull of the ship beneath them, but then they began to back away.

Slowly, quietly, they moved toward the center of the deck.

"What are they—" Gavin started to ask as Tommy came up beside him.

Tommy waited. One breath. Two. Nothing. He saw nothing beyond the rail but smooth water.

But the color was shifting. Looking to the sky, he checked for the cloud that must be passing by the sun, casting a shadow. It wasn't there. Nothing but blue stretched out above him, and he snapped his attention back to the sea.

A black shadow spread across the water—no, through the water. Tommy turned to the starboard side. There, too, the Aisling was darkening, as if a giant had emptied a bottle of ink into the sea.

"That's not good," Gavin said.

"At the ready, men!" Tommy yelled to the crew below him and joined them in drawing his cutlass. "Gavin, you keep us steady as best you can, but be ready to maneuver as needed when the beast attacks. And it will."

Behind him he heard Mikkel speaking words of encouragement to the crew. Such was the man's way with the crew before a skirmish, bolstering their courage like a beloved general of some army rather than a humble bo'sun on a pirate vessel.

Tommy rushed back to Bria, whose eyes hadn't opened despite all the commotion around her. Should she be told what had happened? Should he risk disturbing her concentration in order to tell her about Maura?

Before he could decide, the first scream came.

Aoife helped Renna ease Maura onto Declan's bed, but when she moved to pull a blanket over her, the older fae stopped her with a light touch on her arm.

"She needs the air."

She thought it an odd requirement, though Aoife was far from an expert on fae anything. Maura hadn't felt feverish at all, and a casual observer might have thought she was simply taking an afternoon nap. Her complexion remained flawless. Her hair showed no signs of having been in the sea air for hours. Nothing external gave any indication that Maura was ailing at all.

Aoife started to inquire as to what else the unconscious fae might need to aid in her recovery, but instead of her own whispered voice, a scream, full of agony and surprise, came from outside.

Renna was out the cabin door before Aoife managed to get to the main room. Pulling her dagger out, her heart thumping deep in her chest, she rushed out onto the deck without hesitation.

And stopped.

She could have had a whole year to train with Collins—a lifetime—and she still would not have been prepared for what she found.

On both sides of the ship, snake-like creatures—black and gray, mottled with no visible head, and near-translucent discs on their bellies—writhed in the air, threatening to crush the ship as it came closer.

Not snakes! Why would you think snakes?!

Of course these were the deadly limbs of the kraken. Either way, she froze, unsure how two days of practice and a puny blade would be of any help to the crew and to her friends. To Declan.

Aoife looked around but found no sign of Renna. She must have gone up to the quarterdeck to aid Bria. A glance at the sails, which were full and taut, proved Bria still had control of the wind, though it didn't seem useful now, as the monster clearly had them in its grasp.

A clatter of cracking wood mixed with groans and shouts, and she looked over in time to see an arm sweeping across the deck toward her. At the last moment she jumped back out of its reach, but her feet slipped on the water the creature had brought on board. She fell hard on her backside.

It was utter mayhem on deck. Aoife's attention flitted around the scene as she tried to make sense of it all. Above her head on the mainmast, a young crewman clung to the ship's rigging. Aoife marveled at how the man was able to signal to the men below without falling.

The floor beneath her rumbled with a loud explosion. The cannons. A long shot, but at least they were trying them. Several more booms followed, but the creature's arms—flinching from the few cannonballs that made contact—kept returning to the deck, knocking men into the water. One wrapped itself around a crewman and hauled him into the air before slamming him down against the rail of the ship, impaling him on a sharp point where the wood had splintered.

All around the deck, pirates were reacting and taking different positions. Some were cowering against the wall near her, some were lying on the ground, groaning from the blows they'd taken from the monster. Others did their best to fight back, swiping and stabbing at the massive arms whenever they came near.

A scream—of attack, not pain—snapped her attention back to the starboard side, where a chunk of railing was missing. Blood and seawater were washing across the deck. A man lunged toward the creature, cutlass drawn, his face a frightening display of fury.

Collins.

Aoife held her breath, unable to look away as this pirate—her friend—charged toward his inevitable demise. But just before the hideous arm moved away, Collins leaped into the air, his cutlass held high above his head, its curved edge pointing down toward its target.

The scene slowed before Aoife's eyes.

Collins screaming.

Kraken sweeping.

Cutlass piercing the fleshy limb.

Collins hovering in the air by the grip of his cutlass, which was stuck fast in the still-moving arm.

Aoife's muscles moved on their own, lifting her up to her feet and sending her barreling toward Collins. She ran through the techniques he'd taught her, adjusted her grip on her dagger, and flung herself forward. With a less than graceful hop over a fallen pirate, she managed to remain upright as she came within striking distance.

"Now!" Collins bellowed from his perch above her head.

As she had done repeatedly during their practice sessions, she mimicked the movements he'd displayed and drove her dagger forward. But the blade simply slid along the tough skin, and she flew forward, slamming her elbows and knees onto the deck.

"Aoife!" The pirate yelled her name, prompting her to turn around, but she had no time—wouldn't have even if she hadn't been partially winded—to strike again before the limb swept back out to sea, taking the cutlass and Collins with it.

"No!" Aoife screamed. "Collins!" As if the creature would hear her pleas and bring her friend back.

She had nearly reached the shattered railing when a body came flying at her. Ducking, she barely missed having her head removed by the projectile but still managed to spin around to inspect the person who had been thrown back on deck.

Crawling along, ignoring how her hands turned light red from the watery, bloody mixture covering the ship, she reached the man and recognized the cutlass still in his hand.

"Collins," she said, giving his shoulder a shake. She couldn't tell if he was breathing; her eyes were unable to focus with how the kraken's arms rocked the ship. Bile threatened to rise, but she forced it back down with desperate effort. She needed to wake her friend. Needed him to not be dead. Needed him to be okay.

This route hadn't been anyone's ideal choice, and everyone had known the risks involved, but that did little to quiet the guilt that had taken up permanent residence inside her.

"Collins. Please!" Aoife gave one last cry, but the man lay silent and still. Tears welled, and for a moment she forgot about the battle taking place around her. Collins had been the one to first see her on the ship, the one to take her to Declan, the one who wasn't afraid of her bad luck—though perhaps he should have been.

"Aoife." A familiar voice cut through the noise around her, and she looked up to see Tommy approaching. He dropped to his knees. Within seconds, he had his arms underneath his crewman and was standing, cradling the tall pirate as a mother would her baby.

"He tried to attack—" Aoife shouted the words at Tommy's back as she followed him to the officers' cabin. Once inside the small room, Aoife stood frozen in the doorway, unable to move as Tommy laid the man onto the bunk Aoife had slept in just last night.

"Is he—"

"No," Tommy said, turning a chin toward her before ensuring his friend was secure and safe. For now. "He's just knocked unconscious."

"How can you be sure? He wasn't moving. He wasn't—"

"He's breathing, Aoife. That's all we can hope for right now."

Aoife shook her head, still unable to see what sign of life she had missed.

"Trust me. He's fine," Tommy said, but the corner of his lips twitched. Quickly he moved toward her and the door. "We need to go."

Aoife pivoted out of his way. "But what do we do? What can I possibly do?" She held up her sad blade as if it was nothing more than a spoon. It might as well have been with how little it had done against the kraken.

Tommy's eyes shone with a haunting mix of determination, fear, worry, and anger. "We fight, Aoife. You fight. Until someone wins, you fight."

Before she could say anything more, he was back out on the deck, brandishing his cutlass and dagger as he ran forward to do just as he had commanded.

Focus on the next task, Aoife. Fight. Fight until someone wins.

Sands, she hoped that someone was them.

28

CAIT

Despite being exhausted, Cait couldn't sleep. And not because of Lucy's bizarre appearance.

She'd fallen onto her bed, too tired to even remove her boots, but the few hours of sleep she'd managed to get had brought painful memories and equally disturbing images of what could happen in the future—or was happening at this moment while she slept. She kept her eyes closed, though her mind was far from quiet, and she had been awake for the past several hours. But even all these years later, this apartment—different yet uncomfortably unchanged—reminded her too much of her previous life. A life with family and love and laughter.

And innocence.

Back then she hadn't known—hadn't had any suspicion at all—that her comfortable life on Cregah was a farce, a life made possible only because of the pride and greed of the council.

If only her parents had trusted her back then, before they died. She would have been able to ask them all the questions that had been swirling around her head since first discovering the secret passage and underground office.

How had her parents known about the council's corruption? Why hadn't they acted sooner? What had happened that caused the council to take action against them? And why hadn't the council come for her? And how could she ever hope to finish what her parents had started?

Hope or not, you have to at least try.

Through her closed lids, Cait could sense the late-morning sun streaming in through the window opposite her bed, but she could not urge her eyes to open yet. But avoiding the sight of her childhood home—even if she had purposefully moved furniture around and left the doors to the back bedrooms closed—wasn't enough to keep all the memories at bay.

Against her will, her mind floated from one to the next.

Her mother giving advice before her first meeting with the boy she was courting.

Her father's smile as he worked tirelessly at the pub.

The way they loved each other and their children.

Declan's laugh as he played around the pub tables after closing.

The look she caught her parents exchanging. A look of worry and fear.

That had been mere hours before they'd taken her mother, dragging her into the early morning mist, her father chasing after her. Not that Cait had seen it. She'd had to trust his and Declan's account, as she had been out that night.

Her father had not been able to catch up to the attackers. And as far as Cait knew, they'd never found her mother. Cait hadn't been able to process what had happened, and still now she wondered—as she had ever since—why her father hadn't trusted her enough to let her join the Rogues. She could have helped. Maybe then he'd still be alive, at least.

For several excruciating hours after her mother's disappearance, her family had barely spoken to one another, and Cait had been given nothing more than a single reassurance from her father that he would take care of it. To his credit, her father had played the dutiful pub worker well, while it had taken all of Cait's power to keep a smile on her face and make idle chatter with the patrons. But she'd forced herself to keep going, mimicking the way she had seen her mother act in this role.

But when those two pirates had walked in—the same pirates who had hauled away her mother—her father's expression had tightened, though he'd kept his smile in place. She'd known him well enough to tell when he was uncomfortable, even though she'd only seen it happen a handful of times over her sixteen years. The pirates had stayed until closing, drinking cup after cup of rum as they talked and laughed. Cait thought she remembered seeing them eying her father, laughing at his expense, but she wasn't sure.

Declan had remained oblivious to the tension pulsing through the pub as he sat on one of the stools, still and quiet, no longer the brother she had laughed and played with his whole life. Her breath had seemed trapped within her as she kept an eye on both the pirates and her father, hoping he wouldn't do anything stupid. It wasn't until the men threw some money onto the table and exited out onto the cobblestone street that she'd dared let her breathing return to normal.

But then she'd realized, too late, that her father had also left the pub. Somehow, as she'd been focused on those pirates, she had lost track of him. Before she'd been able to head to the back storage area to search for him, movement through the front window caught her attention.

A low curse had fallen from her mouth, alerting Declan that something was wrong. He'd slid off the stool and turned even before Cait could get around the bar. They'd both run for the door, too slow, pulling it open too late. Her father's feet were scrambling against the cobbles as he was dragged away by one of the pirates. The other pirate lay at Cait's feet, with a weapon she didn't recognize sticking out of his neck, his blood pooling around him.

Her father had killed one, and Cait couldn't stop Declan from seeing the body. He'd been too young to witness it. Even Cait hadn't known how to process all the blood and violence before her when her whole life was built around peace.

So many mistakes. So many regrets.

The rhythmic thud of boots on the stairs had Cait's eyes flashing open as she swung her legs off the bed and stood, grasping behind her back the small blade she kept under her pillow. The memories, too vivid and too fresh, made her mind race, and for a moment she assumed the worst possible scenario was happening now too. And although it was unlikely to be anyone from the council, she refused to be taken by surprise. Better to pull a blade on a friend than to be unarmed against a foe.

"Cait! You decent?" Lucan's familiar voice lacked its usual tinge of humor, and she could guess why.

Slipping the blade into her boot, she rushed to open the door as she worked to hide all traces of stress.

She swung the door open and leaned against the frame in a casual, almost bored, manner.

"Sleep well?" she asked. Lucan pushed past her in a huff.

There was no point in checking to see what he was doing. She'd seen him in this perturbed state more often than he'd ever admit despite that he always tried to be the lighthearted, carefree one.

Though he hadn't been that person since Adler showed up.

Raising a brow in question, she turned to Adler, who seemed relaxed as ever as he stood at the top of the stairs, arms crossed loosely before him.

"What?" he asked.

From behind her Lucan said, "He snores, that's what."

Oh, for crying out loud.

Adler gave a light shrug. "I might. I wouldn't know. I was asleep."

Lucan groaned and stomped back over to them. Leaning past Cait's shoulder, he pointed at the pirate, saying, "I don't believe that for a damn second."

Cait couldn't stop her eyes from rolling. She loved her friend, but he was acting like a baby. "Seriously, Lucan. I highly doubt that's the case."

He stepped back. "You weren't there."

Turning to him, she put her hands on her hips, the way her mother had done so many times when reprimanding her and Declan. "No, I wasn't there. I don't have time to babysit two supposedly grown men." She looked from one to the other. "Work it out."

Lucan opened his mouth, probably to protest, but Cait cut him off with a pointed glare.

"I mean it, Lucan. I don't know what's gotten into you, but you need to get it together. If we're going to succeed, you're going to have to deal. You aren't going to like everyone you have to work with, but we need all the help we can get. And you..." She spun back around to the pirate. "I don't know you well enough yet to know if you're being a pain in the ass on purpose or if it's just who you are, but try to get along. Without him, you would have been dispatched back in that forest. Now, are we done acting like toddlers?"

Adler nodded, and Lucan mumbled his agreement.

"Good," Cait said, though she remained on edge. If she couldn't sleep, she needed to at least take a few hours to relax if possible. And sands knew she needed these men to more than tolerate each other.

Trudging over to the chest of drawers under the window, Cait tried to work the tension out of her body, but it was as stubborn as Lucan. From the top drawer she pulled out a deck of cards, the edges of which were worn smooth from years of shuffling and handling.

"Please tell me one of you brought breakfast," she said as she settled herself at the small dining table in the corner. Why she'd kept all four chairs out for all these years, she couldn't say, but she was thankful for them now. With a nod, she invited the men to sit while she waited for an answer.

Lucan grimaced and mouthed an apology.

Adler's eyes widened with exaggerated innocence. "Don't look at me. I'm new here, remember?"

Cait ignored Lucan's unsubtle eye roll. This wasn't going to be fixed with nagging.

Shuffling the deck, she gave the men a relaxed shrug. "No worries. We can scrounge something up after a few hands."

"Cards, love?" Adler asked, propping his elbows on the table as his large hands worked the cracks out of his knuckles.

"Aye. I assume you've played," Cait said, beginning to deal. Lucan picked his up and shifted them around in his hand without a word.

A grin crept across Adler's face. "A bit."

"Familiar with Royal's Ruse?"

"Might be a bit rusty, but shouldn't take me long to freshen up. Now if you'd said Corks and Bones, you'd both be in trouble."

Lucan scoffed but otherwise remained silent as he took his first turn, picking up a card from the deck and tossing a nine onto the discard pile.

Looking at Cait over his cards, Adler asked, "Twos are wild?"

"For this hand, aye."

A short nod, and Adler played his turn. By the way his brows pinched, the card he'd picked up hadn't helped his hand.

"I see it's going well for you," Cait said with a smirk before taking her turn.

"Or is that just what I want you to think?" A wink capped off his question, and Cait shot a glance Lucan's way to see if his mood would sour more over it.

But her friend was staring out the window, his mind lost in some other place. She kicked him under the table.

"Your turn."

Lucan startled and moved to play his turn. With little emotion, he added a card to his hand and discarded another. And then his hand slammed onto the table.

"No! No way!" Cait yelled as she reached over to pull down Lucan's cards, which he relinquished to her with that smile she'd missed since Adler had shown up.

Adler tossed his own cards facedown onto the table and shot a nod at Lucan. "Fastest hand I've ever played, that's for sure."

Lucan pulled all the cards into his hands and shuffled them several times before dealing the next round. "Luck of the draw, that's all."

The next hand lasted decidedly longer, with Cait growling in mock frustration when Adler discarded a useless card for her and Lucan celebrating when she in turn dropped the card he needed.

But Adler ended up winning, and Cait was happy to see the two men starting to warm up to each other.

At least a little.

"Where you from, Lucan?" Adler asked as Cait pondered over her cards during their fourth round.

"Over the mountains."

"Miss it?"

Cait knew how she wanted to play, but with an actual conversation transpiring between them, she feigned focused deliberation to give them more time to talk.

"Sometimes. But then, what's there to miss about a life of starvation, sickness, and loss?" Again, Lucan delivered this answer with a tone far more level than would be expected.

Adler's hands lowered, his cards folding into them before he laid them on the table. Cait nearly mocked the man for accidentally placing them faceup when she noticed his mouth had fallen open in disbelief.

"What?" The single word fell from Adler with the weight of several kegs.

Lucan shifted his cards front to back, not making eye contact with either of them. Cait had only heard him speak about his past once. She'd made it clear he could always talk about it when he needed to, but she would never push.

He'd never taken her up on the offer, and she had kept her promise.

Now she watched her friend with curiosity. How would he answer? Would he shrug it off like he always did with the other Rogues? Or open up as he'd done with her so long ago?

"You don't know?" Lucan's eyes remained fixed on his cards, though he didn't seem to be focused on them.

"That a village on Cregah battled so much misfortune? No. I

didn't know," Adler said.

"Not just one village," Lucan clarified. He lowered his hands to his lap, letting them slip from view below the table. "Unfortunately."

"More than one?" Adler's brow creased again as it had at the start of the game.

"All of them," Cait and Lucan said in unison.

"I didn't know," Adler repeated, falling back against his chair with a loud exhale.

"No one does. No one beyond our coast, that is."

"How is that possible? How do they—" Understanding seemed to dawn on him, and he didn't finish his question. "Morshan is the only port. It's the only place anyone sees."

With a nod, Cait said, "The council only lets people know what they want them to."

Lucan moved forward. "And most people don't want to know."

"But—" Adler stopped short and snapped his attention to Cait. "So it's not just the exiles you hope to stop."

She shook her head.

"What happened to you? How'd you end up here?" Adler looked at Lucan once more, genuine concern on his face.

"Same as the others, I guess. Lost my family. Came to the council for help they refused to grant. Might have ended up exiled myself had Cait not found me when she did."

Adler, crossing his arms as he placed them on the table, leaned forward with a half-smirk, slowly revealing a single dimple within his beard. Even if Cait's instinct had pushed her away from trusting him, those damn dimples of his might have been enough to pull her firmly into his corner. When his eyes—those epically blue eyes, the color of the eastern sky at dusk—met hers once more, she tried to shoo away the internal flutters he'd triggered.

"Seems you saved us both, love."

Cait wanted to protest, insist she had only acted in self-interest. To cure her loneliness. To further her cause. But Lucan's words—spoken with that familiar and warm optimism she loved—filled the room before she could open her mouth. "She's saved more than us. And she'll save far more before she's done."

She wanted to be encouraged by the smile Lucan beamed at her, wanted to believe in herself as he did, but even with all the confidence she put on display for everyone, she so often felt like that lonely and confused teenage girl who had lost her parents and failed her brother.

Now with Adler and Lucan both looking at her with admiration—admiration she didn't deserve—she needed air, needed space.

"I'll be right back. Keep playing without me," she said, pushing out her chair. As she shut the apartment door behind her, she heard Lucan mutter something about her exit being a lame excuse to force them to become friends.

She didn't care what they assumed about her motives and actions. Her boots thumped down the stairs loudly. At the bottom, she gave one look at the rum behind the bar that seemed to be calling her name but then shook the idea away. Rum was well and good until it became your only friend. Her stomach growled, nudging her toward the kitchen behind the storeroom. The pub didn't serve food, and this small kitchen wouldn't have been able to support that service even if they tried; it was only large enough to prepare meals for a small family.

Rushing to the shelves, she absentmindedly pulled out a large frying pan, several eggs, and some cured meat. Vegetables and fruit were scarce these days, and she wasn't slated to get another ration of them for another couple of weeks. It was a marvel she and

Lucan had managed to stave off illness with how imbalanced their diet was.

As she cooked their breakfast, an image of Lucan's confident smile came back to the forefront of her mind. She had panicked over a damned smile. It had been a long time since she'd had such a reaction, and it wasn't as if Lucan—or the rest of the Rogues—hadn't shown appreciation for her before. But this time, the heartfelt look he'd given her, in combination with his words about her saving everyone, had been altogether too much.

Everyone needed her to be strong, to run the pub, to keep life going. And sometimes she spent so much energy portraying that strength to the world, she had none left over for herself. Like a pitcher of water poured into everyone's glasses over and over, day after day, glass after glass, with no drop left to satisfy her own needs.

How had her mother done this? Cait often asked herself this, seeking some answer in her memories. Although, even if her mother had suffered similarly, her younger self likely wouldn't have recognized the signs.

The memories always reminded her of one thing: her mother had done all of this with a loving husband beside her.

Cait had wanted a love like theirs, even as she had dreamed of traveling the sea and having her own adventures; she always imagined a new life with a love of her own beside her.

"Find a man who cares for you but also trusts you, Cait. Find a man who has your back as much as you have his, a man who would follow you into the siren's lair and never leave your side."

"You've said this so many times," Cait said, *exaggerating the roll of her eyes she loved to annoy her mother with.*

Her mother brushed a strand of hair away from Cait's forehead, tucking it behind her ear. "I know, sweet girl. I know. I say it all the time, because it is so important in this life to give your heart to someone who will care for it as if it were their own."

Cait raised a brow. *"It's only our first date."*

Her mother let out a laugh that felt like a warm hug and a cup of hot cider, especially when paired with her smile, which could melt any cold heart. *"The first may be the most important. I'll never tell you to follow your heart, because sands knows it can betray you for deceptively greener hills. Nor would I have you follow your head alone, as it is weak against fear, talking you out of good but challenging opportunities."*

"So what do I follow then? The sun? The moon?"

Another warm laugh enveloped her. *"Of course not. That voice within you? You know the one. It sounds like you, but it's mysteriously far more. Listen to it. It will help navigate the paths of life, steering you on the right heading, even when storms are raging and other courses seem nicer. Follow that voice within you that knows where you are needed and what you should do."*

"And who I should love."

A nod. A soft kiss on the forehead.

And the memory faded.

The smell of burning food invaded Cait's senses as she snapped back to the present.

"Shit," she whispered as she pulled the pan from the heat and put out the fire before grabbing a plate and some forks.

Looking down at the meager—and blackened—portions she was about to place before Adler and Lucan, a weight thudded into the bottom of her stomach. How could they expect her to save them—or anyone—when she couldn't even prepare a simple meal?

But burned or not, her rations were running low, and she hadn't been able to risk securing extra at the docks. This would have to do. And she would have to ignore whatever bruises her ego developed as a result.

Cait opened the door of the apartment to find the men still

seated at the table, quietly playing another round of cards, though by the placement of the cards, Adler must have convinced Lucan to switch to Corks and Bones. And by the look on Lucan's face, Adler hadn't made empty boasts about his skill at the game.

At the sound of the door clicking shut behind her, Lucan dropped his cards with a rush of relieved breath.

"Saved me again, Cait. Thank you."

At these words, Cait fought back a wince, dropping the plate onto the table with as much confidence as she could muster. She picked up a piece of charred meat as she settled back into her seat and waited for their reaction.

"This looks..." Adler said slowly, grimacing. "Remind me never to piss you off, love." He shoveled up what used to be edible eggs. "If this is what happens to things you like, I'd hate to see what happens to those you don't."

She tried not to laugh as he choked down the bite. "How do you know I like eggs and meat?"

"Because I would never trust someone who didn't. And I'd hate to have to stop trusting you now."

How he took another bite, she wasn't sure, but before she could tell him he didn't have to, Lucan was pulling the plate toward him. He had finished off two pieces of meat already, and with a shrug, he loaded his fork up with a hefty portion of unrecognizable eggs and plopped it greedily into his mouth.

As he went to take another, he caught Cait and Adler both staring at him.

"Oh, did you not want me to finish it for you?" Lucan asked, gesturing the fork toward each of them, causing bits of food to fall onto the plate.

"But it looks—" Cait said.

"And tastes—" Adler added.

Lucan shrugged. "Doesn't matter when you're hungry. Plus, I've had worse. Sure you don't want some, Adler?"

Chuckling, Adler shook his head. "I'm good, friend. All yours."

He'd called Lucan *friend*, and that was not lost on Cait. Even if it was as casual for him as calling her *love*, it was a step in the right direction. Adler flashed her a smile with those dimples again, and something warmed within her.

Tommy stepped into the utter chaos on deck. Men continued to attack the creature's massive arms while avoiding their grasp. Why hadn't it crushed them yet? By the size of the tentacles reaching out of the inky black sea, the legends had not exaggerated the kraken's size. It could easily wrap itself around the hull and tear the ship in two. Yet it hadn't.

He'd left Aoife in the doorway. She'd need to take care of herself.

Declan will never forgive you if something happens to her.

Though that would cease to matter if he didn't focus on getting them free of this monster.

Tommy cupped his hands around his mouth and called for Mikkel. When the bo'sun arrived, he leaned in close. "Get as many men as you can below on the cannons. Aim for the widest sections. With precision."

"Aye, sir." It was the first time he'd been called that since assuming command.

Nothing more than habit for Mikkel though.

"Have some of them keep an eye on the hull and patch up whatever they can with whatever they have."

The man nodded and left to carry out the command. Tommy bounded up the quarterdeck stairs two at a time. Bria hadn't left her position at the rail, and Renna was beside her, silent but attentive. The sails still filled with the wind Bria summoned, but a glance at the sea told him her work wasn't helping to free them.

Rushing over to the two fae, he called out, "Renna, have her stop!"

Renna shot him a questioning look.

"It's holding us in place. Toying with us. We're just draining Bria's magic." He didn't know how to pull a fae out of whatever this trance was. Last thing he wanted was to do it wrong and worsen their situation.

Without so much as a nod, Renna turned her attention to Bria and silently took her hand in hers. A few breaths later, Bria's eyes flashed open and focused on Renna before snapping to Tommy.

"Why did—" she began, but he held up a hand.

"Can you summon it quickly? Strongly?" He sounded like a buffoon, but he had no time to worry about how he phrased things at the moment. "Or do you need to be in that intense state as you have been?"

Her brow quirked up. "I can, but it doesn't last long."

"Are you able to ease back into a steady rhythm without issue?"

She nodded, but concern filled her eyes. "Yes, but I'm running dangerously low. We will need to be careful."

Cannons began firing beneath them, and Tommy turned to watch as the kraken's limbs pulled back and retreated with each blow. They returned as quickly as they had fled, but still, the shots did better than he'd expected. His hope sparked.

If they could time it well, it might work.

It had to work.

"On my signal, summon as strong a burst as you can to propel us. Then maintain it, giving it as much as you can until we get away."

Bria eyed him quizzically.

"Renna," he continued, "you can tell how she's faring, yes?" A solemn nod. "Watch over her and pull her back before she gets to the edge."

He moved to the helm before Renna could ask any questions, before he had a chance to change his mind, tell her to keep her going, and sacrifice Bria's gifts—and long life—if it meant saving Maura.

And Declan.

Somehow, by sheer luck perhaps, none of the masts or the helm had been smashed by the kraken. The only visible indication that they were even under attack were the beads of sweat dripping down Gavin's face and the curses falling from his mouth every few seconds. While there wasn't much he could do from the helm, Gavin had stayed put, watching all of his friends fight around him, in order to be ready to maneuver them away as soon as the opportunity arose.

"How are we?" Tommy asked as he stepped up beside him.

Gavin stopped swearing long enough to reply, "Could be worse."

"Could also be better."

"That's a given. But we've had good fortune so far. What do you think it's doing?"

With a shake of his head, Tommy said, "I've been wondering

the same thing."

The cannons continued to fire, hitting the monster more often than not, but it still wasn't giving them the opening they needed. He glanced behind him. The two sisters watched him with anticipation.

"They need to coordinate their shots. Hit both sides at the same time," Tommy mumbled to himself.

Aoife ran up the stairs toward them and yelled over the thundering cannons, "We need to time our shots better!"

"Agreed. Go! Below. Find Mikkel and make it happen!"

To Tommy's surprise Aoife listened—possibly for the first time since he'd met her—and he couldn't stop his mouth from curling into a small smile.

He'd barely lost sight of her on the stairs when movement to the side caught his eye. One of the kraken's arms lifted high in the air. It seemed to be surveying the ship, as if it had eyes. Impossible. How could it sense their positions? Pointing toward the prow, it swept around, remaining elevated above the ship until it aimed directly behind Tommy.

At Bria.

He turned around, cutlass ready, and ran across the small deck. Aiming for the tentacle as it moved to come down on the fae, he pushed himself to hurry. But before he'd managed to strike, the limb stopped a few inches from Bria's face, which was hidden behind the curtain of hair that now flew up into the air toward the attacker. The arm struggled against the wind that kept it in place, moving this way and that in an attempt to get free of its invisible shackles, but with each move, it met another wall of air.

"Gavin!" Tommy called. The helmsman was by him in a second. "Cutlass, now!"

Throwing his gaze toward the tentacle, he willed his friend to understand his meaning. Thankfully, after so many years of sailing and raiding and fighting and surviving together, Gavin caught his intent without hesitation and scurried under the tentacle to the other side as he pulled his cutlass loose from its scabbard.

The two pirates lifted their blades in unison, moving the weapons far back behind them to give extra force to their strikes. They swung simultaneously, bringing the cutlasses down onto the wriggling arm of the beast. With all their strength, they thrust their weapons down, slicing a deep cut into either side. The limb retreated in pain, dripping inky black blood onto the deck.

A scream tore through the air, and it took a full breath for Tommy to realize it was coming from Gavin, who had dropped his cutlass onto the ground. Cradling his arm in his left hand, Gavin stared down at his forearm, where the kraken's blood—as thick and black and foul as pitch—had fallen onto his skin.

Before Tommy could find his voice, Renna was there, placing her hands on Gavin's wounded arm. His screams quieted. His body relaxed.

But the fight wasn't over.

The kraken's wounded arm was gone, but another limb took its place before Bria could call up the wind again to protect them. It thudded to the floor of the quarterdeck and swiped toward them, knocking both Tommy and Bria down. Tommy, with his clothes soaked and uncomfortably sticking to him, lay gasping for air that wouldn't come at first. He rolled over onto his back to find the arm hovering above him, but it didn't seem interested in or even aware of him. Craning his neck, Tommy peered behind him. Bria had already recovered from the blow and was standing once more, calling the wind to keep the monster at bay.

Renna approached Tommy and lowered herself in front of him, putting a hand on his chest as she caught his attention. "It's trying to wear her down," she said, her concern evident despite the steadiness of her tone.

"How do you—" he started, then looked back up to the massive tentacle held in place by Bria's powers. "You can hear it?"

She gave the slightest of nods. "Just barely. It's faint, but it's there."

"You couldn't have discovered this earlier?" he asked with a chuckle, though nothing about this situation was amusing.

"I didn't know for sure it would work. It's been centuries since I've been near any nonhuman creatures."

"So what do we do?" He turned to watch the turbulent standoff between the fae and the kraken. Bria was still holding on, but unlike before, the creature didn't wriggle and struggle. It seemed to be conserving its energy as it drained hers.

Renna thought for half a second. "We need to wound it—severely—before it drains her of all her strength."

"If only you had offensive powers."

"I've oft wished that myself."

Tommy's shoulders tensed. "Collins is out cold. Gavin is—"

"Healing," Renna said as she looked toward the helmsman, who had managed to return to his station, "but his arm will need at least a few days to rest before it will be of use."

"And Maura...?" Tommy said. The shake of Renna's head tightened his gut.

"We need to get Bria away and get the cannons to hit it in multiple points at once so she can move us out of its reach and these waters. I'll go below. When the time is right, shout the order in your mind, and I'll hear it."

Tommy gave her a nod and didn't waste a moment before he lunged for Bria. Grabbing her around the waist, he turned her around and directed her down the stairs. He risked a look behind them as they descended to the main deck, expecting to see the long arm following them, but he caught the end of it pulling off the side of the ship, moving back down into the sea.

"Where are we going?" Bria asked, and Tommy pointed toward the officers' cabin where Collins slept.

"Not inside. Just next to the door." Once there, with his feet planted on the rocking deck, he surveyed the scene before him. Several bodies lay strewn across the deck. The man who had been atop the mast had long ago fallen from his perch. Tommy winced as he recalled the sight of the pirate's body being snatched in the air by the beast and yanked below the surface.

By sheer luck, they didn't need to wait long for the stupid beast to make a poor decision. Six limbs, three on either side of the ship, rose in unison, and each happened to be in the line of sight of one of the gunners below decks. Before he could even push the thought to Renna, the cannons fired. Every cannon. The force shook the ship, but Tommy barely noticed as he scanned both sides. The cannons had hit their marks—rather effectively—and the monster pulled its injured tentacles away from the ship.

"Now!" Tommy shouted to Bria. Immediately the sails filled with wind. The ship lurched forward, pulling away from the kraken's limbs, which were still raised in the air despite the damage they'd suffered. Their retreat hadn't gone unnoticed though, and the creature moved to follow.

Too slow. They were going much too slow. "Bria. Can you do more?"

She gave him no indication that she'd heard, but the ship increased speed beneath his feet.

Gavin shouted from above, "Tommy, it's gone!"

With a word of encouragement for Bria to keep it up as long as she could, Tommy rushed away, bounding up the stairs once more and running to the rail. Gavin was right. The only sign the kraken had been there was the mysterious ink floating near the surface, slowly fading away.

"That was too lucky," Tommy said to himself. Deep in his bones he knew something was amiss. Coming back to Gavin, he noted, "Hold on. I don't think it's done with us yet."

30

CAIT

Lucan and Adler arrived the next morning laughing at something as they stepped into the pub. Cait quickly finished plait-
ing her hair.

Adler's teasing smirk spread across his face. "Didn't take you
for the vain type, love."

Lucan no longer bristled at the man's use of the term for her.
Instead, he grinned broadly, as though he was privy to some joke
she hadn't heard.

With a shrug, she said, "I'll have you know, this perfection is
far from effortless."

Adler looked as though he wanted to move toward her but
stopped short before saying, "And it is far from unappreciated."

Lucan groaned, his grin replaced with the look Declan used to
don whenever their parents kissed too intimately in front of them.
But nothing between her and Adler warranted such a reaction. She

should be offended, but it wasn't worth the effort, so she settled for a signature roll of her eyes. "We're done flirting now, Lucan."

At that, Adler playfully smacked Lucan's chest with the back of his hand, his jaw dropping open. "Did you hear that?"

Lucan nodded, his face now lit up with amusement.

"Hear what?" Cait asked, hoping she didn't sound as pathetic as she felt for not understanding.

Adler's eyes turned almost seductive. "You agreed you were flirting with me, love."

Embarrassment pooled in her stomach.

"I don't know why you're so excited about that, man," Lucan said with a laugh. "She flirts with me all the time."

"I do not!" This was ridiculous. Here the Rogues were on the verge of executing the first step in their plan to unseat the council, and these two buffoons were teasing her over something as stupid as flirting.

Adler's smile brightened, and when those damn dimples greeted her, she had to look away.

"She responded rather quickly to that, friend," Adler said. "I think you might be right. I'll remember not to let her advances go to my head."

With a huff, Cait threw her hands up and walked in between them toward the door. She didn't bother to invite them to follow and, although it was childish, she allowed herself the simple satisfaction of slamming the door behind her.

Out on the street, she didn't acknowledge the men's presence behind her as she made her way toward Penny's Place. Penny's was a popular eatery owned by one of the more prominent members of town. Penny had been a prominent figure in Morshan for as long as Cait could remember. She was also not fond of the McCallagh's and didn't bother to hide her disdain for the family.

While she had sent her condolences to Cait and Declan after their parents' disappearances, Penny had seemed almost pleased with what had happened, as if she'd had a hand in it.

And Cait wasn't sure she hadn't.

None of that was why the Rogues had decided to target her though. They needed a person of influence, someone the people would listen to, but also someone who wasn't likely to be a council pawn. The Rogues had been watching her—in random shifts, never the same person two days in a row and never in the same order, lest the woman notice and become suspicious—for the better part of the last two years. Based on the reports of her movements and meetings and dealings, Cait was confident Penny was as dimwitted as she'd always imagined.

There was no sign she was working with the council or that she had any suspicion about what the council actually did behind the scenes, how they controlled the flow of goods not for the benefit of the people, as they claimed, but to maintain their hold on the people and the island.

Penny was a staunch supporter of the council and prided herself on how she valued the law of peace on the island. And that made her the perfect person to target for this particular exercise.

The trio remained silent as they entered the building and made their way to a seat by the far wall, near the stairs. They pretended to look over the scant menu as they sat and waited. The dining room, unusually empty at this hour, was a small area cramped with simple tables and chairs. This would be even harder to pull off while there were so few people around. Cait had hoped the typical hustle and bustle of the breakfast crowd would add to the confusion of what they were about to stage.

As Cait wracked her mind for options, Penny approached. "Good morning, Cait. Lucan." The friendliness in her tone was in stark contrast to the irritated look she flashed them. Bitterness was not a flattering trait in most people, but it was particularly unbecoming in this woman. Her beak-like nose was made more prominent by the scowl on her thin lips, and the sharpness of her glare made her brown eyes more of a dull muddy hue rather than the sweet chocolate color they might have been otherwise.

"And who is this? Newcomer?" Penny eyed Adler, a hint of suspicion hiding behind blatant attraction.

"New bar hand" was all Cait offered, turning her eyes back to the menu.

No other words were exchanged after their orders were placed, and the trio sat for several minutes in silence, Adler looking around the room with his jaw in the palm of his hand as his fingers drummed lazily against his temple. Lucan showed no sign of his earlier good mood as he fidgeted in his seat, like a toddler who was antsy to go play. Except it wasn't excitement that had him so uncomfortable, though sands knew this was a vast improvement from when he'd first arrived in Morshan.

Cait reached her hand over the table and placed it atop his. With a squeeze, she donned a reassuring smile, hoping he knew she hadn't forgotten how hard this was for him, even if she couldn't personally understand the difficulty.

Though Cait had learned Morshan wasn't like the other towns and villages on Cregah, there was a vast difference between knowing the hardships her people faced elsewhere and actually living it herself. Morshan was like a decadent palace compared to the squalor they lived in. Starvation was a common way to die, second only to illness and infection. Morshan was a mask, a pleasant veneer displayed to an ignorant public, giving the people a view of comfort and peace while the rest of the country suffered. It was this reminder of the mask that hit Lucan so hard.

Not that it wasn't noticeable in the shops throughout the town he'd called home for years. But the restaurants always affected him more, where the abundance of food and wastefulness of the citizens was on full display.

Cait was forced to release Lucan's hand when Penny delivered the food to the table. The breakfast was similar to what Cait had attempted to make yesterday—a fried egg, a single piece of toast, and a bit of cured meat—but it lacked the charred quality of inattention.

Cait looked up at Adler through her lashes as she leaned over her plate to begin eating. If her actions with Lucan had bothered him in any way, it didn't show in his expression as he took a bite of food and watched as more patrons arrived and took seats. Why would it bother him? And why did it matter if it had? It shouldn't. There wasn't anything to explain beyond friendship—regardless of Lucan's earlier assertion that she flirted with him often. And there certainly was nothing happening between her and the pirate that would warrant any jealousy on his part.

Lucan cleared his throat. With toast in hand, he flicked his eyes up to the door and then back down to his food. Pretending to stretch her neck, Cait turned to see the man Lucan had indicated. Short stature. Not a local—but also not a pirate. Alone, visibly intoxicated. Though Cait didn't know who he was, she had seen him in here often enough to know he was a Morshan regular, and Penny's was his preferred destination in the mornings, especially after a long night of drinking.

Cait returned to eating and gave a nearly imperceptible nod. She stole one more glance at Adler and took his half-smile as an indication he understood.

The man ambled by them, his feet shuffling against the floor before he stumbled, falling against Cait's chair. She cried out as his hand tangled in her hair. Penny rushed over before Lucan or Adler could pretend to react.

"Gregor, come on." It was the gentlest tone Cait had ever heard the woman use. Penny focused her attention on Cait as she supported the man's weight. "Perhaps you shouldn't have your chair out so far."

There was the spite-filled Penny Cait knew and loathed, but Cait responded with the sweetest smile she could muster.

"I'm sorry, Penny. Here, let me help," she said as she stood. She reached out to take Gregor's arm, and as she had hoped, Penny's shoulders slumped as she released a heavy breath.

"Thank you. Just take him to the back. I have a spot where he can rest. It's hard to miss."

"Least I can do. Apologies again," Cait offered before turning to Gregor. "Let's get you settled, shall we?"

Behind her, Lucan struck up a conversation with Penny, asking how business was before introducing her to Adler. Adler must have said something charming or funny or both, because Penny's laugh filled the room, but it wasn't like any laugh Cait had ever heard from her. This one seemed forced, a bit louder than usual.

While her men kept the owner busy, Cait led the drunken man through the dining room, nodding and humming at his slurred and indecipherable questions. They had just made it to the small counter where Penny collected notes and tallied up earnings for the council when Cait feigned a stumble that sent her foot into the path of Gregor's stride. He grabbed for Cait in his drunken haze, and they both tumbled to the ground. Cait noticed the gathered crowd craning their necks to see what had caused the commotion. She raised her hand in a wave as she caught Penny's eye.

"We're okay!" she said, even as Gregor let out a sound that could only be described as groaning laughter.

Keeping the diners in her periphery, Cait righted herself and reached down to help the man up. He was heavier than expected, and in her effort to lift him, she leaned back, far. This was not at all the way to move a louse—and she'd had plenty of practice doing that—but no one seemed to be paying her any attention, having already turned back to their meals and conversations. Cait's hands slipped off Gregor's arm, and she fell onto her backside, more quietly this time so as not to call as much attention to herself.

Swinging her legs around, she moved into a kneeling position and pretended to whisper to the man, who appeared awfully close to falling asleep. She stole a quick look at Adler and Lucan. Penny was still chattering away as she leaned closer to Adler's side of the table.

She'd need to do it now, or they'd lose this opportunity. As quickly as she could, Cait pulled out the small dagger she'd stashed in her boot.

Atop the counter lay a stack of paper, receipts, and menus. With the dagger hidden along her forearm, she rose, careful to keep her arm concealed behind the counter. During the split second it took her to stand, she slipped the blade beneath the mess.

She held her breath for a moment, but when she raised her eyes and saw no one was looking her way, too engaged in their food and talk, she let the air rush from her lungs.

"Okay, Gregor. This is not where Miss Penny intended for you to rest. Shall we?"

No answer. Not that she had expected one. She hauled the man up as she had done with countless others back at the pub, and deposited him on the pile of blankets in the corner of the storeroom. He curled up on his side, mumbling and barely conscious.

"You're welcome," Cait offered before heading back to her seat.

"Have some trouble with that, did you?" Adler asked as she approached, craning around Penny's form to meet Cait's eyes. Penny stepped back a pace to allow Cait room to pull the seat out.

Cait lifted a shoulder. "Not the hardest person I've had to escort in such a fashion."

"Yeah, she's had to move me a couple times, sadly," Lucan piped up, and for a moment Cait caught a glimpse of his earlier goofiness.

"You were one of the worst, Luc," Cait agreed.

Penny, clearing her throat, gestured to Cait's chair. "Please, sit. I'll bring you a little something for home as a token of gratitude."

Cait appreciated the gesture as much as possible, considering it was coming from a woman who had always been so rude to her. And she almost felt bad for what was going to happen in a moment.

"I wish we could, but we really must be going. I'll have Adler settle the balance with you while Lucan and I wait outside so as to free up the table for you."

Penny didn't seem at all put out at the opportunity to spend more time talking with the former pirate, and she didn't bother to say anything to Cait before she started walking toward the counter, waving her hand over her shoulder to signal Adler to follow.

Cait and Adler exchanged a brief look as he stood, and his blue eyes flashed her a wink before he strode past her. His shoulder brushing against hers sent her skin tingling, and she told herself it was nothing more than an involuntary reaction to human contact. It had nothing to do with him personally.

Lucan came up behind her and placed a hand on the small of her back as he motioned for them to exit. When they reached the door, Cait glanced back to where Adler now stood at the counter with the owner, chatting and giggling about who knew what.

When Cait opened the door, a gust of wind—perfectly timed and unexpected—rushed into the space and sent the papers in front of Adler fluttering away.

Cait and Lucan walked out onto the sidewalk to monitor the situation inconspicuously while staging a conversation.

A sudden movement inside caused them to snap their attention to the window. Even from outside, Cait could hear Adler's booming voice.

"Woah! Why do you have that?"

Penny stood before him, holding the dagger in her hand, her forehead wrinkling with her confusion. Her eyes were fixed on the blade she held, and her head began to shake. Adler's question had alerted the others in the room to the situation, and several people had turned to look, their mouths open either in shock or to whisper to their companions. A woman rushed out the door and, as Cait had hoped, headed straight for the pirates currently patrolling the town on behalf of the council.

With his hands up in surrender, Adler remained frozen in place. It didn't take long before the woman returned with two burly pirates who had dull yellow sashes tied around their waists.

Backing up to give the pirates room to pass, Cait and Lucan continued to watch the situation unfold. Penny still held the blade, as if it had been seared to her palm. As the pirates approached, the diners backed away. Except for Adler, who remained rooted in place, though his hands had at least relaxed. From outside, Cait couldn't make out what was said, but as she watched Penny's shock give way to confusion and then anger in a matter of minutes, she assumed it wasn't going well for the restaurateur.

"I don't like it," Lucan said under his breath.

Cait didn't turn to look at him, wanting to oversee everything happening within. "None of us like it, but remember, we have a plan." She lowered her voice. "Penny will get taken to the council. They'll sentence her to exile. But the twins will be ready to follow them. To rescue her at the opportune moment. It will be okay."

"Yeah, I've heard that before."

Her shoulders slumped at the reminder. Those had been the words she'd used to ease everyone's worries over sending Maggie in as a spy.

"We have to hope." When he didn't say anything, she continued. "Positive thinking isn't magic. It can't change the future. It can't bring us victory. But it can keep us from giving up entirely, from accepting defeat at the start."

Whether her words convinced him or not, she couldn't tell. Inside, the pirates seized Penny, whose face was twisted in fright. One of the pirates confiscated the blade and slipped it into his belt, and then the two men began to drag her to the exit. Adler hung back. As planned.

The front door opened.

"Please! You have to believe me! It wasn't mine!" Desperation clung to each syllable.

The pirates paused just long enough for one of them to kick the door closed behind them while the other sneered at her. Although their clothes were clean, their beards trimmed, and their faces washed, they still had that disagreeable quality about them that indicated their profession and expertise in that field. Their teeth were nearly as dirty as their fingernails, their language just as vile.

Cait tracked the pirates as they dragged Penny to the sidewalk. No doubt they would assume she and Lucan were nothing more than curious citizens watching the spectacle. Penny continued proclaiming her innocence, and the pirates continued ignoring her.

"Shit." The whispered curse rushed out of Cait as she watched them turn right.

"What is it?" Lucan asked.

"They're not taking her to the council. That's back the other way." She was moving to follow them before she'd finished talking. But she had no plan. She kicked herself for not having a contingency plan—or rather, not having the right contingency plan. Their handful of preplanned maneuvers had all hinged on the fact that exiles were taken before the council first for sentencing. In all her years, Cait had never known them to allow their hired hands to dispatch citizens on their own.

"Maybe they're taking the scenic route," Lucan said, coming up beside her, easily matching her quick stride.

Cait stayed silent.

"Shouldn't we wait for Adler?"

She stopped to look over her shoulder and spotted the tall pirate jogging toward them. Urgency coursed through her. If they lost track of them, she would have gotten another innocent person killed for nothing.

"Come on!" she yelled at Adler, as she silently urged Penny to keep shouting.

Before Adler had caught up, Cait was off again. The pirates had moved Penny onto another street, but Cait could still hear her shrill, hoarse voice wafting around the buildings.

"The twins—" Lucan started.

"No time," Adler said before Cait could, and she wasn't sure if she was annoyed or grateful. "We'll need to find them, follow them, and take care of it ourselves."

Cait nodded along and pushed her legs to keep going as she followed the woman's shouts through town. When they neared the docks, she wondered what the pirates planned to do. Exile, yes. But how? Where? When Aron had spotted the pirates carrying off

Maggie's body, he hadn't followed them, hadn't discovered where they took the exiles.

As stone gave way to wooden planks beneath her feet, she froze, hesitating.

Left. Right. Nowhere. And the screaming had stopped. They'd need to split up.

"Lucan, head that way toward the docks. Adler and I will go the opposite."

Lucan's jaw tensed, and Cait waited for him to argue, knowing this order wasn't easy for him; it would force him near the sea he feared to possibly face two pirates on his own, and he would have to leave Cait's side in the midst of danger.

He swallowed hard and with a nod to Cait took off toward the water.

Cait grabbed Adler's arm and turned him around so they faced the forest at the edge of town. "Let's go."

"So quick to get me alone in the woods again?" he asked as he picked up the pace and flashed her another wink.

"Whatever keeps you moving forward."

The road seemed to disappear into the trees, as though the town had been lifted from some other world and dropped into the middle of this forest, making the roads lead nowhere.

But there was a faint hint of a path where the grass was sparser.

And there—a footprint, clear as day in the soft ground.

Panic sped up her heart, and she bit down until her teeth hurt in an effort to prevent the inevitable shaking of her hands from starting. Penny needed her to hurry. The whole of Cregah needed her to hurry. This was their best option to expose the council's secret violence. But what if she chose wrong? She couldn't split up from Adler. While she'd love to believe she could take on two pirates unassisted, she knew her limits.

Adler pushed silently past her into the trees, his eyes on the ground. He stopped and called to her in a hushed tone, "Here. More boot prints."

"You sure?" she asked as she met up with him.

"Well, I'm but a humble pirate and no tracker. But it's the best lead we have."

"It's a shaky lead at best."

"It's where I would go if I were going to exile someone." He raised a brow.

She took two seconds to breathe and consider and then continued moving down the overgrown path, not bothering to call Adler to follow.

Let us be right, Penny. And let us hurry.

I may not like you, but that doesn't mean I want you dead.

31

DECLAN

Many of the stories passed around the Aisling were based on true events that had been twisted into outlandish myths, but some had been so horrifying to begin with that no elaboration could have made them any more frightening. The dragons might have long ago left the region—as far as Declan knew—but the sirens remained. And nothing had deterred him from taking their legend seriously.

Still, he hoped the legends were false.

Even from the windowless brig Declan knew when they had arrived at the Black Sound. The air around him hadn't shifted. It was still the dank and musty belly of the ship, with a hint of the scent of oranges. The hair on Declan's arms wasn't standing on end. His skin wasn't tingling. There was no indication they'd arrived except the eerie quiet that settled above him. Even from this far below deck, the noises of the crew walking and talking and shouting reached him at all hours of the day.

But all that had ceased in an instant.

And Declan knew his nonexistent luck hadn't brought him the sudden demise of everyone aboard.

No. They'd slowed. The crew had quieted. A threat lay ahead. Declan waited.

The faint sound of boots moving down the ladder filled the space, pulling Declan's attention to the man Callum had sent to retrieve him. Without a word—without any sound at all—the man unlocked the cell door, careful to keep the ring of keys he carried from jangling together, wincing when the iron hinges creaked in protest at being used.

Part of Declan wanted to say something, to break the stillness with a quip or a jab at the man's expense. Had they been in any other location—or in any other circumstance—he would have, but even Declan didn't want to tempt the sirens.

At least not yet.

So he allowed the man to take him by the arm, doing his best not to comment on how the service on board had improved greatly. Without the ability to joke, though, Declan found it especially hard to ignore the dread that had returned to his gut.

Forcing the bile back down his tightened throat, he ascended the last steps to the deck, desperate to ignore the memory of the last time he'd made this climb to find Killian bound and awaiting his punishment. Blinking hard, he forced away the image of the man being dragged over the railing, body mangled, life hanging on by a thread.

This time, though, the men of the *Curse Bringer* did not jeer at him or taunt him as he walked among them. Their stillness was a drastic change from the crazed enthusiasm they had shown just yesterday. And though Declan never wanted to revisit yesterday's spectacle—not even in his own mind—this atmosphere was almost as unsettling.

Almost.

Though Declan had sailed all around the Aisling Sea, from the black sands of Cregah and the lush forests of Caprothe to the pristine white cliffs of Turvala, none of it compared to the view before him.

The teal water beneath them sat as still as glass, transforming the surface into a mirror that reflected the sheer walls of black rock, which were blanketed in dense trees as green as the hills of Cregah. But these had an otherworldly essence to them, as if each leaf and branch was cut from priceless gems. Wisps of clouds clung to the hills where water cascaded down, cutting through the foliage like the veins of a great giant. And above, stretching toward the azure sky, bare rock reached up, like a solemn observer looking down on all who dared approach.

No sound came beyond the distant rumble of the waterfalls crashing into the sea. No hint of bird or beast could be found—not in the trees, the skies, or the seas. The quiet, as ominous and foreboding as it was, pulled at Declan, drawing him away from the crew. He moved around the mainmast and closer to the ship's rail. The Black Sound was calling him, like it had been expecting him. Or perhaps it was that its inhabitants could sense the depth of his remorse and beckoned him to come and find them.

"You feel it, don't you?"

Declan jumped as Callum appeared seemingly out of nowhere and whispered the question, easily heard in the silence surrounding them.

"Your shoulder lingering against mine? Aye, I do. Makes me uncomfortable," Declan said and eyed the captain without turning his head.

A smile distorted Callum's scar. "Jokes won't protect you in there."

The apprehension pooling in Declan's gut grew turbulent at the words, but he was not about to let Callum know. He turned his attention toward his captor and raised a brow, the corners of his mouth pulling down.

"Perhaps I could try a disguise."

Callum didn't look amused.

Declan raised his still-manacled hands to his chin, tapping it with a forefinger. "I'll need a change of clothes. And probably a new hat."

"A disguise." Callum's tone showed as much humor as his face. None.

"Aye. You could have one too. It'll be a classic Declan-Callum mess-around."

Callum gave a shrug. "Could be rather entertaining to see you try."

Declan's chin bobbed with several nods. "Aye. You're in need of a distraction, and I aim to please."

Silence once again rolled in like the fog hugging the cliffs of the sound. While Declan normally relished any moments void of incessant chatter and pointless noise, here the stillness was far from calming. Even the sea below them seemed hesitant to splash too much against the hull of the ship. The crew barely breathed. No one moved.

Declan leaned his head toward Callum, his eyes still focused on the entrance to the sound, and whispered, "So there's no singing then?"

When Callum didn't answer, Declan turned to find exasperation written on the man's face.

"Are we waiting to be invited in?"

Callum's jaw tightened before he responded. "You in such a hurry to greet death?"

"Why put off the inevitable?" Pivoting around, he stood up on his toes and craned his neck to get a glimpse of the waters behind them. No sails were visible. Not even on the distant horizon. "And it appears my rescuers will not make it in time."

Declan could not prevent his throat from constricting as the memories surfaced. It was as though the sirens' presence had unlocked the chains around them.

Tommy collapsing onto the stone floor. Blood spreading across his chest.

His father being dragged away to be tried for murder.

His mother disappearing into the mist, never to return.

Aoife shaking her head. Denying him. Refusing him.

Tighter and tighter, each memory cut off his air.

He had failed.

Again.

No matter how much he tried to remind himself it wasn't over until his last breath, no matter how often he tried to focus on the next task, the bitter truth drowned out every bit of reassurance he could scrounge up.

He should have kept to himself, kept everyone from getting too close. Nothing good came from being his friend or his kin.

Or his lover.

If not for him, Tommy wouldn't have been injured. Aoife wouldn't have been betrayed. His parents—

Logically, Declan knew he wasn't responsible for their deaths. Logically, his mind understood there was nothing he could have done as a young kid to protect them or to prevent it.

Unfortunately, man was ruled not by logic alone but by experience, emotion, trauma. And those denied Declan any relief. It was irrational, but something within him insisted that redemption could never be his. Others may deserve it, but not him. Never him.

His chest caved, and his shoulders began to curve forward, as they had when he was a young cabin boy hiding in the corner of the ship during a storm. This was what the sirens wanted. This internal suffering. The pain that marred his soul. The regret that ate holes throughout his heart like a worm through an apple.

Clenching his jaw tight until his teeth ached, Declan tried to push away the darkness that plagued him. He would not readily serve his mangled soul to these demons. He couldn't. He had to fight. Not just for Tommy and Aoife and Cait, but for himself too. No matter what he tried, though, no matter how hard he pushed against the darkness, it fought back harder, and he could contain it no better than if he were attempting to hold back the tide with his bare hands.

"Don't fight it, Declan." Callum's quiet voice—emotionless and matter-of-fact—cut through his inner battle. "Remember what I said. It's too late."

Callum was right, but Declan still shook his head in denial as he turned. Despite the apathy in his words, Callum's demeanor had shifted. If the sirens really were calling to Declan's inner demons, they could very well be doing the same to Callum—and everyone else aboard this ship.

"You're not looking too good yourself," Declan said. "Sure it's not too late for you too? I thought you were smarter than me."

Callum's gaze shifted back to the darkness waiting between the rocky cliffs. "I am. Unfortunately, all pain reacts to the sirens' call. But not all pain is equal. It never goes away. Some flicker of it always remains. Like a...scar." He seemed to struggle with that last word. "Like you, I betrayed someone. Someone close to me. But she betrayed me as well. Left me with this." Callum gestured to the scar that ran down his cheek.

"Are you about to share your story with me? Should I be honored?" Declan looked around with suspicion. "Good thing the crew's fear is keeping them back or they might hear it all."

Callum ignored the questions but shook his head and gave a light laugh. "You know, I just might miss your ridiculous chatter, McCallagh."

"I'm touched." Declan cleared his throat before lowering his voice. "So who was she?"

"A pirate. One of the best damned pirates I've ever worked with."

While Declan hadn't met many female pirates, Callum couldn't have been referring to the one who had helped him get Aoife away from the council. Halloran.

"She must be if she managed to wound you like that. What'd you do to earn it, exactly?"

"Are we stalling now? Not so eager to die after all?" Callum asked, though he didn't wait for Declan to answer as he leaned against the railing and looked down at the water. "She was my quartermaster, actually. And no, you wouldn't have heard about it. It didn't last long enough to make it into the gossip channels."

"The betrayal would have, though, right?"

A shrug. "Perhaps that was the last consolation she offered—allowing my reputation to remain intact, even as she made off with nearly all of the prize and a handful of my crew. Secured her own ship. Hired a bunch of women as her officers. Made a name for herself."

"Halloran."

A silent nod. This was interesting.

"But you betrayed her first?"

"Aye."

"What happened?"

Callum straightened from the railing. "That's a story for another time. We could call it an incentive for you to survive in there."

Declan scoffed. "Not much of an incentive, is it?"

"Take it however you wish to. Try to make it, try not to, I don't mind either way as long as you keep them preoccupied long enough for me to locate and grab the blade." Callum raised a hand and signaled someone behind Declan with a quick wave. Before Declan could turn to see who was approaching, a rough hand grasped one of his forearms, keeping it steady as keys fit into the lock of the manacles. The satisfying metallic click of it releasing might have brought relief for Declan had he been facing something else.

Try to make it.

Callum might think Declan had already given up. Perhaps that was what most people would do, but he'd made his choice the first day on this ship, and nothing had changed that.

He would survive.

Or he'd die trying.

32

AOIFE

Pride coursed through Aoife as she returned to the main deck. Though it would have been better if Declan was here to witness their success. Her success. As angry as she still was with him, she couldn't ignore the warmth that flickered within her when she thought of him—even if it was quickly overrun by fear and worry that they would be too late and she would never see him again.

That thought pushed her feet faster, and by some miracle she didn't lose her balance as the ship suddenly surged forward. While she was on the ladder, though, another burst of movement came, perfectly timed to fling half of her body from the rungs and rails. She let out a loud huff of surprise and irritation as she struggled to get herself steady once again so she could climb.

She'd once commented on the lack of excitement aboard this ship, but now, as she clambered up ladder after ladder before crawling up onto the deck, she wished she'd never made such an observation. Against her will—and despite all her effort to focus on the task at hand—a memory swept over her. His hands on her wrists. Her back pressed against the bed. His warmth and his breath and his touch. It barreled into her like a wave against a rocky shore, but she continued pushing forward, ignoring the images that threatened to pull her under and distract her.

By the time she had ascended the stairs and made it to the helm, where Tommy stood watching the aft as Gavin looked ahead, her legs and lungs burned, and a stitch in her side ached with each breath as she tried to suck down air and find relief. Two days of training with Collins hadn't been enough to make up for two decades of sedentary living. Tommy had warned her body would tire quickly, but she hadn't expected it to feel like this.

Bending over, she rested her hands above her knees and widened her eyes to focus on the wooden floor beneath her as she breathed. Everything hurt. She'd never been in so much pain.

She stood and focused on Gavin, who was manning the wheel with only one hand. His other arm hugged his ribs, and his hand rested against his midsection like he was preparing to be sick. But he'd been on the seas for basically his whole life—as far as she knew. He wouldn't get queasy now.

"What happened?" Aoife looked from one man to the other.

Gavin raised his brows above unamused eyes that were dimmed by fatigue. "The damn thing bled on me."

Confused, she turned to Tommy for an explanation. He looked away as he said, "Its blood is toxic, it seems."

"What?" Her panic rushed forward, but Gavin shook his head. "Don't worry. Renna helped. I'll be shipshape soon enough."

Aoife's shoulders fell as her breath escaped. "I'd be a lot less worried if you both didn't look so concerned. We got away, right? It worked?" She paused to look at the sails above, which were still full of the enchanted wind Bria brought them. She must be teetering on the edge of burnout. So why had Tommy—the man who had been so adamant about avoiding that outcome—suddenly stopped caring? Why hadn't he called for Bria to stop?

Without a word, Tommy walked away toward the aft rail, and Aoife followed, unsure if that was what he wanted. He stood stiffly beside the rail instead of leaning against it as he normally did. Not that anything about this was normal. Men shouted behind her, calling for others to help them move the wounded and the dead. The injured let out cries of pain as they were lifted and carried away from where they lay. Perhaps this was normal for them. They were a pirate crew, after all. But the look on Tommy's face—a look she'd seen on Gavin's too—told her something was different now.

She leaned her shoulder against Tommy and gave him a gentle nudge before speaking. "Why is Bria still..." She didn't know what to call it. Working? Conjuring? Magicifying? But Tommy didn't seem to notice her floundering for words.

"It's not done," he said through tight lips, focusing intently on the waters behind them. But Aoife saw nothing. No sign of limbs breaching the surface. Even the monster's inky warning had completely disappeared.

"How can you know that?"

"Gut feeling. We got away too easily. It gave up too quickly."

"Perhaps it wasn't hungry anymore," she said with a shaky breath, though she had never been good at using humor to defuse awkward situations. Usually she just made things worse, but thankfully Tommy showed her some much appreciated pity with a half-hearted, breathy laugh.

"Doubtful," he said.

"Well, can't we simply do what we did before? Wouldn't that tactic work again?"

He shook his head. "No. I don't think so. We got lucky. It moved precisely where we needed it to be when we needed it to be there. I don't believe in destiny or fate or whatever, but something about it feels off. We won't get that kind of fortune a second time."

Aoife tightened her brow as she considered their situation and all he was saying. "So we just push Bria to the edge? Risk her powers? Her long life? Isn't that the very reason you were being such a stubborn ass before?" Her anger flared too quickly for her to hold it back.

He refused to look at her as he gripped the railing so hard his knuckles whitened and his tendons flared. Aoife waited for his harsh response, but instead he closed his eyes and said in a low, determined voice, "I made a mistake, Aoife."

"You think?" She still couldn't get a handle on the rage that simmered under her skin.

His voice remained quiet. "Not the mistake you think."

He didn't look at her, and for several silent breaths, Aoife's impatience grew. If he was right and the kraken would reappear, his taking his sweet time with this conversation was a mistake too.

"Am I supposed to guess?" Aoife lowered her face into his line of sight to snap him out of whatever daydream he'd lost himself in.

"You know, I miss the old Aoife. The nice one. The sweet one—" Tommy's amber eyes flashed with what Aoife could only describe as desperate anger. It was what she assumed he saw in hers.

"I'm sorry I'm not feeling sweet or nice at the moment, Tommy." With these final stinging words, she deflated, slumping her shoulders and dropping her head as all the rage fell away. She immediately wanted it to return and hide the heartache it had been shadowing. "I'm sorry, Tommy."

"I am too," Tommy said and angled himself toward her as he leaned against the railing. "It's just so—"

"Exhausting?"

A sad half-smile pulled at his lips. "That, and stressful. How can I lead this crew?"

Aoife surveyed the ship. "What do you mean? You *are* leading them. You snapped me out of that haze after Collins was wounded and got me to keep fighting."

"And look around you." He swept an arm out, gesturing toward the bloody deck and broken rails. "I got them killed. And I may very well get Declan killed with my failure."

Lifting her hands, Aoife grasped Tommy's face and gently forced him to look at her. Something flickered in his expression at her touch. It was either embarrassment or shame, not that it mattered which. She ignored it so she could focus on what she needed to tell him.

"Declan trusts you. I trust you. The *crew* trusts you. All know the danger of these waters. All know the risks on these seas. They could have stayed behind in Morshan. But they didn't. When they all heard about Declan, they knew they'd be serving under you, and they stayed. Trust them. Trust yourself, Tommy."

Before he could protest, a shout from Gavin made them both turn toward the helm.

"Tommy!" Gavin quickly pointed to the port side with his good arm before barking orders at the few uninjured crewmen on deck. He grabbed the wheel and swung it hard to the right.

"What is that?" Aoife asked Tommy as he rushed back to Gavin's side. From her perch at the rail, where she held on as the ship changed course, she could see the sea churning unnaturally, not from wind at the surface but because of something beneath.

Tommy called back over his shoulder, "Nothing good!"

He could say that again.

The swirling sea increased in speed around a point not one hundred meters away from them, the center point darkening and dropping below the surface, like a monster slowly opening its mouth to swallow them whole. Fear plunged her gut into her feet, weighing her down. She couldn't move. Couldn't release the rail she now clung to.

You fight. Until someone wins, you fight.

She repeated the words over and over, letting them circle her mind like the waters before her. No one had won. Not yet. So they needed to fight. She needed to fight.

But how?

How could you fight a sea that obeyed the enormous creature within it? They had gotten away from its grasp, yes, but perhaps this was why it had been so easy. It had known it would get them one way or another. It had allowed them one bit of hope before claiming its prize. There had to be something they could do.

Aoife swung her attention to Tommy and Gavin, who were frantically talking and gesturing erratically. She couldn't hear a damn thing they said. If she was going to help, she needed to get closer. She needed to move. Hopeful Gavin didn't need to make another drastic turn, Aoife forced her hands to release the rail and pushed her feet to move her forward.

She had nearly made it when the ship rocked to the port side, sending her body slamming into Tommy's. How the man managed to stay upright with such a move, she didn't know. But she doubted his sea legs could be the sole explanation.

The ship still hadn't completely righted, but Tommy held her steady. Before Aoife could ask him what the plan was, his eyes darted into the air behind her head, and she turned to see what had startled him. Her breath caught in her throat, and panic rose sharply at the sight of the sails dropping all at once. Lifeless.

"Bria." The name was out of Tommy's lips at the same instant he moved. Aoife might have fallen had Gavin not caught her with his good arm.

Aoife turned to search Gavin's eyes for any hint they would survive this, but they didn't shimmer with the humor and kindness she'd always seen before. Instead, they were full of despair.

And it was then, in that moment, that Aoife let go of all hope.

33

Tommy

Tommy's feet slipped and slid as he ran down the stairs and across the tilted deck. More than once he worried he was about to go right off the side of the ship through the gap in the railing. Somehow, though, he stayed on his feet and in control of his limbs long enough to reach Bria, who lay in a crumpled heap, soaked through by sea spray. His knees scraped against wood as he fell to the floor to check on her. His hands scrambled to find her wrist or her neck or some other pulse point so he could ensure her heart was still beating, the whole time cursing himself under his breath.

Maura.

Collins.

Bria.

Declan.

How many people would Tommy let down before his last

breath?

"Thoughts like that won't help you," said a stern but kind voice behind him. Of course Renna would be listening in on his thoughts.

"Yes," she said.

"I didn't ask you anything," Tommy said without turning to her.

She knelt down, keeping a respectful distance between them. "I don't listen in unless I have cause to—"

"I don't care," he muttered as he leaned forward to pick up the limp fae before standing. She felt so similar to Maura in his arms, and he tried not to think about the youngest sister who had fallen first on this cursed course. Waiting beside the door to the officers' quarters, he ground out a command for Renna to open the door.

She remained silent as she obliged, entering the small room and holding the door open for him. Tommy surveyed the room briefly. Collins hadn't budged since being brought in, which was fortunate since the ship was still pitched at a sharp angle. The cot near the ceiling was too high for him to lift Bria into easily at this angle. When Renna moved to lay out bedding on the floor, he nearly thanked her for invading his thoughts again.

With Bria lying down, looking as though she was taking a mid-day nap, Tommy continued to monitor her shallow breathing.

"Will they be okay?" he asked.

"I believe so," she replied, sounding more relaxed than the current situation warranted.

Pivoting on his heel, he turned to her awkwardly as the ship continued to circle the maelstrom. "It's not good."

"You know it's not."

"So how do we get out of this?" he asked. They had no wind, no weapons with which to fight the creature. There was no escape from the trap the creature had snared them in. Renna didn't answer, at least not with words, her eyes closing and her lips tightening into a line. "So that's it then. And exactly why am I not supposed to blame myself for this? Why?"

His nails dug into his palms as he tightened his hands into fists and inched closer to her. She didn't back away.

"A solution may still present itself," she said, and the optimism in her words punched through his chest. How could she be so calm? They were circling down toward certain death, and she acted as though they had simply run out of cheese or misplaced a favorite book. In answer to his silent chatter, she said, "I'm calm, Tommy, because the opposite won't help any of us right now."

"So we simply take a stroll out on the deck and hope for this *solution* to fall on us? Is that what I'm to do, Renna?" She didn't respond with anything more than a blink, so he continued, stepping closer still. "I am captain right now, and I am failing everyone. Why Declan ever named me his quartermaster, I'll never know. If he were here—"

"But he's not. You are." Renna's tone took on a new edge. "And if you give into those thoughts, if you let them become the truth you see in yourself, you will surely fail. But what did you tell Aoife earlier?" She paused, as if listening to some far-off whisper. "*'We fight. Until someone wins.'* Well, Captain, no one has won this fight just yet. So if you don't mind, take your own damn advice, stop wallowing in your self-pity, and think. Not of what Declan would do or what any other pirate would do, but what you can do right now."

He didn't say another word but stormed past her and out onto the deck.

Where he was going or what he was going to do, he wasn't entirely sure, but he hoped some idea would come to him as he returned to the helm. Mikkel came up from below decks just as Tommy rounded the corner to the quarterdeck stairs.

"Tommy," he said, grabbing his arm and stopping him from ascending.

"What is it?"

"I have an idea."

"Well, bring it with you," he said and motioned for the man to follow him. Once they were at the helm, he looked from Gavin, who struggled to keep the wheel steady, to Aoife, who was holding on to one of the spindles of the railing. Her head was down, but her eyes were open, staring at the deck before her. "Go on, Mikkel."

"I've seen these whirlpools before. Not of this magnitude, of course, but back home in Turvala, they sprang up often, and it was part of our—"

Tommy held up a hand to stop the man's rambling. "You know how to escape it?" Reflexively he turned to look at the churning water they were caught in. How long had they been trapped? Felt like nearly an hour, but they were still fairly close to the surface.

"Aye. Though I've only ever done it in a small fishing dinghy with oars to propel us out. We don't have any oars."

He was rambling again.

"Explain."

"We get it to spit us out."

Of course this is when the man would be brief.

"And how do we do that exactly?"

"We need to position ourselves near the outer edge of it and keep our heading in the same direction as the currents, until we pick up enough speed that we get tossed outside of its grips."

Tommy and Gavin looked at each other. "Could it…" Tommy started to ask.

Gavin offered a shrug. "We don't have any other options at the moment."

"Try it," Tommy said with a determined nod. Mikkel turned to leave, but Tommy stopped him. "Stay. We'll need you to tell us when we need to make our move to be...spit out, as you said."

"Aye," Mikkel replied, though he didn't look too thrilled at the order to remain here, his face becoming paler than usual and taking on a slight tinge of green.

No one spoke as the ship continued on its path. Around and around. Gavin moved the wheel to stop fighting the current, and Tommy wondered if it felt as backwards to Gavin as it did to him. With the change to the rudder, they picked up speed. Tommy couldn't see how this would keep them from getting pulled down into the dark pit at the center, but Mikkel seemed confident, and as Gavin had said, they had no other option.

So he waited and breathed. They were creeping down the steep walls of the whirlpool, little by little, and Tommy eyed Mikkel. "What—" he started.

Mikkel stopped him with a raised hand, paused, and then shouted to Gavin, "Now! Starboard!" Before Gavin could voice his request for help, Mikkel sprang forward and grabbed the wheel with him. Both men pulled and pushed, trying to get the ship to turn away from the maelstrom, and Tommy had nearly given up hope of this working when the ship made her escape. It was as if the fast-moving water had indeed tossed them aside, like someone spitting out a seed.

The seas they settled in were so calm, Tommy might have thought the entire ordeal with the whirlpool had been a figment of his imagination.

"Shouldn't we move?" Aoife asked as she attempted to pull herself to a standing position. Gavin rushed over to offer her his good arm, and she thanked him quietly before raising her eyes to Tommy and Mikkel. But it was Gavin who answered her.

"Aye. We should, but with no wind and no fae to summon any, we are dead in the water."

Tommy stepped forward, eying their helmsman. "You couldn't find a better phrase to use?"

Gavin offered an apology, but Aoife's voice drowned it out. "He's not wrong though. Is he? I mean, it's not as though we've killed the beast. We've probably made it angry."

At her words, Tommy instinctively turned to look over his shoulder to see what had happened to the whirlpool. He blinked several times. It wasn't possible. Pivoting, he spun around completely, nearly smacking an elbow into Mikkel as he did.

"What in the..." Aoife spoke the exact words Tommy had been thinking.

"How?" Gavin asked as he stepped up beside Tommy, who had frozen in the middle of the quarterdeck and now stared out at the calm, dark teal waters of the Aisling Sea.

No churning, spinning, or foaming.

Nothing.

It was still as glass, the blue sky and billowing clouds above reflected perfectly on its surface. If the creature was toying with them as Tommy suspected, it was doing a damn good job of it. His heart pounded. His breathing sped up. His eyes scanned the waters. It was going to come back, and now they had no defense against it. No offensive capabilities either.

Aoife and Gavin gasped, stopping the thrumming of his heart cold, and he turned once more. Mikkel growled out a curse seconds before throwing himself across the quarterdeck and down the stairs, calling out commands on the way.

Tommy swallowed hard as he watched water cascade down

from the monster as it rose from the surface. It was like the sea itself was draining, its level dropping to reveal an island of flesh underneath. The tentacles themselves—which now remained hidden in the sea—had been terrifying enough, but the sight of the creature emerging gave that word a new meaning, chilling the very blood in his veins. The kraken's head—or was that its body?—was radically different from the smooth-skinned fish they had caught off the western coast of Cregah when he was a kid. Instead, its flesh jutted out in sharp, haphazard angles between the pits and craters that left darkened shadows all over its grayish-purple skin. Around its eyes—two pits of blackness that would have looked completely empty had light not bounced off their slimy outer layer—the skin lightened from purple to brown before turning a sickening yellow, giving the monster the appearance of a massive bruise in various stages of healing.

A bruise with teeth.

Teeth—row upon row of teeth—which looked more like hundreds of snake's fangs, filled the cavernous mouth that remained half-submerged in the sea. With horror, Tommy watched as the water began to rush toward the spear-lined cavern. It was pulling them in.

He had no oars.

No wind.

No magic.

No idea what to do.

34
CAIT

Cait and Adler had walked along the trail—if one could call it that—for a couple of hours and still hadn't come upon Penny and the pirates. She was about to break the silence and express her doubt, when a turn in the path thrust them onto another. While it was far from being as well-kept as the roads and trails leading to the council hall, this new path, with its distinct outline, was a welcome improvement over the one they'd been stumbling down.

She hesitated at the edge, and Adler did the same. To the right, about a hundred paces away, this new path ended abruptly at a large boulder. Before Cait could begin to ponder why a path would simply stop, her eyes caught the light that lay beyond the rock. A clearing. No... If her eyes could be trusted, it looked like a road.

If the pirates had brought Penny this way, it seemed improbable they would have taken her to a main road. Or even a side road.

Adler must have seen the same thing and come to the same

conclusion, because he tapped Cait on the shoulder and gestured to the left with his head. Not waiting for her agreement, he started off in that direction. Cait growled in the back of her throat at his presumption that she would simply follow him. Was he being disrespectful of her leadership? He hadn't grown up on Cregah, hadn't been raised under its matriarchal rule. Perhaps in Daorna the roles were reversed, and certainly he hadn't had any women in his crew on Tiernen's ship.

Or he's confident you were smart enough to understand why he took this route.

Either way, his motive didn't matter when an innocent citizen was about to be killed. Cait had sacrificed Penny; her fate had been sealed as soon as Cait had chosen her. There had always been a risk they wouldn't be able to catch them in time, that this whole plan was destined to fail.

Following Adler, she pushed herself to stay on his heels, desperate not to lose track of him as well. After traveling for several minutes down the path, Cait swore she heard voices up ahead. She reached up a hand and pulled on the back of Adler's shirt. He stopped and looked at her over his shoulder.

With a finger to her lips, she urged him to remain quiet as she crept forward, continuing to listen for the sound she'd heard. But all she could make out was the soft padding of her boots on the leaf-covered ground. Adler silently came up beside her and joined her in listening. Waiting.

There.

Voices. Unmistakable.

She caught Adler's attention, grateful to witness a glimmer of hope in his eyes. He nodded toward the voices as his arm swung wide, inviting her to lead the way. She obliged, but when his other hand landed on the small of her back, she stopped and turned to him in confusion and curiosity.

The warmth from his touch disappeared as quickly as it had arrived, and he pulled his mouth into a grimace—more sheepish and apologetic than disgusted. He mouthed an apology, and because she couldn't think of anything else to do, she offered a one-shouldered shrug before continuing on down the path.

A few voices ahead of them became clearer, but Penny's didn't seem to be one of them. Either they were too late, or the pirates had simply knocked her unconscious or otherwise quieted her. She still couldn't decipher what they were saying, but they seemed to be finding some part of their task humorous, as every few words were interrupted by light laughter.

A few more near-silent steps and Cait caught a glimpse of the men through the branches of the pines. They stood in a clearing, bathed in sunlight. Beyond them came a steady thrum of sound, like a hand passing through sand, but louder.

The sea.

They were at the coast.

Or at least the cliffs that made up this part of the coast.

Adler stood close to Cait, his shoulder pressing into hers as he watched the scene with her. The two pirates were chatting at the edge of the cliff, except it wasn't the edge, for the ground stretched out beyond where they stood.

"It's a pit cave," Cait said, not realizing she'd spoken aloud until Adler responded with a single syllable of agreement.

"I've heard of this place," he said, lowering his mouth close to her ear so he wouldn't have to risk speaking louder than necessary. His whisper came out strained. "Pirates don't talk about it much. A mention here and there. After a few cups of rum, secrets come out eventually."

Cait turned her chin slightly toward him. "If they've spoken about it, why doesn't everyone know by now?"

It was his turn to shrug. "Perhaps no one trusts a man who reeks of drink."

He had a point. The council must be trusting the pirates to keep their mouths shut—in exchange for safe haven while in port—knowing if they ever spilled their secrets while intoxicated, few would believe them.

"What is it?" Cait asked, even though she already had a good idea.

Adler didn't berate her at all but provided her with a straight answer. "The graveyard. Or one of them, I imagine. They used to *exile* people in actual fields, so I've heard, but eventually the exiles became so frequent, they needed a more inconspicuous location."

"How—" Having lived her whole life under the guise of peace, even losing her parents to the council, it was nearly impossible for Cait to grasp the reality of where they were and what they were seeing.

"That hole. Where they stand." Adler gestured with his hands as if pushing away an invisible attacker.

Cait's breath caught, and although some part of her was ashamed for being shocked and horrified by this truth, another part of her gave thanks that life with the Rogues—and the knowledge of what the council did—hadn't desensitized her too much.

Until it hit her.

If this was where they exiled citizens, then she was likely staring at the last place her parents had taken their final breaths before being—

She forced her eyes shut against the painful sight. She hadn't cried in years, and while the tears for her mother and father had long since dried up, grief she had thought she'd conquered welled up in her throat.

I'm going to be sick.

What would Adler think if she broke down here?

Adler.

Cait's gut tightened with another wave of sadness. It had been so many years since she'd lost her parents—and years since she'd essentially lost Declan—and though time could only dampen grief and not erase it, she could not fathom being here just one week after losing a loved one as he had. She turned to him, expecting to see some sign of mourning, but his expression was blank. She fought to conceal her shock. He might as well have been back at the pub cleaning up.

"How are you so calm?" she asked.

He breathed deep before whispering back, "Looks can be deceiving, love."

When his blue eyes met hers, she tried to see what might be hiding behind them, if only to know she wasn't standing here alone getting her heart shredded and reopening old scars she'd tried so hard to ignore.

But his scars are fresh.

"Don't worry about me," he said with a wink, though no humor lined his words and no playfulness flashed across his features. "I'm a big boy. I'll be okay. And we have a job to do. Can't do that if I'm busy licking my wounds."

"I just can't—" He raised his hand and looked away, and she took a step toward him. To do what, she didn't know.

"I'm okay," he repeated, and she wondered if he was trying to convince himself of that as much as her.

Cait wanted to say something, to do something. Their sorrow, similar though not shared, was almost palpable in the air between them. It sent pinpricks up her arms and down her spine. She'd pushed aside all of these kinds of feelings because she'd had to.

She'd had a job to do, to run the pub and care for Declan. Not that she'd done well with the latter. Never had she found anyone who understood her pain quite like this. Not Lucan, not Kira, not the twins, not any of the Rogues. They'd all lost someone—or multiple someones—but none of them managed their grief as she did. Others mourned outwardly, breaking out into tears randomly, for years upon years, but she hadn't the luxury of time and rest. She couldn't afford to be vulnerable or weak.

And that was what she saw now in Adler.

That same determination to keep moving, to keep going, to not forget those lost but to honor them by continuing to live. Those who mourned privately still mourned; she knew that all too well.

"I'm sorry for assuming you were feeling nothing. That was callous of me."

He lowered his head to look her straight in the eye and wrapped his hands lightly around her arms. "You have nothing to apologize for. I'm not sure whether to be flattered that you care for me or offended that you think so little of me."

Cait tightened her lips into a line, unsure of what to say and not trusting herself to not say something stupid. Again.

Adler straightened and dropped his hands. "Before we start swapping sob stories, we should probably focus, no?"

With a nod, Cait moved her attention back to the pirates, who were still chatting quietly. "Where is she? Do you see her?" Her questions came out as a breath, so light she didn't think he'd heard her until he moved up beside her. From the corner of her eye, she watched him crane his neck slightly this way and that to peer around the branches and scan the clearing.

"There," he said, pointing out something to the right.

On the ground a few paces away from the pirates, Penny lay.

Whether she was still alive or already dead, Cait couldn't tell from this vantage point. Why hadn't they tossed her over yet? Why had they left her on the ground? Didn't they have other things to do?

As if Adler could hear her thoughts, he said, "They're probably waiting for her to regain consciousness. They want her awake when they..." He didn't finish the sentence, and Cait was glad for that.

"Any ideas?" she asked, shoving aside her embarrassment over asking him for help. She was the leader of the Rogues, and here she was asking for input from a pirate.

Adler pulled back and looked at her. "You mean the great Cait McCallagh doesn't have a plan already in mind?"

She rolled her eyes. "I wasn't supposed to be the one to do this, remember? It was to be the twins. And I don't dictate how they do their jobs. So no, I don't have a specific plan in mind."

"And I suppose pushing them into that chasm isn't acceptable?" Cait shook her head.

"Then we will just have to knock them unconscious long enough to grab her."

"Except we need her awake first, remember? We need her to realize what was about to happen to her."

"Ah, right," Adler said. "Then we wait. They aren't going anywhere."

Looking back at the pirates, who were still chatting and laughing as if they weren't here to kill this woman for the council, Cait swallowed hard. "Why don't they wake her themselves?"

Beside her, Adler lowered himself to the ground and rested his back against a nearby tree where he could still keep an eye on their targets. "If I had to guess, they're in no hurry to get back to their post in town. The longer they stay here—the longer this takes them—the less work they have to do overall."

Cait glanced at him over her shoulder. "So pirates are lazy."

"No." He paused to pull one side of his mouth into a smirk. "Selfish and greedy? Sure. But lazy?" He shook his head.

Selfishness and greed certainly plagued many of the pirates she'd hosted in the pub over the years, but neither characteristic seemed to apply to the pirate accompanying her on this task.

Former pirate.

"Plus," he continued, "what would their incentive be to rush it? It's not like she's bothering them at the moment. Nor does the council offer bonuses for quickness. Or anything really."

Not bothering to say more, Cait simply shrugged and settled herself onto the ground, propping her elbows on her bent knees as she continued to watch for any sign Penny was waking. But the woman remained still, so still Cait seriously questioned whether she was still alive. If only there was some way to wake her without alerting her captors of their presence.

"So you and Lucan..." Adler said, his low voice barely hiding his amusement. "I take it you two aren't—"

"No. We aren't." Immediately her face grew warm, though the topic didn't warrant such a response.

A breath of a laugh escaped him. "So defensive. I hope he never hears you dismiss the idea so quickly. Men bruise easily, you know."

"He understands—"

"That you're not attracted to him. That's fair."

"You know that wasn't what I was going to say."

"Do I?" Adler looked pensively up to the treetops, his finger tapping against his lips. "Then why? And don't claim the *cause* doesn't allow for such things. I saw several pairings of Rogues at the ruins."

"It's just not something I'm looking for." Cait tried to appear as uninterested as possible. Not that she minded the discussion. It did help pass the time, but Adler seemed intent on not accepting her answers, and that was going to get old quickly.

"Ah, careful about that though. These things have a way of falling into your lap whether you're looking for them or not." He raised a brow, and Cait couldn't tell if he was still referring to Lucan or not.

"Is that how it went with Lani?" The words were out before Cait could rethink them. She'd been so desperate to divert attention away from her. Her discomfort must have shown on her face, because Adler laughed again, low enough to keep it hidden under the rumbling of the sea beyond.

"It's okay, love. I meant it when I told you not to worry about me." His smile remained, though his eyes seemed to dim.

"Would hate to think I bruised you so easily though."

"Well, now I am flattered. Thank you. But yes, to answer your question. That is basically how it happened between us."

Cait had no reply. She didn't even know why she'd asked the question in the first place, and it wasn't like her to slip up as much as she was, saying things without forethought.

It's just the stress.

Her stress had greatly increased over the past couple of days. Her mind was on high alert at all times, all her worries and concerns churning away, unwilling to be quieted or set aside, like they feared she'd forget about them if they didn't stay at the forefront of her mind.

"What about when this is all done though?" Adler's question snapped Cait's attention back to him.

"What about what?" Her brow tightened as she tried to remember what they'd been talking about. *You're losing it, Cait.*

Adler's smile returned, his dimples greeting her before they disappeared with his response. "You. Lucan. Future?"

"I don't see how that's any of your concern."

"Are you that repulsed by him that you refuse to talk about it?"

"Seems an odd topic given our current circumstances."

Adler's shoulders lifted in an easy shrug. "What can I say, love. I'm a bit of a romantic."

"I see." She glanced quickly past the trees into the clearing. The pirates were still talking, though they had taken to sitting on the ground. "So, how long do you think it will be, Mr. Romantic, before someone else falls in your lap?"

"The real question is when will I be ready to let someone stay once they've fallen."

Cait couldn't refrain from rolling her eyes at his confidence. She considered him carefully. Did he don this false bravado to hide a scorched heart? But all she saw in his jewel-like eyes was a sarcastic glint. Either he really hadn't been that hurt by Lani's death, or he had perfected his ability to hide himself from others.

Looks can be deceiving.

Perhaps he was right.

Adler must have noticed her scrutiny, because he raised a brow again and asked, "Not finding what you're seeking here?" and circled his hand in the air to indicate his face.

"I can't figure you out." Again, the words were out before she was able to stop them. What was happening to her?

"Well that was far more honest than I expected from the notorious leader of the Rogues. Speaking of which," he said, his expression darkening, "if you are indeed so notorious, why does the council not know who you are by now?"

Cait's mouth tightened as she shook her head. "I honestly don't know. Every day I wake up wondering if this will be the day they decide to make their move against me. So far, they haven't. And I can only assume either they're not as powerful as they've made themselves out to be, or they're waiting for the best moment to—"

"Spring their trap," Adler offered. It wasn't a question, but Cait still nodded. "So, what about me is tripping you up?"

He hadn't forgotten her stupid confession, and now he expected an explanation. Should she be honest with him? If she was going to work with him against the council, it seemed best to be able to trust him implicitly. And yet, regardless of her gut feeling that he could be trusted, she hadn't opened up to anyone but Lucan in years. Even before her parents had disappeared, she'd been a closed book. Some feelings and thoughts needed to be held close, protected. Even Lucan didn't know the extent of the dark thoughts she kept concealed, the ones she'd learned could be best hidden behind a quick wit, a sharp tongue, and a friendly smile.

Would she ever find someone she could share all of herself with? All of her inner demons and fears? Adler might understand her better than most, but it took more than common trauma to build a connection. And she wasn't sure she even wanted such a thing.

He asked you a simple question. He didn't request you court him. Get a hold of yourself.

"I just can't figure out if all this carefree attitude and easy smile"—she cleared her throat and gestured to his face with her hand—"is the real you or if it's a mask to cover someone who is still hurting."

"Why can't it be both?" Adler cocked his head.

"How would that work at all? How can the real you also be a mask? That doesn't make any sense."

"Doesn't it though? The mask we choose to wear around others is as much us as the emotions we hide. They don't have to be an either-or, mutually exclusive. After all, it's not as though we can steal the personalities of others."

"But we can pretend; we can put on an act. Are you claiming such is still reflective of our true self?"

"We cannot separate our personality from our words and actions even when we try. Some part of us will always seep through. Perhaps only a small part, but we cannot erase ourselves no matter how hard we might try or hope to."

Adler's explanation brought images of Declan to Cait's mind, and she contemplated how his actions had varied each time she'd seen him since his recent return to Cregah. How he had effectively been a different person during each visit. The confident, snarky pirate at the pub. The belligerent younger brother in her office. The concerned and doting lover with Aoife. They were all indeed him, each exaggerating a different part of his personality, but each a part of him regardless.

"Makes sense, I guess," she admitted. She rubbed a hand behind her neck, wishing Penny would wake already so they could get this over with and not have to continue this conversation.

Adler looked as though he was about to speak again, and she might have stopped him had another voice not sounded first.

"Up. Both of you." A pirate wearing the same yellow fabric as Penny's captors loomed over them as he emphasized the command with a wave of his knife.

35
DECLAN

The entrance to the Black Sound provided no indication of the darkness that resided within, nor did it match its moniker in the slightest. Something in the air soothed Declan's nerves, having the same calming effect as that of his mother's hand on his back when he'd had trouble falling asleep as a kid. The sun, still hours away from setting, shone through clouds high above the mountain peaks. The entire scene reflected perfectly in the still water of the sound. The sheer beauty of it all, combined with the rhythmic sound of their small boat's oars in the water, was strangely comforting.

With what Callum had explained about the sirens' tastes, this environment seemed counterproductive. If they desired the most sorrowful and regretful souls to come to them, why calm them first?

"Don't let it fool you," Callum said, his rough voice cutting through the tranquil atmosphere. "It's part of their devilry."

"Beautiful scenery and calm seas?"

"Aye. They may not use song to lure you in, but they have other ways of attracting their prey. Like offering a banquet of tantalizing food—"

"—only to poison it."

"Basically."

"And what type of poison should I expect to find?" He tried to keep the question casual, though his nerves were starting to fray despite their serene surroundings.

"I would not be surprised if we find your lass waiting for us. But remember, it isn't really her. Whatever you see in there isn't real. The longer you can resist the queen's baiting, the more time I'll have to locate the dagger, so I'd rather you not die too quickly."

"Well, I am rather fond of living."

"You won't be once she gets a hold of you."

"And we know for sure it will be the queen who—"

Callum gave a firm nod. "The queen is the only one with that strong of an ability. The others can't enter your mind like she can. They can pull your mind toward them, get you lost in what they offer, but only the queen can stow away in your thoughts, change them, make you see what isn't real, believe what isn't true."

Declan shivered reflexively and shifted to look at his companion. "How do you know so much about the sirens? How does anyone? They don't seem to be the type to suffer some to survive and leave."

"Seems it happened more often centuries ago, which is how we ended up with the various texts about them. Not that most folks see them as anything more than myths and legends. The sirens. The dagger. The dragons. Even the fae, to an extent, have become little more than fanciful tales. But there are still some who believe. Like you. And me."

"What makes you see it as truth and not a fable?"

Callum raised a brow. "I could ask the same of you."

Why did Declan believe the stories? He had honestly never asked himself that question or wondered what made him so different from the skeptics. Looking out over the prow of the boat and taking in the beauty around them, Declan chewed on the question.

His parents had always told him not to take anything at face value but to question everything, warning him that nothing could be trusted beyond family bonds. So when his schooling with his father had turned to the subject of the Aisling legends, he'd treated them as the opposite. *All legends have some truth to them.* His father had repeated this often, and Declan had taken it to heart.

Declan cleared his throat with a hoarse rumble and said, "My father."

"Same."

"And here I thought you were spawned from some devil." He tried to picture Callum as a child, sitting on a barstool like he had often done, being taught lessons by his own dad. It wasn't easy to imagine the pirate as a child, let alone one with a father and a family.

Callum said, "My father was one of the few to have seen them with his own eyes, to face them and live to tell the tale."

"And you believed him?"

"Of course. I had no reason not to. You believed yours."

"Why was he even up here? What happened to him? How did he survive?" The questions fell out of Declan's mouth, and an image of Aoife rambling flashed in his mind.

"It's the age-old story. Boy loves girl. Girl's father disapproves. Boy seeks treasure to prove his worth. He found a crew leaving Caprothe, heading north to Turvala. Convinced a few of the men to sneak away on one of the lifeboats to get to the sound and the legendary treasure. Out of the four who ventured in, only two came out, one of them being my father."

Like the four of us in this damned boat. Declan couldn't help but wonder which two—if any—would survive today.

Callum continued. "He managed to pocket a handful of gold coins before escaping, enough to support a wife and eventually a child."

"You."

"Aye." For a long while, Callum stared at the water, seeming lost in his story. "He never liked talking about his life before starting his family. Whenever I asked him to describe his childhood or how he had made his riches, he waved me off, saying it was of little interest, before diving into some fanciful tale of dragons and fae. But later, when I was grown, he and I shared a bottle of rum on the day we buried my mother. And he told me the tale of how he ended up in these waters, how the queen had appeared before them, how she had shown a different vision to each—dependent on their personal histories and pains. One of them went mad quickly, throwing himself into the water where the other sirens waited for him. Another fought against it as long as he could before breaking down into a heap of remorse and pain. They left him writhing on the stone while they watched him hungrily, like he was a roast turning over the fire. My father said he believed he was allowed to leave—along with the fourth, who was little more than a boy still—because his heart was untainted by darkness and had little appeal to the creatures. Whether that is true, I don't know, but that was the only reason he ever gave."

"And they simply let them leave? No sneaking away necessary?"

Callum pulled his mouth into a tight line before answering. "As far as I know, they granted them that gift. Though I don't know how much of a gift it was. His sleep was never restful. Always thrashing and screaming himself awake. He said he never regretted what he did, because it brought him my mother and me, but when he did finally pass, he seemed relieved and ready to leave it all behind him for some actual rest and peace."

Declan let the story soak in, picking out what might be helpful for him when he faced the queen and whatever tricks she had in store for him. He couldn't see any obvious holes in Callum's tale, but he heard his own father's reminder to question it all, always. Callum wouldn't like the one question he had, but even still, he needed to consider it, especially if Callum was as serious to get to the dagger as he claimed.

"And what if he was wrong? What if all the legends got it wrong?"

Callum simply raised a brow, though no annoyance showed on his face. "I've pondered that same thing all these years. But if all the stories describe the same thing, it is only logical that there would be at least a fair amount of truth to them."

"But couldn't the sirens use their compulsion powers to shape the survivors' stories to fit their needs?"

"Aye. Anything's possible. So we plan for the worst—that we are walking into an awful trap completely blind—but we hope for the best."

"You mean hope that I resist long enough for you to retrieve an enchanted dagger with the power to bring you victory over all your adversaries?"

"Pretty much."

"Great," Declan muttered under his breath. His skin should have been tingling with the anticipation of facing the queen, but whatever magic existed here had covered him in a blanket of comfort and calm. Though he consciously knew of the danger, his body refused to react or prepare for it. It was the perfect way to have your prey arrive at your doorstep, so comfortable that resistance was unlikely.

Put you at ease before they rip you to pieces.

They spent the rest of the journey in silence, the four men in the small boat casually watching the scenery as it passed by. How mere rock and water could appear so majestic, Declan couldn't explain. So simple yet so grand. He peered up at the rock wall closest to him and wondered if anyone at the top was able to see them. That question led to several more pressing ones.

Where did the sirens live exactly?

What would they show him?

Would he survive?

He marveled at how his body and mind didn't react naturally. His heart rate and breathing remained steady, his mind gliding from question to question as easily as their boat through the water. He should be preparing himself mentally for the fight that lay ahead, but his mind refused to acknowledge the coming threat, as if he was approaching the peace of his cove back on Cregah.

The cove.

Though the memory flooded his mind, he didn't drown in it as he had every time before. He saw her face, his bloody hands, him pleading on his knees, and her walking away from him, all as though it had happened to complete strangers.

No emotional response.

No pain.

Only numbness.

All part of the plan.

The waters of the sound cut through the land, winding around the cliffs. Callum had his men row them as close to the inside of each turn to cut down on time. After an hour, Declan opened his mouth to ask when he expected them to arrive, but just as he did, they rounded another corner and the scenery changed, the narrow passage between the cliffs opening up into a vast body of water. It was surrounded by the same tall mountains, but they no longer dropped straight down into the water. Instead, beaches peppered the shoreline all around the basin.

But unlike the beaches he'd visited, these lay barren. No trees. No animals.

No animals anywhere, actually. No birds in the sky, and the crystal-clear water showed no sign of fish.

But the water was far from empty.

From his perch, Declan spotted the remains of boats, some with holes in them and others completely intact. How many captains and crews had been lured into these pristine waters, called by the calm serenity within, only to end up at the bottom of this watery crater? It didn't appear particularly deep, but it was far from peaceful.

A flash of light danced through the water, under their boat. Not a light, Declan realized, but a reflection of it. *Sirens.* For the first time since they'd arrived, he felt a twinge of panic.

A splash of water to his left pulled his attention, and he turned in time to see delicate fins, feathery and flowing, slide below the surface. Callum's men stopped rowing, and Declan waited for the captain to bark at them to resume. But the order never came.

Callum sat as still as his men. No one moved. Declan wasn't sure any of them blinked or breathed. Their eyes were wide, their fists tight.

The boat jolted. Declan clamped his hands down on either side to steady himself.

Before he could say anything, the boat jerked again, this time struck from the other side. The once still water now churned around them as tails flicked in and out of the water.

Declan was nearly convinced his heart had altogether stopped when something emerged to his right. Not a tail but a woman. Or what looked like one. To an extent. Gold hair, wet and clinging to her, framed her face. Her otherworldly beauty was marred only by her horrifying silver eyes, which were so light the irises were nearly invisible. Giving them a smile with her deep pink lips, she raised her arms out of the water, snatched the rower closest to her, and pulled him under. The water swallowed his screams.

But even with her unnatural speed, Declan hadn't missed how her smile had shifted into a deathly grin before she plunged her teeth, terrifyingly sharp, into the man, ripping the flesh between his neck and shoulder and turning the water around them red with his blood.

Declan's heartbeat thundered in his ears as he waited for the next attack, wondering who would be snatched next.

But the boat went still. The surface of the water became glassy and calm once again—albeit no longer clear—as the sirens retreated from them. Still, no one spoke.

Don't be so surprised, Declan.

This had been his expectation, after all. This was what they did.

Yet he remained stunned, staring at the water where the man had slipped below, broken and dying. Declan hadn't known the man, and he had no reason to feel any remorse over the loss. But it brought questions all the same.

Would anyone mourn that pirate?

Had he been supporting a family?

Was he of the rotten and vile variety?

Will anyone mourn you?

He hoped so.

With a shake of his head, he snapped himself back to the matter at hand.

"Do you know where to go, exactly?" Declan whispered out of the corner of his mouth, but Callum didn't respond. Declan tried to see what had caught his attention, but there didn't appear to be anything of interest on the far-off beach of bone-white sand.

Declan waved a hand in front of Callum's face, but the man's eyes—though they blinked—didn't shift away from the beach, which lay straight ahead.

Declan.

His name was whispered into his mind in a voice decidedly more feminine than his own. It sent him spinning his head round to see if someone was nearby, but the only other person there besides Callum was the remaining crewman, who had somehow found the wherewithal to resume rowing.

Declan.

The voice came again, all too familiar to him, like the whisper of a pleasant dream that fled with the fluttering open of one's eyes, comforting but blurred, leaving behind only a trace of the emotion it had caused and no clue as to its origin or essence.

How could you?

Declan stilled. He didn't need to ask for clarification, though had this been Callum—or even Tommy—posing the question and not an eerily familiar voice speaking to him within his mind, he would have made some snarky comment.

You said you loved me.

Declan's chin snapped up. They had rowed almost all the way across the water now, and the beach with white sand lay less than fifty feet ahead of them.

And it was no longer empty.

Movement in the water to his right, and then to the left, nearly pulled his attention away, but even if a siren were to appear on the boat beside him, he would not be able to look away from the woman who stood on the beach.

This wasn't real. It couldn't be. It was merely part of the sirens' games.

But it seemed too real.

She seemed too real.

It had been a week—or more?—since he'd last seen her, but there was the face that appeared every time he closed his eyes. The sweet freckles sprinkled across her nose and cheeks. The clothes he'd helped her with that night. And it was the same look of pity and disappointment in those gold-flecked green eyes. She didn't speak. She didn't move.

But she spoke to him all the same.

I trusted you.

She wasn't real.

She wasn't real.

She wasn't real.

It wasn't her voice.

It wasn't her on the beach.

The sirens were shifters and tricksters, feeding on heartache and suffering. This was a siren, not Aoife, and yet the sight of her stabbed him in the chest, hollowing it out just as she had that night in the cove.

I can't.

Declan couldn't pull his eyes away as they rowed closer. When the boat brushed up against the soft beach, his limbs remained still. More from remorse than fear.

Odd. He'd thought he would feel hope when he next saw her. Hope for redemption and forgiveness.

But that hope was dead. Pulled into the bloody waters behind him.

"Didn't you miss me, Declan?" This time she spoke aloud, her lips grabbing his attention as they formed the words. He didn't answer, but he couldn't look away from the sweet face he'd been longing to see again.

Something pressed against his back, and before he could protest, it pushed him forward until he had no other choice but to step over the side of the boat and head ashore. He didn't need to look behind to know it was Callum who had forced him out, but now, having seen the sirens' territory, he didn't know how the pirate hoped to find the dagger. It could be anywhere, from the mess of rotting wood in the water to somewhere on this barren beach.

Declan's feet splashed in the water as he walked slowly up the sand toward Aoife.

Not Aoife, he reminded himself.

But as he got closer, he couldn't help but marvel at the resemblance. The waves of her hair, still cut short. The tiny quiver of her lips. The desperate tension of her fisted hand at her chest.

Yearning to touch her once more, to hold her again and soothe away the sorrow on her face, he lifted a hand, but before his fingers met the skin of her cheek, he froze, blinked, and tilted his head.

He dropped his hand and donned his favorite smirk.

"That is quite the trick, I must say. Near perfect."

Aoife lowered her head into her hands as if ashamed, but when she straightened once again, smoothing her hair back as she ran her fingers through it, every familiar feature dissolved into someone else's. Her unruly brown hair now lay well past her shoulders in dark waves—a raven black that shone blue or purple depending on how the sun's rays hit it. Aoife's gold-green eyes darkened to a haunting deep purple, and her freckled skin became as pristine as the sea's surface on a windless morning. Her pirate's attire dissolved into a black dress that plunged to her navel and didn't cover much beyond that. Before, her expression had been filled with anguish and regret, but now it showed little more than a sinister wickedness and delight.

"I knew it would be hard to fool you, Declan." The woman's sultry voice no longer matched the one he loved, though it was nearly as lovely. A twisted sort of lovely. "But I had you at least for a moment. Perhaps two."

"Not surprising for one of such power, Your Majesty," Declan said, though he kept his features cold and emotionless.

"So you have heard of me then. And you still came to visit."

Lifting a shoulder, he tightened his lips. "Honestly, I thought you'd be taller. With a crown."

"And I thought you'd be more of a challenge," she said, the fire in her eyes seeming to dim as her features sagged with disappointment.

"Well, the day is still young, and I've only just arrived. Perhaps I'll surprise you yet."

The queen turned before he finished speaking and began to walk toward the face of the cliff, calling back to him, "Are you coming? Or am I mistaken and you're not here for the dagger?"

Declan glanced over his shoulder, expecting to see Callum and his remaining man already rowing away to start their search for that very blade. But Callum and his crewman had stepped onto the beach, and both wore blank expressions ill-fitting for the situation.

"You too, Callum," the queen called in a song-like tone. But only Callum moved, leaving his man behind and walking past Declan without any acknowledgment. Declan knew he should move; he should obey, get this over with. But he couldn't look away from the last man standing tall on the beach, the water lapping at his ankles as he stared straight ahead.

Even when the sirens surfaced beside him, the man's eyes remained blank and unseeing.

Declan couldn't budge as he watched the sirens emerge from the water. Three. Four. Five deathly beautiful women hauled their bodies over the white sand, dragging themselves forward with their slender forearms. At their hips, their pearl-like skin shifted into mesmerizing scales of shimmering golds and blues and teals and reds. Legends told of their fish-like bodies, but nothing could have prepared Declan for witnessing it firsthand. Nor for the transformation that occurred as they exited the water, scales and fins melting away until they stood on lithe, feminine legs. In any other scenario, Declan might have found their unabashed nakedness appealing, but knowing their intentions, his gut twisted, and bile climbed his throat.

When they made their move, Declan forced himself to turn away and tried to block out the sound of tearing flesh and tortured screams. But he couldn't, even as he quickened his pace to follow after the queen and Callum.

After a hundred or so paces, the sickening sounds behind him faded away, though he wasn't sure if it was due to the distance or because the sirens had finished their meal. He focused on his surroundings and found nothing but water, sand, and rock.

No doorways. No obvious secret nooks where she might conduct her ghastly business in private. Though if Callum's father's account was accurate, this siren didn't shy away from an audience.

"So, what's your name?" Declan asked as he caught up with them.

The queen spun around on him, and he nearly ran into her. Her brow tightened. "I thought you said you'd heard of me."

"I only noted your height. You assumed the other."

She simply blinked. Once. Twice. Aoife would have rolled her eyes.

She's not Aoife.

"No, I'm not Aoife. I'm Triss."

Her intense glare burned a hole right through him, but he refused to flinch, even when her eyes roamed over his face, her head leaning from one side to the other. The seductive scent of mountain mist and iron engulfed him. And then she had him. Her hand gripped his hair and yanked his head back. She wet her lips with her tongue in a slow, deliberate motion, like she was looking upon a gourmet meal.

Stepping closer, she let her breath caress his cheek for one long, slow, painful moment before she whispered to him. "I'm going to have fun with you, Declan McCallagh."

36

AOIFE

Of all the visions Aoife had had for her future, being swallowed whole by a legendary creature of the sea had never occurred to her. Yet here she was. Staring into the maw of a beast she'd thought only myth until recently. She'd never considered herself brave. Not when she'd run. Not when she'd approached Callum. Not when she'd stood up to her mother in the library. Not even when she had tried to help Collins during the kraken's initial attack.

And even if she had found some courage hidden somewhere within her, no doubt it would have melted away in this moment as the abyss yawned before her.

No one moved around her, causing her to wonder if these men—pirates who had seen more than their fair share of danger and risk—had lost their fearlessness. She hoped not.

Although her feet remained frozen to the deck—her eyes

wide and her fingers trembling at her sides—her mind raced on, searching for some way they could survive this. Explosives were not available, and their cannons would be of little help—if they had any ammunition remaining after all the shots they'd already fired. Bria and Maura had collapsed from overexertion, and Renna's talent didn't provide much help in this situation.

Aoife might have wept. She wanted to, actually. At least crying would be doing something more than simply standing here, lifeless. But she had gone completely numb, and even her anxiety refused to manifest, leaving her an empty shell, as if her soul had already decided to pack up and vacate.

"Declan."

His name fell from her lips in a whisper, and her mind flooded with memories of him. The cove. The alley. His cabin. The birthday party. The beach in Foxhaven. The kiss—the real one. The looks of protectiveness and remorse and then despair as she walked away. The memories gave way to nightmares. Declan alone in the brig of a ship, being tortured by Callum. Then him standing before the sirens awaiting their attacks.

Every thought grieved her until she envisioned him lying bloody and lifeless on whatever sands the sirens called home. Then the grief turned to anger, a burning rage below her ribs that slowly spread throughout her body, like a deep well of boiling water had been unstopped within her. It now rushed to fill every bit of her. She gritted her teeth as she clenched her eyes shut and closed her fists tightly. The heat intensified, but instead of fighting it, she welcomed it.

While numbness had its uses, so did rage.

And perhaps rage was what she needed right now.

With her chin lowered, Aoife opened her eyes and focused on the beast. Slowly, little by little, it pulled the ship closer. Or perhaps time simply seemed to slow down as she focused on her target. She had no idea what she hoped to accomplish simply by staring at it angrily, but she was willing to try anything at this point. She might not be fae, but fae weren't the only ones with powers. Maybe Aoife had something hidden deep within her, something that could help her friends and Declan.

Tommy had moved around behind her to whisper with Gavin, but Aoife couldn't hear what they said. Then all sounds were drowned out by the rush of water around the hull. They were picking up speed.

For Declan.

For me.

For us all.

She concentrated on the creature's mouth, imagined pulling out every fang, envisioned taking those fangs and stabbing its haunting eyes with them. But nothing happened. Not even a wiggle from the sharp teeth that threatened them. So she moved on to the water. If she couldn't control living things, maybe she could do something with the elements like Bria could. So she let the sound of the sea engulf her, envisioned it shifting its course and carrying them away from the danger instead of toward it.

And she felt like an imbecile.

More so as she noticed they seemed to be increasing in speed, as though the kraken had noticed her attempts to thwart it and had intensified its efforts.

Her rage dissolved. Like a candle being snuffed out.

Only her hopelessness remained.

What was she even hoping to do? She was nothing but a human, awkward and clumsy. Humans didn't possess supernatural qualities.

Her chin dropped to her chest in defeat, and she once again

let her eyelids fall closed. Words of regret and guilt and sorrow echoed in her mind as she prepared for whatever end was about to befall her and her friends.

Sucking in a deep breath, she recalled her favorite memories.

Her and Lani enjoying a picnic lunch on the lawn of the council hall, lying down in the soft grass and pointing out the shapes of clouds to each other and laughing at the ridiculous stories they created from what they saw. And then Declan under a sea of stars at night, his hands taking hers as she spun out of Tommy's grasp, seeing that nervous spark in his eyes.

Her hand reached up to his face, to cup his jaw in her palm, but before her fingers could touch him, two large splashes in the water sent the memory fleeing, and her eyes flashed open.

There, right in the middle of the monster's mouth, water sprayed up from the sea. Before she had any time to ponder what could have caused that, the loudest sounds she'd ever heard came at her—louder even than the cannons below decks all firing at once—and before she could determine what was happening, the world seemed to fly at her.

Water crashed over her. So much water she thought she'd fallen into the sea or the ship had sunk below the surface. But then something else began to fall. It splattered onto the deck, making a squishing sound that had Aoife's stomach turning even before she opened her eyes.

All around her the deck was covered in chunks of flesh—purple and gray, fatty, slimy globs—resting in black pools of what looked more like, well, Aoife didn't know what. It was thicker than normal blood, and it clung to the wooden planks of the deck, adhering the bits of meat to the ship.

"Aoife! Are you okay?" The voice pulled her attention away from the gooey mess, and she turned to find Gavin rushing over to her, careful not to step in any of the creature's remains.

"Yeah," Aoife said, blinking. "I think so. What was that?"

"But—you should be hurt."

He looked genuinely concerned, but still, his lack of confidence in her was rather offensive.

"Gee, thanks, Gavin." Before he could respond, she swung her head back to the sea where the kraken had been waiting to swallow them. The surface of the Aisling looked much like the deck of the *Siren's Song*—littered with small pieces of the creature's remains.

"No, Aoife. Look!" Gavin had stepped closer to her, but she turned to find him keeping a wider berth than she'd expected. His finger pointed at her torso as he spoke again. "That doesn't hurt?"

Looking down, Aoife realized she had not miraculously avoided being hit by any of the falling pieces of carcass as she'd originally thought. The kraken's thick blood had splattered across her clothes, from her chest down to her boots, making her look like one of the spotted pigs some townspeople kept in Morshan for food. She reached her fingers toward one of the splotches and saw Gavin's whole body tensing. That's when she realized the blood had hit more than her clothes. A part of her arm just below the elbow felt stiff with quickly drying blood.

She looked up at her friend slowly. "Is this the same thing—" Her eyes dropped to his arm, which still lay in a sling across his ribs.

He gave a nod, his eyes wide and roaming over her.

"Well, it doesn't hurt. I'm fine." Twisting and bending her arm, she demonstrated her point. "I can't say it's particularly flattering, but it's at least painless."

Gavin didn't release his breath as she'd expected, and his shoulders remained tight. Every muscle in his body was pulled taut, actually. He seemed to be leaning away from her, but Aoife assured herself it was her imagination. He was her friend after all.

"Wait!" She spun around on the deck, taking in the state of things. Somehow the entire ship beyond the helm appeared untouched, unmarred by the gore she stood in. "What happened? And how did you not get hit with any of this, whatever it is? And where's Tommy?"

"He ran down to check on Maura." Gavin's shoulders loosened enough to offer a shrug before he said, "I don't know how I got so lucky, to be honest. But I think they might be able to answer your first question." He pointed toward the starboard side.

A ship, larger than the *Siren's Song*, sailed toward them. No, it didn't exactly *sail*, for their gold-lined sails hung lifeless. Long oars protruded from small openings in the sides of the hull, cutting through the surface of the sea and bringing the ship closer far faster than Aoife would have thought possible. Especially with no wind.

"Who?" she whispered, but it didn't matter if Gavin had heard her or not, because the answer came on its own.

There at the prow of the ship, Captain Halloran stood in an understated dark gray coat well-fitted to her curves, with a gold sash tied around her waist. Even from this distance, Aoife found her intimidating. The captain's eyes were hidden in the shade cast by her large hat, and her lips were curled up into a half-smile. Raising her hand to her hat, Halloran dipped her chin in greeting to Aoife and Gavin.

Aoife could have sworn the woman's smile grew.

Gavin took in a breath. "I should get the captain." He started to step away, but Aoife held out her arm to stop him, careful not to touch him as she did.

"No. He's had a tough day—as we all have—but I think we

can let him rest, can't we? We can handle this. I mean, what's the likelihood she's here to do us harm?"

Gavin seemed to consider her words, narrowing his eyes slightly, but said nothing for a moment. He finally blinked and shook his head, saying, "Aye. You're right." He started toward the stairs before turning to add, "And if you're wrong, I'm not taking the blame."

〜

Captain Halloran and her three officers had boarded the *Siren's Song*, and now they stood facing Aoife and Gavin on the deck. Her officers were just as imposing as their captain. Though two of them weren't much taller than Aoife, she still felt quite small in comparison.

"Glad to see you again," Aoife said, extending her hand to the captain.

Halloran glanced down at it, her eyes roving over Aoife's gore-spattered arm and attire before she pulled back one corner of her mouth and raised a brow.

Aoife, flustered and embarrassed, clasped her hands behind her back with a quiet apology.

"I'm not one to normally be so picky about cleanliness," Halloran said, "but I'd rather not risk any injuries from that stuff." The captain's eyes narrowed slightly, and Aoife waited for the inevitable question, the same one Gavin had asked. But instead, Halloran turned to Gavin with a shallow nod. "Apologies for not getting here faster."

Gavin straightened but remained several inches shorter than the captain. "No apologies necessary, Captain. You arrived just in time. One more moment and we would have been in the gullet of that beast."

"And now we're wearing it," Aoife said.

Someone had to keep the mood light, right?

Gavin ignored her comment and cleared his throat. "But how did you find us exactly?"

"More importantly," Aoife interjected, "how did you save us?"

Halloran looked from one to the other before asking, "And where is your captain?"

"Tommy is—" Aoife started to reply, but Halloran's warm hazel eyes widened with concern. Once again she looked from Aoife to Gavin and back again.

"What happened to McCallagh?" Her tone betrayed some hint of emotion, but Aoife couldn't quite tell.

"You didn't hear?" Aoife immediately regretted asking the obvious.

Halloran's expression shifted into one Aoife had seen many times on her mother's face, albeit less harsh. "Yes, this is the face of someone in the know."

"Callum—"

Gavin only managed to utter one word before Halloran interrupted, tension stiffening her body. "What in the sands did that blasted man do now?"

"So you've met him then," Aoife said.

Stretching her neck, Halloran said, "You could say that. So what'd he do? Something stupid, no doubt."

"He took Declan."

"He took the captain."

Aoife and Gavin spoke at the same time.

"Any idea why he took him?" Halloran shifted her gaze between them again, and they shared a glance, searching each other's eyes as if they could silently discuss how to answer. "Honestly, you two. I'd like to think saving your sorry asses from the kraken would be proof enough that you can trust me. If Callum has Declan, I assure you, I'm as worried about his wellbeing as you are."

Had Declan even told the crew what they were chasing? Or had they found out when they'd learned of his capture? Would he tell Halloran now? He had trusted her enough to get Aoife away from the council hall safely. He wouldn't have done that without reason.

Aoife said the words quietly. "They're going after the dagger. In the Black Sound."

Halloran's eyes closed as she pulled a breath deep into her lungs and let it out with a whispered string of curses. She turned to look at her officers.

"And what is Tommy doing then? Why isn't he here to—"

Renna stepped forward with a confidence that only came from centuries of living. "He's attending to my youngest sister."

"And who are..." Halloran's looked over the fae. "Impossible." The word came out as a whisper.

"Says the woman who eviscerated an ancient sea creature less than an hour ago?" Renna asked with no challenge in her tone. No humor either. The eldest fae looked exhausted.

Aoife raised a hand. "You never said how you did that."

"Nothing special, really. We always keep large barrels of explosives on hand. And Lara here"—she gestured to the tallest of her officers—"she's our master gunner. Rigged a weapon on the *Duchess* that allows us to send those barrels flying at a target far away."

"I've never heard of such a thing," Mikkel said from behind Renna.

Lara eyed him, though not in an unfriendly way. "Aye. A design from my country, far from the Aisling. We used it on land, but

Captain here allowed me to try it out on the ship."

"And it worked," Aoife said.

Halloran turned her attention back to Renna. "So the stories are true then."

Renna shrugged, an elegant and graceful rise of her shoulders. "Depends on which stories you're referring to."

"You're who Declan was rescuing from the council hall."

A smooth nod.

"You didn't know?" Aoife asked Halloran, wondering if perhaps Declan didn't trust this captain as much as she'd assumed.

"First thing you learn as a pirate is always say less than necessary. He didn't say. I didn't ask."

Aoife's face scrunched with confusion. "Why agree to help him then?"

The familiar look of exasperation washed over Halloran's features, like Aoife was an irritating pebble in her boot that needed shaking out and discarding. "Long story, and one we don't have time for at the moment. Unless you aren't actually interested in saving Declan."

"Right," Aoife said as her face went hot. She looked up to the masts. "But how? These waters seem plagued by a lack of wind."

"With their help," Gavin said, nodding toward the *Duchess*.

"Aye," Halloran confirmed. "Do you have enough men to secure the tow lines?"

"Enough men, yes, though I'm not sure what state they're in."

Mikkel stepped up alongside Renna. "We have enough who aren't wounded, yes, but most could use a rest, especially since we still need to sail the rest of the way to the sound."

"Not a problem," Halloran said. She nodded to her other two officers, and without a word exchanged, they were striding back over to the *Duchess*. "We can help with that. Our crew will help secure the lines for you. It will take us some time to get you out of these dead seas, but that should offer at least several hours for your men to recharge."

Aoife wanted to ask what would happen after that, but it didn't matter if she knew or not. What would happen would happen, and the best she could do was prepare for the various paths they might find themselves on. And focus on the next task in the meantime.

The pirate grabbed Cait's arm and shoved her toward the clearing. Her toe caught on a rock, and she would have fallen to the ground had Adler not rushed forward to catch her.

"Careful, love," he whispered in her ear as he helped her straighten.

She turned her head to thank him, but before she could, the pirate nudged them both forward—placing a flat hand on Cait's shoulder blade while he held his knife against Adler's ribs. Adler didn't resist but let the pirate prod him along before suddenly pivoting and slamming his forearm down hard, knocking the knife into the dirt and sending his fist to greet the man's temple.

It happened much quicker than Cait would have ever expected, but she had acquired quick reflexes—both mental and physical—during her years at the pub. As soon as the blade thumped against the ground, she was kneeling and wrapping her fingers around its handle. She remained in a crouch as she watched Adler send the guy stumbling away. Blood already flowed freely from where the man's cheek had split open, and his hands rushed up instinctively to protect his head. Cait took that opportunity to swing her arm, knife firmly in hand, across the front of his legs. While it wasn't as effective as a strike to the ankle, it did as she had hoped, and the man's knees buckled beneath him. His scream of pain was cut short when Adler's fist connected with the middle of his face.

The pirate fell to his knees, and his hands rushed up to his busted nose. Though he was obviously dazed and looked far from being an immediate threat, Adler still gave him a solid kick to the shoulder that knocked him down. His head made a sickening sound when it struck a rock on the side of the path.

"You made that look too easy," Cait said, wiping blood from the knife onto her pants before securing it into her belt.

"They will have heard that," Adler said, nodding toward the clearing behind her.

Leaning forward, he offered his uninjured hand to her. If he had been looking at her, the gesture might have seemed romantic. Instead he remained focused on the clearing. She twisted her neck around to get a glimpse herself, but he moved at the same time, pushing and turning in an unfamiliar maneuver that brought her whole body around so his arm guarded her front and her back pressed against his torso. A sense of déjà vu swept over her.

His breaths, even and measured as they warmed her ear, contrasted starkly with the tension she felt coursing through his arm and chest. His jaw flexed against her head, a slight movement she might not have noticed if she hadn't already been hyper-focused on him.

Moving her head away from his face, Cait tried to see around the trees and into the clearing, which was now silent except for the distant roaring of the sea.

"Where are—" she started to whisper, but Adler's arm tightened around her rib cage, and he whispered for her to stay quiet.

Leaning close once again, he breathed his command, "When I let you go, move quickly to the right. Stay low. Aye?"

Piecing together his plan—or what she hoped was his plan—she dipped her chin in affirmation. No sooner had she answered than his arm slipped away. The unexpected emptiness she felt—not only at her waist—surprised her, but she gave herself a mental slap in the face and scurried her way into the trees, keeping as low as she could while still maintaining a brisk pace.

When she was sure she had gotten far enough, she turned and peered back around one of the trees to see what had happened to Adler. The pirates who had captured Penny had ventured down the path—likely to check out the commotion—and now approached Adler. Cait's gut tightened and her breath quickened as she waited to see how this would play out.

He might be double-crossing you.

The thought stung, and she tried to convince herself she hadn't made a mistake in trusting him. From her hiding spot, she couldn't make out the words exchanged, but it was evident Adler had said something to appease them. They shared a hearty laugh over their fallen mate—who she hoped was merely unconscious and not dead—and left the man behind as they led Adler toward the clearing. She waited for him to look her way, to give her any sign that his plan was working, that she should move, that she had done well. That last one left a bad taste in her mouth. Why should she want his approval?

But he never glanced back, and the emptiness returned.

What is happening to you?

You told him yourself there's no hope for...

She couldn't even allow herself to finish that thought, promptly drowning it and the unwanted feelings with a deep breath.

There was a job to do. And she would get it done.

Trying to creep through the forest without making a sound took longer than Cait wanted, but she didn't seem to have many other options. So she continued on, carefully watching where she placed her feet before glancing up to make sure she was heading in the right direction while staying hidden.

The trees became more densely packed the farther she moved into the forest, making it nearly impossible to see what lay ahead. Focusing on the men's voices—and the now familiar sound of Adler's deep laugh—she hoped her course would bring her to the clearing and to Penny, and not off the rocky cliffs into the Aisling.

A shiver sent her shoulders squirming, and she cursed her inconvenient fear of heights that could make her uneasy with a mere mental image.

Sands help me if I pop out at a drop-off.

After several excruciatingly long, tedious minutes of trekking through the forest, the trees began to thin out once again, almost as if the forest was announcing to any travelers within that something was about to change.

She relaxed at the sight of grass just beyond the forest's edge. As beautiful as the waters were, and as much as she dreamed of leaving this cursed island, she had no desire to greet the sea from so high.

She slowed her pace even more so she could focus on the conversation ahead. She could almost make out what was being said. Cautiously she ventured forward until she was near enough to the clearing to get a decent view—of the pit cave and of Penny still lying beside it—without risk of being spotted by the pirates. Pirates who seemed to still be having a grand time. Their short stories were resulting in round after round of guffaws.

Penny fidgeted—first a foot and then a hand—and began to regain consciousness. Cait waited. She needed the woman to rouse fully and understand their plan for her rescue. Trying to get herself into a comfortable position, Cait crouched down, careful to keep the leaves from making too much noise as she lowered a knee onto them. Her heart pounded in anticipation, and she tried to steady it with several slow breaths. Penny's restlessness had ceased, and Cait rolled her eyes. Perhaps she could throw something at her, help her along in the waking-up process.

But as Cait turned to look for a stick that would do the trick without injuring the poor woman, the pirates' conversation called her attention.

"You never told us what you were doing here, Jensen." Cait didn't recognize the voices, and she held her breath as she waited to hear more.

"Yeah, last I heard you were near set on earning a promotion with Tiernen. Odd time for you to bail."

Cait's breath caught as she waited for Adler's response. Would he tell the truth? And did Cait even know what the truth was? She winced at the thought that maybe this time her gut had led her astray, led her straight into a trap. For what, a pretty face?

It's not that pretty.

"What can I say?" Adler started. "A better opportunity pre- sented itself."

Cait could picture that smug look of his as he spoke, and she gritted her teeth when the image sent her stomach fluttering. No time for such thoughts or feelings. No time. No hope.

"Better than an officer under a lord, eh? Not sure I believes you," the first pirate said.

Adler gave a relaxed laugh as the other pirate spoke again.

"What could be better than that though?"

Silence stretched, and Cait worked to keep her breaths quiet since the pounding of her heart in her ears made it hard enough to hear their conversation. Would he name her and the Rogues? Or would he mention Lani?

And why did the thought of the latter sting just as much as the former?

"What," Adler finally said, "is the one thing that gets a man to head ashore? To walk away from the sea? To put down roots?"

"Is this a riddle?"

"No, stupid. It's a damn woman."

"You sure?"

"It is, isn't it?"

Cait couldn't keep straight which of the pirates spoke when. She was only able to identify Adler's voice. Not that it mattered.

He laughed. "No, not a riddle. And aye, a woman."

"I knew it."

"Whatever. So who is she?"

This time Adler didn't laugh. "Alas, gents, there is no hope for me there."

Cait couldn't tell if the sorrow in his words was genuine. Of course he would still be mourning Lani's death, even with all his attempts to put up a strong and healthy front. It was exactly what she had done after her parents' deaths. Locking up her pain and grief, only letting it out when she was alone. She also knew it was impossible to keep it contained perfectly, and she still remembered the first time she'd let the depths of her pain show with Lucan. The tears. The screams. The tremors. The rage. It had all escaped her vault, and it was a wonder Lucan hadn't left after seeing such insanity.

But this wasn't Adler screaming and lashing out from pain.

This was a barely evident change in tone, and by the way the other pirates responded, it had gone unnoticed.

"That's a tough break, lad."

"Aye," the other pirate agreed. "So what now?"

Adler answered, "I haven't completely decided, to be honest. Couple irons in the fire at the moment though."

"Good to have options, but I do have one question for you."

"Oh?" Adler asked.

"Aye. You never answered the question. What are you doing out here?" Suspicion coated each word.

"I didn't? You sure?"

"No. You didn't."

No answer. Tense silence. Did Adler have a plan? Or was Cait failing to play her part in that plan? It would have been nice to have been privy to his plan—assuming he had one.

"Oh," Adler said finally, speaking with a confidence that re-assured her he wasn't flying blind. "Well, in that case, I'm here to save that lass over there."

Cait's breath caught.

"What?"

"Why would you do that?"

Another of Adler's laughs filled the clearing. "You really going to waste your time asking why when you could be trying to stop me?"

As the scuffling of feet began, Cait snapped into action, breaking free of the protection of the trees to reach Penny before the pirates could. She shook the woman awake as she glanced over her shoulder to find Adler taking on the two pirates, who—based on their clumsy display of strikes and blocks—had not seen much fighting in recent days. And Adler, with his quick reflexes, seemed able to anticipate each of their poorly executed maneuvers. As they continued to throw punches and kicks—all blocked or countered with ease—they seemed oblivious to the fact that Adler was gradually easing them toward the pit cave.

If Cait didn't get Penny roused soon, this whole ordeal would be for naught. She turned back to the woman and, grabbing both shoulders, gave a few firm pushes while saying Penny's name in a low voice. Penny's legs shifted, but her eyes still didn't open, and Cait half contemplated smacking her across the face. As satisfying as that would be for all the snide comments the woman had made to her over the years, somehow it felt inappropriate.

So instead Cait pinched her.

Right on the underside of Penny's arm, Cait plucked a bit of skin and squeezed as hard as she could.

Penny's eyes flashed open as she let out a yelp.

"Quiet, Penny," Cait whispered as she ducked to get into the woman's line of sight.

"What? Cait? What in the sands are you doing here?" She tried to sit up. "Where am I?" Her head turned from one side to the other and then stopped when she caught a glimpse of the scene behind Cait. "What is that man doing? They shouldn't be fighting. Where did they get blades? That's the man from the shop. What is he...? What am I doing here? Why am I not at the council?" Panic began to fill her dull eyes as they darted around the clearing. "What is this place?"

"Adler and I followed you here."

"Why would you follow me? They weren't hurting me. They were merely escorting me, doing their job," Penny protested as she slowly pushed herself up to standing.

"Oh." Cait stood as well, placing her hands on her hips. How silly she felt arguing with this woman while Adler was busy fighting. "Is that why you screamed then?"

"Well, no one wants to be exiled, Cait. Of all the people on Morshan, you should understand that better than most." No sympathy showed on the woman's face, and Cait wished she had indeed slapped the woman awake.

"I do. It's why I'm here now."

"Surely it's a mistake and they just stopped here for a break on our way to the council. And how do I know that man—your man—didn't instigate this violence?"

Cait should have known it wouldn't be so easy to change her mind. Penny had grown up in Morshan with a family who believed wholeheartedly in the mission of the council and trusted them implicitly. Some people didn't want to see the truth lying behind the veil of perfection and comfort. They never doubted. And now Cait needed to convince one of the council's most devoted believers.

Turning her chin over her shoulder, she found the fight had quieted down—which she might have noticed sooner had she not been entertaining all of Penny's questions. One of the pirates was kneeling on the ground, groaning. He had his forehead pressed against the grass while his hands, covered in his own blood, held onto his nose. Adler had pinned the other pirate's arm behind his back and was working to keep him in place as he struggled.

"Adler?" Cait called in her most innocent tone.

"Yes, love? How can I help?" His half-smile quirked up until that dimple appeared, and Cait worked to focus her attention elsewhere.

"That's enough. Let him go. Miss Penny here would like us to allow them to continue escorting her to the council hall."

One of his brows angled up. A bit of mischief flashed in his blue eyes before he released the pirate and took a casual step back. "Of course."

Cait moved to meet Adler on the other side of the clearing,

happy to see the pirates were slow to rise and return to their senses. As Adler came alongside her, the warmth of his shoulder brought back all the sensations she'd experienced when he'd held her earlier in the trees. With a clearing of her throat, she pushed all of that to the edge of her mind and turned to the two pirates, who were still shaking their heads clear of the stars Adler had gifted them.

"Gentlemen. My apologies. Please continue with your exile," Cait said, offering the words in her sweetest and most amenable tone. She gestured toward Penny before turning back to Adler and weaving her hand into the crook of his arm. "Let's go, love."

She'd known using his own term of endearment on him would get a reaction, but nothing could have prepared her for the way heat engulfed her from her toes up to her ears and down to her fingertips at the sight of his smile, as genuine as she'd ever seen it. That warmth only increased when his hand hovered over the small of her back and he began to lead her back to the path through the trees.

"Careful there, Cait. Don't be using that with me too often. Especially not around Lucan," Adler said in a low voice. "I'd hate to make him even more jealous."

"Don't lie. You would love to do that to him," she said as they stepped into the trees.

"Aye, I would." He let out a single, quiet laugh, then stopped, drew in a long breath, and turned her to face him. "But honestly, and in all seriousness, please don't call me that."

Cait's forehead tightened. His words sparked confusion she couldn't conceal. "Oh, but you can—"

"Old habits die hard," he said. She waited for that smirk to appear within his beard, but he remained somber. "But you didn't say it out of habit. You used it deliberately, and while I may be a lying, murderous pirate, I do have a heart. Albeit one a bit broken of late. And unless you mean it—which I think we both know you don't—then please refrain."

Cait's mind emptied. A basin drained of all water. No thoughts. No words. She had no response for him. But he didn't seem to mind her silence. He offered her a tight smile and turned away to see what had happened back at the pit while they had been talking.

"Now to figure out how to make this work," he whispered, flicking his chin back to the clearing. Penny was approaching the pirates, who now seemed more than eager to get this job over and done with.

"Any ideas?" Cait asked, the words coming out scratchy and strained.

Adler's eyes narrowed, and he pursed his lips to one side for a moment before he spoke. "It's too bad we don't have a whip." Turning toward her, he added, "You don't have one, do you?"

She raised a brow at him. He couldn't be serious. "No. I don't. Didn't go with this outfit."

He nodded, like this was a perfectly reasonable answer. "What about a crossbow?"

"Fresh out, I'm afraid."

"Well, what do we have exactly? Anything useful? You know, beyond my strength and your tongue."

"How about this?" Cait asked, pulling the knife from where she'd stashed it in her belt.

Adler's face lit up when he reached for it. "This will do."

"But there are two of them and only one blade. How—"

"Will you need this back?" He held up the weapon.

"No?" Why she said it as a question, she wasn't sure. "It's not mine."

"All right then."

"Just be ready to use it."

"Always am." His words didn't carry the same bravado she'd become accustomed to, but she brushed that away to focus on the scene playing out before her.

Penny, her chin raised high in her most dignified posture, no longer looked like the frightened criminal being dragged away to her exile. "I do apologize," she said. "I should not have struggled as I did. You were only carrying out the rule of our land. A rule I wholeheartedly believe in, and therefore I am ready, gentlemen, to proceed on to the council hall with you so I may explain the situation to our fair councilwomen."

Cait's heartbeat once again filled her ears until she wasn't sure she'd be able to hear the pirates' responses. But the men didn't reply immediately, instead dropping their heads toward one another and conversing quietly. To her credit, Penny didn't show any sign of worry or panic.

Cait wished she were a tough and fearless fighter like her brother. Sadly, though, she had little more than a sharp tongue and a quick mind, neither of which would help her physically conquer her opponents—or her fears.

You've been in dire situations before, and you were fine.

But even as she reminded herself of that, she knew this was different. Watching Adler take on those pirates earlier had both thrilled her—giving her a glimpse of the adventurous life she'd always dreamed of—and crushed her, and she'd wondered if she would be capable of doing what was needed when the time came. She had stood up to Adler in the woods, and she had fooled those pirates in the pub when they'd come asking after Aoife. But in both instances she'd wielded words, not fists.

The pirates took a couple of steps toward Penny, who grew an inch or two as she straightened.

"Apologies, miss, but the council won't be seeing you," one of the men said, his face smeared with nearly dry blood.

"Excuse me?" Penny asked.

"You should have accepted the rescue when you could."

Penny took a step backward, her head shaking in disbelief as she stammered. "What—what do you mean? I'm to see the council. That is my right as a Cregahn. You have made a grave error."

"Oh, have we now?"

Another step forward for the men. Another two steps back for Penny.

Cait's stomach curdled as she watched Penny inch closer and closer to the pit behind her. "Come on," she whispered to herself. The pirates needed to tell the woman the truth soon so she and Adler could rescue her before she stepped back to her death. Adler didn't seem to be having the same response to what was unfolding. When Cait peered at him, she saw no tension in his body or anxiety in his expression. Rather, he looked calculating, calm but distant, separated emotionally from it all.

Penny's voice snapped Cait's attention back to the clearing. "When I get to the council hall, I'll report both of you for usurping our laws and disobeying the rule of the council. You'll be exiled for your impertinence."

"Ah, but you see, miss, we are actually carrying out the very orders of your beloved council."

"What?"

"Aye, it's true. There are no trials—anymore—and no pleas for mercy."

The other pirate interjected. "Well, you could beg for mercy, but if we granted that to you, it would be us falling to our deaths, not you. And we rather enjoy being alive."

"Aye," the first pirate agreed. "Indeed we do. So if you don't mind, we—"

"What do you mean, *death*?" Penny asked, and her eyes widened with renewed panic.

Adler shifted forward, but before he could move, Cait stopped him with her arm.

"Not yet," she said in a hoarse whisper.

"Why not?"

"We need her to clearly understand."

"She's inching her way toward that clarity," he said, gesturing with his chin toward Penny, who was still moving closer to the drop.

Before Cait could once again insist on waiting, Penny's shrill words pierced the air. "Let go of me! What are you doing?"

The pirates had each grabbed one of Penny's arms and were attempting to lift her, but the injuries Adler had gifted them must have made that task difficult, as they had barely gotten her more than an inch above the ground when she began to kick and stomp, wriggling in their grasp.

"Council's orders, miss," one growled as she squirmed.

They made slow progress toward the pit cave, but still Cait didn't move. Cait could sense Adler was getting antsy waiting for her to give the word. One breath. One step. Another and another. If she waited too long, though, she risked Penny tumbling over the edge by accident.

The other pirate struggled to stay upright as Penny flailed to get away. "I hate this job!" he moaned.

"They aren't usually this troublesome," the first said.

"Please," Penny whimpered. She looked from one of her captors to the other and then back as she spoke. "Please, let me go. I'll leave. I'll catch a ship. I'll never come back."

"That's not how this works. This is our task. This is our lot. And that"—he gestured to the pit behind her—"that right there is yours."

As the pirates moved her feet nearer to the edge and her whimpers turned into sobs, Cait bounded out of the trees with Adler on her heels. She sprinted toward the pirates and registered the sound of a knife hitting its mark in one pirate a second before she dropped to the ground and used her momentum to slide into the other's legs, kicking them out from under him.

The pirate's boots slipped. His legs jutted out over the darkness of the cave, but his grip remained firm on Penny's arm, and he pulled her hard to the ground with him. Cait scrambled to get herself away from the edge, kicking her feet at both the ground and the pirate equally.

Where was Adler?

As if in answer to the thought, he said, "Be right there."

Cait pulled in a sharp breath at the sight of the other pirate's body going over the edge—or being thrown over. No scream came from him as he fell. Cait had barely taken another breath when she heard Adler again.

"I'm right here," he said as he slipped his arms around Penny and pulled her easily away from her remaining captor, who appeared to have given up any effort to complete his job for the council.

Instead his eyes went wide with fright. His hands fought unsuccessfully for purchase in the grass and dirt as the weight of his legs pulled him slowly toward the drop. He growled again, and his hand brushed against Cait's pant leg. Her heart raced.

She couldn't let him.

Wouldn't let him.

With a determined kick, she shoved her foot against his shoulder, forcing his body fully over the lip of the cave, but at the last moment, his fingers once again grabbed for her leg, and he managed to secure a firm grip on her ankle. Her backside ached as it slid across the ground, dragged forward by the weight of a full-grown man and his squirming body. But that discomfort was nothing compared to the terror that ripped through her and pulled a scream from her lungs.

"Adler!"

Her feet went over, her legs stretching painfully as the pirate pulled her along in his descent. With her arms stretched out to the sides, Cait had as much success grabbing onto the grass as the pirate had.

Don't give up. Don't give up. Don't give up.

But it wasn't that easy.

Her arms ached.

Her leg throbbed from where the man's fingers dug into her.

Cait stared up at the bright blue afternoon sky. This was it. She'd failed, and now she was going to plunge to her death from an unimaginable height.

Opening her mouth, she tried to shout for Adler again, but no sound came. Or if it did, she didn't hear it. The world became muffled, like she'd plunged her head underwater and every noise was distant and soft.

Another frantic breath, and the ground fell away.

She closed her eyes, not wanting to see her death coming at her. A jolt of pain shot through her arm as her body came to a sudden stop and the weight fell away from her legs. She couldn't look down, couldn't look to see what had happened, but she felt rocks jutting into her back, digging into her skull. Something gripped her forearms tightly.

"I've got you, love."

Adler.

Cait wanted to look up at him, but she couldn't force her eyes open, couldn't even open her mouth to answer him. She should do something, maybe press her feet against the wall of the pit to help propel herself to the surface, but she had no control over her limbs.

Even when the roughness of the rocks was replaced with the softness of the grass in the clearing, she didn't open her eyes. But when the ground beneath her head moved and she realized she was lying on Adler's legs and not the ground, her eyelids flashed open to find his deep blue eyes sparkling down at her.

"Looks like you've fallen into my lap."

Cait knew she should get up. She should move, stand, get back to work. But all her energy had been used up trying to stay alive, and if she was being honest, she didn't want to pull herself away from Adler's warm, comforting arms. Once again she found herself swimming in those azure eyes of his, as inviting as the sea on a sunny day.

"Will you let me stay here?" Her question came out as a whisper. Did he remember what he'd said earlier, or had it been a flippant remark, forgotten as soon as he'd uttered it?

Adler didn't move except to search her eyes, shifting between them, looking for…what? Cait didn't know why she'd asked. She had no time for distractions, no matter how good-looking they might be. Her focus had to be on ending the council's rule.

But sands help her, none of that seemed to matter when his hand moved and he cradled her face in his steady palm. His thumb brushed her lips so lightly she might have imagined it, but when his caress moved to her cheek, she couldn't constrain her gasp. Such a simple gesture, a whisper of a touch. Yet it sent sparks through her entire body.

Her heart screamed at her to sit up and taste his lips, while her mind begged her to get up and leave. Before she could do either,

Adler blinked and looked away, lifting her up so he could stand.

Whatever spell had trapped them in that moment, Adler had managed to free himself from its grasp.

Unfortunately, Cait had not.

From the inside out, Maura burned.

It had been so long since she'd experienced this—and even then, never to this extent. She'd forgotten just how painful it was. It seemed counterintuitive to her that when a fae's magic fizzled out—or got close to it—their bodies warmed. No. Warmed was the wrong word for the fire that blazed through her.

Every nerve frayed.

Every hair singed.

Every breath constricted.

Every thought consumed.

Her last thought, before her body had gone up in flames, had been of Tommy.

But the image of him watching her, of the worry in his amber eyes as she and Bria prepared to dive into their powers, had quickly turned to ash, and now all she had to focus on was the never-ending attack of a thousand knives stabbing into her over and over. There was no respite from the torture, and every time she sensed it subsiding, it would flare back up, like a fire given new life with a bit of air.

Several times she'd tried to push beyond the pain, to sense where she was and who was with her. Anything to let her know she was still alive.

But there was nothing. Nothing but her own agony.

Experiencing that—excruciating as it was—meant she hadn't yet succumbed and her magic was still hers. While it was impossible for her to know exactly what it was like to completely lose her powers, she'd met others who had experienced it. They all described it as a haunting desolation, like their insides had been poured out and all that was left behind was a dry shell. Numb. That's what they all said. Not that they ceased to have emotions— though Maura wasn't completely convinced that those didn't at least become muted.

Maura had no sense of time. She couldn't even recall how long she'd managed to keep the glamour in place over the ship before she'd collapsed. Had anyone moved her? Or was she still on the deck of the ship? Had they gotten away? Had they survived?

The scorching heat lessened enough for her to notice new sensations along her skin. Cool air soothing her arms and face. Softness caressing her legs. She wasn't on the deck.

Little by little, and with caution, she studied each new feeling as if her torment was a living thing that could be startled into returning should it discover her waking. And each second that passed without the searing pain intensifying brought more than simple relief.

Each second brought hope.

Counting her breaths, she struggled to listen to the world

around her. Silence engulfed her. Not muffled quietness. Terrifying silence. The air rushed in and out of her lungs, but she heard none of it. She tried to speak. Or at least she thought she did. Nothing. Reaching a hand up to her throat, she tried to make another sound, and her vocal cords vibrated under her fingertips.

And then the heat returned, and she stiffened once more.

But this heat wasn't like before. It wasn't scalding, but comforting. And it wasn't over her entire body. It was focused on the hand still resting at her collar.

Open your eyes, she commanded, but her body refused to obey.

The warmth at her hand began to move in light strokes back and forth and around.

Another two breaths, and a new sensation flooded her senses. The scents of mountain air, pine forests, and spice entered her silent world, painting it in warm amber behind her closed eyelids. It was so familiar, but she couldn't place it. Her heart raced as she chased after memories that refused to materialize. She was a ship chasing the setting sun, seeking but never reaching the images she could sense at the edges of her mind.

Then the amber in her vision darkened, like a shadow had passed over her, and she held her breath. Was this the end? Was this what happened before the numbness set in? A dulling of all her senses? A dimming of the life within her?

But then warmth landed on her forehead. Soft. Delicate. And sad? She couldn't be sure. Couldn't trust herself to analyze any of this right now. Reality seemed to be dissolving around her, if it had ever existed at all, and all she knew seemed to be falling away.

Maura.

That was her name. Echoing in her mind. At least that hadn't faded from her consciousness.

Maura. Wake up.

She mulled over the words. Something about them seemed off, like they weren't coming from within. But that was impossible. Not without her hearing restored.

"Maura."

Her breath stuck in her throat. Not merely a thought or a feeling then, but an actual word, spoken. She strained to hear more, but nothing else penetrated the silence. Drawing air deeper into her lungs and ignoring how her chest shook from the effort, she fought back the tears pooling under her eyelids.

"Maura, I need you."

The circling warmth on the back of her hand stopped, spread over it, and then moved slowly up her arm. And before she could contemplate what was happening, that same comforting heat lined one side of her body, pressing against her shoulder, hip, and knee. Half of her melted into bliss.

"Please. Please be okay. I can't lose you."

The desperate words tugged at her heart. Focusing on the scents in the room and the warmth at her side, she forced her mind to try again, to try harder. The amber hue surrounding her intensified. She knew that color.

Knew it. Loved it.

A pair of eyes appeared in her mind, but instead of startling her, the image brought another wave of comfort. Her breath eased. Her heart slowed. Her body swayed.

No, her entire world swayed, rolling in time with her breath.

The smell of seawater and wood pushed their way in, and little by little, the image in her mind came into focus, like a black fog was dissipating, revealing the memories she'd feared were gone. Amber eyes. Kind and worried. A stubbled chin. A ship at sea. A bed that wasn't hers.

Swallowing hard, she pried her eyes open. She blinked away

the tears that hadn't escaped and took in the deep brown of the wooden planks above her. Sunlight streamed in from the windows to her left. She wiggled her toes and flexed her fingers.

And the warmth vanished. Her body suddenly went cold, but before she could look to see what had happened, the voice returned.

"Maura?" Now a question. Clear as day.

Another swallow and a clearing of her throat, and she managed to respond. Not with words, but a sound at least. A sound she could hear, not just feel within, but hear with her ears.

Slowly she directed her attention to where the voice had come from, and there she found those amber eyes. A pair of eyes she desperately loved and had come so close to forgetting entirely.

Tommy.

She thought she had said it, but when he didn't move or react, she realized she must have only thought his name. Her smile seemed reluctant to form along her lips, and for a moment she worried he would see a grimace instead. Still unable to speak, she reached out a hand toward him, and he moved faster than she thought possible, taking her hand in his as he sat down beside her.

His eyes became melted honey, sweet and warm.

"Are you okay?" Tommy's voice was low and carried a hint of concern. More than a hint, she thought.

With a slow nod, she moved to sit up, thankful when his hands rushed to help her.

"Did you—do you—what—" He stumbled over his words, and a silent laugh tickled her chest from within. No doubt he was trying to ask about her powers without sounding callous, but she wasn't sure how to answer.

Looking down at her hands, she rubbed her thumbs along her fingertips and urged her mind to turn inward, to look deeper and call out for the magic she hoped hadn't been extinguished. But there, where she feared emptiness had settled in, she felt it. A weak and tiny spark, but a spark nonetheless, buried deep within her chest.

"Tommy."

She marveled at the sound of her voice in her ears once more and then laughed—not a silent laugh this time but the type that comes from sheer happiness and relief.

He scooted himself closer and ducked his head down into her line of sight, and when she smiled again, he smiled back.

"I guess this is when you tell me *I told you so*?" she asked, hoping he'd take it as the joke she meant it to be.

His smile twisted slightly. "There'll be time for that later. I just need to know you're okay. You're not—"

"Going to die anytime soon? Not if I can help it."

With a roll of his eyes, he rubbed a hand over his mouth and down his chin, but he didn't say anything more.

"How long was I out?" she asked.

"Not as long as I expected you to be, in all honesty. Half a day. If that."

Surprise hit her, though it was quickly replaced with the confidence that she would have remained unconscious far longer had he not been with her. All the words she'd heard from him replayed in her mind, but she couldn't tell if they had been truly from him or born only from some foolish hope she couldn't set aside.

She raised her chin and searched his eyes before asking, "Did you mean it?" Probably not the best way to go about this, but fatigue was beginning to crowd her mind, keeping her from finding a more tactful way to broach the topic.

"Mean what?"

"You need me? Can't lose me? Or did I dream that?" Sudden

embarrassment pushed her chin down, and her gaze settled back to her hands. It was not a familiar emotion for her, and she didn't like how vulnerable it made her feel, but she also couldn't bear to look at him as he told her it was all in her imagination.

His hand reached forward, his finger sliding under her chin before lifting it. She closed her eyes once more, still too scared to look at him, sure he was going to reject her as he had before. Only this time, she wasn't strong enough to pretend it didn't hurt or she didn't care or she could live without him.

"Look at me, Maura," he whispered, and when she finally obliged, she fell heart-first into that liquid amber that shined with hope and promise and love. "I said it. All of it. And I meant it."

His lips were on hers then. Tender yet strong. Desperate yet thankful. Her eyes slid closed as his lips moved with hers, patiently seeking her permission one second before giving in and demanding it the next. Even though she could feel his hands cradling her jawline, his fingers caressing the nape of her neck, she feared letting herself believe wholly that this was real. That he was real. That this wasn't some hallucination brought on by her fatigue and waning magic.

When he leaned into the kiss, she retreated, immediately regretting it when his lips pulled away. She risked opening her eyes. She'd loved his eyes from the first moment she'd seen them, but they had never shone quite like this. Somehow he had lured the stars out of the sky and convinced them to shimmer in his eyes just for her. With only a glance, he managed to pick up all the scattered pieces of her heart and hold them together with tenderness and care.

If this was an illusion, it was a particularly cruel one.

Here was all she'd wanted and hoped for.

"Is this real?" She winced when he flinched ever so slightly in response. In the silence that followed, she could hear his pulse pick up speed, and she waited for the truth—that while he cared for her, he couldn't be with her.

But instead, one brow angled up, and he muttered a single word. "Ouch."

"Ouch?"

"Aye," he said. "If you couldn't tell it was real, then that doesn't reflect well on me." A hint of a smile played at his lips.

"Oh." It was the only word she could manage, the only thought she could form.

"Let me try that again," he said, and this time when his lips found hers, forcing them open so he could caress her tongue with his, her doubts dissolved.

Maura didn't hesitate now. She reached for him as his hand explored her body, running over the rise of her hip down into the valley of her waist before resting on her ribs. Her fingers brushed past his ears and slipped into his hair.

Tommy was a sea she would happily drown in, over and over for all eternity.

She pulled him closer, deepening the kiss as she let her hands whisper down his neck before slipping across his shoulders. All doubt was gone. All fear had fled. All worry had been washed away. Now it was only Tommy and her, their lips and tongues and hands exploring each other. It wasn't enough. It would never be enough.

She waited for him to push her away as he had before. Waited for him to remember all the reasons they couldn't be together. And part of her wondered if she should be more responsible and remind him herself.

But that thought was shoved aside as Tommy's kiss deepened, his movements becoming more passionate, his hunger keeping pace with hers. She shifted in her seat, trying to find a way to somehow get him closer still, and he stopped.

The kisses. The caresses. It all stopped.

This time she couldn't contain that sting of rejection that pierced her chest. Why didn't he want her? Why had he told her he did, if he didn't really?

She couldn't look at him, couldn't watch him reject her again.

He pulled further away, and the emptiness between them was bitterly cold, like an icy breeze in the dead of winter. Her chin dropped once more to her chest as he shrugged his arms out from under hers. But he didn't leave. Instead, he took her hands in his.

"Maura?" He paused for a breath. "Why do you look as though I'm going to bolt out that door any moment and never return?"

Her eyes blinked open, and she stared at their clasped hands. She shook her head and offered a weak shrug.

"Did you really not believe me when I said I need you?"

"I did," she said with a meekness that sounded foreign to her. "But I also believed you when you said you could never be with me."

Leaning forward, he pressed his forehead against hers and whispered, "Things change."

It would have been logical to ask what had changed his mind— or his heart—but a different question had her fingers tightening against his hands.

"Then why did you pull away just now?" She cringed at the weakness she was showing. She was fae. She was powerful. She was confident.

But she was also vulnerable and scared, and the seconds seemed to lengthen as she waited for his answer. She didn't feel much better when he laughed. Though it wasn't mean-spirited or mocking, it still chafed her bruised heart.

Tommy pulled back once more, still squeezing her hands.

"Unfortunately, Maura," he started, and she forgot how to breathe. He was going to say what he'd said all along. She could handle this. She could learn to live with her love being unrequited and unwelcome. "We don't have the luxury of time, and I remembered that at the most inconvenient moment."

"So…" Maybe it was the lingering fogginess in her mind, but she couldn't quite get a mental grasp of his words.

"I didn't want to stop. Sands help me, I didn't. I'm not entirely sure how I did. Not sure if you know this, Maura, but you're not easy to turn down."

She quirked a brow at him in challenge.

"I know, I turned you down before, but it was far from easy. I couldn't even escape you in my dreams. I've wanted you since I opened my eyes that evening. And now I want nothing more than to rip off that dress and claim you as mine right here."

Heat emanated from him, and the desire she'd tasted in him earlier now flared up in his eyes. Her body tensed with anticipation, silently begging him to do all that he said, her hands itching to tear his own clothes from him.

"But it has to wait. I…have to wait. Because when I do take you—and I fully intend to—it won't be in my captain's bed. And it won't be rushed. You were meant to be savored, Maura."

The flames he had ignited with his touch flared with those last words, her mind racing ahead to imagine all the ways he intended to delight in her.

Leaning toward her, he brushed her lips with a soft, gentle kiss and the whispered promise, "Soon, but not yet."

Her entire body sighed as she leaned into him. He'd given her more than she'd expected, even if part of her remained unsatisfied. She would accept what he offered. Comfort. Love. And hope.

"By the way, you missed quite the excitement with the kraken while you were out. I actually missed the last of it—"

The kraken. She had completely forgotten.

"Why did you miss any of it?"

He cleared his throat and grasped her hands a little tighter. "Because if we were going to die—which it appeared we would—I wasn't going to let you die alone. I wasn't going to die anywhere but by your side."

"And you're sure we're not dead?"

Tommy pursed his lips and frowned as he pretended to ponder the question. "I'm fairly certain we aren't. But if we are, and I get to spend an eternity with you? I'll take it. Gladly."

Maura moved to meet his lips with hers once more, but the cabin door opened, and she stopped her advance. To her surprise, Tommy didn't turn, didn't retreat, but remained close beside her with their hands still clasped between them.

"Hi, Aoife," Maura said, her eyes never leaving Tommy's, never wanting to be pulled away from them.

"How did you—" Aoife started as she rounded the corner of the doorway to the bedroom. "Oh right. Fae hearing. I'm going to have to get used to that."

Maura laughed. "You have a very distinctive walk, friend. Doesn't require fae senses to identify."

Tommy flashed Maura a wink before turning his chin over his shoulder. "She's not wrong. But that doesn't mean we aren't happy to see you."

Maura had to stifle another laugh as Aoife strolled over to the windows, noticeably trying to change her gait as she did but when Aoife turned and leaned back against the window frame, Maura could see this was not the time to tease the girl. Her pallor clearly indicated she was not interrupting their moment with good news.

Tommy pulled one hand from Maura's, and she swallowed

her disappointment. It wasn't like he could hold onto her forever. Running his hand across the back of his neck, he asked, "Or should we not be happy to see you?"

With her eyes cast down, Aoife toed the floor—a nervous habit of hers that Maura had witnessed on several occasions.

"Halloran mentioned seeing Callum's ship. She didn't know Declan was aboard, and I believe her when she says she would have gone to his aid had she known." Tommy moved to speak, but Aoife held up a hand to stop him, her eyes slowly blinking as her jaw tensed. "She saw—they were stopped. And they were punishing someone. Over that distance, she couldn't make out who they had strung up, but it was clear they were—"

"Keelhauling," Tommy said in a whisper.

Aoife gave an almost imperceptible nod. "What if it was—"

"Callum's not that dumb. He wouldn't do that to Declan. Not if he needs him."

The words didn't seem to bring the girl any comfort, and Maura's heart ached in sympathy as she considered how she'd be just as scared if it were Tommy on that ship instead of Declan.

Aoife's voice remained steady though, despite the worry tugging at her features. "Are you sure? He wouldn't do it to torture him?"

With a shake of his head, Tommy answered, "No, keelhauling isn't something you do to someone until you're ready to kill them. But I wouldn't put it past Callum to use it to torture Declan all the same."

"What do you mean?"

Tommy looked at Maura and then back at Aoife as if contemplating whether his next words would be suitable for present company. Maura gave his hand an instinctive squeeze.

"You know better than most that Declan is more than the callous and uncaring man he displays for others. And unfortunately, Callum knows this too. If someone on that ship dared to help our captain? Callum wouldn't be above punishing that person with extreme harshness—especially knowing it would emotionally wreck Declan."

None of this appeared to put Aoife at ease, and Maura wasn't quite sure what she could say to help her friend. The girl looked like she was going to break down into tears at any moment, her brow furrowed, her bottom lip twitching.

"Aoife, friend," Maura said, waiting for Aoife to look up at her, "we will get him back."

Or we will all die trying.

She kept that thought to herself though.

Tommy wasn't going to lie. When Aoife had come in with the news Callum was implementing such a punishment aboard his ship, his gut had tightened with the thought it might have been his best friend. But that wasn't Callum's style. As much as he relished inflicting physical pain—hence his being one of the few pirate captains who still sentenced people to be keelhauled—Callum far preferred to draw out the abuse, to watch someone suffer emotional torment. Especially if it could be stretched out over days or even weeks.

Callum knew that Declan would carry guilt—even unwarranted guilt—over someone being hurt because of him.

Aoife had settled into silence over by the windows, and Tommy searched for any additional words that could offer comfort, but he had none. Nothing, save finding Declan, would ease the anguish plaguing her. Still, they couldn't stand here forever either; they still needed to develop a plan for when they arrived at the sound.

Turning back to Maura, he offered her a half-smile before saying, "I'm going to go gather folks up. Do you want to rest some more? Or—"

Maura interrupted. "Rest would be good, but I'd still like to help if I can."

He nodded. "I'll have them meet here then."

"Not in here," Maura said and nudged her chin toward the main room of the cabin. "Out there. I'll have Aoife help me over to the chair. Now, go."

His smile widened. Though he knew theirs was a doomed future, a story with no possible happy ending, he couldn't deny her—or himself—any longer. A short time loving her—and being loved by her—was far better than a lifetime of regret over what could have been.

Leaning forward, he cradled her face in his hands once more and pressed his lips against hers, stealing one more taste. He didn't want to back away. Didn't want to lose the feel of her skin against his, but duty called. Without another word, he left before he could change his mind and give in to the desire to have her completely.

Out on the deck, the emptiness in his hands seemed to magnify, numbing his senses. How much more would it hurt when he had to let her go permanently? He shouldn't be distracted by that thought, he knew, but it was a reality he couldn't escape. She was needed in Larcsporough, and though he hadn't been told the specifics, he'd gathered it wasn't a task he could help with. Nor was it a task he could even be by her side for.

We'll deal with that when the time comes.

They still had to survive the sound and the sirens if they were going to even reach that future. If he was to ever make good on his promise.

As Tommy headed toward the quarterdeck stairs, he spotted Collins and offered his hand in greeting. "Glad to see you up and about."

"Me too. Not one hundred percent yet, but my body was going to mutiny against me if I forced it to stay in that bed one more moment. How's Aoife?"

Tommy couldn't keep the corner of his mouth from lifting at the question. The crew had been staunchly against her being aboard the *Siren's Song*, and even though Collins had never been one to let superstition and prejudice sway him, his concern for Aoife was nice to see.

"She's Aoife."

"Stubborn and awkward?"

"Aye, and still going despite all she carries."

"No surprise there. That girl may have her quirks, but she has the spirit of a pirate."

"What bad influences we've been on her, Collins," Tommy said with a laugh, though neither of them thought of that spirit as a negative thing. He cleared his throat. "Is Mikkel up—"

"I believe he's belowdecks checking on the crew. If the racket they've been making is any indication, they've been working tirelessly to do what repairs they can."

"Good, good. Can you find him and send him to the captain's quarters for me?"

"Aye, s—Tommy." The man turned before Tommy could correct him over his near slip in addressing him. He wasn't ready to be a *sir* to this crew. Acting captain or not, he would remain Tommy to the men until... He didn't want to think about the circumstance that would warrant his becoming their true captain.

As he stepped onto the quarterdeck, he noticed the scenery for the first time. This part of the Aisling Sea was far different from any other he had sailed. They had left behind the vast open-ness of the sea between Caprothe and Turvala, and they would be approaching the entrance to the Black Sound soon.

Great rocky cliffs, spotted with trees and capped with clouds, loomed high some distance away. On the opposite side, the sea was broken up by smaller islands jutting out of the water like uneven stepping-stones covered in moss. Although a steady wind filled the sails above his head, the surface of the water showed no disruption apart from the lines cut through by their hull. It was as though some invisible shield guarded the water from the winds above. Or the winds dared not get too close to these waters. Tommy had never seen anything quite like it.

Either way, the wind was a welcome change from the dol-drums they'd endured in the kraken's territory.

"We're getting close," Gavin said, eyeing him from the helm. His face sagged from exhaustion. Had the man gotten any sleep?

Stepping closer to his friend, Tommy looked out over their prow as he asked, "How close?"

"If the map is accurate—which it might not be given how few survivors…" His voice faded. "But, map or no, the air is changing."

Tommy needed no clarification on that statement, as he had sensed a shift as well. The air had sparked to life around them, tingling along his skin, sending shivers across his shoulders, and giving him an altogether disturbing feeling in his gut.

"If you get a chance, get some sleep," Tommy said, putting a hand on Gavin's shoulder. "You're no good to us if you collapse from fatigue."

"Aye, Tommy. I know. I'll try, but I assume you're here to call a meeting of sorts. Unless you've already devised a plan all on your lonesome? Or with your fae beauty, perhaps?" Gavin flashed him an almost smug smile.

But Tommy ignored it and simply stated, "No plan yet. Can you hand the helm over? Or would you like to stay to navigate the waters?" Something inside him begged him to drop anchor, to not get any closer to the sound and its dangers until they had a plan in place. But Declan was somewhere ahead of them, hopefully alive. For how long was anyone's guess.

"Whatever you decide I'll support, Tommy. The others have been waiting for you though."

At that, Tommy turned his attention to the two women standing at the railing. Both were standing almost regally. Although Halloran was decidedly rougher around the edges than Renna, Tommy had little desire to cross either of them. Yet he had already gone against his word to the fae by stepping over the line with Maura, and he swallowed his dread, wondering how she would react to what she likely already knew.

"How is she, Tommy?" It was Halloran who voiced the question as he approached.

"Conscious at least, but I'm not sure she'll be strong enough to go into the sound with us," he said, hoping the depth of his concern wasn't evident.

"Not the fae. Aoife," Halloran clarified. Tommy raised his brow at that, and his surprise must have been clear, because the renowned captain rolled her eyes. "I know what you're going to say. Don't."

Tommy could imagine how Declan would have responded to such a statement, and he nearly smiled.

"Say what?" he offered, and when the captain remained stoic and annoyed, he conceded with a slight shrug. "She's scared."

"As she should be," Halloran said. She swung her attention to Renna beside her, who seemed to be ignoring their exchange, but she didn't address the eldest fae.

"I'm actually surprised to still see you, Captain," Tommy said. "Not that it isn't a welcome surprise. I thought you would have sailed on your way after offering us the tow."

"Aye, my ship will be sailing on shortly."

Tommy noted her odd phrasing. "And will you be on it?"

Her chin rose in the air slightly. "I'd like to remain here to help however I can, if you'll allow it."

"I appreciate it. Truly."

"If you're both done with the idle chatter," Renna said, her harsh tone cutting through the charged air, stinging Tommy with a power of its own. "We should discuss what exactly we will do once we get there."

With a nod, Tommy pivoted on his heel and motioned for the pair to follow him to Declan's quarters.

As he made his way down the stairs, he wished—for the millionth time—that his friend was here with him.

◦◦◦

Once again Tommy found himself leaning over Declan's desk, his mind whirring with all the decisions that had to be made. But when he looked around him, it was painfully clear how things had changed since that first meeting. Renna stood where she had before, but now one of her sisters was sitting in Declan's chair beside Tommy, and the other was absent, still laid out on the floor of the officers' cabin, recovering. On Tommy's other side, Aoife leaned onto the desk. Opposite him, Captain Halloran, Mikkel, and Collins stood tall and serious.

"Declan didn't tell you how he anticipated using their magic?" Aoife asked Tommy, nodding her head toward Renna.

Tommy roughed a hand over his mouth and shook his head.

"We had planned to decide that on the journey north, but obviously he didn't make it to that meeting." He cringed internally at his casual reference to Declan's abduction. "When we went to the council hall, we had no indication of the powers they held, so we couldn't very well plan how to use them when we didn't know what they were."

Halloran widened her stance slightly and said, "And why did Declan's absence warrant not going forward with planning?"

He bristled at the question but recovered quickly. Tensions were high for everyone. "Unfortunately nothing has gone quite right for us. Between the storm and the kraken and thinking we were all going to drown or be eaten, we didn't find the time to plan that far ahead. But we're here now." He straightened and forced himself to ignore Maura, who was looking up at him from her seat as he addressed her sister. "Any ideas, Renna?"

Also, thank you for letting me ask the question aloud before you answered. If the fae was listening in on his thoughts, he might as well offer his gratitude. A tight smile appeared on her lips, the only sign she might have gotten the message.

"The sirens are a tricky lot, to be sure," Renna said, looking at each person gathered in turn. "All are shifters, as you might be aware, but different than others you might be familiar with."

Others?

He'd never heard of the existence of other creatures capable of shifting, and by the looks on his crewmen's faces, he wasn't alone.

"Their primary state is much like our own, though you will only find females among them. They can alter their appearances to look like other sirens, humans, or fae, but they're only able to shift half of themselves into another creature."

"What does that mean?" Aoife asked.

"They really didn't teach you much as a council heir, did they?" Renna asked her, seeming more sympathetic than judgmental.

A breathy laugh escaped Aoife. "I think that's fairly obvious to all of us now. No point in being taught about evil flesh-eating creatures in the north when you're to lead a life devoted to killing your own people."

Maura leaned forward to look around Tommy at Aoife. "Technically only *some* of your people."

Aoife gave another awkward laugh. "Regardless, I don't know much beyond their being rather dangerous and crafty and hungry."

Tommy caught Aoife's eyes and gave her a smile. "That's as good a starting place as any."

"Indeed," Renna said, showing more patience than Tommy would have expected given where they were headed and how many times she was being interrupted.

Though he did notice she did not look directly at him or Maura.

No point in dwelling on that now.

Renna cleared her throat. "They can only change into two types of creature: fish or bird. And even then, it is only a partial shift. It's a bit disconcerting, honestly, a woman with a fish tail for legs or the wings and legs of a bird. As you can imagine, they are stronger than humans, similar to fae in that regard. They delight in tempting their prey before making them suffer. So most of the time they lure you in and then throw all your mistakes in your face until you are close to drowning in your own sorrow. That's when they eat you."

Tommy wasn't sure if it was the subject that had caused his skin to crawl or the casual way Renna was speaking. *They eat you.* It was one thing to know about all of this, another to hear someone say it aloud. His stomach tightened, threatening to push its contents upwards. But he managed to keep it under control.

"Okay. So they pull you in, push you down, and then—" Aoife stopped short, and Tommy could have hugged her for not finishing that sentence.

"Pretty much," Renna said.

Tommy held up a hand. "You said most of the time. What about the other times?"

"Like the rest of us, if they're hungry enough, they'll settle for what they can get. But their queen has more powers still."

"They have a queen?" Aoife asked, eyes widening.

"I feel like the queen having *powers* is more reason for shock than just her existence," Tommy said, but Aoife only shrugged.

"Yes, they have a queen, who—given her fixation on power and control—will likely keep the dagger close. Probably on her. She is not going to be easy to face. Particularly for those who wear their guilt like a cloak about their shoulders." Renna didn't hide the way her eyes focused on Aoife as she explained, but Aoife, to her credit, didn't seem to take offense. In fact, she didn't seem to react to the insinuation at all.

"What does she do, exactly?" Halloran had spoken up this time, her impatience worn plainly on her face.

"Compulsion."

The word fell from the fae's lips and slammed into the wooden floor at their feet.

The quiet that filled the room made Tommy even more uneasy. He had to end it.

"Right, so, what can counter that power? Anything?"

Renna looked at him for the first time since they'd gathered. "Like counters like, though not perfectly."

Tommy pulled in a breath. "We fight compulsion with more compulsion?"

The fae gave a nod at the same time Aoife said, "Isn't that part of your gifts, Renna?"

But it was Maura who answered for her sister. "As long as she's rested, but even then, it's not as strong as the siren's."

Halloran, her hand resting casually on the hilt of her cutlass, flicked her eyes slowly between the sisters. "How is it that you've come to know so much about these demons?"

"Because we helped to confine them to the sound."

Somehow Tommy managed to keep his jaw from dropping as he looked to Maura for confirmation. She replied with a tight-lipped smile and a lift of a shoulder.

"How?" he asked, and Maura turned away as Renna began to answer.

"It took all the royals. Ten of us. Combining our powers to ward the entrance against their kind."

"Okay, wait. You can't just drop all of these things on us at once!" Aoife said, her voice rising. Tommy didn't blame her. The amount of information Renna had provided them with during the last half hour had his head spinning. He leaned heavily onto the desk.

"Well, to be fair, Aoife, she asked," Renna said, levelling a finger at Halloran.

Aoife opened her mouth to give a retort, but Tommy stopped her with a look.

Pinching the bridge of his nose, he closed his eyes and said, "Okay. So. The sirens are evil. Their queen has the dagger on her— we assume—as well as the power of compulsion. Renna can use compulsion—within limits—to counter the queen's." He dropped his hand and opened his eyes, though he kept his head down. "And all of this information is accurate because Renna and her sisters are fae *royalty* who helped trap them in the sound. Centuries ago."

Tommy glared sharply at Renna and Maura, the former looking far less apologetic than her younger sister.

"Surprise!" Maura said in a quiet voice, as if it would make any of this easier to swallow.

It should have hurt Tommy that she had kept this secret from him, but he wasn't so much hurt as he was disappointed. He had been right all along. There could be no future with her. Not when she was a royal. A royal with a duty to her kin. No wonder she was needed in Larcsporough.

But could he walk away from her? After he'd given himself the permission to walk over that threshold, to let that dream take root, *to kiss her*? Could he give it all up? Could he take all of his actions and words and promises back?

"Tommy?"

He looked up to find everyone staring at him. Aoife's expression displayed genuine concern, her eyes asking him silently if he was all right. He gave her a nod before forcing his mind back to the matter at hand.

"So what is the plan then? We don't have ten royals to bring together to kill them."

"And you won't need that many," Renna said.

"What do we need?" Tommy asked.

Aoife added her own question. "And is the goal truly to kill them?"

"Yes. Undoubtedly," Renna said. Her grave tone sent another shiver across Tommy's back.

Maura touched his arm and, looking up at him, said, "At least the queen. With her gone, the others will scatter."

"How? If the sound is warded to hold them—" Tommy started.

"Because the ward is tied to the queen's life specifically,"

Renna answered. "Once she dies, the other sirens will no longer be under her compulsion and can leave."

Aoife stepped forward. Her arm brushed against Tommy's, her eyes seeking an answer from both sisters. "Why would we want them to leave though? Won't they simply wreak havoc across the Aisling?"

"Thankfully no. Triss—the queen—compelled them all to serve her. They've lived under her power for so long, they're long past the point of fighting it. The only way to free them is to kill her. And, believe it or not, they were once peaceful, providing aid to sailors, saving them during storms, guiding them toward safety."

"So where did she come from? How does she have more power?" Aoife asked, each word laced with impatience.

Renna stiffened and shared a glance with Maura as she answered, "She is part fae."

Before Aoife could react to this, Maura added, "She is our sister. Well, half-sister."

Tommy swallowed hard. He could almost hear the air being sucked from the room by the collective breath being drawn.

"Excuse me?" Aoife asked, brows lifted as far as they would go.

"It's a long and not altogether relevant story," Renna offered.

Tommy nearly lost it at that. "Not relevant?! I'm starting to severely question your judgment on what is relevant and not!"

Maura slipped her hand into his and gave it a squeeze. Part of him wanted to toss it aside so she'd understand his anger. But the brush of her thumb over the back of his hand cleared away some of his frustration. Their future might have been doomed from the start, but he refused to let his anger and hurt ruin whatever time they had. He squeezed her hand back and offered her a half-smile.

"The short version, if you think it would help to know, is that our father was tricked by a siren who took the appearance of our mother, with the hope that any offspring would inherit some of his power. And that's exactly what happened. We didn't know—no one knew—until Triss was grown and sought out our family, in search of the man who had sired her."

"What happened?" Aoife asked.

Maura moved to stand, using Tommy's hand to help her up. "He was angry over the trickery, unwilling to accept a reminder of his infidelity, so he turned her away. She didn't take it well and called her kin to meet in the sound to plot her revenge. We only heard about it because one of our friends, a siren, warned us. We followed them there—the four royal families."

"And you know the rest," Renna said.

Mikkel and Collins shared a look. Halloran seemed to be chewing on the information, her stoicism locked into place.

Aoife cut through the silence. "But that still leaves the dagger."

Renna dropped her head to one side. "What about it?"

Seeing Aoife's face redden as her temper flared, Tommy stepped in. "I think most of us know the basics about it, but if we're going to retrieve it from this queen, a refresher might help." He hardened his glare at Renna. "Along with anything you might have forgotten to tell us about?"

"What basics do you know?" Renna asked.

"It brings victory to the one who possesses it," Aoife said, her irritation barely starting to subside.

Mikkel's voice chimed in. "The king of Tyshaly used it to end the Aisling War."

"And apparently," Collins said, "it ended up in the Black Sound guarded by hungry magical creatures."

Tommy looked around at the others.

When no one else spoke up, Renna's shoulders slumped.

"Seriously? That's all you know?" She glanced toward the window. "With time getting away from us... the queen of Cregah enchanted it for King Csintala to help him end the war in exchange for his promise to return to her. He won the war, but he lost in the end because the dagger—enchanted as it is—does not suffer betrayers to wield it. He had claimed to love her, but when the king broke his promise and refused her, the dagger worked as it was created to. It led him to his death."

"In the sound."

Tommy had said it to himself, but Maura affirmed his statement with a quiet, "Yes."

"But why—" Aoife paused. "Why doesn't the siren queen use it for her own victory if she keeps it on her?"

Maura, with her eyes locked on her sister, said, "Magical beings can't wield it for themselves. Look at it as a check on its power."

"Okay, so we get in, get the dagger, kill the queen, save the sirens, save Declan." Aoife listed off each task on her fingers, eyes wide with incredulity.

Tommy offered her a smile. "Easy as pie."

40

AOIFE

By the time the planning session had concluded, Aoife felt as though she was back in the kraken's whirlpool. Around and around her thoughts swirled and spun, making her head dizzy and her stomach uneasy. Sitting down on the edge of the bed, she looked down at her arms, which were now wiped clean of the kraken's black blood, though it still clung to her clothes and would likely never wash out of them.

Aoife had meant to ask the fae why she hadn't been hurt by it as Gavin had. She wasn't quite sure it could be chalked up to mere adrenaline as she'd assumed at the time. Her fingers traced the swirls of black that were etched into her forearm—up and down, around and around—as her mind continued to churn. She'd never been told what the purpose of the inked art was, and before— before death and pirates and fae and kraken and evil sirens—she had thought nothing of it. It had simply been a mark to set the councilwomen apart from others. But now, after hearing of all the magic that existed in her world—after seeing magic firsthand—she wondered if perhaps the design dancing across her pale skin held a power of its own. Was this what had protected her from the kraken's blood? Could it perhaps protect her from the siren queen's compulsion?

Neither Renna nor Maura had offered any indication that was the case, but she also hadn't gotten a chance to ask directly, as the discussion had rapidly turned toward strategy.

Now the plans were finalized—or as finalized as they could be, given all the unknowns. And Aoife was once again alone in this bedroom. Only a few days ago, she'd stood in this room with Declan preparing to go ashore. Yet it felt like months had passed. And now she had to enter these dangerous waters and rescue him from ravenous, evil monsters. Even though she had faced the kraken and lived, that didn't ease her fears in the slightest. She'd gotten lucky. They all had. If Captain Halloran hadn't arrived when she did, they would now be in the belly of that beast instead of sailing north toward Declan.

Could she expect similar luck at the sound? She wasn't so sure.

Above her head, footsteps sounded on the quarterdeck, and each one was like a hammer tapping against her sternum. With each tap, her stomach turned and her chest tingled as the familiar sensation of anxiety settled in. Even after all these years of panic attacks, they had not become any more bearable. Remembering Declan's advice only helped a little. With every reminder to breathe, she saw his face and heard his voice, which sent her back under the waves of this internal tempest.

Counting silently to herself, she tried to focus on the air being pulled into her lungs.

Breathing in.

One.

Two.

Three.

Four.

And out.

One.

Two.

Declan.

Damnit.

Breathing in.

One.

Two.

I love you, Aoife.

A growl rumbled in the back of her throat, and she threw herself back on the bed, closing her eyes so she didn't have to see the familiar wooden ceiling.

It wouldn't do her any good to be unfocused, but every other thought brought his face to mind. Perhaps that wasn't a bad thing. Maybe it was good to be reminded of what she was fighting for. But it wasn't only Declan she needed to save. It was all of Cregah.

The weight of that increased the tightness in her chest, and her breathing became shallow and rapid.

She reached up to the collar of her shirt and, finding the delicate chain, pulled the vial of black sand out. She clutched it in her hand, wishing it contained more than mere sand, like perhaps some magical properties to help her heal and relax and prepare.

She'd made up her mind to forgive him. After the kraken attack and facing almost certain death—after being saved at the last moment and being given a second chance of sorts—she had decided to offer him the same. Maybe it wasn't the same as being rescued from the jaws of a monster, but this forgiveness seemed equally important. It was a different type of monster that held Declan, a torment Aoife knew all too well, as it had clutched her own heart since the day she'd chased that carriage and failed her sister.

But her guilt might still be her undoing.

Their undoing.

Renna had said the sirens favored the souls pained by guilt, darkened by remorse. Would they find Declan alive when they finally caught up to him? Or would the queen already have finished playing with him? Would he be dead?

Whether he was or not, Aoife knew she, too, would be targeted by the queen. No doubt the sirens would sense the guilt she still carried. While it had been shoved aside of late, shadowed by more pressing matters, it whispered to her all the same. She had betrayed her sister. And she could never take that back or make it right. The only thing she could do was work harder to avoid repeating the mistake in the future.

But it was one thing to know what she should do and another to actually manage it.

How could she prepare, exactly, for a powerful ancient being picking at her emotional wounds? Aoife wanted to be brave, to walk into that sound with her chin up as her mother always did, to hold her own as she had in that library.

She wanted to believe, too, that she could find the same confidence and courage even without Declan beside her, but the void he'd left behind—*When you shoved him away, you mean*—seemed to swallow any she possessed.

They had another day or so before they arrived at the sound, and Aoife knew now why Declan had always been impatiently checking his pocket watch. Sailing seemed a tediously slow way to travel, although she had nothing to compare it to, really. It had to be faster than walking, after all, but still, she had to spend so much time waiting, cooped up in the cabin, with nothing but her thoughts for company.

With her eyes still closed, she slowly began to give in to the sleep that beckoned her. She hadn't rested since before they'd entered the kraken's waters, and now, every inch of her seemed worn thin, drained of all energy. Even if she'd wanted to keep pondering what she would do and say when they arrived in the sound, her fatigued mind wouldn't allow it. But still, the heaviness in her chest and the rapid beating of her heart refused to let up, and she slipped into the darkness of sleep with all her nerves pulled taut, her thoughts troubled, her dreams darkened.

Aoife's boots crunched against the white sand of an unfamiliar beach. But this wasn't like normal sand. Even through the soles of her feet, she could feel the coarseness of each grain, which was far bigger than the sand she'd encountered at home or in Foxhaven. An uneasiness settled in her gut, warning her that this beach wasn't like any other.

Something moved in her periphery, swept up onto the disconcerting shore by the dark tide. Her mind screamed at her to not look, but curiosity got the better of her, as it always did. She saw red first. Not the color of blood but the color of falling leaves in autumn, spread out across the ground in thick waves. She knew those waves. She'd envied them.

Lani.

With a swallow, Aoife let her eyes travel from the long strands of wet hair to the body of the woman they belonged to. Her sister's face stared at her. Her green eyes were open but lifeless and dull, her normally radiant complexion gray and placid, and her mouth showing the slight curve of a frown.

Aoife fell to her knees, ignoring how the sharp shards of sand bit into her skin.

"I'm so sorry, Lani. I didn't mean to. You know my damn tongue always gets away from me, and my mind always seems blind to all possible scenarios.

It's no excuse. I screwed up." Her words flooded out of her but fell empty upon the ground, surprisingly flat, as though she were making small talk over tea. No one would ever believe it had been an accident, that she could have possibly been that naive to trust her family and all she'd been taught.

The guilt wrenched her heart, squeezing it until she was sure it would be crushed into a million pieces and scattered across this white beach. But instead, her thoughts darkened, and she moved from sorrow to loathing. Loathing of herself. She'd been right to run away. She was no good to anyone. She couldn't do anything right. She only got people hurt, killed, kidnapped. A whisper called to her from a great distance, her name on a breeze she couldn't feel against her skin.

"Declan. Tommy. Gavin. Collins. Maura." The whisper repeated the names of those she held most dear, a desperate attempt to remind her that people cared about her.

But the darkness within her wouldn't listen, and with each name she heard, a harsh truth echoed back.

Declan. Gone.

Tommy. Burdened.

Gavin. Injured.

Collins. Wounded.

Maura. Weakened.

And Lani. Dead.

Everyone was better off without her. She couldn't do anything right. Why even try? What was the point?

But then another voice cut through the whispers, this one familiar and comforting, like a loving embrace around her shoulders or a gentle stroke upon her hand.

"It's not your fault, Aoife. None of it."

She balked at it, but the voice continued.

"She forgave you. Lani did."

Aoife's gaze snapped up. Only one person could know such a thing, and *he now stood a few feet away from her, looking just as he had when she'd left him standing in that cove. Declan.*

Bloody. Distraught. Desperate.

Yet his eyes—those stormy grays that threatened to pull her under—held nothing but the love she'd seen in them in his cabin before he'd kissed her.

"What?" She tried to say the word, but no sound came. He heard it all the same.

"Before I—before she died, your sister gave me a message. If I ever came across you, I was to tell you that she forgives you."

Aoife's pulse sped up as her mind whirred, processing his words, and a slew of emotions hit her in turn: gratitude, peace, frustration, anger. Her jaw clenched. Her eyes burned into his.

"And you tell me this now*?" she screamed, her voice finding new strength in her fury. "You knew how guilty I felt! You saw how it plagued me! You saw how I struggled! And you stayed silent. For what? To save your own heart? To save yourself from the discomfort of confessing what you'd done?"*

"Yes." A single word. A single, emotionless word. No remorse. No sorrow. Empty. Hollow.

His eyes dulled, becoming as vacant as his voice, and they glazed over, no longer seeing her but seeing through her. He gaped. His head lolled to one side. His legs gave out. And when he crumpled to the ground, his body as lifeless as Lani's, Aoife tried to scream, but all the air was sucked from her lungs at the sight of the woman before her.

Her hair was as black as the kraken's blood, and her dark eyes pulled Aoife into them. A cruel smile graced her beautiful, wicked face.

And Aoife lost all hope of getting Declan back—of saving anyone.

41
DECLAN

Declan knew he still had feet because he could see them standing beneath him on the white sand of the beach. But he could no better control them than he could control the siren who sat before him atop a large rock, her legs—bare and delicate but strong—crossed at the knees. At least he still had some power over his mind.

For now.

Was that his own thought? Or her voice invading his mind? He wasn't sure.

"Nice throne you have there," he said, forcing his face to relax.

"You're trying too hard, Declan," she crooned and switched her legs to cross the other way. He didn't answer but raised a single brow in question. "Trying too hard to remain calm."

"Well you can imagine how this current situation might make it a challenge."

"Also trying too hard to fix the brokenness within you." She clicked her tongue as she lifted a hand to point to his left. "Didn't Callum here warn you it was too late? Sounds like it, if I'm getting his thoughts adequately."

Declan couldn't move his head to turn toward the other pirate, but out of the corner of his eye he could see the man kneeling in the sand, his hands clasped behind his back, bound with invisible manacles, just like Declan.

"Aye, he did. But I tend not to heed those who hit me over the head and throw me into a dank brig."

Triss laughed, her deep purple eyes sparkling. "One of the many mistakes you've made."

"So it would seem," he replied. "Are we to sit around here all day making idle chitchat? Or did you want something from me?"

Though her laughter had ceased, her wicked smile remained. "Always so impatient. Always so ready for action. But one thing I've learned over these many centuries, it's good to slow down once in a while and savor the moments. Especially the good ones."

"Can't say this tops my list of good moments."

Leaning forward, her arms resting on her legs, she winked at him. "Ah, but does it top the bad?" Her eyes flitted up to the sky as if she were searching her thoughts. Or searching his. She let out a disappointed sigh. "That's too bad. I had hoped to at least make your top five. Oh well. There is still time for that."

Declan tried to keep his memories at bay, shoving them back into the far reaches of his mind, but they wouldn't listen. Triss had control of them now: visions of his parents disappearing, of Aoife walking away, of Tommy being stabbed, of Lani's face before he'd pushed her, of Killian's tortured body. They ran in a loop in his mind, each one vying for attention like children trying to get their mother to notice them.

"Ah," Triss's viciously sweet voice cut through the images. "There it is. That's the darkness I crave. The despair. The sorrow. Makes your blood that much more…"

"Potent?"

Her lips curled up once more, and she shook her head. "Delicious."

Declan dug deeper into his resolve, and with another push, he managed to get each scene to dissolve into the void, leaving his mind—and his expression—calm once again.

Triss frowned as she studied him.

"You're stronger than I expected."

"I get that a lot."

"Well, we'll see how strong you are once she arrives."

Aoife, the only *she* who he knew—hoped—was on her way here. Before he could respond, though, Triss was speaking once more, but not to him.

"Callum Grayson." She dropped her head to one side as she studied the man. "You look just like your father. To be honest, I didn't expect him to follow through with his word. I could see all his plans unfurl as we made our deal." She continued as if speaking to herself, not bothering to wait for any response or reaction from either pirate. "And yes, before you argue, I did compel him to fulfill his agreement. But wouldn't you know? The further away someone gets from me, the weaker the compulsion becomes. It wasn't always that way, mind you. Before, I could make anyone do anything for as long as I wanted, even if they left my side. As it turns out, the ward those fae scum placed around this sound dampens the compulsion. And I didn't know that when I let him leave. He was the first I'd ever granted freedom to. Serves me right, I suppose. I've learned my lesson since."

What did she want from Callum's father? Declan wondered. Triss answered as if he had asked it aloud.

"What I want from everyone, dear Declan. Blackened souls. Burned hearts. Rancid blood. Unfortunately, Tobias Grayson had none of those things when he came to me. All full of virtue and hope. Utterly disgusting and useless." She paused to listen to Declan's silent question. "Ah, you haven't figured that out yet? You're losing your touch there. Or perhaps the rumors of you are more far-fetched than people know. Tobias Grayson fought me on it, of course, with all that goodness inside him. He didn't want to pay the price for his freedom. He refused. He would have rather died here, never to take the treasure I offered to win the hand of his love back home, never to have a family. So I did what I had to. And I compelled him. To send me his firstborn."

Triss released her hold on Declan's body enough that he was able to look toward Callum, who still hadn't moved, his eyes staring blankly ahead.

"Don't look so worried, Declan," Triss said, her voice far more pleasant than it had any right to be. "You will get your turn soon enough, once I'm done with him."

Before Declan could respond, Callum's face contorted in pain, his body going rigid and tense before starting to shake. Triss stood and strode slowly over to the kneeling man.

"Stop fighting it, Callum," she said in an eerily sweet tone. "I'm not showing you anything you don't already know, anything you haven't already done."

As if on silent command, Callum's body went still before he rose to his feet, coming face to face with his tormentor. She cupped his face with one of her slender, perfect hands, stroking the length of his scar with her thumb, acting more like a lover than a hungry monster.

"You were the price," she said. "You were the cost Tobias had to pay to take the riches I offered. And yet you still admire him. Fortunately—for me—you never lived up to his virtue, and that blackness in your heart will be your demise. And my treat."

What was she referring to? Callum had been so confident his past would be no issue, so sure he had conquered his own demons sufficiently. That had obviously been a mistake, as the queen now gripped his chin in her hand, and it was no longer the sweet touch she'd shown him earlier. With a growl, Triss pulled his jaw hard to the left. Callum's scream echoed off the rocks around them. Declan saw no blood, but Callum's jaw hung askew. When Callum tried to move it, he screamed again, and Triss's laughter joined in.

Without turning her attention away from Callum's broken face, she answered one of the million questions coursing through Declan's head. "What did you expect, Captain? Did you really think we didn't play with our food a bit?" She paused, no doubt listening in some more. "Ah, well, that was rather naive of you. No, our fun here doesn't merely affect the mind. As you might have witnessed earlier with my friends' welcome party, we like to get our hands a little dirty first."

Callum's eyes were now closed tight, arms once again shaking from shock. Triss smiled, a maniacal glint in her eyes as she waved a hand behind Callum and called out, "Come. Sit. Watch."

The sirens passed by Declan, stroking his neck with cold, wet hands, and he clenched his eyes shut. He had no desire to watch them attack Callum as they had the man on the beach.

His heart went cold as all hope washed away.

42

CAIT

The walk back from the pit cave was nearly unbearable. An awkward silence remained with Cait, Adler, and Penny the entire way. It wasn't intentional, at least not for Cait, but after finding herself in such an intimate position with Adler, all words had abandoned her. Every time she settled on something to say, she second-guessed it and stopped herself. And now the silence had gone on for so long that anything she said would feel even more awkward, regardless of what it was.

So she continued walking, focusing on her breathing and the sound of their footsteps on the trail. Every now and then she gave a sideways glance toward Penny, who walked between her and Adler. The woman stared blankly ahead, not even looking down when her foot tripped on a stick or a rock, and not responding to Adler when he caught her by the arm and righted her once more.

Cait could see Adler looking at her, but she ignored him. Why should she be embarrassed about how she'd fallen into his lap? She could have thanked him for saving her life. She should have thanked him. But she didn't know how to talk to him anymore.

They had shared more of their past during their wait than she had intended, and she didn't know where that left them. She'd allowed him into the Rogues because she wanted to grant him his revenge on the council. Nothing more. But it wouldn't be bad to be friends with him, would it?

No friends. Friends were a liability.

It was why she kept a certain emotional distance from Kira and Aron and Eva—and Maggie. Her chest tightened. How much stronger would this guilt be had Maggie been a friend and not just one of her Rogues?

You still care for them though.

But not like she did for Declan. Or Lucan.

She'd let him too far into her life before realizing the danger of having such an attachment, but loneliness had kept her from pushing him away completely.

No, she couldn't be friends—or anything else—with Adler.

When they reached the outskirts of Morshan and the path gave way to cobblestones, Cait gently pulled Penny's arm to get her to stop. Turning the woman, she peered into her eyes, which were still lifeless from her earlier trauma. The plan wouldn't work if Penny couldn't snap out of it, but this wasn't one of those things you could slap someone out of. Or pinch them out of.

It took time.

Time that was quickly running out.

"Is there somewhere we can take her?" Adler asked, his voice rough from going so long without speaking.

Cait blinked rapidly as she looked at him and shook her head as she thought. "I don't know. I had planned for her to be able to—and eager to—spread word to the people immediately, which was obviously stupid of me. I should have expected this."

With a casual shrug, Adler's mouth curved into that upside down smile. "You were uncharacteristically optimistic. Nothing wrong with that."

A snarl started in the back of her throat, but she pushed it back down. "No, there *is* something wrong with that when it means I didn't plan for any contingencies. I wasn't prepared, and now—"

"Now we figure it out."

She wanted to interpret his tone as mocking or condescending, but part of her nearly swooned at his patience and desire to help her.

Nearly.

He's just helping himself and his own interests.

And Cait needed to do the same.

"We need to get her back to the pub without anyone noticing, but it's the middle of the damn day, and we have no cloak or anything to put on her. We can't exactly wait until dark either."

Turning away from her, Adler shifted his weight and peered around the trees toward town. Cait breathed through her impatience and counted four deep breaths before he finally spoke.

"Wait here. I'll be right back."

Before Cait could protest, he was gone, leaving her to wonder where in the sands he thought she would wander off to with their near catatonic charge. When he didn't return as quickly as she'd hoped, she opted to try and pull Penny from her stupor, knowing it wasn't likely to work. But it seemed better than standing here doing nothing.

"Penny," she started, trying to get into her line of sight once more, but the woman's eyes looked through her. Cait took Penny's hands and was surprised to find them still trembling slightly. Giving the unsteady hands a gentle squeeze, she tried again. "Penny, I'm sorry you had to go through that. But you're safe now."

Even as she uttered the words, she tasted them for the lie they were. If anything, Penny's life was in far greater danger than it had been when she'd woken up that morning. And that was on Cait's conscience.

But it was the only way.

Except it might not work, and then what? She'd put an innocent woman in the crosshairs of the council for nothing. This felt a million times worse than the guilt already simmering in her chest, because unlike Maggie, Penny hadn't signed up for this. She hadn't had a choice. She'd been forced into this situation and used.

The only way.

No matter how much she repeated the words, though, her inner discomfort wouldn't be soothed.

Refocusing on the woman before her, Cait attempted to clear the emotion lodged in her throat.

"We could use your help though. If you're able. I know we haven't been close—"

That's an understatement!

"—but now that you know what the council does, we need to inform everyone else. We need you to tell the others. Please."

Cait waited, counting several slow breaths as she searched Penny's face for any sign of acknowledgment. Seeing nothing, she dropped her chin to her chest in defeat. Where was Adler? What was taking him so long? Had he run all the way back to the pub to grab a cloak? Had something happened to him?

Her mind spiraled through all the dangers that could have befallen him.

Kidnapped by pirates like Declan.

Discovered by more of the council's hired thugs.

Fallen into a hole somewhere.

Or maybe he had ditched her and abandoned the plan.

Maybe he had never been on her side at all.

This time Cait didn't suppress the growl that pushed its way out. This cycle of thinking was becoming tiresome. Would she ever fully trust him? Would she ever stop doubting his word?

Before she could answer those questions for herself, he returned, stepping onto the path so casually that Cait wanted to throw her shoe at him for making her worry. He might as well have been whistling a lighthearted tune as he strolled up, with that dimple-creating smile of his and bright blue eyes. When they met her own—which must have quite clearly shown her ire—his smile immediately vanished.

"What?"

Cait ground her teeth and pressed her lips into a tight line. "Nothing."

"Clearly," he said, his expression the epitome of innocence. He shuffled his feet, fidgeting in place like a boy caught stealing a cookie from the kitchen rather than the rugged pirate he was.

Former pirate.

"Did you at least find something useful while you were gone?"

"Will this do?" he asked, pulling a bunch of deep brown fabric from under his arm and shaking it out to reveal an old cloak. How had she not noticed that when he'd arrived?

He held it up behind Penny—who still hadn't moved—to show how it would cover her whole frame. And then some. The cloak was about a foot too long for the slight woman, but it was better than nothing.

"It will have to," she said and began to situate it around Penny's shoulders with Adler's help. "Let's hope she doesn't trip on it. Where did you get it anyway?"

"On a ship near Turvala."

Cait raised a single brow at him. Other people might fall for those kinds of teasing answers, but Cait had grown used to them with Declan—even with how little he visited.

"What? It's true." Adler frowned.

"You got it off a ship?"

He nodded.

"Just now?"

He cocked his head to the side and gave her a quizzical look. "Well, no, obviously not. A couple years ago, I think."

Cait drew in a deep breath as her eyes rolled toward the treetops. This man was going to be the death of her, one way or another.

"And where were you keeping it?"

"Do you really want to know where I stash my hard-earned yet sadly depleted goods? Or would you like to get her back to the pub before sundown?"

Cait had the niggling suspicion he was dodging the question, but he wasn't wrong. The sun was fading fast, and his errand to retrieve the cloak hadn't helped them in their urgency. Though it had helped them more than anything Cait had done.

Don't sell yourself short.

Lucan had said those words to her right after she'd sent Declan off, yet no amount of repeating them kept her self-deprecating inner thoughts at bay. But she could at least shove them aside. Even if only temporarily.

Without another word, Cait took Penny's arm and guided her out of the trees. Adler strode behind them.

At the pub's back door in the alley, Cait paused before stepping into the back hallway. Silence. Just as expected. The pub wasn't due to open for another hour or so, which gave them enough time to get Penny situated in the spare bedroom upstairs—the room that had once been Cait's, before she'd moved her bed into the main living area for convenience.

A flash of movement caught her eye as she neared the stairs though, and she stopped in her tracks, causing Penny to run into her. Adler pulled the woman back gently. Without looking behind her, Cait motioned with her hand for Adler to take Penny up the stairs.

Stretching her neck, Cait peered into the pub. Chairs sat upside down on the tables, and beyond them, standing near the door, Naeve fidgeted, her hands trembling as they clutched at her skirts. Swallowing back her irritation that the girl had the stupidity to come back to the pub so soon, Cait stepped forward. Glancing around, she confirmed Naeve was alone.

"Tell me." There was no time for pleasantries today.

The girl blinked rapidly and drew in a lungful of air. "The council. They're coming."

Cait's eyes widened, but she kept her surprise in check. No need to get worked up until the situation called for it. "Explain."

"To Morshan. They're on their way right now," Naeve said. Her eyes darted around the room and over her shoulder, as if the council might have arrived already.

"For what, do you know?"

A rapid string of nods. "Aye. A town meeting with the people."

Confusion swept through Cait. In all her twenty-eight years, she'd never heard of the ruling council coming to Morshan—heirs, yes, although not after they were matched—let alone holding an official meeting in the town. "Why?"

Even as she asked, though, she knew.

Two heirs gone.

A known spy caught.

They were vying for the love of the people.

"I don't know," Naeve admitted.

"Where exactly? And when? We'll need to be there."

"The square. On the steps of the old library." She glanced to the clock above the pub. "Two hours past midday, I believe."

That gave them twenty minutes. Cait mentally calculated the fastest route from the pub before offering a nod to the girl. "Get back to the council hall, before anyone notices you were gone."

Naeve flashed a small smile, dipped into a curtsy, and turned toward the door.

"And, Naeve?" Cait asked. The girl stopped and looked over her shoulder. "Good job."

It wasn't until she was gone and the door was shut once more that Cait allowed herself to turn back to where Adler and Penny waited. Adler's lifted his chin with a silent question, while Penny looked as out of it as ever.

"You mean you weren't listening in on that conversation?" Cait asked.

"Of course I was, but I'd hate to assume what you're planning."

"First, let's get her upstairs to the spare room." She nodded at the stairs, but Adler didn't make any effort to move.

"I think she should come with us," he countered. "The council isn't likely to know about her exile, since the pirates took her straight to the pit."

Cait's thoughts caught up to his logic, and she interrupted his explanation. "And if we bring her to the square, someone will see and ask the council about her."

"If we're lucky, she'll snap out of this funk in time to tell the entire town the truth."

Cait couldn't help but smile. This just might work. Perhaps not all hope was lost.

But as they walked back out the door to the alley, not wanting to take a chance of someone spotting them escorting her, Cait realized she'd forgotten one thing.

"Lucan," she said, trying not to bump into Penny as Adler stopped walking in front of her.

"What?"

"Where is he?"

Though Adler loved to tease her best friend to no end, his regard for him was evident now in the way his blue eyes softened. "I'm sure he's fine. He probably went back to his place to lay low for a bit." Cait breathed out a sigh in time for Adler to add with a shrug, "Or he fell into the Aisling."

Let's hope not.

Adler and Cait kept to the alleys and lesser-traveled back streets as they led Penny toward the square. The plan wasn't a great one, but that wasn't particularly new for Cait. They'd done well with worse in the past.

As they neared the square, Cait clicked her tongue, and Adler stopped at the corner, remaining in the shadow cast by the building. The passageway they were in was smaller than most in Morshan, providing them with a limited view of the public space beyond. A few people walked in and out of sight, about the same number as any other afternoon, meaning the town hadn't gotten notice of the council's impending visit.

Leaning around Penny, who still appeared dazed, Cait whispered to Adler, "Stay here until they arrive and the crowd gathers a bit. I'm going to go around to the other side. I'm trusting you to find the right time to present Penny to them."

"Aye," he said, and his eyes dropped down to her lips so quickly she was sure she'd imagined it. "And after?"

"Pub."

She turned without another word and headed away from them, but Adler whispered her name, stopping her before she'd gotten far. "What if things go south?"

"Same. But in the storeroom."

Once she was back out on the street, Cait lowered her hood and began walking toward the main road. She didn't necessarily want to intercept them, but allowing them a chance to see her in town, being a model citizen of Morshan, seemed the best way to keep suspicion off of her. Before long, she heard the rumble of hooves and wheels on the cobbled stones, a sound not often heard here, where no one owned a horse, let alone a carriage. Most residents had no need for anything more than a simple cart, and even then, it wasn't that common to even own one of those. Only those responsible for making deliveries for the council had one.

So it was no surprise to Cait when people's faces, full of confusion and wonder, began to appear in the open windows and doors along the street. Someone called down to her, "McCallagh! What is it? Do you know?"

She feigned ignorance, donning a bewildered expression as she shrugged. "I'll find out." As she walked away, she could hear the doors behind her thud shut, and people began to trail after her. No point in looking back. This was what the council wanted. And what Cait needed.

An audience.

But why would the council be doing this? And why now? They governed from afar, preferring only to be seen when a citizen had a grievance to report or for the annual harvest offering, and even then, they kept their distance, claiming that a hands-off approach to ruling was best for everyone, even as they passed down law after law to control everything from curfews to business hours.

How had things gotten this bad? Her parents had told her

stories of a time before the treaty, before the war, when the land was prosperous, the people free to pursue the families they wanted and the futures they dreamed of. They'd never lived that life themselves, but their own parents had passed down historical accounts to them, protected and kept secret through the centuries, lest they get damaged by war or fall victim to the council's strict rules about appropriate reading material.

The library—now looming before her, its regal facade kept pristine—had been closed decades ago, its contents sorted, cataloged, and removed. What remained inside, no one knew. Although it was unlocked like all other buildings in Morshan, no one dared enter, the fear of exile always looming over them. Even the Rogues didn't tempt fate with that one. It simply wasn't worth the risk and—as far as Cait knew—offered no benefit to their cause.

The thundering of the carriage grew louder behind her, and she instinctively moved to the side of the road, pressing her back against a building as she turned toward the sound. The horses, a pair of chestnut brown mares with black manes, cantered into view, pulling a simple but elegant closed carriage behind them. The driver, a sullen-looking woman in black, stared blankly forward as they passed Cait and the others lining the street. Murmurings began all around, like an echo of the horses' hoofbeats. She didn't have a moment to think before the crowd began to push her toward the library and the square.

Somehow Cait managed to get to the far edge of the growing mob of people who were rushing to see what was going on in town. As soon as they reached the library and everyone entered the square, Cait veered off and moved behind the building, wanting to be nowhere near where Adler and Penny emerged.

As Cait made her way around, her mind wandered to Lucan. He'd managed to get the message to Tommy on the ship just fine without incident, though he had later complained profusely about how he'd almost been taken out to sea against his will.

Lucan could take care of himself. He was a grown man, after all. But still, an ache grew behind her sternum, and she worried about all the possible tragedies that could have befallen him since they'd parted.

The crowd quieted as the carriage door opened, everyone—even those at the front of the group—craning their necks to see who had come to visit. Cait didn't. Assuming Naeve had been honest and heard things correctly, she knew who this was. When all three passengers had stepped out, the driver shut the door once more, climbed up into her seat, and drove the horses on into the crowd, forcing everyone to move aside or be trampled.

Three women ascended the steps to the library, their movements regal and refined. About halfway up, they halted, and as one, they turned to face the crowd. Two were markedly older than the third, and none of them held any resemblance to Aoife, though Cait couldn't clearly identify any of them. They were obviously all councilwomen, the swirls of black ink visible on their forearms as they clasped their hands before them and looked over the square. The woman standing in the middle, whose waves of red hair reminded Cait of the vibrant sunsets of summer nights, raised her chin and spoke, her words ringing clear in the gathering space as they bounced off the surrounding buildings.

"Good afternoon," she said with a tone that was surprisingly flat compared to the dynamic nature of her appearance. Her hands remained clasped elegantly against her green dress that was simple in style but made from a material no average citizen would have in their wardrobe. "Our visit to Morshan has been long overdue. Thank you for being here on such short notice. We had hoped our first visit to meet with you would be on better terms, but that was not to be." Her chin lowered, as if she were fighting back tears. The women beside her lifted hands to her shoulders, seemingly to comfort her, though Cait saw no tenderness in their demeanor. Once again, the councilwoman looked out at the assembled crowd.

"Unfortunately, our eldest sister, Melina, could not join us, as Lord Madigen has extended his visit to see her. She sends her apologies and hopes to see you at the harvest offering next month. For those who may not know me, I am Fiona, and this is my sister, Brigeh, and her daughter, Darienn." She gestured gracefully to her companions as she named them.

Cait looked out over the crowd and marveled at how quiet everyone was. Apparently, the presence of the councilwomen had put them all in a trance. Except, their expressions were not blank and unseeing, but uneasy and cautious. Like a child when they first see the sea.

Brigeh's blonde hair—which had less red in it than her daughter's—flowed down her back, and even from this distance, Cait could see how vibrant her blue eyes were. She now addressed the people. Although her voice was harsher than her sister's, it was far sweeter than most of the people Cait served on a daily basis.

"There have been rumors about two of our heirs, and we have come today to lay those to rest." She paused. "The rumors are true."

The councilwoman must have expected the instant chatter that spread through the assembly, because her hand shot up to quiet it as soon as it started.

"But, in an effort to be completely transparent with you, our people, we wanted you to know what happened, because rumors left unchecked will undoubtedly put at risk the peace we have worked so hard for all these centuries."

Cait stifled a cough at the lie, thankful she wasn't near anyone who might notice her contempt.

Brigeh continued, "We did, sadly, have to exile two of our own." A gasp rose from the people, though it seemed not all were shocked by this news. "We do not want to defile their reputation any more than their exile already has, so all we can tell you is that they broke their allegiance to you and to our country. We cannot afford to have heirs to the council who do not have the Cregahn people's best interests at heart."

A voice pierced the air from the back of the crowd. Cait couldn't see who spoke, but she didn't need to. Penny had recovered.

"Excuse me, Your Grace, but can you tell me if you took their lives yourselves? Or did you have your pirates drag them off to be pushed into the pit?"

To their credit, the councilwomen showed no reaction. The people of Morshan shifted, presumably to allow Penny a clear path to the library steps. Once again, whispers rustled through the space like a rushing stream.

"And you are?" Fiona asked, looking over Penny casually.

"Penny. The restaurant owner you tried to have killed—I mean, *exiled*—today."

The three women looked at one another, their eerie smiles turning into equally disturbing laughter. *Like three witches cackling,* Cait thought.

"My dear lady," Fiona offered, "when we granted your appeal today at your hearing, we did not expect you to disrespect our mercy so openly."

Penny's scoff filled the air, echoing off the buildings. "What hearing? What appeal? When was I ever given such a chance to request your *mercy*?"

Some of the people closest to Cait murmured to one another, and she could see a seed of doubt beginning to sprout in their minds just as she had hoped it would. But she needed more than mere seedlings to convince the people to stand up to the council.

Brigeh took a step down, then another. "It appears we should have carried out the *exile* after all. Our mercy was wasted on this one. Cregah has no need for liars."

A man called out from deep within the crowd. "How do we know it's not *you* who is lying?"

A few people voiced their agreement, but most remained quiet, waiting, tension thrumming and pulsing among them.

"Who has fed you?" Brigeh asked.

Fiona stepped forward. "And who has maintained peace on our shores?"

Both women turned to Darienn, who took a few confident steps forward to stand beside her mother, before her voice— youthful but powerful—rang out. "Who has kept you safe from pirate raids and our enemies' assaults?"

"And who is to keep us safe from *you?*" another voice responded. Cait's eyes slid closed at the familiar tone and cadence.

Lucan.

Perhaps it would have been better for him to have fallen into the Aisling, if it would have kept him from doing something this stupid.

The councilwomen didn't respond, but their attention was now effectively directed away from Penny. Cait inched her way around the mass of people, trying to hide behind the taller individuals as she went. But Lucan had already begun speaking again before she could reach him.

"Who cares for those starving in the other villages? Who ensures they get the medicine they need? Who protects them from poverty while we—" He was cut off with a sickening thud, and he doubled over.

Cait moved faster but stopped when she saw blood dripping from Lucan's face, and then she saw Adler—with Tiernen's colors tied around his waist—standing there shaking his hand from the impact.

43

AOIFE

Sleep had evaded Aoife since they'd started this chase, the night-mares refusing to release her. They were growing more and more vivid too, and even hours after waking fully, she could not forget the woman who had appeared in this latest one.

With vicious beauty, the woman had eyed Aoife like a tasty morsel instead of a person, but there had been more in her eyes than insatiable hunger.

Recognition.

Like they had met before.

It was preposterous of course, but she remained unsettled by it nevertheless. She might have asked Maura or Renna about it, since they knew all about the creatures they were heading toward. But Renna was busy tending to Bria as best she could without using any more of her power than was absolutely necessary. And Maura…

Aoife pressed her lips together. Why did she feel so uncomfortable approaching her and Tommy? They were both her friends, after all, and she had confided in each of them separately. But still, it didn't feel right to cut into what little time they had together.

From the doorway to Declan's quarters, she could see them standing against the intact section of railing, looking out at the sea as they conversed. She took note of the little gestures they used with one another, the subtle smiles, the near touches.

She shook her head and pulled her attention away. If she wasn't going to interrupt them, she should also avoid staring. But she couldn't awkwardly remain here either.

Closing the door behind her, she made her way out onto the deck and spotted Gavin at the helm as usual. He had been oddly silent with her since the kraken had exploded all over her. It reminded her, unfortunately, of how the crew had initially reacted to her presence aboard the ship. To his credit Gavin didn't appear to want to throw her overboard, but he did seem wary of her.

She didn't recognize most of the other crew working on the deck, and as she spun in a circle, she realized staying at the doorway would have been less awkward than what she was doing now. There had to be something she could do, some way she could be preparing. Sleep was impossible. Maybe Collins would be willing to train more with her. But he was still recovering from his injuries, and dagger skills weren't likely to come in handy against the sirens anyway. She certainly couldn't help the crew with their duties.

Which left her with nothing to do but agonize over their situation. They had discussed everything to death while planning, and no one would want to spend more time discussing her silly musings.

Something touched her shoulder, and she jumped, letting out an embarrassing shriek as she spun around. Captain Halloran looked on the verge of smiling—something Aoife wasn't sure the hardened woman remembered how to do, assuming she ever had. With a hand pressed to her chest, Aoife pushed her breath out and quickly drew in another. "Don't do that! You can't sneak up on someone like that!"

Halloran crossed her arms. "I don't sneak."

"Well, what do you call it then?"

"I call it getting someone's attention when I've been calling their name with no response."

Aoife's eyes widened. She glanced around, pleased to see no one was gawking at her as she'd expected.

"Sorry, Captain," Aoife said, returning her attention to Halloran, who stood regally before her now—not impatiently either, which helped ease Aoife's still-pounding heart. "What was it you needed?"

"I wondered if you might have a moment to talk." The tall woman looked almost bored.

"Are you sure?"

"Why wouldn't I be? Is there some reason I should not—" Halloran didn't get a chance to finish her question before Aoife was waving her hands between them.

"Oh, no, I mean, I have nothing to hide, if that's what you're thinking." She paused. Halloran gave no indication that had been the case. Aoife fumbled with her words once more. "It's just we've spent the last however many hours talking. Figured everyone would be tired of it. Seems like all we do is talk and talk and talk."

"You mean when you're not breaking the fae out of their prison or fighting the kraken?"

Aoife pursed her lips to the side and then shrugged. "Well, that's only two things. The rest of the time we're either talking or sleeping or..."

This time there was no question it was a smile—albeit a small one—gracing the captain's full lips. "The pirate life not providing enough action for you, is that it?"

The words punched Aoife right in the chest, so hard she was shocked it didn't physically knock the air from her lungs. *Don't beg for action if it's not what you want.* She could almost feel Declan's breath in her ear now, repeating what he'd said before, challenging her. It had been frightening at the time, but looking back, she understood why he'd done it, could see it for the self-preservation tactic it was. He'd needed to push her away.

But then something had changed.

"Aoife?" Halloran asked, and for a moment Aoife worried she had fallen or tripped or done some other stupid thing. Thankfully, though, she was still on her feet.

"Yeah, I guess. Well, no, but you don't want to know about my drama with Declan," Aoife said, and she once again waved her hand in front of her face as if batting away the captain's question.

Halloran's hand shot up, grabbing Aoife's wrist and stopping it. Aoife snapped her mouth shut and widened her eyes, fearful of what this captain was about to do. But Halloran didn't appear angry at all. More tired than anything else. With more care than Aoife expected, Halloran lowered their hands, dropping Aoife's at her waist.

"Stop" was all she said before she pivoted on her heel and walked toward the prow of the ship. Aoife didn't know exactly what had just happened, and she gawked at the woman as she retreated. But Halloran's hand appeared over her shoulder, gesturing for Aoife to follow her as she called out, "Come on, Aoife. Let's talk."

Aoife settled herself beside Halloran, who had taken to leaning back against the railing. For several moments, they stood there in silence, causing Aoife to wonder if maybe she hadn't heard the captain correctly and she wasn't supposed to have followed her. But as she opened her mouth to say something, Halloran began, her voice quiet. "How much do you know about Declan?"

Aoife, startled and curious, stared dumbly at her.

Halloran didn't look at her as she repeated the question, this time with an edge of annoyance to her voice.

Aoife shook her head. "Very little actually."

Halloran nodded.

The silence stretched out long enough to make Aoife wonder if she was supposed to be saying more or not. Should she keep looking at the woman? Look out to the sea? What should she do with her hands?

Aoife dared to study the captain's face, which showed no hint she would speak again soon. Ignoring the nervous tightening of her gut, Aoife said, "Why do you ask?"

"What happened after I left you on that rock?" The question came out so quietly, Aoife wasn't sure she'd heard correctly.

"What—"

The captain cut her off with a shake of her head and repeated the question, barely louder this time.

Aoife shifted her feet. "I thought you didn't want to know about—"

Halloran lifted a hand. "I didn't. But I told him..." She paused. "But I need to know. If I'm to help rescue him, I don't need to go in blind to whatever is going on between you."

"Why do you think something—"

A growl escaped Halloran this time—not angry but annoyed.

"Don't. Don't think you can fool me. Now, talk."

Aoife hadn't discussed it—not in such detail—since Tommy had demanded to know why Declan hadn't returned with her. But the words still burned her throat as she forced them out, keeping them limited, as Halloran was undoubtedly less willing to tolerate her spilling all of her emotions.

When she finished, Halloran's eyes slid shut, and Aoife wondered whose side the captain would be on. She'd beaten herself up enough over what had happened—walking away from him and stepping all over his heart in the process. She didn't particularly want a lecture from this woman.

"And will you forgive him?" the captain asked, eyes still closed. When Aoife didn't answer right away, she looked to her.

"I already have." The words came out quiet, meek. Aoife cleared her throat and clarified. "I have. Though he doesn't know yet."

"Good."

"Why do you care exactly? I mean, it's one thing to know the situation. Another to have an opinion about it, no?"

Halloran's mouth pulled into a half-smile. "You're more perceptive than I gave you credit for. You don't get to where I am being ruled by emotions. But you also can't ignore them entirely. I made a promise, years ago."

Aoife opened her mouth to ask a question, but Halloran continued before she could.

"To the McCallaghs. Ada and Carthach. Declan's parents."

Questions spun around Aoife's head, but she knew better than to let them all tumble out. Surprisingly enough, her tongue obeyed, and she managed to ask only one. "How did you know them?"

Captain Halloran remained quiet for so long that Aoife thought she might not answer at all. But when she did finally respond, her voice held only a hint of its typical roughness.

"They gave me aid when I came to Morshan. Alone. No money. No connections. My home had been hit hard by illness. Supplies had stopped arriving from Morshan. With no medicine or healers, many died, if not from the fever then from starvation. My betrothed among them."

Aoife's heart threatened to pound its way out of her chest as understanding hit her. No supplies from Morshan. From the council. It wasn't just the exiles. The council was letting their people die. Did they know? Was it intentional? Why would they let their people die for no reason?

"You didn't know." Halloran's voice sliced through Aoife's frantic thoughts. Aoife could only shake her head. "I didn't either, until I got to Morshan, with its wealth and its comfort. After so much loss, the sight of it dropped me to my knees right in the middle of the cobblestones outside the pub. Must have looked crazy, but Ada didn't treat me as such when she fetched me, took me inside, called for her husband to get me a drink. I couldn't pay, but she insisted it was a gift."

Aoife struggled to process all of this, but her mind was hung up on how this wasn't the Halloran she'd met before. Why was she opening up to her? Why now? Why...ever?

"You look confused." That sounded more like the Halloran Aoife knew. Words cold and sharp.

Before Aoife could think better of it, she blurted out, "Why are you telling me?"

Looks like you haven't gotten control of your tongue after all.

She braced herself for Halloran's gruff rebuke, but the response, while certainly not friendly, wasn't as harsh as Aoife had expected.

"Because you need to know. What the council is doing. What

your *mother* is doing. I lost my entire family and my home. Finding the McCallaghs and their fight to save the country? I promised to help them."

"How?"

An annoyed huff from Halloran accompanied a hard glare. Aoife needed to stop interrupting.

"My plan was two-fold: discover how the council carried out exiles and somehow get the truth out to the other lands, to make the hidden violence there known. It was to be a lengthy ploy. Years spent working my way up the ranks on pirate crews. Doing whatever I needed to—" She paused, and a shadow of sadness passed over her eyes. "Whatever I had to, to get a ship of my own."

"And infiltrate a lord's fleet," Aoife whispered.

Halloran nodded. "We needed to find weaknesses—if there were any—in the allegiance of the lords with the council. My merciless reputation caught the attention of Lord Madigen. But not a month after he recruited me for his fleet, I sailed to Morshan only to find my friends gone. Exiled."

Aoife's throat closed shut. Declan had lost his parents. That must have been why he fled for the sea.

"Their kids—Cait and Declan—handled it as well as anyone could. She had thrown herself into running the pub. Declan had bottled up all emotion, closed himself off. From what Ada had told me of her family, I knew that wasn't like him. But there was little I could do, so I kept an eye on them from afar, even when Declan joined a crew and later led his own. Ada and Carthach were good people. They would have been proud of him."

Proud of him? For being a murderous pirate? How could they—and then Aoife remembered what she would have had to do as a councilwoman, what her mother would have expected her to do.

Halloran breathed out a hollow laugh. "The McCallaghs welcomed many a pirate into their pub, befriended them, knew the life they led out on the sea. Yes, Declan did some despicable things early on to establish his name—just as I have. But his tactics shifted once he found he could coast along more on rumors and stories than actual deeds."

Moving away from the railing, Halloran turned to look out at the water and fell silent. Aoife joined her, careful to keep a respectable distance between them. She didn't speak again until Aoife turned her attention back to the sea.

"Declan will never be a guiltless or moral man, Aoife. But he is still a man of loyalty and honor. His parents would have been proud of how he has weathered his brokenness, let it drive him forward. Even if sometimes it drives him in the wrong direction."

"I still don't understand why," Aoife said. "Why are you telling me this? About Declan. About his parents. What did you promise them?"

Captain Halloran turned slightly, leaning on her forearm. "Perhaps you're not as perceptive as I thought. To watch after them if anything happened. To protect Declan and Cait as best I could without sacrificing the overall mission. I don't make promises lightly, Aoife. I've had to become this"—she pointed to herself—"this cold and callous pirate, but I still care. I care what happens to him. And that means I care about what happens to you and him. The only way this works between you is if you accept him for who he is."

"How did you even know about us? I didn't meet you until that night."

"The beauty of having ties to the leader of the Rogues." She turned back to the sea. "Cait got word to me as soon as we landed. Described what she observed between you two."

Aoife's face warmed. Cait had noticed? She should have expected her to. Cait was a McCallagh.

"Through her, Declan had laid out his plans if things went badly in the hall. As they did."

As she listened to the slapping of the water against the hull, Aoife counted her breaths in time with its rhythm. So much information to process. So much insight into this man she'd fallen for. Wringing her hands in front of her, she kept her eyes down as she broached a question.

"What do I do then?"

"Beyond the forgiveness you already plan to offer?"

Aoife could only nod, wondering if perhaps the woman wouldn't have any other advice.

"Do whatever you can to heal from this. Forgiving him is not lightly done, I know. It won't magically heal the pain his betrayal caused you. But learn from me, Aoife. I know what it is to betray someone you love. There is no winner in these circumstances. It leaves us haunted by the ghosts of possibility, with fading images of what we could have had. Spare the both of you a lifetime of regret. If you can. Forgive. Heal. And love him back. The boy deserves something good in his life. That could be you. If you're willing."

Before Aoife could press her further, a voice from across the deck called for Captain Halloran, and she moved quickly to attend to whatever matter had arisen, giving Aoife a stern yet surprisingly warm look as she passed by.

Aoife had made the decision to forgive Declan, and it had stitched up the wound his lies had left on her heart. Would seeing him open that wound again? Would forgiveness be enough to make things right between them?

Save him first. Deal with the rest later.

44

TOMMY

It took every bit of Tommy's will to keep the world around him from falling away as he watched Maura. Memorizing the lines of her silhouette as she looked out at the sea, he wondered what she was thinking about, with that slight upturn of her lips. If he wasn't careful, he'd lose all track of time and purpose.

They didn't touch, hadn't since they'd followed the others out of the captain's quarters. Standing inches from her now, though, with that sliver of space between them as cold as the northern waters below, Tommy kicked himself for insisting she could use the fresh air. His hands itched to hold hers as they had in the cabin, but that was more than he was willing to do yet out in the open, if for no other reason than he didn't want to distract anyone from the task ahead.

Out of the corner of his eye he saw Aoife chase after Captain Halloran, and before he could wonder too much about what they were discussing, Maura's voice pulled his attention back.

"I wouldn't worry," she said.

"About what?"

Tossing her hair over her shoulder, she nodded toward Aoife and the captain as she turned to face him. "About them."

"Who said I was worried?"

She smirked at him with a slight tilt to her head. Either he was becoming regretfully easy to read, or she understood him better than most.

"The captain is filling Aoife in on Declan's parents. Among other things."

He quickly glanced at the pair and then turned back to Maura. "Even I don't know about his parents. Not beyond their disappearances."

"I'm sure he had reason for not sharing that with you." Maura placed a hand on his arm.

He didn't retreat, but he also didn't lean into her touch as he wanted to.

"I don't think even Declan knows much about them. Especially not Halloran's connection to them."

"Guess the captains will have a lot of catching up to do when we're all reunited then."

Hope swirled in Maura's golden eyes, or maybe it was simply what Tommy wanted—needed—to see. He needed someone to believe they could succeed and that Declan would survive.

She returned her focus to the sea, but instead of smiling as she took in the view, her lips tightened.

"Are you truly comfortable with me coming with you into the sound?" she asked, with more hesitancy than Tommy had come to expect from her.

"If I wasn't, I would have said something back there." He

nodded toward Declan's quarters.

"No, Tommy. If you wanted to stop me from stepping off this ship, you would have said something. But simply allowing something to happen and being at peace with it happening are two separate things."

Leaning forward, he propped his forearms on the railing, if only to keep himself from pulling her close. He steadied himself with a couple of breaths as he searched for words. She mirrored his movements and took up a spot next to him, letting her shoulder press against his.

"I will never be comfortable putting you in harm's way, Maura. I believe in you, but I'm afraid of losing you. This need to protect... My crew, my captain, my friends, and you. Especially you. It's—"

"Much like a mother with her children, I imagine," she said softly. "I may not know exactly how you feel—no one can truly know another's emotions—but I know what it looks like. Fae, especially our males, are quite protective of those they love. I told you the bonds aren't unbreakable connections, but those myths likely sprang up because to any observing human it would appear as such. The loyalty and devotion fae show their partners—and by extension, their children—is a great deal stronger than human hearts are capable of."

Something about the words pricked Tommy's heart like a barb digging into him, pinpointing his shortcomings and his inability to ever give her what someone else could. And after they got the dagger to the Rogues, she would be on her way to a land full of someones. But he hid the cringe by closing his eyes, hoping she would assume he was merely tired. Which he was.

"I didn't mean..." she started, but the way she paused twisted that barb. "I'm not minimizing your loyalty. Simply saying I might understand your need to protect better than you expect."

The sting eased a bit. She wasn't insulting him, even if his treacherous mind insisted she was.

"I meant it though." He waited to see if she would prompt him to continue, but she only hummed a response. "If I'm going to die, it's going to be beside you."

She cocked her head as she peered at him. "So you're saying if you're going to die, you want me to die too? Is that supposed to be romantic?"

"Sounded romantic in my head," he said, keeping his voice low, and he thought she might have laughed, but if she did, it was too faint for him to be sure. He counted a few more breaths. When she still hadn't said anything more, he said in explanation, "It should be obvious I don't want either of us to die."

"Well, that's good at least," she said, her smirk teasing him.

"But I want you beside me wherever I must go."

Any hint of amusement vanished from her expression. "Even with my powers weakened?" Something about her tone betrayed an insecurity that might rival his own.

"You're more than your powers. Far more. I don't want you to die with me. And I don't think you need me to protect you. But we can fight together, by each other's side. It's where we belong."

For as long as we can.

Before she could respond, he pulled her close. He no longer cared who was on the deck, who saw, who objected. Their time was limited, regardless of how things went with the sirens, and he refused to waste it pretending this was nothing.

It was far from nothing.

Licking his lips, he lowered his face to hers as she lifted herself to meet him. And when their lips touched, he couldn't contain the smile that spread across his face. Maura laughed, pulling back enough to say, "This would be easier if you weren't smiling."

His grin vanished, the corners of his mouth dropping low.

Another laugh, sweet and light. "That's even worse!"

He moved to turn away from her, to play up the feigned hurt. No sooner had his eyes left hers than her hand reached for his chin, and before she could guide him closer, he was there, his lips leading hers in a dance that was uniquely theirs.

And he never wanted it to stop.

ᕬᕰ

The rowboat bobbed in the water, knocking against the side of the anchored ship as it waited to be boarded. It had room for six—seven in an emergency—so Tommy had assigned Collins to accompany him, Maura, Aoife, and Halloran.

"Are you sure Renna can't come with us?" Aoife asked yet again, though they'd been over it several times.

"Yes, I'm sure, Aoife. Now drop it," Tommy said, his words unnecessarily harsh.

Renna's tone wasn't much gentler. "Once I've compelled the five of you, I'll need to rest, and there's no benefit to having me close to you. Besides, Bria is still recovering. I'd like to be there when she comes to."

"It'll be okay, Aoife," Maura said, giving Aoife's hand a light squeeze.

While they gathered around Renna to start the process of protecting their minds, Tommy glanced at the entrance to the sound. He had never seen anything like it, but as beautiful as it was, he had no desire to stay here any longer than necessary.

"I wonder where Callum's ship is," Aoife said. "Do you think we're wrong about them coming here?"

Halloran shook her head. "Doubtful. More likely his crew sailed the ship out of sight somewhere."

Renna called everyone closer. "Tommy, may I?" She held her hand out, palm up. He hesitated, unsure what she wanted from him. "Your knife, Captain."

Confusion tore through him. Perhaps he should have had Renna explain what the process entailed before agreeing to it. But they had no other defense against the siren queen.

"How exactly does this work?" Collins said, looking far more curious than Tommy felt, almost like he was eager to learn a new trick with a blade.

After sliding the knife across her palm, Renna did the same to Tommy's hand, saying, "While I can do little more than offer suggestions within someone's mind, mixing of blood during the compulsion makes it more potent, more likely to hold. More likely to keep you safe in there."

No one spoke when Renna squeezed her hand into a fist above Tommy's open palm, letting three drops of her blood fall into his open wound. He looked from his hand to her face, surprised to see her staring at him, not standing in a trance as her sisters had been while in the kraken's waters. After another silent minute, she smiled at him and nodded for him to move aside.

"Do you feel any different?" Aoife whispered to him.

Did he? Aside from the sting in his hand, he couldn't tell. How would he know it had worked? Was facing the queen the only way to test it?

Renna answered Aoife's question. "Everyone reacts differently to it. Some won't notice any change. For others, it's similar to thinking of a memory you can't quite recall, hovering at the edge of your mind."

She paused as she performed the ritual on Captain Halloran,

who looked almost bored, as if this was something she did every day.

"But while it may feel differently for everyone, its effects remain the same as far as I can tell. Fae. Human. All have appeared to respond to it in the same way, so you needn't worry if you don't feel something and someone else does."

Renna spent a few minutes preparing Collins and Maura before turning to Aoife, who seemed more hesitant than anyone else. Holding her hands together tightly at her chest, Aoife eyed the fae with suspicion. Tommy stepped up beside her.

"Aoife, it's okay. What's the matter?" he asked her, but she didn't look at him.

"I don't like it. I mean, in theory it sounds... But the thought of having my self-control taken from me—" Her eyes dropped to her feet with apparent embarrassment.

Tommy looked around at the others and gestured them back. "Give Aoife and me a moment to talk." Once they had moved away, he turned Aoife to face him, lifting her chin with his hand so that she was forced to look at him. "Aoife. What is it really? You may be awkward, a little gullible at times, but you're not stupid. Far from it. So I know it's not the compulsion bothering you—because you know if you don't let Renna do this, your mind will be—"

"Subject to the sirens. I know." Her lower lip quivered a bit before she forced it to stop with her teeth.

Tommy placed his hands lightly on her shoulders, hoping she didn't think he was about to shake her. That certainly wouldn't help in this situation, no matter how impatient he became. "So what is it?"

"I'm scared." Two timid words whispered between them.

"We're all scared, Aoife." That didn't seem to help, so he continued. "The sirens, the queen—"

Aoife shook her head with her eyes closed—not just closed, squeezed tight like she was trying to ward off some nightmare or vision. "Declan." His name fell from her lips like sand through splayed fingers.

"For him or *of* him?" Tommy's gut told him it might be the latter despite how preposterous that seemed.

"Both." She opened her eyes. Fear and worry swirled in the greens and golds. "What if he's already dead? And if he's not... what if he's no longer himself? What if the queen has twisted his mind so badly he doesn't remember me, us, any of us?"

Tommy swallowed hard. How he had failed to consider these possibilities, he wasn't sure, though he had admittedly been distracted by Maura. Still, that worry couldn't keep them from trying. "Aoife, we've come this far. Are you really wanting to stop now? When we're this close to getting him back?"

"Of course not, but my stomach is tied up in knots so painful I'm not sure how to keep going. I've already failed my sister and Declan and...and I—"

"Will certainly fail if you stop now. The longer we wait, the longer the sirens have to hurt him, Aoife. Please. We have to go. You won't be alone. I'll be with you. Maura will be there. Collins and Halloran. We're doing this together, okay?"

He watched her for several moments, waiting to see some shift in her eyes, some indication that his words had struck a nerve or sparked some courage within her. But nothing changed as she whispered an "Okay" and looked over his shoulder to get Renna's attention.

Standing beside Aoife, he wrapped an arm around her shoulders while Renna drew the knife across her palm. When Renna stepped back, indicating all of them were ready, he looked down to see how Aoife fared. "You ready? How do you feel?"

Aoife took a bit of cloth Collins offered her and began to wrap it around her hand as she answered. "I feel...okay? Like something new is there, but I can't quite pinpoint what."

"Well, she did say that could happen for some. Will you be able to focus?"

She nodded and smiled. "I think so."

"Let's go then. Declan's waited for us long enough."

As Tommy watched the others climb the rope ladder down into the rowboat and waited for his turn to follow, he pondered Aoife's words. Would Declan be the Declan they knew? Tommy's gut twisted upon itself at the very real possibility that his friend might already be gone, whether he was dead or not.

The entire square went quiet, and for a moment Cait wondered if it was simply her own shock that had caused her world to go silent. She couldn't look away from the two men. Her thoughts twisted into a confused tangle of shared stories and tender moments and careless hopes.

This whole time, he had been playing her. How had she missed it? Was she truly that distracted by an attractive man? Had her instincts failed? Tapping into those instincts now, she found nothing but a gray void. No feeling one way or the other.

Was he her enemy? An enemy she'd allowed into their innermost circle? An enemy she'd hoped would kiss her?

Or was *this* an act? Another mask?

The latter would be decidedly better, yet it tasted bitter as she mulled it over. If he hadn't planned this, then why did he have his old sash? And if he had, why hadn't he trusted her enough to tell her?

But it wasn't as if her reaction mattered in this instance. She had no intention of making herself known, not even as a regular citizen of Morshan, lest it lead to the councilwomen determining she was part of the rebellion.

If Adler was aware of her watching him, he didn't indicate it. He simply stared as Lucan spit out more saliva and blood onto the ground.

Don't do it, Luc, she silently urged him. The two men might have warmed up to each other, but she knew her friend. And he wasn't one to not fight back.

"You two," one of the councilwomen called out over the crowd, "come closer."

Adler took Lucan's arm and yanked him toward the council. Cait inched forward to keep an eye on them, but the gathered masses parted and closed around the pair of men, like a snake devouring its lunch. Refusing to miss this exchange, she pushed around people as politely as she could, offering whispered apologies and requests to be let past, stopping only when there was a single row of people between her and her friends.

Or your friend. *Singular.*

The councilwoman named Brigeh spoke again. "Pirate—"

Adler shifted forward, but the woman lifted a hand.

"Stop. You will listen and not speak."

His head dipped, and he inched back slightly, his hands clasped behind his back.

"While we appreciate your defending this council and the integrity of the rules of our land, violence is never the answer."

Cait's breath stopped mid-exhale. This was not going at all as they'd hoped. They were supposed to catch the council off guard, trap them into exposing their secrets, but the council was using

Adler's actions to strengthen their false image of peace and mercy. The councilwoman's next words, addressed to all gathered, confirmed this.

"This—this is why we have the rules we do! This is why our land is ruled by women. This is why we have survived—prospered, even—since the end of the war, a war that began because of the dangerous and vile tendencies of men. It is men who got us into that war. It is that war that tore families apart, leaving behind mere shells of those who had gone off to fight, leaving them too broken to return home. But we did not turn our backs on those men. Those who returned to the seas became our allies through the Muirnaughton Treaty. Those who stayed were cared for, nurtured, and healed while our ancestors rebuilt the land into a place of peace and prosperity. It seems, though, if today's events are any indication, we still have much work to do."

Brigeh glided down the steps until she stood before Adler, just out of his reach.

"But, we are a people of mercy, regardless of what this man claims." She waved a hand toward Lucan. "And as you are one of our allies, pirate, and you acted out of loyalty, we will grant you leniency."

Adler offered a quiet "Thank you" as the councilwoman shifted to the side and directed her attention to Lucan. The crowd seemed to take a collective breath and hold it as one, waiting for their rulers to pass judgment upon him.

"You, sir, are out of line." Brigeh's chin lifted into the air until she was staring down the bridge of her nose at Lucan.

He spit on the cobblestones again, inches from her feet.

Cait caught the twinge of anger at the corners of Brigeh's eyes. The woman clenched her fists at her sides but kept her voice steady as she asked, "And how is it that you have the audacity to speak to us, this council, directly? Where is the head of your household? Or do you have no woman to claim you?"

"I am a citizen of Cregah, as much a citizen as anyone else, and I am the head of my own household. I speak for myself," he said with confidence.

Adler lifted an arm as if to elbow Lucan in the face but stopped. Brigeh nodded—likely in thanks for his restraint, but at this point, Cait wasn't sure what to make of anything. She fidgeted before daring to make her way to the left, little by little, keeping her movements small so as not to call attention to herself. But when Fiona's voice cut through the air, she halted and looked up.

"Who are you?" The councilwoman glared down at Lucan.

Lucan's chin rose. "Just a man mourning the family that was taken from him."

"The family you lost," Darienn clarified, and even from where Cait stood, with her view partially blocked by the women in front of her, she could see the young heir's cold glare.

Lucan only scoffed as Fiona leaned to whisper something to her sister, who nodded.

"You, *citizen of Cregah*," Brigeh said mockingly, "are hereby *exiled*."

Cait's knees nearly gave out, and her mind blurred, unable to focus on any particular thought.

Brigeh continued, "Let the good people of Morshan bear witness to our land's laws rightly applied and justice fulfilled in line with our founders' vision. Pirate, you are tasked with overseeing this exile. Report back to us when it is done."

Adler nodded before taking Lucan's arms and locking them behind his back. Lucan struggled, his feet slipping on the cobblestones as Adler dragged him through the mass of people who were slow to part for him.

Panic rose in Cait's throat, making it hard to swallow, let alone think. Why hadn't she reminded Lucan to keep his shit together? To not goad them like that? How had this all fallen apart? And had Adler been lying to her this whole time?

Tightening her hands into fists and slamming her teeth together, she forced her head to clear as best she could, throwing the random thoughts into the shadows of her mind. She had lost her parents and Maggie to this council. Her Rogues had already had so much stolen from them. And now Declan might also be taken from her because of them.

She would not let them take Lucan.

She had to stop Adler, however she could.

46
DECLAN

Declan had no concept of time as he stood on the beach, his limbs hostage to Triss's compulsion. He'd reminded himself many times that he shouldn't care what happened to Callum, the man who had tortured someone simply for helping him.

The five sirens who had joined Triss now gathered on the stone dais she'd been sitting atop earlier. Unlike their queen, these creatures didn't bother with clothing, leaving their human forms on full display as they lounged. He might have reacted lustfully to their appearance—as any man would have—if not for the blood gracing their chins and chests and hands, which prevented him from seeing anything more than monsters.

Triss, still grinning, approached Callum. "Funny that you should want to save him, Declan. Given all he's done to you."

Declan pulled his attention away from the nude sirens before addressing her. "I'm just as surprised as you by that," he said in a flat, bored tone.

"Who said I was surprised? You're an easy pirate to read. An odd one; I'll give you that. But easy."

A half-hearted laugh escaped him. "I should hope so, given your ability to read minds and pillage memories." As much as he urged himself not to form any thoughts she could use against him, he could no better control them than he could the tide.

"No, Declan, there is no tide here. The waters here are as stagnant as the futures of those trapped here."

"If I didn't know better, I'd think you're rather bitter about your plight."

She didn't snap around to look at him. Rather, her head pivoted slowly with a deadly grace. "Of course I'm bitter." The look in her eyes shifted from irritation to something far worse. "I'm also hungry, Declan."

Kneeling, she took Callum's face in her hands and looked him over, like someone inspecting a fish she was about to cook.

"Is he done yet?" Declan asked, his gut roiling.

"Let's see." She licked her lips before taking his hand in hers. She lifted it up as if to examine it, but then, without warning, she snapped his little finger off at the base. His scream was cut short by her sharp glare and whatever silent command she gave. Turning, she tossed the finger to the other sirens, saying, "Try it. Is he done?"

In an effort to avoid watching the sirens fight over Callum's severed digit, Declan asked, "How does that work exactly?"

Triss offered a smooth shrug. "Same as it does for anyone else. Open our mouths. Chew. Swallow."

"And this"—unable to gesture with his hands, Declan resorted to jutting a chin toward Callum—"does what?"

"You mean, besides being gloriously entertaining? It enhances the flavor."

Though he'd attempted to steel his stomach at the expected answer, it still tightened, threatening to push bile into his throat.

"But you already knew that, Declan," Triss crooned. "It will do you no good to stall."

"Perhaps not, but it at least helps pass the time. This isn't my type of spectacle."

At this, she laughed, a low rumble sounding from deep in her chest. "Pretend all you want. You can't hide your fear from me."

"Oh, shit, I forgot about that. Silly me."

She didn't respond but turned back to Callum, whose hand she still held. Shaking her head, she spoke to the tortured pirate. "How did you endure this man's incessant blathering for the entire voyage here?"

Declan remained silent, forcing his mind to go as blank as possible. He painted the invisible walls of his thoughts with the teal and navy of the Aisling and tried to lose himself in the dark calm. It worked, as far as he could assume, but a piercing sound of pain stripped away the colors and forced him back to the present.

Callum's face twisted in anguish as Triss focused on him. Beyond holding his hand, she didn't appear to be doing anything to him physically.

"What are you doing to him?" Declan asked, thankful the words came out with more curiosity than fear.

"Nothing he couldn't have done to himself."

"That's barely an answer."

A sigh fell from her lips, though it sounded more like a growl. "Shall I show you?" She dropped Callum's hand and pushed him down to the white sand, then came toward Declan with the slow progression only someone facing an eternity of isolation and suffering could possess.

She had time. All the time in her cursed world.

And Declan's was quickly running out.

∾

Declan blinked. Callum was no longer lying in the sand. And the sand was no longer white. His boots sank into the fine black sand of home, the tide washing over them once, twice, three times. The sheer walls of the Cregahn cliffs stood prominently above him, protecting this spot—this all too familiar location.

A woman sat in the sand, her back leaning against one of the white boulders that peppered the beach.

Aoife.

But she didn't look at him. Didn't seem to notice him at all. He thought this might be their first meeting, but then he realized her hair ended above her shoulders, which meant she had already run away from the council.

But this didn't make sense. If this was meant to be a memory of when she'd been taken here by Halloran after the disaster with the council, it would have been nighttime, not the middle of the day, with the sun glimmering on the water.

He looked closer at Aoife, whose face was lit up with an expression of peace and happiness he'd only caught a glimpse of once before. But not like this. This Aoife before him now held none of the fear and worry she'd been carrying since he met her. She appeared as he'd hoped to find her someday—happy and unburdened.

What was this? A vision of her life had he not entered into it?

His answer came when another person stepped onto the beach, emerging from the trees guarding the hidden path to the cove, and his breath caught. It was like looking in a mirror, but not.

While he was looking at himself, this Declan was different.

Happier.

Content.

Free.

He remained standing in the water as he watched his counter-part sit down beside Aoife and wrap his arm around her shoulders. His other hand reached across to rest on her belly. A belly showing the unmistakable signs of being with child.

Breath refused to come to Declan as he observed this alternate reality. He noticed the ring gracing his other self's hand. They were married, happy, expecting. A dream he'd tried to ignore and bury, convinced it was a life that could never be his. He would never have the happiness he'd seen in his parents.

But here, before him, it seemed so real.

His heart ached with the crushing realization of what this was: a future he would never have. A dream he'd thrown away with his lies and deceit and betrayal.

Dangling from Aoife's neck was the vial of black sand, the necklace she'd gotten from her sister. The sister he had killed. But perhaps he hadn't done that in this reality. Maybe he had let Lani go, found a way to get her off the island.

As if in answer to that thought, his mirror-self whispered to Aoife, "Thank you. I didn't deserve your understanding or your love. I still don't. But I will be forever grateful for it."

Her next words echoed what she'd spat at him at the cove in the dark. "I don't blame you for what you did for them. That's on them, not you." But instead of anger, Aoife's voice was filled with warmth and love. "Thank you for telling me the truth. I know it wasn't easy, but I will be forever thankful that you trusted me."

When they leaned in to share a kiss, Declan forced his eyes closed.

This was a reality that could never be. This was a reality that could have come about had he not been selfish and stupid. A coward.

It didn't matter that this was only a vision, an image created in his mind by the siren queen who had him frozen on a white-sand beach thousands of miles away from this cove. Because he understood now what Triss had meant when she'd said she did nothing he couldn't do to himself.

How many times had he nearly pictured this scene in his own mind, only to dash it away before it could completely take shape?

Triss had merely taken his own nightmare and forced him to live it.

When he opened his eyes again, the black sand was still there, but the light above came from the moon now, casting an eerie light over the cove. This was the scene he remembered, the one that refused to budge from his mind no matter how much he pushed.

Aoife standing over his blood-covered form as he knelt before her. Him standing, begging for her forgiveness. But this Aoife didn't stop at the words that had cut him so deeply that night. This Aoife railed against him.

"I hate you, Declan! I hate you! I could never love someone who would deceive the one they claimed to care for. How could I? Don't follow me. Don't try to fix this, because it cannot be fixed. It can never be fixed!"

She shoved past him and disappeared into the trees.

This was what he'd expected from her that night. He could never make this right. He could never earn her forgiveness.

He had done this with his own bloodied hands and cowardly spirit. And he would have to suffer the consequences, live with the burden of her hate.

His head fell, chin pressing into his chest and eyes closing once more. His hands—clenched into fists—trembled until he forced them to open, stretching his fingers wide. The bitterness of his failure—his multiple failures—coated his tongue, and no matter how much he swallowed, it would not leave.

Halloran sat alert in the prow of the boat as Tommy and Collins rowed them into the sound. Maura and Aoife sat together in the middle. Aoife tried to calm herself by focusing on the soft splashing of the oars pushing through the water.

Questions gripped her insides, wringing them into a tangled mess of nerves.

How far was it?

Was Declan still alive?

How many sirens were there?

Would they come across any along the way?

Something glimmered in the water to Aoife's right. She sucked in a breath and tightened her grip on Maura's arm.

She wanted to ask Maura if she'd seen it, but fear kept her silent and still.

"We've entered their domain," Maura whispered beside her.

"This is where we trapped them."

The shimmers of light increased under the surface, and Aoife jumped as something splashed.

"They don't seem too happy about that," Halloran said over her shoulder in a hushed tone.

"I wouldn't be either," Maura said. Aoife could have sworn she heard a slight tremor of fear in her friend's voice. Before, that might have made her smile, to know that the fae weren't entirely perfect. But here, now, fear was not to their benefit, and if Maura was already afraid, that did not bode well for their party.

"Maura, take the knives from my belt. And Collins's," Tommy instructed, shifting his body so she had easier access to the weapons. "We'll keep rowing. You three need to be ready."

I can't do this.

Yet she had attacked a kraken. This couldn't be worse than that, right?

"Steady, Aoife," Maura said, handing her one of the knives. "Just strike at anything that moves, and try not to tip us over when you do."

If Maura meant it as a joke, Aoife didn't find it funny. At all.

For the next several minutes, they crept along at an agonizingly slow pace. Aoife remained tightly wound as she watched and waited. Her eyes were painfully dry from refusing to blink much. Her hand ached from trying to hold the knife steady in her sweaty palm. Her teeth hurt from clenching her jaw. If she kept this up, she'd have no energy once they found the queen.

When she glanced at her companions and noticed none of them were as tense as she was, she urged herself to loosen up. She uncurled her toes, unclenched her backside, rolled her shoulders, stretched out her jaw, and blinked several times. Finally, she loosened her grip on the knife, ready to place it in her other hand so she could wipe off her sweaty palm on her pants.

She'd just about gotten the knife to her bandaged hand when the attack came. Something—or someone—slammed into her side of the boat. She groaned as her shoulder collided with Maura's, and the knife fell onto the floor of the boat.

With a curse, Aoife bent over. Before she could grasp the weapon, something cold and wet and strong had a hold of her arm and began to pull her toward the edge. Even her scream seemed to be absorbed by their surroundings, coming out fainter than expected. Maura reached around her but couldn't get to the creature before it clamped its teeth down on Aoife's arm.

A shout came from Tommy, though Aoife couldn't see what happened, as the siren drove its teeth in further and blinding pain shot through her.

Her flesh was ripped away from the bone, fat and muscle and tendons tearing as someone fought to get the thing off her. Her vision blurred. If her screams continued, she didn't know. The world around her swayed and spun until she didn't know which way was up or whether she was even in this world anymore.

Then everything went dark.

48
MAURA

"Do you have her?" Tommy asked.

Maura looked up and gave him a nod as she moved Aoife into a more comfortable position in her lap. He was trying hard to conceal his concern, but he had to realize it could have been far worse.

"She'll be okay."

Frowning, Tommy surveyed the damage to Aoife's arm. A section of her jacket sleeve was torn away, revealing a mangled mess of skin and flesh beneath. He didn't seem convinced.

Collins, rowing with Tommy as fast as he could, looked squarely at Maura—seeming more worried than angry—and asked, "How exactly is she going to be okay? A chunk of her arm is gone! She lost a lot—"

Pinning him with a stern glare, Maura stopped the young pirate but kept her voice calm. "You underestimate her. We all do."

"Underestimated or not," Halloran called back, "she needs her wound wrapped. Here." A pile of gold fabric floated through the air between the men's heads and landed on Aoife's chest.

Maura was so engrossed with the task of removing Aoife's jacket and binding her wound, she didn't hear the approaching danger.

The sirens surfaced with such quickness that Maura had no time to shout a warning before one had Tommy in her clawed hands. A second siren appeared at the prow, grasping for Captain Halloran's legs. But the captain had been ready, and with a swift motion, she slashed her blade across the creature's throat before kicking the body back into the water.

But Tommy had no blade ready, only an oar, which now clattered into the boat as the siren's grip forced all strength from his hands. Maura, helpless and useless with Aoife unconscious across her legs, shouted to Halloran and Collins, who was already moving. Collins rammed the handle of his oar past Tommy's head and into the siren's face. It did little but anger her, and her mouth opened in a sharp screech, revealing multiple rows of sharp fangs.

Then time slowed as Maura watched those fangs latch onto Tommy's shoulder. His pained scream echoed off the rocks as Halloran drove her knife into the side of the siren's head. The siren's jaws and hands released him. But as Halloran worked to get the lifeless body over the edge, Tommy's eyes rolled back, and he collapsed backwards into the boat, his head thudding against one of the wooden seats.

What hope did they have of succeeding now?

Don't underestimate them, Maura. Don't underestimate yourself.

Having gotten Tommy's shoulder bound with his teal sash, Captain Halloran took up his oar and worked with Collins to keep them moving. They were granted a bit of luck somehow, and no more sirens came near their boat. Although Maura saw the occasional feathery tail splash at the surface, the sirens kept their distance. Whatever the reason, she was thankful for the reprieve.

The sound gradually narrowed. The rock walls closed in on them, and Maura had to push away the reminder of what life had been like in that room at the council hall for all those centuries. She closed her eyes, hoping to ease the discomfort, but doing so made her stomach uneasy as the boat swayed gently in the still water. When she opened them, they were rounding a bend and arriving in an open basin of water. It wasn't so big she couldn't see its rocky edges, but it was still large enough to give Maura pause.

"The beach," Halloran said, and Maura turned to see where she indicated.

Across the water, a pristine beach lay waiting. While she saw no boat on the shore, she could make out the pool of blood on the white sand.

Please don't be Declan's.

Aoife stirred in her lap.

"How in the sands…" Collins said in a low voice as he spotted the movement in Aoife's still unconscious body. Maura offered him an easy shrug and a bit of a smirk, though it disappeared when she noted how Tommy still lay motionless next to her.

It wasn't until the bottom of their boat crunched against the rough sand that Aoife's eyes flashed open. Blinking, she asked, "What happened? Why am I in your lap?"

An airy laugh escaped Maura, and she helped her friend sit up. "You nearly became a siren's meal. But we didn't let them get more than a nibble."

"Much appreciated. Thank you," Aoife said, but a half a breath later, she noticed Halloran sitting where Tommy had been originally. "Where's Tommy?" Maura didn't get to answer before Aoife spotted him on the other side of the rowers' bench. Halloran and Collins stepped out of the boat to pull it up onto the sand, and Aoife rushed forward.

Maura waited for her to ask the inevitable question, but Aoife's fingers hovered over Tommy's bloodied shoulder.

"Will he be okay?" Aoife asked without looking back at Maura.

"I believe so, but he will need to rest."

Now Aoife faced her, her green eyes ablaze with curiosity. "Why did I recover so quickly? How long will he need?"

"Longer than we have, unfortunately," Halloran said, pulling their attention to the beach where she stood. "Let's get him moved."

Maura opened her mouth to protest, but there were no other options. They couldn't wait for Tommy to recover, and her magic was depleted enough that she couldn't risk healing him even a little bit. Declan was here somewhere, and they hadn't traveled all this way to settle for retrieving the dagger without him.

Aoife placed a reassuring hand on Maura's arm as they watched the two pirates lay Tommy's unconscious form behind a pile of black rocks.

"He'll be okay, Maura. Let's get this over with."

The four of them trudged away from the water's edge, and Aoife purposefully stepped around the bloody mess that lay nearby. She'd seen enough of the remains to know it probably wasn't Declan's blood. There was a bit of torn burgundy fabric nearby—the same color Callum's crew wore. Whoever the sirens had killed here, they had left no piece of his body behind, only bloody clothes strewn about.

"There," Halloran said, pointing ahead of them where faint indentations appeared in the sand.

"Footsteps?" Aoife asked.

"Aye. Two sets," Collins said as he stepped up beside her.

A spark of hope flashed within her, singeing her nerves and making her skin tingle. Uninvited memories flooded her mind, calling forward the guilt that had been her near constant companion since the morning Lani had been dragged away. Instinctively she grasped the pendant at her chest and held the small vial in her uninjured palm as tightly as if it were her sister's hand. Lani had always been the brave one. When storms raged with bright flashes of lightning and booming thunder or when their mothers were in particularly ill tempers, Lani had not shaken as Aoife had, always facing those moments with stern determination.

Had she faced Declan with that same attitude?

Declan.

Beneath Aoife's hand her chest tightened, like it wanted to guard her heart from him and his lies.

Clamping her eyes shut, she pushed back against that thought. No, she had forgiven him. She would forgive him. It was what you did when you loved someone.

"Aoife." Maura's voice had Aoife's eyes snapping open once more.

She found the fae standing in front of her, stooping her head low to peer into Aoife's eyes. Was she searching for a hint she was going to break? A sign something was seriously wrong with her? A part of her wanted to cower under this intense scrutiny.

"What?" Aoife asked, voice strained.

"You can do this," Maura said. "I'm right here with you."

In silence they worked to catch up to Halloran and Collins, who had already gotten a hundred or so paces ahead of them. The pirates turned a corner Aoife hadn't noticed. From the shoreline, the cliffs looked solid, but now, as she approached, she found the dark gray stone hid the entrance to another section of the beach.

The two pirates stopped short.

When she stepped between them, her shoulders brushing against theirs, she saw what had them frozen.

A woman, tall and beautiful and regal, stood in the middle of the space with several women—who wore nothing but blood—

lounging on a pile of stone behind her. To her right, a body lay in a heap on the ground. From this distance, Aoife couldn't tell who it was or if the person was even breathing. Directly in front of the queen, though, a man stood. Even without his teal sash, even with his back to her, even with his hair a bit shaggier, Aoife knew it was him.

She called his name. A question. He didn't move. Didn't even flinch.

Before Aoife could stop herself, her feet were carrying her toward him, kicking up sand behind her. A few times, she nearly fell, but she managed to stay upright somehow. She had intended to not seem so eager and to not give the sirens any information that could be used against her, Declan, or their friends.

But all those plans had vanished like a fading mist, and she was far from graceful or impressive. She was a desperate, scared but hopeful woman so close to the man who needed her.

He stood unnaturally still, and panic tore through her as she imagined him already dead. Was she too late? With twenty paces to go, she cried out his name again, and this time he turned.

Declan was here. He was alive. He was here. She had made it.

But something was terribly wrong.

Those stormy gray eyes she'd been dreaming of for the past week were the same, and yet they weren't. How many times had she envisioned their reunion? Each time she'd imagined him being thrilled to see her. But now his eyes held no hope, no eagerness, no happiness.

He looked almost scared of her, cowering away from her like she was going to strike him. His trembling lips and empty stare pricked her heart. Should she stay back? Should she refrain from getting too close?

He needs you. He's hurting. He needs you.

With that thought, Aoife ran into him, her arms finding their home around his neck, but he didn't make any move to return her embrace. Nestling her face under his jaw, she relished his scent, which had already begun to fade from his cabin.

But he remained a statue.

Still, she refused to let him go. Not for anything.

Then the siren spoke.

"Welcome, Aoife. We've been waiting for you."

50
DECLAN

D eclan?" A familiar voice called for him. A voice he would
forever cherish and be haunted by. A voice that had kept
him from giving up in the brig on Callum's ship.

But it wasn't real. Like the visions he'd seen, this was a trick.
Triss's doing. Screwing with his mind and his heart to push his
sorrow and pain into every fiber of his body for her own pleasure.

But the call came again. Clearer. Brighter.

"Declan."

No longer a question, Aoife's voice sounded urgent, desperate, scared.

His eyes flashed open, bringing back the view of the white
sand, Callum's now unconscious body, and Triss standing before
him. But she was looking past him, over his shoulder. His body,
once held by Triss's silent commands, now listened to him once
again, and he turned slowly, every muscle and joint stiff from

standing frozen for so long.

Aoife was here, her green eyes wide as she ran toward him. This was what he'd been waiting for, but the sight of her brought no hope, only a fresh reminder that he had hurt her and would never be good enough for her. And when her body pressed against his, his limbs began to shake, and he tried to pull away, but he couldn't move any more than he could speak.

Triss had taken control over him again.

Declan wanted to pry Aoife's arms away, tell her he wasn't right for her, remind her of how he'd hurt her and how she couldn't trust him. But he also wanted to hold her close to him and never let her go, to spend every day making it up to her, proving that she meant everything to him.

But he could do neither.

All he could do was try to memorize this feeling of her clinging to him and tuck it away for safekeeping.

When Triss's voice called out in greeting to Aoife, every inch of him wanted to guard her from this demon. He half-expected Triss to laugh at his thoughts, but she continued to speak as Aoife held fast to him.

"You took your time getting here, didn't you? Have some trouble along the way?"

Aoife loosened her grip on him, and he couldn't bring himself to look at her as she pulled away and inched to his side. "You must be Triss," she said, her voice warbling a bit.

"The one and only."

Declan could picture Triss's smug smile.

Aoife, her tense arm pressing against his, spoke again, this time with a bit more confidence. "I'm here for him."

Declan's eyes flashed open, and though he couldn't turn his head to look at her, he could see in his periphery how she stood taller, surer of herself.

"Just him?" Triss asked.

"For now."

Declan's body pivoted against his will. He would never get used to this part of Triss's powers. Now he faced Triss, who dropped her head to the side and flashed him an insincere smile. "Did you hear that, Declan? She's here just for you. For now."

He didn't react, but he wasn't sure how much of that was Triss's doing.

Triss focused once more on Aoife. "And why would I let you take him?"

Aoife's confident posture remained, though her voice betrayed that it might be starting to unravel a bit. "Certainly not from the goodness of your heart. If you have one."

A cackling laugh reverberated off the rock walls, and Triss's expression turned dark and taunting. "Oh, I have one. Two now, actually." With a wave of her hand, she gestured to Declan first and then to Callum, whose body was still slumped on the ground to the siren's right.

His stomach lurched when Triss raised her other hand, holding another of Callum's severed fingers, still bloody. She flashed Aoife a wink before popping it into her mouth like a grape. Closing her eyes, she made a show of enjoying her snack, savoring each crunch of bone before licking her lips and swallowing. With a contented sigh, she opened her purple eyes once more.

"Not quite done, but still rather delicious."

A oife couldn't tear her eyes from the siren standing before her. The woman's terrible dark eyes roved over Aoife with a burning hunger that sent pinpricks across her skin, but Aoife steeled herself as best she could.

Wracking her brain, she searched for the words they had planned for her to offer, but her mind refused, fixated instead on the mental image Triss's words had created: Callum and Declan dead and broken. Hearts ripped out.

"Interesting," Triss said quietly as her eyes narrowed on Aoife once more. "I can't seem to get a read on your thoughts. Your mind appears to be cloaked."

With this, her head snapped away, and Aoife turned to where the others stood watching, waiting. Why were they just standing there? They should be searching for the dagger while she helped Declan. Aoife surveyed the area, which was empty aside from the dais the sirens sat upon, and she knew it was as they'd feared.

Triss had the dagger on her.

The queen stood and moved forward, not toward the others as Aoife had expected, but toward her. Her movements reminded Aoife so much of her mother—a regal, confident, lethal grace—as her sheer black dress swished around her hips and legs, concealing little of her body.

Aoife swallowed, realizing she hadn't responded at all to the siren's last comments.

Triss stopped just outside of Aoife's reach, her haunting eyes intensely studying her, like she could unlock Aoife's thoughts with a glare alone.

Look away! Aoife's mind pleaded with her, but there was something about those purple-hued pools of ink. Something in them. Power? Hunger? Magic? Aoife wasn't sure which of these held her captive. It wasn't until something bumped into her shoulder that she blinked and cut off whatever spell had been cast on her. She turned, and although Declan still faced ahead, she saw him watching from the corner of his eye, and his shoulder hovered lightly against hers.

He couldn't move, really. Yet he'd been able to push his muscles just enough to lean into her. Aoife tried to give him a reassuring smile, but her hope was slowly dying, like a candle nearing the end of its wick.

"Yes, yes, that's very touching," Triss said, though it was obvious she hadn't found Declan's gesture to be anything remotely endearing. "Looks like you had a bit of an accident on your way here?" Her dark eyes flashed down to Aoife's arm.

"Oh, that? Just a scratch."

"That's a lot of blood for a scratch." Aoife only shrugged, trying to mimic the bored attitude Declan displayed in tense situations. "Can I ask you a question, Aoife?"

Aoife responded with a silent lift of her brow.

"Who is your mother?"

That wasn't exactly the question Aoife had expected, and her already flustered mind stumbled around the answer.

Triss released an exasperated breath. "You do have a mother, don't you?"

For an ancient, presumably immortal creature, this siren was certainly impatient. The thought elicited a nervous chuckle in the back of her throat, but she quieted it before it could escape and earn her a harsher response from the queen. Still, that didn't mean she had to rush through her answer.

"Aye," she said. Her hands itched to reach for the necklace hidden beneath her shirt, but she kept them steady by weaving her fingers together, clasping them in front of her waist. The itching in her arm beneath the makeshift bandage threatened to derail her thoughts completely, but she pushed out her response. "I'm merely surprised you hadn't already collected that information by pillaging the young captain's mind."

"Ah, yes, he did unknowingly give me her name and a rundown of all her despicable qualities. But alas, his mental image of Melina is fuzzy at best. And since I can't get through the clever cloaking trick here"—she waved a finger at Aoife's head—"I hoped you might be able to describe her to me."

"Why? Are you wanting to paint her portrait?" Pride might have swelled in Aoife's chest over the retort had she not also been scared of what Triss might do when goaded.

But Triss once again turned to Declan. "You didn't tell me she was so feisty."

Though his body still couldn't move, he was able to say, "Technically I didn't tell you anything about her."

Triss waved her hand in dismissal, muttering something about *semantics* before addressing Aoife again. "No, Aoife, I am not painting. We are sorely lacking any art supplies, as you might have noticed during your inspection of my home here. But it's simply that you look so oddly familiar is all. Curious if she might look familiar to me as well. Or perhaps you're fae or elf or nymph? Are you sure we didn't meet long ago before those bitches imprisoned me and my kin in this stagnant pool?"

"Those bitches including your own sisters? Oh, excuse me—half-sisters."

Triss's eyes narrowed as her lips slid into a thin line. She turned her attention back to Aoife's companions, and a surprisingly friendly smile lit up her face. "Speaking of *half*-sisters. You brought one with you, I see. Maura. Come, come." Before Maura had reached Aoife's side, Triss was already asking, "How long has it been?"

Maura's normally carefree voice came out tense and cold as she said, "Not long enough, Triss."

"Never thought you'd come back here, did you? And how are our sisters? Still alive? When that war broke out, I wondered if any of the fae survived."

"Aye, we survived."

Triss clicked her tongue. "And what a shame that is."

No one responded, and a heavy silence fell until Triss broke it with another cackle. "So I assume I have Renna to thank for this." She tapped a clawed finger at her temple. "And where is she? I would have liked to say hi. To her and to Bria."

Maura didn't answer her and instead held the siren's intense stare.

With a flick of her fingers, Triss freed Declan's limbs from their invisible prison, but he still didn't appear to be back in control of them, as he left Aoife's side to join Triss. When he turned to face them, his eyes remained down for several breaths before snapping up. Those stormy greys she had dreamed about since she'd abandoned him flared with a kaleidoscope of strong emotions.

What was the man thinking? Did he have any hope remaining within? Was he already lost to the siren's call? Had they arrived too late?

Triss shifted a bit, looking from Aoife to Declan and back with that smug look she'd had before. As she moved, her skirts swished again, just as they had when she'd first walked toward them, but now something flashed from within the fabric. A reflection of the sun on some kind of metal. Aoife tried to catch a glimpse of what it was, but Triss dropped a hand to her hip and pulled open a fold in the skirt, retrieving a dagger.

Its gold hilt was intricately designed, and its blade was etched with a pattern that seemed familiar to Aoife. This was the dagger she'd read about. The legend. The thing coveted by so many and needed by the Rogues to free all her people.

"The Csintala dagger," Triss said, twirling the blade's point against one of her fingers. "That king didn't know what he'd been gifted, sadly for him. I, of course, was quite appreciative. Had he known a thing or two about enchantments—or the queen he'd vowed to return to—he would have known better than to go back on his word. Funny thing about fae enchantments. They always have a catch."

The siren paused to stare into Aoife's eyes.

Triss continued. "The queen certainly pulled a fast one on the world with that little lie about a shield too. Aye, we are not so secluded up here that we do not catch wind of rumors swirling about. Many have come to find this, you know. Few live long enough to even catch a glimpse. What can I say? Sometimes my hunger can't bear to wait for them to properly marinate in their pain."

She shrugged, as if she weren't discussing torturing and eating people.

Aoife steeled herself against her gut's reflex at the mental image that formed.

"I suppose," Triss continued, "it's odd for me to hold onto such a blade when I can't wield its magic. But then again, why hand it over to those who could use it against me?"

The siren let out a breathy laugh, a slight smile turning up the corners of her mouth as she continued to spin the dagger. "Let's make a deal, shall we? Despite my hunger, I'm feeling rather generous today. So I'll give Declan to you, if that's what he wants."

Aoife's gut twisted even tighter. Her mind picked apart the words. "And the dagger?"

"It's either Declan or the dagger. Choose."

There was no question in Aoife's mind. It had to be Declan. Surely the others could get the dagger from Triss, even without Tommy. Aoife merely had to bargain for Declan's safety. Breaking Triss's compulsion over him wouldn't be as easy as stealing a blade from her hand.

As if either could be considered easy.

Aoife contemplated the options before her, working through each word of Triss's proposed deal. On the surface, it seemed acceptable, but she'd be foolish to think there wasn't a catch.

Triss slipped the dagger back into the sheath at her hip. "I don't need access to your mind to know you've made your choice. That should warm your heart, Declan."

"I'll agree, if—"

"If?" Triss didn't look at all shocked at the answer.

"If you agree he won't be compelled to want to stay...or to

kill any of us."

Triss nodded and whispered to Declan, just loud enough for Aoife to hear, "You chose a smart one here. It's a shame she's just not smart enough."

When Declan's eyes closed, panic coursed through Aoife's veins. Before she could rush forward to help him, it was done. And it was far from good. Triss's smile brightened, lighting up her entire face as Declan opened his eyes once more.

With a new and terrifying madness, his glare bored into Aoife. He charged toward her in a murderous rage.

"Move!" Collins yelled, and then Aoife was falling hard in the sand, with Collins on top of her. Collins scrambled to turn around. Keeping Aoife at his back, he lifted his hands toward Declan, who growled as he stopped short.

Declan stood over them, jaw clenched, muscles tensed, gripping his own dagger tightly in his hand. "Get out of my way! My fight is not with you! It's her!"

What had Triss done to him?

Had she compelled Declan to kill her?

Aoife had been a fool to believe Triss would adhere to any agreement.

Collins pushed to his feet and swiped Declan's hand—and blade—to the side. Stepping forward, he forced Declan to take a step back.

Maura ran in and grabbed Aoife by the arm to pull her away, but Aoife resisted, wanting to remain and listen to their exchange. She needed to know why he hated her enough to fight his own man.

"I don't want to hurt you, Captain," Collins said. His hands were lifted between them, his body ready to react.

Declan scoffed. "I'm the one with the blade, Collins. Even if you wanted to—" He didn't finish his sentence before thrusting his dagger forward.

But his blade struck steel rather than flesh. Collins had pulled out a dagger hidden at his wrist. Declan laughed. "Ah, new tricks, I see."

Collins nodded, drawing another dagger—Tommy's—from his belt, and inched closer to his captain. Maura pawed at Aoife, urging her to move, but still she stayed, straining to hear their words.

"I don't want to hurt you either, Collins. I really don't," Declan said, his rage softening briefly before flaring once more. "But I will if you don't let me at her."

"What did she do to you?"

"She handed me over to Callum! And it's *her* fault Tommy is dead!" He shouted the accusation over Collins's shoulder, pointing his dagger at Aoife. His voice lowered into a snarl as he glowered at Collins once more. "My oldest friend. A brother to me. And she got him killed. Gutted like a damn fish."

Collins stumbled backward, as if the words themselves had shoved him away, but he recovered as quickly as he could, yelling at Declan, "Tommy's alive! Whatever you think Aoife's done, it's a lie, a trick of the siren!"

Declan rushed him once more, knocking one of his daggers into the sand. But Collins held his ground, pushing all his weight against his captain. Their weapons were now pressed against each other's throats.

"Don't you dare defend that bitch. Don't you dare." Declan spat the words in his face, but he held fast, unflinching.

"I'm just trying to help—"

"Bullshit! If that were true, you'd be chasing her down yourself, stringing her up so I could give her what she damn well deserves. But instead you're here! Knife to my throat. Loyal crew indeed." Declan's lip curled into a sneer. "You let her follow you onto my ship. Maybe I should hurt you for bringing down this curse!"

Maura stopped pulling her, halted in place by Declan's shouts. Aoife's head began to shake in disbelief. Triss could not win. Especially not like this, with Declan hating her, thinking she'd betrayed him and killed his best friend. She had to do something. Something other than crouch in the sand and wait to be killed.

With a burst of energy she flung herself away from Maura, but the fae held her.

"Aoife, stop," Maura pleaded with her, but it only made Aoife try harder.

"Let me go. I need to stop him. To end this," she said with a growl.

"And how in the hell do you think you'll stop it? Aoife! Think!"

"I don't know! I don't know..." She repeated the words over and over, and each time, they grew softer as her body lost its fight against Maura's iron grip. "But I have to try."

She stilled and resorted once again to watching Declan trying to get at her, Collins standing in his way.

"What has she done?" Aoife asked no one in particular.

Maura answered, "Compelled him to believe a new memory."

"But why? Why not simply compel him to kill me if that's what she wants?"

She winced as Collins landed a blow on Declan's ribs, thankful it had been with his fist and not his blade. But it did little to slow Declan down in his pursuit. For each step Collins pushed Declan back, Declan gained two. Or three. They were getting closer to her, and Aoife wasn't surprised when her friend pulled her further away.

Maura answered her as they scrambled on the sand. "That wouldn't be as entertaining for her. It wouldn't have this amount of emotion and passion behind it."

So it was for Triss's enjoyment—and the enjoyment of her audience. It wasn't merely Aoife's death she sought.

"She wants to hurt him more," Aoife said, and Maura nodded. "If he succeeds, she'll take the memory away—"

Maura finished the thought. "And leave his heart even more tarnished with guilt. And loss."

A fire flared within Aoife's chest, and she dug her toes into the sand as hard as she could, but it did little to stop Maura from pulling her along.

"Let me go," Aoife repeated, but this time she filled each word with the flames raging within her. "Let me try."

When the tightness around her arm lessened, she didn't hesitate to take advantage. She didn't run. She needed to maintain her strength for what she needed to do. It was a long shot, she knew. She had no skills to help her combat a siren's magic, but she hoped—beyond all hope—that maybe the stories were true.

Love conquered all.

And if Declan truly loved her, it could break this evil cloud he was trapped in. It had to.

Maura followed close behind but didn't seem keen on dragging her away again.

Love conquers all. She repeated it to herself, as if doing so could give the words power, make them true.

Less than twenty feet separated them when Declan feinted, drawing Collins to one side so he could drive his knee into his stomach. Collins rallied and stood, but Declan must have anticipated his move, because in a blur of movement too fast for Aoife to track, Collins's blade was dropping to the ground.

Declan's hand slammed into him.

They both stilled.

Wrapping an arm around Collins, Declan pulled him closer, but there was nothing friendly about the move.

What was happening?

Then Collins collapsed to his knees, and Aoife's eyes went wide as she watched him slowly sway.

Get up! Get up! Get up!

She silently screamed at him over and over.

Declan stood and lifted his blade, which was now dripping with blood.

"No!" Aoife screamed. Or did she? She couldn't tell what was real anymore.

Collins's head lolled to one side. His arms went limp. Even if Aoife hadn't been frozen in place, Maura wouldn't have allowed her to go help him, so she waited. And watched.

He was fine. He had to be.

Aoife's breath caught as Declan pushed him. Collins didn't resist. He simply fell to the ground and lay motionless.

Declan's lips moved as he muttered something, but Aoife couldn't hear him over her heartbeat thundering in her ears. Adjusting his grip on his blade, he stalked toward her, eyes pulsing with hatred.

And now she heard his words.

"You claimed to love me, Aoife, and I believed you. Like a fool. You've taken everything from me. My pride, my heart, my friend. And now you're going to pay. Slowly. Painfully." His spewed vitriol ripped her heart to shreds.

Aoife channeled the pain into her next words, directed not at him but at Triss. "How are you so heartless?"

Triss replied with a wide grin before baring her teeth, which transformed into a hideous mess of needle-like tines. She laughed, the most maniacal cackle Aoife had ever heard.

Then Maura was there, standing in front of Aoife, protecting her.

No, no, no, no.

This time she knew the words remained in her mind, silent to the world, but it was the only response she had to seeing another friend rush toward a threat to save her.

To save Declan.

Declan showed no mercy to the fae though, and he didn't hesitate to attack. Maura held her own as best she could, her arms taking nicks from the blade as he swiped it this way and that, but still she held strong. Twice she hit her mark. An elbow to his chin. A fist to his ribs where Collins had struck him before. And though he recoiled, the hits did little—even with her inhuman strength— to slow him down. Blood dripped from her arms, peppering the white sand between their feet. And then Declan landed a lucky blow, an elbow to Maura's temple. She tried to remain standing, tried to keep going, but her feet were quickly faltering.

Aoife was there to grab her before she fell, and she grunted under the sudden weight of her friend's still body. Aoife feared the worst but managed somehow to focus on the spot where Maura's blood should still flow in her veins, and after seeing the pulse there, slow and sure, she released a breath of relief.

But that relief was short-lived, and now Declan had a hold of her hair at the crown of her head, pulling her out from under the fae until she stood mere inches from his hate-filled face. The weight of his animosity slammed into her chest, and she couldn't breathe, couldn't think.

Aoife wasn't afraid to die. She'd expected death to come for her at some point on this journey. But she'd never thought it would be like this. At the hand of someone who loved her.

The tears welled up without warning. She had no strength remaining to fight them from spilling over and trailing down her cheeks. She should plead with him, as he had done in the cove, but the words stuck in her throat, and she was frozen in fear. He was staring at her with such disgust.

"Don't you dare," he started, his voice low, gravelly, terrifying. "You aren't allowed to weep. Not after what you did. I gave you *everything* I had. I *trusted* you. My sister trusted you."

Aoife tried to protest, even though she knew it would do no good. "I didn't. I didn't."

He whirled her around until her back pressed against his chest and his dagger pricked her throat. His breath warmed her ear, and the flood of memories drowned her. The man she had grown to know and love was the Declan she wanted to remember. The one who, though dangerous, had a heart, even if it was a bit burnt. The Declan who brushed away her tears, who talked her through the panic, who held her hand, who knelt in the sand and begged for her to understand.

Would pleading work for her now? It hadn't swayed her, but it was her only chance now.

"I'm sorry, Declan," she said, her voice barely over a whisper. He scoffed, but she continued. "Please forgive me. I need you."

"Shut up," he hissed in her ear.

She refused.

"No. I won't shut up. You need to know."

Before she could say more, her eyes snapped to the action unfolding near Triss's dais.

Callum, now conscious, rose to his feet and didn't hesitate before running at Triss, hands flexed and eyes ablaze. Triss didn't see him. Her eyes—wide with anticipation—were focused solely on Aoife. Aoife's breath caught as Callum launched himself at the queen.

But she hadn't been oblivious after all.

Her hand flashed up, caught Callum by the throat, and squeezed.

52

DECLAN

Yo u've failed them, Aoife," Declan whispered into Aoife's ear, and he grimaced at how close he had to stand to this woman who disgusted him. But it would be over soon enough. After she felt a fraction of the pain he did. "Look around. They're all dead or dying. Because of you. It's all you're good for. Getting people killed. Lani. Tommy. Collins. Maura. You're next."

A pathetic whimper squeaked out of her, and he allowed himself a laugh if only to keep the pain of his sister's death from bowling him over once more.

"Who is that?" Aoife asked, risking a nick from the blade as she nodded toward the siren who now held Callum by his neck. The man's toes barely skimmed the surface of the sand as he struggled.

"Doesn't matter," he continued, "you'll be dead before you have a chance to meet her. And you'll never get the precious dagger you're searching for."

Callum's kicks lessened, his face losing color as his lungs failed to pull in any more air. He was going to lose this fight, and Declan was glad for that. Served him right for how he'd plotted with Aoife to snatch him off the street. For how he'd tortured Killian.

Lowering his blade, he spun Aoife around in his arms to face him. He wanted to see her life drain away.

She stared at him. Her unblinking gold-flecked green eyes called up visions of home and rolling hills. At one time, these eyes had been his hope and promise for a love-filled life like his parents had had, but now all he saw was her deceit and her lies.

He clenched his jaw. This bitch needed to pay. She needed to hurt as he did.

They stood so close he could feel her breath on his chest. It was far steadier than he might have expected—or wanted. Gone were the tears that had spilled earlier. Now she exhibited determination and strength, as if he wasn't holding a dagger to her throat. As if she were daring him to get it over with.

"I'd offer you the chance for last words," he said, "but I honestly don't give a shit what you have to say. Nothing you say could make me forgive you."

He paused, searching her eyes for any hint that his words had an impact on her. But if anything, they seemed to bolster her, and she stood an inch taller as she straightened. The movement brought her face closer to his, and her eyes drifted to his lips. He sneered at her. But she didn't seem to notice, her eyes once more finding his.

She swallowed and drew in a deep breath. "I love you, Declan McCallagh, and no one can change that—not a siren, and not you. I forgive you."

Before he could respond to her outrageous declaration, a flurry of movement pulled his attention back to where Triss still held Callum, pale and weak, in her grasp. A flash of sun on steel skimmed across Declan's line of sight. A moan of pain escaped from Callum. Triss loosened her grip and examined the knife now lodged in his shoulder before turning toward the one who had thrown it.

Captain Halloran? What was she doing here?

She approached the queen and her captive. The sirens on the dais, still watching, writhed on the stone, licking their lips. Yet they didn't budge. Even as Halloran walked past them, they remained, glancing at Triss every few breaths.

Triss clicked her tongue at her kin and gave a shake of her head, and this had them snarling in protest, but she didn't seem to care as she focused on Halloran.

"You missed," Triss said with a laugh.

"I meant to hit him. The bastard deserved it." Halloran's stride remained confident as she continued forward, not once glancing away from the queen.

"Oh, really." Triss faced Callum once more, shaking his head a bit and finally slapping him across the face to get his eyes to open. When they did open, just barely, she stared into them. "Is this the one you've lamented over? The one that got away? The one who betrayed you before you could betray her?"

As he listened to their exchange, Declan tightened his fingers in Aoife's hair to keep her steady, ignoring how she stared at him. One swipe and it would be over. She'd bleed out, he'd have his revenge, and then he'd get that dagger from the siren. He'd delayed too long. Flexing his arm, he prepared to pull the dagger across her throat. But it was yanked from his hand by someone or something. It clattered against the rock wall to his right and fell to the ground.

What in the sands was that?

Aoife's mouth gaped in bewilderment. But he didn't need a

blade to kill her. Using her shock against her, he moved his hands to her throat before she could try to stop him. Yes, this would be better. He smirked as he thought of how much more pleasant it was to squeeze the life out of her, to crush her windpipe, to feel her last shuddering breath.

He tightened his fingers, adjusting them slightly to get a better grip. She didn't smack his arms or try to wriggle free. Instead she rested her hands on him. Her eyes held none of the terror he'd hoped for, nor did they plead with him for mercy. This was the look he'd seen pass between his parents, a look of unconditional love, a look of trust and adoration.

Who was she to look at him like that? How dare she? He wouldn't make this mistake again. Wouldn't trust her and her lies.

He squeezed harder. Her breathing became ragged and shallow as she tried to pull in air. And still she looked at him with those damn adoring eyes. Her mouth formed words, but she didn't have the air to give them sound.

I love you.

Declan couldn't look at her anymore. As much as he wanted to watch her die, he couldn't. Not when she looked at him like that.

He looked over her head to where Halloran now crossed the last bit of sand before coming to a stop an arm's length away from the siren. With one deft movement, Triss released Callum's throat and kicked him back down to the ground. She struck Halloran across the face with one hand, grabbing the captain's hair with the other, then leaned in close. Even from this distance, Declan could hear every word she said.

"Captain Halloran. You're a fool. You're all fools. Did you really think a little cloaking of the mind could protect you? I don't need in here"—she shook Halloran's head around for emphasis—"to hurt you. It's a shame he never told you how he felt about you. Did you never guess it? Or did you ignore all the signs so you wouldn't feel so bad when you double-crossed him? When you sliced up his face?"

Halloran spat at the queen's face. "I'm a pirate. Slicing people up is what I do."

Triss threw her head back with a harsh laugh. She had barely quieted down when Callum pushed himself up from the ground. This time he didn't lunge for the queen as he had before, instead pulling the knife from his shoulder and throwing it at Triss. But she must have heard the plan in his head because she easily deflected the blade with her arm as she laughed again.

"Seriously, Callum," she said. "Will you never learn? I know all that you think and all that you plan. There's nothing you can do that I won't foresee."

The sweat pooling beneath Declan's palms forced his attention away from the queen. He readjusted his hands, surprised that Aoife still made no move to escape even when his grip loosened for a moment. He looked down at her, which was a mistake. Those eyes once more pleaded with him, and they remained devoid of fear or anger or remorse. There was only love. Why in the sands did she look at him like that? If she loved him, she would never have turned him over, would never have given up the names of the Rogues, would never have sacrificed his sister to the council's ruthless judgment.

The familiar sound of a blade against leather pulled Declan's attention up once more, and his hands tightened reflexively as he watched the scene play out.

With a growl, Callum bounded across the sand, pushing Halloran away as he gripped her cutlass to unsheathe it. Pulling his arm back as he turned, Callum sent the curved blade slicing deep across the siren's belly. Triss bared her teeth again, snarling and hissing as she worked to keep her innards from spilling out onto the sand.

Callum stumbled backwards, and Triss looked ready to lunge for him, but from the left came a flash of movement and light before steel met ancient flesh. Triss howled as a dagger buried itself in her chest, and she turned to see who it had come from. Declan nearly stumbled backward at the sight of Tommy staggering toward the queen, determination and pain written all over his face.

Tommy was here? He was alive? How? Declan had seen his lifeless body on that library floor.

No, this had to be a trick of Aoife's. Somehow she'd gotten in his head, making him see what she wanted him to. That wasn't really Tommy. It was someone else, someone she was forcing him to see as his best friend.

But Triss wouldn't be beaten so easily. With a wave of her bloody hand and another snarl, she sent a silent command to the sirens.

Declan watched the creatures—who were mad with hunger—bound off the dais toward the man.

What if that was Tommy? And Declan was just standing here instead of helping him?

But another look at Aoife sent his rage spiraling again, and his fingers quickly found new strength around her throat.

It was time to finish this.

53

TOMMY

The blade flew true, slamming into the siren just as Tommy had intended. Pain tore through his shoulder, but he would get no rest, it seemed, as the queen gave a silent command without hesitation.

A group of sirens leaped off the pile of stone, their hands outstretched toward him.

He had no more weapons. No way to defend himself against their inhuman strength and razor-sharp teeth.

But weapons or no, he would not go down easily. He didn't know how, but determination swelled within him as he caught a glimpse of Maura lying in the sand.

The eyes of the sirens, sickly and white, turned his stomach, but still he stood firm.

Dried blood clung to their flawless skin. It was smeared up their arms. Down their chins. Across their chests.

With a final inhale, he set his feet and braced himself for the impact. Ready.

His eyes snapped shut as the first of the five reached him. Her clawed hand reached for his face, cutting open his cheek.

And then the winds changed everything.

A gust of air rushed across the sand, past Tommy, slamming into the sirens. Their bodies were flung backward until the wind crushed them against the rock wall with a sickening yet satisfying sound. Tommy whirled around to find Bria standing there, lowering her hands as she released her control on the air. Beside her, Renna assessed Maura.

"You're too late, sisters." Triss's words came out strained as she choked on her own blood. "It's already done."

Tommy, pivoting quickly, turned to find Aoife's head falling to one side. Her face was the color of death, and Declan smiled as he squeezed harder.

A deep growl echoed off the stone walls, and in his periphery Tommy saw Halloran reach over to pull the dagger from Triss's chest and draw its sharp edge across the siren's neck.

Blood sprayed, and Triss—her eyes glazing over before turning toward the sky—fell to the white ground, her blood seeping into the sand.

54

DECLAN

Declan blinked, slow and steady. His head pounded. His hands ached.

Something slid off his forearms, and he looked down to find Aoife's arms falling lifeless at her sides. Aoife. Only his hands at her throat kept her upright. Why was he choking her? His hands released her, and his arms moved to catch her as she crumpled to the ground.

What had he done? What had happened?

He tried to recall, but the last thing he remembered was Aoife bargaining with Triss to let him go. Beyond that there was nothing. A section of time had been cut from his life and discarded.

"Aoife!" he called, but she didn't stir.

Falling to his knees—a painful echo of what had happened on that fateful night back in the cove—he lowered her down, cradling her in his arms. Stroking her hair, that unruly and unkempt hair that fit her freckled face so perfectly, he whispered her name again and again.

He could see her pulse thumping away at her neck, although much too slowly. Still, her heart was beating, and that was what mattered. But he needed her to wake up, needed her to be okay. Had he really come all this way, endured all of that, to fail her again?

Tommy inched his way toward him, wincing and holding his head in his hand.

"Tommy!" he yelled, his voice cracking in desperation. He needed his help—Aoife needed help—but he couldn't get any other words out. Stumbling over, Tommy cringed at the sight of a body he passed. He didn't kneel down. Didn't offer to help. He simply stared, his features twisting and flinching, as if he didn't know how to feel, what to think, or what to do.

"Maura," Tommy muttered, and Declan looked across the sand to where Renna and Bria knelt beside another body lying on the ground, but this one stirred, trying to sit up. "Maura?" Tommy called again.

"I'm okay," a voice, weak and strained, said. "Help Declan."

Tommy hesitated for a moment but then looked back down at Declan and Aoife.

"You don't remember." It wasn't a question. And Declan could only stare blankly at him. Tommy crouched down, his fingers checking for Aoife's pulse. Maura approached and placed a gentle hand on Tommy's injured shoulder before she caught Declan's attention and explained what had happened. How Triss had compelled him to believe Aoife had betrayed him and gotten Tommy killed, how he had fought Collins and Maura in order to get to Aoife and kill her himself.

Each word carved out another piece of his heart. It wasn't his fault, he knew, but it hurt all the same.

"But I'm okay," Declan said. "She'll be okay. We'll all be okay."

Tommy flinched, and Declan's eyes dropped to the ground behind his friend where a body lay lifeless. He worked his way back through the day's events, trying to recall who all had arrived with Aoife.

"Collins." The name fell from his lips as a whisper. "But the fae…"

Maura shook her head. "I'm sorry, Declan. It's too late for us to help him."

"I killed him."

No one moved.

What did they all think of him? Would the crew still want him as their captain? Would Aoife…

Declan looked down to where Aoife lay in his arms, at the face he'd dreamed of every night in Callum's ship. Had he scared her while he was under Triss's powers? How would she forgive him for this when she had refused to forgive him before?

Just one more thing he'd need to make right.

A throat cleared, and Declan found Captain Halloran striding toward him. There was a cut below her left eye, but it was no longer bleeding. Maura offered to hold Aoife so he could talk to the captain, but he shook his head rapidly. He had finally gotten her back. He wasn't about to let her go. Not unless she told him to.

As Halloran closed the distance and knelt before Declan, his mind flashed back to his youth. His parents had taken up this stance whenever he had fallen down or gotten hurt. There was only kindness in the woman's dark eyes. He should thank her, endlessly thank her for all she'd apparently done for his crew and for Aoife and for him, but words eluded him.

"Captain Halloran here," Tommy started, waiting for Declan

to look at him, "if she hadn't found us, we would be at the bottom of the Aisling or deep in the kraken's belly."

Maura offered a tight smile. "And if not there, we'd surely have been siren food."

For the first time, Declan noticed the bloody tangle of gore and delicate black fabric on the ground behind Halloran.

Triss.

Reluctantly he pulled one hand away from Aoife and extended it toward the captain. "Do I owe you a word of thanks for that? For killing her?"

Her lip twitched. "Only partly. Callum deserves your gratitude as well."

Declan's eyes closed as his chin dropped to his chest. He ran a hand over his brow, clenching his jaw. How could he thank the man who had snatched him off the street and tortured a good man simply for helping him?

Halloran spoke again, but he couldn't look at her. "I won't say he's a good man, McCallagh. Sands knows he's done his share of evil. But he didn't have to do what he did. He didn't have to help us."

Declan's gut tightened as visions of Killian's shredded body filled every inch of his mind.

Halloran added, "You don't have to like him. No one really likes him anyway. But his evil deeds don't make his good ones null and void."

Drawing in a deep breath, Declan began to nod. Halloran spoke true. Callum might still be punished for all eternity for his heinous actions and ruthless nature, but that didn't make him any less worthy of thanks when he did right—no matter how seldom it was.

Opening his eyes, he looked at those sitting around him. "So where is he?"

Heads turned, and everyone searched for the pirate captain. But aside from Triss's remains and Callum's blood staining the white sand, the beach was empty.

"And I can only assume the dagger is gone too?" Before Declan could finish the question, Tommy was up and running toward Triss's corpse. Frantically he searched the remnants of the queen and her garments.

Tommy punched the ground and lowered his head. He didn't need to relay the news for Declan to know.

Callum was gone.

The dagger along with him.

That bastard.

CAIT

Cait sneaked out of the town square and started down a road that ran parallel to the one where Adler had taken Lucan. When she popped out from between the buildings onto the road running along the harbor, she looked to the right, toward the path that led to the pit. But they were nowhere in sight. It didn't make sense. It was nearly a straight shot to the trees where they had turned that morning.

Where was Adler taking him if not to that pit?

Scanning the docks that jutted out along the coast, she continued on her way, craning her neck to see around the random sailors and pirates loading goods onto ships or meandering into town for a hot meal. Nowhere. No Lucan. No Adler. Where in the sands were they?

A flash of bright fabric caught her attention, standing out in stark contrast to the dull browns and grays most of the sailors wore.

Lucy.

Cait picked up speed, keeping her eyes firmly locked on the woman's bright attire. She dodged one pirate swigging a bottle of rum and then a pair of travelers making their way into the city.

Lucy turned onto one of the docks, her gait sure and confident. Cait's intuition pushed her forward. She was sure Lucy was involved somehow. Continuously scanning the dock, Cait searched for any sign of the two men.

Still nothing.

Perhaps they had headed to the pit and she'd just been late?

Maybe she was wasting her time following this crazy woman from Foxhaven.

Cait turned around in circles, not caring if people thought her mad. She searched.

Two tall men.

One blonde. One with brown hair.

One a victim. One a damned traitor.

She had completed two full turns before she thought she caught a glimpse of Adler. Her vision was a bit dizzy from spinning, but when she looked closer, she was sure it was him. In front of him, Lucan's familiar face grimaced as he trudged along.

Cait's feet took off running through the crowd once more, and she weaved around boxes and luggage and people, her footfalls becoming hollow thumps as the stones beneath her gave way to the wooden dock. People shouted at her, but she didn't care. Lucan and Adler were just up ahead and about to board a small ship.

She pushed her legs harder, faster.

Lucan hated water. Didn't just hate it. He was deathly afraid of it. Perhaps more afraid of drowning than he was of dying in any other way.

Adler shoved Lucan up the gangplank, following him closely. Cait's mouth nearly dropped open at the sight of Lucy—*damned Lucy*—standing aboard the ship, her hands reaching out to take Lucan's arms.

Making a sharp turn, Cait nearly lost her footing as her shoes slipped across the wet wood of the dock.

"Adler!" she cried as she ran the last fifty feet toward him, hoping her anger would give the word more power.

He turned, and his eyes widened before his lips creeped down into that upside-down smile of his. With a flourish of his hand, he offered her a grand bow before kicking the gangplank back toward the dock. Their crew had worked fast, faster than she'd thought possible, to untie the lines and get them moving. She gauged the distance from the dock to the edge of the ship as she ran, her feet pounding hard against the wooden planks, her legs burning from the effort.

But she skidded to a stop, her toes creeping out over the edge, when she realized they'd gotten too far away for her to make the jump.

Cursing Adler and Lucy, she stood there until their sails disappeared beyond the bay of Morshan.

☙

It was the middle of the busy hour at the pub when Cait finally ambled back. Not bothering to use the alley door, she slammed the front door open and ignored how the patrons stared at her as she stomped across the floor. She bumped her shoulders into pirates and merchants alike, paying them no attention as they grumbled and cursed and finally fell silent when they realized it was her.

Kira was behind the bar. She'd been dutifully manning the business while Cait had been out working.

You mean failing.

Her muttered curse fell to the pub floor as she shoved herself behind the bar. Reaching underneath, she pushed several bottles aside until she found the rum she'd been saving for after the council's fall. They were all doomed now, so there was no point in saving it.

No parents. No brother. No friends. No nothing.

Cait let the dark thoughts take over, her own malicious and barbed words cutting into her more painfully than if anyone else had said them. Standing with the old bottle in hand, its dark amber liquid glistening in the light of the lanterns, she said nothing to Kira or to anyone else as she made to retreat to her room upstairs.

Before she could leave, though, Kira grabbed her arm. The girl's kind, concerned eyes searched hers as though to ask if Cait was all right.

Of course I'm not all right! Cait wanted to shout back at her, and she hoped that message was clear in the glare she shot back.

"Get some rest," Kira said, grabbing Cait's free hand firmly and giving it a squeeze before releasing it and nodding toward the stairs.

Cait had barely gotten the door closed when she stopped and read the note Kira had slipped to her so expertly.

Tomorrow afternoon. Calypso cove. It's not what you think, love. - Adler

With a scowl at the bottle she carried, she gritted her teeth once more, knowing she very well might regret trusting the man again. But this drink could wait a few more days.

Perhaps not all was lost just yet. Perhaps her instincts hadn't completely gone to shit as she'd feared.

56
AOIFE

It hurt to swallow, but then, it hurt to simply lie here. Aoife hadn't yet opened her eyes, almost too afraid to see what reality she would find—if she was still alive at all. Wiggling her toes, she tested out little movements. She listened for any sounds, but everything was muffled, as if she were underwater.

"Aoife?" Declan's voice pushed through the fog, and she slowly opened her eyes.

He lay on his side, his head resting on his arm, looking at her. Worried he would disappear if she blinked, she tried to keep her eyes open and focused on him.

"I'm sorry," he said before pulling a breath of air deep into his lungs.

Her heart pushed her to reach for him, but she hesitated and retreated slightly.

"Am I still alive? Are you?"

He looked around the room before offering her a slight smirk—although it wasn't half as attractive as the one he normally donned. "I would hope paradise doesn't look like my ratty old cabin on this battered ship."

There was a hint of humor amid the deep regret and sadness she'd seen in his eyes under the moonlight in the cove. The memory of that night—of her denying him forgiveness—pulled her insides tight.

"I forgive you, Declan," she said as she inched her hand toward his. "For everything."

He closed his eyes and sighed deeply, like she'd just offered him the world. And perhaps she had.

As their fingers touched, she examined his face. "I assume we won if we're back on the ship then?"

"Aye," he said, his eyes flashing open. "Thanks to Halloran and—as much as I hate to admit it—Callum."

The way he ground out the pirate's name told Aoife he didn't fully appreciate the man's help.

He provided her a short rundown of what had happened after she'd lost consciousness—how Callum had snuck off with the blade, how they planned to give chase and recover it as soon as they got Halloran back to her ship, which was waiting nearby.

It could have been worse.

But that thought rotted around the memory of Collins falling, his blood on Declan's dagger. Had they recovered his body? Would he receive a proper burial at sea? Before Aoife could ask, Declan was talking again, a boyish look on his face. "It's too bad you missed seeing the sirens."

"I think I've had enough sirens for a lifetime." She frowned at him.

"No, the other sirens."

Aoife lifted her injured arm in protest, to remind him of how those *other* sirens had treated her, but the gold fabric they'd tied around her was gone, replaced with clean linen.

"Yes, I know, but they were under Triss's control when they attacked you. Once she was dead and they were freed, we found they weren't like Triss at all. Like me, they couldn't remember anything about their centuries with her. Probably for the better too. They won't be haunted by what they were forced to do and can now live how they wish. Where they wish. Some swam alongside our boats as we left. Others shifted into their bird form and soared high above us before drifting off east."

"That would have been an interesting sight." Even as she said it, she still didn't regret not seeing them. Gentle or not. All she could think of was the pain from their fangs and the sight of Triss's snarling mouth. She shuddered again, and he reached for her.

Scooting across the bed toward him, she let him pull her in close and tuck her in his arms. His lips met her forehead. She altered her breathing to match his and let herself settle into the comforting rhythm of his heartbeat. The best sound in the world. Steady and true and strong.

"You're sure you're not still angry with me?" he asked.

"Do you not remember all that I told you?"

"If you said it while I was not myself, then no. I know nothing beyond what Maura could relate to me." At this, she sat up, and he did the same, propping himself up with a hand before he said, "Was it something good? I hope it was something good. Or something dirty. That would be nice too."

With a slap of her hand on his shoulder, she shook her head at him and rolled her eyes. "You're awful, you know that?"

"So I've been told." He offered up her favorite smirk, and it took all her willpower not to tackle him right then. But that had to wait.

Clenching her hands tightly in her lap, she searched his face, as if the words she needed were written upon his features. Her lower lip quivered, and she bit down on it to force it to be still.

"Why was this so much easier to say when you were trying to kill me?" She meant it as a joke to lighten the mood, but as soon as the words were out, she worried they'd sting him unnecessarily.

But he let out a soft laugh. "Probably because you thought it was the end."

"Seems much more appropriate for a beginning though." She wrinkled her nose as her stomach fluttered.

"Oh?" Light in his eyes danced with that humor she'd missed, even when she'd been so angry with him.

A deep breath couldn't steady her racing heart, but she couldn't withhold this from him any longer.

"I love you, Declan McCallagh."

His lips were on hers in an instant. She'd had more to say, but this was good too. Letting herself sink into him, she met his hunger and need and desperation with each move of their lips and tongues. His arms pulled her close, trapping her against his chest, and still she couldn't get close enough to him.

"I missed you," he whispered around her lips, and she hummed in return, melting further into his touch, getting lost in the growing heat within her that flared with each move of his hands along her back.

She was about to pull back and stop them when his hands came to a rest on her hips and his mouth planted tender kisses along her jaw. Her hands traveled up his neck, her fingers getting lost in his hair. It all felt amazingly delightful, and she never wanted him to stop.

But she knew he had to.

"Declan," she whispered.

"Yes?" he murmured against her skin, kissing across her shoulder as he moved the fabric of her shirt aside.

"Where is Maura?" She thought this would snap him out of whatever spell he was under, but it didn't.

"Why?" The word tickled her ear, which he nipped with his teeth, sending a shock through her whole body.

Aoife shuddered but tried again, moving her hands back down to his chest and giving him a gentle push. "I need to ask her a question."

"And it can't wait?" he asked, allowing her to move him back until she could see him clearly.

Looking at him now, with his hair falling into his face and his gaze burning with desire almost had her tossing aside the question that had plagued her even in unconsciousness. She shook her head. With a bob of his chin, he took her hands in his and pulled her off the bed.

"Then let's find her, shall we?"

They found Maura with Tommy up on the quarterdeck, which was still stained with kraken blood. After exchanging silent greetings of smiles and nods, Aoife blurted out, "Something happened back there with Declan."

They all looked at her like she had just declared water to be wet or the sea to be salty. She tried again.

"When he had his dagger to my throat…" She forced herself to ignore the way his mouth twitched at the reminder. "He wasn't able to use it, because he dropped it. Except he didn't drop it. It flew from his hand. How?"

Maura shifted her weight and gave Tommy an almost apologetic look, which simply confused Aoife more.

"I wanted to tell you," she said, "but there never seemed to be a good time."

"Tell me what?"

"It was you. You did that." Maura's stony expression indicated her words were genuine, but that didn't make them any easier to understand.

"What do you mean, I did—"

"You moved the dagger."

"That's impossible," Aoife said, glancing around. Everyone else appeared as perplexed as she felt.

"You're a demi-fae, Aoife," Maura said.

Three jaws dropped open. With wide eyes, Aoife stared at her friend, looking for any hint that this was a joke. This had to be a joke.

"A what? That's not possible," she said, shaking her head vehemently. "For me to be any type of fae, my mother or father would—"

"—have to be fae," Maura said. "It's your mother."

Aoife felt the floor fall out from under her as her stomach plunged into her feet. She couldn't breathe. What did this mean? How was this at all possible? How many more surprises would she discover? How much did she not know?

A lot, apparently.

All her muscles tensed, and she snapped her eyes up to Maura's again. "What do you mean there was never a good time? This seems like rather pertinent information, Maura! I had a right to know!"

"You did, but it wouldn't have helped. We didn't know for sure if you'd inherited any powers. There was no reason to distract you with it when we weren't certain."

"And when did you figure it out exactly?"

Maura shifted her feet. "Once Renna compelled you. Somehow it awakened whatever magic your mother passed on to you. We could sense it. And I planned to tell you once you awoke."

Aoife knew this was all logically sound, but it still didn't quell the sting or lessen the shock of this revelation.

Declan squeezed her hand reassuringly before asking his own question. "In order for Aoife to inherit any *daemari*, though, Melina would have had to be a royal. So why would she need you and your sisters?"

Maura grimaced as if she were about to offer up more disagreeable news. "It's a long story, and I promise you'll hear it, but not without my sisters present."

"Can you give us the short version?" Tommy asked, his voice tender.

Looking from him to Aoife, Maura nodded slightly. "She lost her *daemari* when she enchanted the dagger for the king."

"What dagger?" Aoife asked, immediately realizing how stupid the question was but not caring.

"How many enchanted daggers do you think there are?" Maura asked with an awkward laugh.

Her mother. The dagger. The king.

The legend.

Aoife's jaw fell open once more as Declan voiced what they were all probably thinking.

"Well, shit."

57
TOMMY

Tommy watched Declan and Aoife disappear down the stairs and continued to stare in their direction long after.

"What's bothering you?" Maura's melodic voice pulled his attention back to where she stood beside him.

Taking her into his arms, he wrapped her in a hug and held her head against his chest. He searched the sea, which was black beneath the night sky. The *Siren's Song* sailed along as fast as they could with the available wind. So many things had gone well.

But others…

Maura didn't pressure him to answer her question, instead settling herself against him, her arms tucked between them, her hands clutching at his shirt.

"It's just a"—Tommy cleared the scratchiness from his throat—"a bad feeling. Like a chill over my skin or an uneasiness settling within me."

"What do you think it's about?" she asked.

"I wish I knew. Or maybe I don't."

At this, she pulled back to look him in the eye, her brow creased in question.

"Does it help to know the doom that lies ahead?" he said. "Or does it distract you from relishing the present moment?"

Maura's eyes rose to the sky as she pondered his words. "Or would it force you to live the present moment to its fullest? If I had known I would be imprisoned in that room for centuries, I would have done more to enjoy the years beforehand. I would have traveled, seen the world, had more fun."

"Or you would have spent all those years trying to find a way to prevent it from happening and ended up sacrificing them all." She lifted her shoulders in concession and flashed him that coy smile he adored. "Maybe we're both right."

"Well, in that case..." Tommy said as he moved a hand to her neck, enjoying how she shivered under his fingers. Cradling her jaw, he lowered his lips to her shoulder, kissing and nibbling and breathing along her skin until he reached her ear, where he whispered, "Perhaps we should do more to enjoy this moment."

She leaned into his lips and let the full length of her body press against him as she tangled her fingers in his hair and held him tight.

Tommy continued to taste the sweetness of her skin even as he lowered his hands to lift her up, delighting in the way her legs instinctively wrapped around his waist and her whole body sighed with each of his kisses.

Somehow, with his eyes barely seeing the world around them, he managed to get down the stairs and to the door of the officers' cabin. He pulled away long enough to catch her eye, hoping she could hear his silent question. Maura leaned her ear toward the door and, presumably hearing no sign of her sisters within, took a half breath before pulling her lips into a mischievous grin and gesturing for him to continue inside.

The click of the door closing behind them was like a match to a fuse, setting Tommy ablaze. His kisses became hungrier. His hands gripped her tighter. His body ached for her.

It must have done the same for her, as she was soon leaping down from around his waist and pushing him against the wall. Her fingers had his shirt unbuttoned and on the floor before he even realized what she was doing, but he didn't hesitate to reach down to her waist and pull the length of her dress up, bunching it around her hips.

"There's entirely too much fabric between us," he said.

Before he'd gotten the words out, her hands were at his belt, working to remedy the situation. But he stopped her, moving her arms away from him as he lifted her dress the rest of the way off, slipping it over her head and dropping it to the floor.

His heart took off without him, racing ahead, beating feverishly in response to her utter beauty. She hadn't lied when she'd said she was no mere woman. He'd been with women, even beautiful ones, but they all paled next to Maura.

"You're staring," she teased, placing a hand on her hip.

"I know," he said as he allowed his eyes to greedily run over every inch of her, slowly, as if he could memorize every curve.

With an exaggerated inhale, she looked to the ceiling of the small room. "When you talked of savoring, I thought—"

Tommy had her against him before she could finish her taunt, claiming her mouth with his, loving the way she tasted and enjoying the dance her tongue did with his. Her hands moved lower, but he pulled her hips closer to block her.

"Not yet," he whispered against her lips before blazing a trail of kisses down her neck, over her collarbone, and onto her breasts, which were more delightful than anything he had envisioned. He couldn't hold back a smile when she gasped and shuddered as his tongue brushed over one peak, and he delighted in the way her back arched as he continued to devour it and then the other. When he pulled away, the most adorable whimper of protest filled the space, making it impossible to keep his mouth off her for long.

This time when her hands met his waist, he didn't object. But she was taking her sweet time, making him nearly beg for her to hurry up. Why had he mentioned savoring? This was torture. His need for her increased with each flutter of her fingers against his skin and each inch of his pants she lowered.

She paused and looked up at him. The passion in her eyes had clouded over with hesitation that left him confused. And slightly panicked that he'd done something wrong.

"What?"

"Is this okay? Here? Now?" Her questions came out with humor, though Tommy thought he picked up on a hint of concern as well. "It's not your captain's bed, but—"

Tommy ran his hands along her bare waist and pulled her against him once more. "Are you asking me if I am sure? If I really want this?"

Placing a kiss on his chest, lighter and more innocent than he would have expected from her, she whispered the words against his skin, "I don't want to rush you. I don't want you to regret..."

Her shoulders slumped, and she wrapped her arms around his middle. Tommy kissed the top of her head, then closed his eyes and pressed her closer to him.

"I could never regret any moment spent with you, Maura. Especially a moment like this." Inching his mouth down, he kissed her ear before whispering, "I am yours, if you still want me."

With a sigh, she melted into him and turned to find his lips with hers, whispering against them, "And I am yours, Tommy."

Lowering his hands, he traced the curves of her hips and backside before lifting her up effortlessly to wrap her around him once more, telling her of his intentions in a way words couldn't. He laid her down on the pile of blankets covering the floor of the cabin and smiled against her neck when her hands found the last of his clothes. She didn't hesitate this time, pulling them off and tossing them aside, leaving their bodies heated with passion and writhing in desperation.

"I love you." Her words came out as a silken whisper in his ear, and she pulled him ever closer, raising her hips to lure all of him in. He repeated her words back to her before showing her the depth of that love by claiming all of her—heart, soul, and body—as his own with every inch of him.

✿

I love you, Tommy.

Her words invaded his dreams as he slept beside the first woman to ever steal his heart. He hadn't slept so soundly since before losing Declan a week ago, and when the sun peered through the small window of the cabin and warmed his face, he couldn't contain his contented sigh. His lips pulled into a smile as memories of their night echoed in his mind. Even on the floor of a tiny cabin, it had been everything he'd hoped for and more.

She was his. Even with no ceremonies performed or promises uttered, in his heart he knew. She was his. He was hers.

And he would not waste another moment with his Maura.

Turning onto his side, he opened his eyes, eager to see her greeting him.

But he saw only tangled blankets and the worn floor of his cabin.

Sitting up, he looked around the small room. His heart thrummed faster and faster. His gut clenched in panic, and no matter how he tried to assure himself she had just left to fetch them some breakfast, the dread tightened its hold with each movement as he dressed.

He winced at the brightness of the sun as he stepped out of the cabin and nearly collided with Declan.

"Tommy." His heart fell to his feet with the way his friend uttered his name.

"Where is she?" Tommy asked, not caring how desperate he sounded. He searched Declan's eyes, seeking the answer he desperately needed, that these fears plaguing him were unwarranted.

But his friend's extended silence told him more than any words could.

He brushed past him, ignoring when Declan called after him. His feet couldn't carry him up the quarterdeck stairs fast enough. She wouldn't be there, but maybe he could find some answers.

None of them would be adequate or acceptable.

Gavin's eyes locked on his, and with tight lips the helmsman nodded to the starboard side.

Sails. On the horizon. Even without the spyglass, he knew.

Halloran.

She had needed to go south for some business.

South.

But she hadn't offered to take the fae. Had she?

And even if she had, why would Maura go with them?

After all they had declared, all they had shared, she'd simply left?

Running both hands through his hair, he kept his eyes on

those sails. She couldn't have. She wouldn't have.

She had to have been forced. He could not accept or believe any other explanation.

"Tommy," Declan said from beside him. "I'm sorry. I couldn't change their minds."

The sails blurred and the horizon melted as tears surfaced.

Tommy balled his hands into fists, his nails threatening to draw blood from his palms. He couldn't look at his friend. Everything hurt. His chest was splitting open. His head was pounding, his gut twisting.

Declan spoke again, treading lightly with each word. "We can't follow. Callum was spotted going east toward Turvala. We can't—"

"I know."

The moments ticked by. The sails disappeared.

Maura was gone.

My Maura.

Relaxing his hands, he repeated the words silently. Declan was staring at him, but Tommy just needed a moment to think. He traced back through the events of last night, searching for some explanation for her sudden departure.

But he found nothing.

No reason. No justification.

It made no sense.

He was only certain of one thing, and every echo of every minute he'd spent with her strengthened this conviction.

His pain slowly gave way to the confidence he had in her, his Maura.

"I trust her, Declan. She'll find her way back to me."

The story concludes in

with these last breaths

Aisling Sea Book 3
August 15, 2023

Acknowledgements

To my besties: Crystal, Merrit, Jourdan, Vicki. You've stood by me through some really hard days, and I appreciate you more than I can ever say! Thank you for loving me for me, for not letting me short-change myself, and for being there day in and day out.

To my team of early readers: Amanda, Athena, Beth, Crystal S., Heidi, Jamie, Jen, Jess, Kari, Katie, Lauren, Megan, Morgan H., Morgan M., Natalia, Rachel, Rayleigh, Shannon, Tralyn, Haley, Erin, and Chelsea. Thank you thank you thank you for your encouragement and enthusiasm.

To my fellow authors who make this community great, thank you for all the giggles over writing romance scenes, the hugs from afar, and the chats about characters taking over. I am so blessed to know so many amazingly talented and encouraging creatives. I will forever be thankful that my writing heroes let me slip into their DMs and trick them into being friends with me.

To my publishing team: Emily, Maria, Gerralt, Caitlin. This book would not be what it is without you and your genius.

To all the readers: Time is precious and fleeting, and our TBR piles are ever-growing. You could have picked up any number of amazing books to read, but you read mine, and that will never cease to astound me.

To my kids: I hope you're not too mad at me for redacting parts of this book before I let you read it (you'll be older before you know it). Thank you for always supporting me and this crazy job of mine.

To my husband: Thank you for loving me. Through all the down days and the tears, the morning walks and the laughs, the gin and the sad songs. Thank you for believing in me when I wanted to quit my job so I could write full-time. Thank you for always listening to my rambling about publishing and character arcs and plot holes. I'm sorry I never took you up on the offers to act out some of the scenes in the book. Maybe in book three.

Finally, as always and forever, to Christ Jesus for His saving grace.

CPSIA information can be obtained
at www.ICGtesting.com
Printed in the USA
LVHW090906240723
753027LV00094B/288/J